Catherine Hughes, a high school English teacher, was first intrigued by the story of Mary Grant and Domhnull Donn after visiting Scotland's Urquhart Castle, the site of their courtship and Donn's later imprisonment. Forbidden to be together in their own time, the laird's daughter and the rebel poet cried out from beyond the grave, beckoning someone to listen. Catherine, who resides in Long Beach, NY with her family, heeded their call.

To the voices of yesterday that can be heard in the silences of today…

Catherine Hughes

IN SILENCE CRIES THE HEART

AUSTIN MACAULEY PUBLISHERS™

LONDON * CAMBRIDGE * NEW YORK * SHARJAH

Ordering Information
Quantity sales: Special discounts are available on quantity purchases by corporations, associations, and others. For details, contact the publisher at the address below.

Publisher's Cataloging-in-Publication data
Hughes, Catherine
In Silence Cries the Heart

ISBN 9781649797360 (Paperback)
ISBN 9781649797377 (Hardback)
ISBN 9781649797384 (ePub e-book)

Library of Congress Control Number: 2023914911

www.austinmacauley.com/us

First Published 2023
Austin Macauley Publishers LLC
40 Wall Street, 33rd Floor, Suite 3302
New York, NY 10005
USA

mail-usa@austinmacauley.com
+1 (646) 5125767

Thank you to my family for their encouragement and support throughout this project, to my mother for reading each chapter as it was completed and to my niece, Allison, for her assistance with all equestrian matters. Thank you to my two wonderful friends, Barbara and Laura, who listened to snippets of the book (enjoying some of the bawdy Gaelic terms) as we walked the LB boardwalk together. Thank you to Kathie Snyders for getting me to Scotland and for putting me in the location where Mary and Donal's story came to life. Thank you to my students who teach me on daily basis to be fearless and to dare greatly. And thank you to my all-time favorite person, Sister Nora Doody, who fostered my deep and abiding love for the written word.

Undlay Dungeon – 1665

His finger, damp with moisture and blackened with dirt, outlined the edges of the unyielding stone as he sat in silence in the darkness. How strange that, just a short time ago, that same hand had traced the inviting contours of his lover's soft lips.

And now?

The cold made him shiver—or was it the memory of what he had recently lost?

There are many bargains one makes in life: honor for power; integrity for wealth; character for renown. And while most men readily surrender virtue for worldliness, Donal was not like most men. For him, there was only a single prize worth sacrificing one's name, one's reputation, one's very life for. He had made such a trade and felt no pangs of regret. For even though that transaction brought him here—to this dungeon where the chill fastened upon his bones—his heart remained impassioned with thoughts of her.

His tactile musings were interrupted by the sound of clanging; someone was coming. He supposed it must be time then. *Time, what a peculiar concept,* he wondered. How foolish, how vain to think that he could conquer time through his verses, through his songs. A feeble attempt to immortalize events—and to a certain degree, himself—by the power of his words. But here he was, facing the movement of time, and none of the poetry he had ever written could do anything to slacken its advance.

Words betrayed him now. What were they but an empty compilation of lifeless sounds? They never truly captured the flashes of emerald in his lover's eyes or the dancing rays of light as they shimmered off her russet tresses. *And yet, that is all I had,* he thought to himself, *mere words, brief melodies to describe the indescribable. Tonight, they offer no comfort.* He clung to images of her as clouds of his icy breath formed and dissipated with the rise and fall of his chest.

A jangling of keys and the lattice iron door creaked upon opening. A man motioned to Donal to get up. Wiping his dampened finger on his ragged clothing, he stood tall and walked forward to meet his appointment with Time.

Loch Ness – 2018

The sea spray spattered her cheeks, so she fluttered her eyes to clear her vision. Beneath her feet, the bottom of the boat lifted and retracted in uneven motions as the craft coursed its path over the murky waves. Despite her unsteady footing, she was never more at ease. She welcomed the breeze and the spray and stood tall at the rail, fighting the droplets in order to gaze around her.

There were seven passengers on this journey—not counting the tour guide or the ship's captain—pilgrims they were, seeking to recapture a sense of mystery proffered by a country much older than their own. In a century that seemingly had an answer for all life's mysteries, how refreshing it was to be in a place and among a people comfortable with the unknown. There was something quite liberating about that, about the idea that sometimes things can just "be."

They were a mixed assortment of travelers: a mother and daughter who hailed from the Cumberland Mountains of Kentucky; a pair of childhood friends who lived next door to one another on the South Carolina coast; a married couple born, raised, and still residing in Louisiana; and the unaccompanied sojourner, a die-hard Patriots fan from South Boston. Though their points of origin differed, they all converged upon this same path, an avenue paved with wonder and edged by awe, a journey to an ancient land of mist and shadows.

The engine slowed, allowing the guide to seize his mic. "We'll pause a wee bit here, for ye to have a chance to take some photos and admire the setting," explained Graham.

Beneath the gray skies above, Graham capitalized on its menacing look to begin his tale of the monster. "Aye, so when does the story of the monster begin, ye may wonder? Well, ye must go all the way back to the 500s for the first sighting of Nessie when St. Columba sent one of his monks to swim across the loch to fetch a boat. The creature crashed through the surface and rushed

11

after the swimmer—most likely viewing him as a delectable morsel. 'Go no further, nor touch the man! Go back!' Columba shouted. And like a good little heathen chastised by an irate clergyman, Nessie vanished beneath the surface, leaving the swimmer unharmed." Graham's eyes twinkled as he recounted the tale. "Over the years, there have been thousands of sightings—photographs and videos—but are they real or just hoaxes?"

"Yeah," observed Michael, Ann Marie's spouse, "I think I read that some doctor once took a picture of the thing, and it looked a little bit like a dinosaur, but later it turned out to be fake, right?"

"Well…" Graham paused, "yes, it was a bit doubtful. The man's name was Dr. Robert Kenneth Wilson, and the picture became known as 'The Surgeon's Photo'. There was speculation that it was a plastic or wooden head attached to a toy submarine and that it was really all a prank, but that didna' stop others from trying to locate the creature. In the 1960s, a search party detected a vast underwater cave near Undlay Castle. Could this be the dragon's lair?" Graham swept his hand over the side of the boat for dramatic flair.

"Sounds a bit like the Beowulf story to me," added Caitlyn. "If Grendel and his mother had their own underwater accommodations, why not Nessie?" Returning to the topic of the submarine investigation, she asked, "But did the researchers find anything in the cave? Treasure? Weapons? I always did think it was kind of weird that Grendel's mother had swords in her pile of plunder. I mean, what dragon *needs* swords, right? I guess it's not enough to have fangs, claws, and fire-breath?"

"They have not found anything yet, Caitlyn. No gold or diamonds or such. Just a huge trench that may be just the right size for a monster like Nessie to hide in," Graham explained. "And so the mystery continues. As recently as 2007, someone took video footage of a jet-black creature, about 45 feet long, moving verra fast in the water. Even better, just this year, one of our local boat skippers captured a remarkable sonar image of a 25-foot fish, 115 feet below the surface!"

He shifted away from the railing over toward the center of the boat in order to let his listeners have a closer look. "So ye've got both sides then, the naysayers and the believers, many of whom have devoted their entire lives to uncovering or denying Nessie's legitimacy. But regardless of where ye stand on the issue, it certainly has boosted the Scottish economy by a few billion pounds!" He laughed amusedly. "So as we cruise through this stretch of sea, keep yer cameras at the ready, just in case you notice that ripple on the surface…"

The small size of the touring group allowed for a smooth change of position as each picked out the best vantage point and clicked away. The breeze continued to blow and the clouds tumbled above, compelling Caitlyn to consider, "Well, if there ever *were* to be a perfect setting for dragons and monsters, this certainly is the place!" She grinned to herself, knowing how she relished these kinds of stories, the inexplicable occurrences, the "it's possible/it's not possible" see-saw that engaged the mind, personally preferring to always be atop the teeter-totter, amidst the airy world of chance.

Not seeing the vessel in the distance, only the swell it left behind, Christina's mother pointed at the water and shouted, "There, look over there! To the right! Did anybody see that?" Her eyes were lit with a mixture of surprise and delight.

"Good one, Doris. I'm going to video that and see if I can pass it off as a bit of 'Nessie gas' to my fantasy football buddies when I get home," Michael countered, noticing the boat responsible for the rippling water.

The captain signaled to Graham, so the guide announced, "All right, guys, time to steam ahead; we have a little ways to go before our next stop."

As Caitlyn put her phone back into the pocket of her raincoat, she thought how awesome it was not to have to always come up with the answer.

***

That's what Caitlyn's life back in Boston was all about: solving problems, finding answers. Whether it was teaching her students how to identify the subject and predicate of a sentence or figuring out what had to be done in order to make her boyfriend happy, her life was all about solutions. And she was tired of that. She was tired of pretending that she knew the symbolism intended by a particular poet. She was tired of finding weekend jaunts to inject a little excitement into her relationship with Brian. She was tired of managing the household budget so that they could cover all their expenses. And she was tired of believing that the answer to her own happiness was to put comfort and predictability above passion.

I don't have answers, she thought, *and there's nothing wrong with that. Why can't I accept my own limitations in that regard? Why do I interpret my "lack of answers" as being a failure? A sign that I'm not trying hard enough or exploring far enough or researching deeply enough? Sometimes it's okay to just "be," right? Sometimes it's even better to leave things open-ended, to have that question still ringing in the air after the poem's been read or the argument has ended. What's wrong with that kind of silence? It's okay to put down the mantle of Grand Keeper of the Solution once in a while, isn't it?*

This trip was a nod to that surrender. For inexplicable reasons, Caitlyn had always been drawn to Scottish history and culture. A fierce people, impacted by their landscape and climate, the Scots recognized their own vulnerability in the face of those challenges, and yet that vulnerability never devolved into weakness. Rather, its seed burgeoned into courage, resilience, and conviction. A country that embraced superstition—indeed its ghosts, fairies, and mythological creatures were woven into the very soul of a Scot as tangible as the tartan threads that enveloped his body. And Caitlyn liked that. She liked the inexplicable, the hushed warning, the slight but palpable feeling that not all things can be neatly structured into a four-paragraph essay or a day trip to the Cape. No, it is better to recognize powerlessness, to accept fallibility, to acknowledge those forces greater than oneself.

In fact, it was one of those forces that struck her hard and fast just a few months ago. For years, she had been teaching British literature to her high school students, and while she loved all the course material and even did her Master's thesis on Chaucer, it was the haunting melodies and tragic storylines of the Celtic ballads that captured her imagination most of all. Moved by an earlier class discussion on "Edward," Caitlyn visited the campus library of her alma mater, Boston College, to delve deeper into this poetic tradition, pouring through Nigel Fulton's *Anthology of Poetry from the British Isles*. There, ensconced in a snug cubicle as the waning light of the afternoon sun shed its rays upon the open text before her, she came across an evocative piece she had never read before:

O where hae ye gone, O Mary, my luve,
I'm here but I canna find ye.
In a place far beyond the world we'd known
I'm lost till yer heart comes back to me.

Their love it began in the forested glen
At a time when enchantment was swirling.
He carried her home once he found her alone
And from there, his world had stopped turning.

But their love was denied by the sway of mankind
So they met by the loch but in secret.
Till a rival looked on with a wish to do harm
'Twas his ruse that was meant to defeat them.

With an axe thru his neck, he went to his death
Loving her was the crime he committed.
When she heard he was gone, she couldna' carry on
Thus, to sorrow and grief she submitted.

So he walks by the loch, looking near and then far
For a maiden who resides out of reach.
Though the nights seem so long with a heart this forlorn
He stays true to the words that he speaks:

O where hae ye gone, O Mary, my luve,
I'm here but I canna find ye.
In a place far beyond the world we'd known
I'm lost till yer heart comes back to me.

Caitlyn could not crawl out from under the power of these verses that blanketed her, consumed her, overpowered her. The ballad was cloaked in mystery, the only credit listed beneath, "Anonymous, 17th Century." Although it would have been easier to walk over to the xerox machine to photocopy the page, she felt compelled to write the words with her own hand, bequeathing them to her private journal. Not knowing the people involved or the specific

15

details of the tragedy added to her interest in the piece, heightening Caitlyn's attraction for the inexplicable.

Journeys, not destinations, were what life was all about so, for her, this trip to Scotland was undertaken for the sheer pleasure of it and not for any specific reason. There was no goal she hoped to achieve, no mandated course she had to fulfill, no real answer she was searching for. And the longer she spent in this windswept country of mystery and chance, the more she began to realize it was time for her to let go.

***

Upon the horizon, a fortress loomed. A single stone tower began to emerge, haloed by mist and surrounded by clumps of angry, gray clouds. Like a lone sentinel with furrowed brow, the tower scrutinized the movement of the approaching vessel.

Despite its arrogance, the structure was in disrepair, its rim resembling the top of a chipped rook from a long-discarded chess game. As the boat drew closer, the passengers beheld the full view of the once majestic castle. Extending from the stone tower were the remains of the citadel's foundation, curving and twisting along the banks of Loch Ness, some sections in better condition than others. Only when the vessel drew closer did the travelers begin to appreciate the immensity of the place and its dominance over the landscape.

"Take out those cameras and iPhones, folks, because ye'll definitely want to take a few shots of what stands before us," encouraged Graham. "This is Undlay Castle, a place that has been in existence in some form since the 6th century. Over the course of those hundreds of years, it has certainly witnessed the vagaries of life in the Highlands. At one time, it was the largest medieval fortress in all of Scotland."

With the travelers' interest piqued, Graham continued, "We must go back in time, far back in time to an event that occurred in 580 A.D. when St. Columba—remember our Nessie exorciser—apparently came to this region to baptize a Pictish nobleman by the name of Emchath. There may have been a broch here at that time, but the present ruins date back to the 13th century when Undlay played a role in the Wars of Scottish Independence."

Graham paused here to wipe the lenses of his glasses which had been doused with spray. "Ownership of the castle fluctuated between the Scots and the Brits, and the time was marked by battles, power struggles, and theft. In the 1500s, James IV gave the barony of Undlay to the McElroy clan, commissioning them to restore the castle and estate. So, that tower ye see there, that five-story structure we noticed on our approach? It was built by the McElroys during that century."

"But what happened to it all? Why is it in such poor condition?" queried Vivian. "Did that happen just because of the passage of time?"

Her traveling companion, Paula, jumped in, "I would imagine, Viv, that would be the case. Right, Graham? I mean, take into account all those wars and struggles. Gosh, even just the harsh weather of the Highlands probably had a hand in its disintegration. After all, not everyone can sit on their front porch like we do and make it through an entire calendar year wearing nothing more than a light sweater!"

Graham nodded in agreement. "'Tis true that the castle was affected by all of those forces ye just mentioned, Paula; in fact, a portion of the tower even crashed to the ground because of a violent storm. But the primary reason for the disarray came from an intentional action. When the British abandoned the castle in the early 1700s, they purposely blew it up to prevent its use by Jacobite forces," Graham explained.

"Good God! All that beauty destroyed? What a waste!" lamented Doris. "Hundreds of years to build and mere moments to obliterate."

"Indeed. I believe it was Churchill who said, 'To destroy can be the thoughtless act of a single day.' Ah, well, such are the consequences of war, I suppose," Graham responded. "Later, the locals did even more damage by plundering the site for stonework and other materials. In the 20th century, the castle was eventually transferred to Historic Scotland for restoration, and today 'tis one of the top three visited castles in all of Scotland. How about that?"

The boat's engine churred to a low hum as the captain began to navigate his way into a slip by the entrance pier. The rocky cliffs above gave way to a small patch of sand below, sandwiching the dock on either side.

"Grab yer gear, everyone," Graham announced cheerily. "We're disembarking here for our own appointment with Scottish history. We'll be spending an hour or two on the grounds of Undlay Castle, so be sure to bring anything ye might need with ye for that time."

From the moment the fortress came into view, Caitlyn was silent. It was as if she knew the exact configuration of the structure's layout and could envision it in its entirety. In her mind's eye, she beheld the flags flying from an intact stone tower, she observed the formidable walls enclosing the Great Hall and kitchen, she perceived hallways and chambers contained within. This knowledge, however, made her uneasy not content.

The intensity of the sensation made Caitlyn tremble as her hands grew clammy and her throat constricted. Weighed down by an overwhelming sense of despair, she felt her vision blur from unshed tears. Moving mechanically as if by rote, Caitlyn grabbed her belongings and stepped onto the pier, leaving behind a single salty droplet to mingle with the sea spray on the boat's railing.

***

Caitlyn's faltering misstep when her feet met with dry ground did not go unnoticed. Ann Marie reached out and grabbed hold of Caitlyn's elbow, steadying her. "Darlin', you okay? Feeling a bit queasy from the ride, are you?"

"I...I...suppose so. Just a bit lightheaded, I guess. I'm sure I'll be fine once I get myself going," she responded with just the slightest hint of doubt in her intonation.

Their feet crunched upon the shales that blanketed the shoreline as they made their way to the stone staircase carved into the cliff. Tuffets of grass and weeds peeked through the cracks in the stairs, marking Nature's attempt to erase humanity's intrusion into her domain. At the top of those fifty-some-odd steps stood a stone archway with an iron gate, an apparent threshold into the past.

"Oh, boy, I'm not a big fan of heights, guys," confessed Ann Marie as she leaned on Michael for literal and figurative support. "It's not so bad right now because at least we're out in the open, but I'm not sure if I'm going to be able to handle any narrow passageways up into those towers ahead of us."

"Not a problem," assured Graham. "There's plenty to see here even if ye decide not to climb the towers. I'll give ye the layout of the land, so to speak, and then ye can pick and choose what ye'd like to do."

One by one the tourists ascended the steps and passed through the iron gate, assembling on the stone path that led to the castle entrance. When Graham began to discuss the history of the fortress that stood before them, Caitlyn politely interrupted, "Uh, I'm so sorry. I guess I'm not doing so well after all, everyone. Graham, is there a public restroom nearby? I think I just need a moment or two to pull myself together."

"Of course, my dear," Graham answered, his eyebrows downturned with concern for his traveler. "Just follow the path to the right and up to the top of the hill. There ye'll find a visitor's center where the lavatories are located. By the time ye finish, ye can probably just meander round the grounds with the group or on yer own. My talk here will be somewhat brief, and then everyone is free to explore."

Strangely enough, Caitlyn didn't really wait to hear Graham's full response. Moving in what seemed like a distracted trance, she walked directly up the path as if she were a metallic object drawn to a magnetic pole. Rather than head toward the top of the hill, however, she made a hard left at the first available turn, a path that led her directly to the castle ruins.

Her step quickened as she climbed higher toward the fortress. To an observer, she moved with the alacrity of one who was late for an appointment of great significance. Despite the chill in the air, beads of sweat glistened on her forehead, and the back of her neck became damp and sticky from exertion and worry. Her arms began to pump faster as she drew closer to the structure before her. "Hurry. I must hurry," Caitlyn agonized. "*Is tusa gaol mo chridhe. Leatsa, tha mi criochnaichte.*" O love of my heart. With you, I am complete.

But was she too late?

The narrowness of the staircase and the film of moisture on each step should have forced her to slow her pace, but Caitlyn continued to move with complete abandon, caring nothing for her own safety. Lower and lower into the dark depths of the castle she rushed, twisting and turning with the spiraling steps until at last she came to the bottom.

Her feet now firmly planted on the earthen floor, she stood before a prison cell. With a sharp intake of breath, she leaned closer to peer through the lattice grating into the narrow cave within. Empty. A barren floor bounded by walls of impervious stone. She was too late.

Her anguish culminated in a single primal howl—more animal than human—a sound that reverberated off the dank recesses of the uninhabited dungeon. And after that wail, utter silence. Her body lay twisted on the ground outside the portal that had once contained her soul.

Undlay Castle – 1665

"Aw, now, lassie. Why so woeful, child?" Devin asked as he came upon Mary, outside the McElroy stables. After his momentary pause to witness Mary's quick shoulder shrug, he walked briskly past her, sounds of harness and gear jingling by her as he made his way toward the supply area near the inner stalls and continued going about his work.

The sun's rays sent streams of golden light through the side window of the stable, casting the scene with a warm yellow glow. As Devin arranged the reins in their proper storage places, he heard the plodding steps of the forlorn girl.

"Why won't Da' let me go? Hmm? I'm one of the best riders in the glen, and I'm not afeard of being unable to keep up. I'm actually better at tracking than Robby, aye? So why does he take him and not me on the hunt?"

Placing the remaining tack on the wall, Devin patted the stool next to him, motioning for Mary to sit down. They'd often had these conversations—young child and wizened hostler—indeed, Mary felt more at ease asking questions of Devin than she did of her own father, the imposing laird of Undlay. The stablemaster had patiently taught her many things about riding and caring for horses, about nurturing the tame and appreciating the wild, about reveling in the seasons and respecting Nature's power. Life was his canvas, and with every brush stroke, Devin bestowed upon his young pupil a never-ending masterpiece, teaching her how to be vibrantly alive with joy and wonder. At his knee and in this humble setting, Mary was in her element here more than anywhere else.

"For sure, my lintie, ye're all those things, Mary, but ye must keep in mind that there are some matters that are meant for sons and some meant for daughters. The hunt, aye, is something for the gentlemen to endeavor, and ye'd do well to learn to move on from it and shed nary a tear over things ye canna control. Someday, when ye're the fine lady of yer own estate, ye can make up rules that better suit ye. But for now, why don't ye lead out old Arwen so as she can be brushed and groomed." It hurt Devin a bit to see his favorite child so discouraged, for he knew in his heart she *was* the finest rider and tracker in the glen. They had journeyed out together countless times from when she was barely able to mount lil Enbarr, the pony, to just last week when she was atop Hubert and managed to locate and pursue an elusive red fox. But Devin knew unequivocally that Laird McElroy would never allow Mary to cross the line and be part of a formal hunt.

After tethering Arwen to the post, Mary filled the bucket with water from the spring and began cooling down the old mare's coat. While whispering gentle words into the animal's ear, the young girl put the horse into a state of sweet surrender, and the two kindred spirits found their own sense of peace as the sun dipped deeper along the horizon, embracing them both in beatific light.

The task liberated Mary from her earlier disappointment, and her feelings began to shift from anger and resentment to tenderness and serenity. As she later guided the contented mare back to her stall, a trill of laughter jostled the silence, thanks to the chaotic arrival of Mary's younger siblings, Deirdre and Aidan, and her friend, Annag, daughter of the McElroy's chambermaid.

"MARY, come!" shouted Aidan. "We're playing hide-n-seek, and 'tis much better when there's more people!" With those words, Aidan's running feet slid to a halt once he caught sight of Mary, but he nearly crashed into the back of Arwen's stall trying to slow down.

"Och, now, Aidan, git out of the stalls NOW, what with yer bellowing and yer stomping feet! Can ye not see ye're spooking the horses? Git out and give me some time here to calm her down again, ye eedgit!"

"But will ye come play with us?" begged Deirdre in the softest of whispers, clasping her hands together as if in prayer.

"Maybe, but for now, git out. Both of ye," Mary said with determination.

"God's body, Mary. Please rescue me from those two midges," implored Annag. "I've been with them all afternoon, and I'm losing what little sanity I have. O, and besides, if ye can come join me, when they are hiding, I've got a great story to tell ye about Shannon Waterson and what's become of her love potion." Annag's eyes twinkled with the promise of the latest gossip, and Mary's own widened with interest as she nodded to Annag, assuring her that she would definitely be along momentarily.

As Mary bid farewell to Devin, the gray-haired fellow gave her a wink and raised one of his thick, gnarled fingers back and forth between them both, saying, "We'll go out together, ye and I, tomorrow if ye like, and see if we can find that red fox again, eh?"

"I'd like that very much, Devin. And thank ye…for listening to the babbling of a silly girl like me," Mary responded quickly and then ran up the hill to where the three were waiting.

***

"Okay, so ye two go hide together, and Mary and I will come for ye after we count to fifty," suggested Annag, as she stealthily shifted her eyes over toward Mary and raised her eyebrows up and down a few times.

But before the two young ones could head off to their secret place, the thunder of approaching hooves stopped them in their tracks. "They're back!" yelled Aidan. "They're back from the hunt. Wait, let's see what they've brought. That'll be me someday, ye ken," he announced proudly to the three girls who surrounded him.

"Not if ye're still too scairt to ride Hubert, ye're not," countered Deirdre with a smug look on her face.

"I am NOT too scairt. It's just that Devin willna' let me right now. But I'm ready, ye ken. He just doesna' believe me, is all."

"He doesna' believe ye because yer knees knock together, and yer voice gets all wobbly when he asks ye, that's why," Deirdre declared, lifting her chin in the air and turning her back on her brother.

Aidan snarled, "I'll show ye," as he spun Dierdre around, grabbed her hands, and wrapped his foot around her leg, dropping the girl to the ground.

"Stop, ye fools. We're going to miss their arrival," Mary reprimanded. Curious in spite of herself, Mary wanted to hear about the hunt, yet found herself conflicted. She knew she should be hoping that the men were successful and that there would be additional food for the family and for the guests, but she secretly wished they had failed so that maybe, just maybe, she, with her expertise, would be summoned to join in on the next trip.

Riding at the front, ahead of her own father, was Mary's younger brother, Robby, bursting with an excitement that bubbled over into a tumult of words: "Mary, I did it. I did it. I came upon the boar all on my own. The group had split into three, and I found it. I speared it, right through its side. It was *my* kill." As Robby proclaimed these words, he pointed to the litter trailing behind that carried the bloodied corpse of the animal.

"Fine," Mary uttered half-heartedly while in her own head she thought, *I could've done that myself three years ago, ye dumb twit.*

With the taste of victory in his carriage, Robby led his father and the other four hunters down the hill toward Devin and the stables, but not before one of the riders looked down upon Mary and quipped, "Hey, there. What are ye doing out here when we're coming to sit at table with ye? Have ye already prepared the feast for us starving fellows, have ye? Is that why ye're not in the kitchen as ye should be?"

These words came from George Campbell, the eldest son of Laird Campbell and heir to the great estate just west of Undlay. Tall and lean, with eyes and hair as black as the stallion upon which he rode, George was known for his sarcastic wit and sense of entitlement. Many a time he disparaged Mary for her unseemly outdoor habits and her lack of interest in all things domestic. When they were younger, George often needled the girl with wry insults until she could contain herself no longer and either lost her temper and exploded outright or was forced to stomp off in a huff. It was no secret that both the McElroys and the Campbells felt that a bond between the two families could be forged more securely by a marital union among the children. Unfortunately for Mary, she was, in her eyes, the likely sacrificial lamb.

"Awa'n' bile yer own heed, Georgie Campbell," Mary retorted, unable to avoid scrunching up her nose and pursing her lips simultaneously at the arrogant young man as he snickered in derision and then sped up to rejoin the group once again.

"Well, come on, let's get on with the game then already," Mary snapped impatiently.

***

With the two children safely off to their hiding place, Annag, like a summer storm that gently rises over the Highlands with slow rumbles of thunder until the noise becomes deafening, delivered her story with an ever-building pace that erupted in a single, sensational truth.

"Ye ken how Shannon Waterson has been ogling Malcolm Gordon for nigh on two years now? Well, he didna' have any time for her at all, so what do ye

23

think she does? She goes down through the glen to the shack by the loch, she does."

"No," Mary interrupted in disbelief.

"Aye. She did just that. She did. She told me all about it. She knocked on old Hilda's door, hoping no one followed her or saw her knocking, and the old witch crooks her finger like such and says, 'Come in, lassie; I'll be knowing what ye're after, aye?' And without Shannon even saying a word, Hilda comes back with a small vial of liquid. Now, Shannon says, hanging from the ceiling of her hut meanwhile 'twere all skinned animals and dangling herbs and vines and such, so eerie that Shannon didna' even have a sound coming out of her throat when she did try to speak."

"I canna believe she even *went* there, Annag. She must've been sorely desperate to get Malcolm's attention, no?"

"Aye, and so Hilda tells Shannon 'tis a love potion and that she must somehow pour its contents into Malcolm's drink on the same night as a full moon, which of course, was just Sunday last. So, when Shannon does croak the words, 'thank you' out of her mouth, she goes to put the coin in Hilda's hand, and ye'll never guess what..."

"What?" Mary asked with an intake of breath.

"The old witch darn had two thumbs branching off one another, she did!"

"Och, nooo!"

"Yes," Annag confirmed, wide-eyed.

"But what about the potion?"

"Aye, okay, so's now Shannon must figure out a way to see Malcolm on that Sunday AND she must get him to have a drink with her...oops, wait... 'We're close to finding ye, we are, ye little rascals, Deirdre and Aidan. We're smelling ye out by your stinking bodies, aye!' Okay, so's she bakes some bannocks and sets out in the late afternoon for the Gordon estate with a jug of water bound to her saddle and the vial tucked into the binding of her sleeve.

"Before arriving on the grounds, she lathers up the horse with the water and concocts this story that, while on her way to bring the Gordons the extra bannocks she had made and didna' want to waste, she was chased by a raider. When Lady Gordon sees Shannon and the horse in such disarray, she summons Malcolm to come look at the horse and brings Shannon into the kitchen and asks Shannon what she needs—to which she says, 'Maybe just a wee dram of whiskey, Lady Gordon?' When she returns with the drink, Shannon tells her

24

she wants to go check on her horse's condition and asks, 'Should I bring a dram for Malcolm too, do ye think?' So now, with no one else around, as she is walking toward the stables, she pours the potion into Malcolm's glass and delivers it to him as he's examining the beast. Masterful, no?" Annag asks, nodding her head up and down as if affirming the answer to her own question.

"It may be, but yer not finished yet, right? What happens next?"

"So as Malcolm's busy drying down the horse, Shannon offers him the whiskey, he drinks it, and then he *stops working on the horse*!" Annag exclaims.

"So…? That doesna' mean anything. He had to stop working on the horse in order to take the sip, no? He was probably done calming down the horse anyway, is all," Mary observed.

"No, because then he looks at Shannon. I mean he *really* looks at her for the verra first time in his life, she says. *And* he asks her if she wants him to escort her home! Now, how about that!"

All this while, the pair was so caught up in their story that they didn't hear or notice that the two young ones had simply materialized before them, until Aidan exclaimed, "Ye two are rotten. Ye didna' even look for us, did ye? Flapping your lips and telling your tales. I do not even want to play this game with you anymore!" With that, he folded his arms and stuck out his bottom lip.

"Me, too," Deirdre echoed, assuming Aidan's stance.

"Ah, no, don't be sourpusses, ye two," Mary offered. "Let's not work in pairs any more, all right? I'll go and hide by myself, and ye three can come search for me. How's that?" Anything, Mary thought, to avoid having to sit at table with George Campbell.

And then, quietly to Annag, she murmured, "One escorted ride home doesna' mean the potion worked, ye ken." With a toss of her head, Mary darted off into the woods as the sound of three voices counting off to fifty cut into the silence of the twilight air.

Mary – The Forest

Lifting my skirts for clearance, I commanded my feet to run, rejoicing in the liberation of movement over the grassy knoll on my way toward the wood. Having spent many a day exploring and investigating the forest near the western side of our estate, I ken exactly where to tuck myself away and bide my time till my three pursuers would draw near.

When I run like this, I feel as if my feet spring effortlessly and soundlessly off the earth and that the ground is not hard and rigid but soft and bouncy like a pillow stuffed with fresh down. As I sliced through the wind that broke on either side of me, I felt my hair ribbon loosen and fall in the trail I left behind.

The trees began to thicken, and the ground beneath my feet grew more uneven as I ventured deeper and deeper into the sylvan landscape. My destination was a hollowed-out trunk that rested horizontally, one I ken perfectly fit the contours of my body, a brilliant place to make myself simply disappear.

It was long past twilight now, and as the shadows began to lengthen so too did my thoughts begin to darken with the memory of the afternoon's events. Slowing from a sprint to a brisk walk, I found myself irritated all over again at the constraints under which I lived. I had no voice, no influence, no power to make decisions, decisions that even affected my own life. 'Och, no, she canna go on the hunt. Who cares about her skill or talent? It's just not acceptable, and it will *never* be acceptable, and that's that.'

I'm continually crushed by rules that are as entrenched and immovable as the pines that gather around me. And with that nod to my local surroundings, I looked down and noticed at my feet a shattered egg belonging to a gold crest chick, doomed, poor creature, before it ever had the chance to fly. I stood there for a moment in the silence, touched by its frailty and its grounding. 'Twould never taste the freedom that comes from fluttering its wings, its brief life snuffed out before it could ever ascend.

The luminous glow of the shell provided a stark contrast to the darkness that had enveloped me. *Hell mend ye.* Did I turn where I was supposed to? Oh, dear, I'm not so sure. Foolish girl, getting so caught up in her thoughts that she forgot what she was doing. Maybe I did turn already; I best be heading straight to my hiding place then, I decided. And as I continued to move forward, my thoughts irrevocably paced backward.

And even beyond the hunt, what about having a say in my own future? Look at Shannon, I mused. She sees what she wants, and she's going after it. Course, she may be partaking of some questionable tactics along the way to secure Malcolm's affections, but at least she is paving her own way down the path of true love. And what do I have? A possible—no, a probable—betrothal to a rude, scheming, choleric man who will act more like an overbearing laird than a devoted husband.

If I feel confined now, it'll be a thousand times worse to be under George's authority. All of his vile comments about my complexion ('Yer face is looking quite leathery these days, Mary. Ye must be hanging about the stables again'); my interests ('I was going to buy ye some fine linen when I visited the market, but alas, you canna sew verra well, now can ye?'); even my faith ('What's that I see danglin' from yer hands there, Mary? Surely, ye wouldn't want Reverend Edwards and the Covenanters to be hearing about no rosary beads')—listening to him speak is akin to having to eat the spit-out portions of food ol' Gram McElroy leaves behind on her plate.

And it's not just his words either. His entire presence is utterly revolting: the way his top teeth are crusted in a brown moss near the gums; the anemic sliver of hair above his lip he calls a moustache; the chin that recedes so far into his neck that he doesna' even have a jawline. My skin gets all itchy just thinking about him, and my stomach turns queasy when I remember the time when I was looking for shells by the loch, and he grabbed me from behind, slathering my neck with drool, his deplorable version of a kiss. As I shivered and shook my head, shoulders, and arms in unison, I stopped to get a sense of my bearings. All this deliberation has put me far past the time for playing. I was quite certain that by this hour Deirdre, Aidan, and Annag had probably given up and returned to the castle. But where *was* I?

Despite it being summer, the night chill was in the air, and my surroundings seemed to be wrapped in black velvet. I couldna' make out any discernible features of anything at this point, and I berated myself for being so engrossed in my own misery that I was actually now quite lost…and scared. What was it that Devin always told me? 'What are ye going to be, lassie? A candle or a fire? When the wind come at ye, are ye going to give up and sputter out or are ye going to blaze with power when the hard times come?' From the safety of the barn surrounded by the comforting smell of the horses I so dearly loved, it was easy to claim I'd be the fire, but here, on this ebony night as the screech of the long-eared owl pierced the air, I crumpled beside a different tree, letting the tears dampen the shawl that I wrapped tightly round my body. Detecting no difference between keeping my eyes open or closing them in defeat, I allowed myself to be extinguished.

Donal – The Reckoning

Aye, so we spak of the brae Johnnie
'Twas known throughout the land.
So gallant a man was yong Johnnie
That all here bowed to his command.

The King he hears of Johnnie's valour
And a missive to him he sends,
Requesting a meeting at a certain hour
In the guise of making amends.

The men ride out and convey the King
To a sumptuous feast at Gilnockie,
And Johnnie is sure that the King will bring
Good wishes and honor a'plenty.

With drink and venison and the finest fare
Johnnie walks toward the King with grace.
But the man only looks with covetous stare
Determin'd to show Johnnie his place.

"Be gone, be gone, thou traitor fool
I have come here but to destroy ye,
For how dare ye refuse to honor my rule
And hide these goods and wealth from me!"

"O King, O King, preserve my life
I'll surrender to ye what I own.
My steeds, my cattle, just cause no strife,
And leave me and my raiders alone."

But the King only laughs and signals his men
To seize Johnnie and all his fellows.
"Ye'll not be reiving here ever again;
Yer going straight down to the gallows!"

And to this day, if ye go to that glen
Where young Johnnie and his boys lost their lives,
The faint echo of hooves pounds again and again,
As their spirits forever will ride.

Four voices sang out these verses in unison as we went about checking our gear and watering our horses. Although the night had settled into a rich darkness, beneath it throbbed the scintillating energy that arises from the promise of adventure. Tonight we would raid again, the first in quite some time. It had been a changing landscape for us, the men who lived on the border—not on the literal border, of course, as we were not in the lowlands, but figuratively, in the sense that we occupied a netherlands of sorts.

Future inheritance for each of us was negligible. Not one of us was an eldest son; we would stand to gain nothing once death seized upon a father. So we danced upon this boundary between lawlessness and decorum because we were forced to, compelled to, finding ourselves, more often than not, in the latter circumstances rather than the former. And to be quite honest, it was undoubtedly the more exciting place to be.

Our goal this eve was to lift about 25 cattle from MacKinty lands, but the night was yet too young to begin our journey. So as we waited for the hours to slip into deeper ebony, we sang, we joked, and we justified our actions. The MacKinty clan were notorious for stealing and cheating their neighbors and tenants. Just last week, they took four chickens from one of their cottars— William and Kirstine—because they felt the couple had been holding back on their rent payments. Too dumb or perhaps too cold-hearted to realize that

William was not able to work for nigh on two months as his ribs were broken in a fall from his roof, Callan MacKinty cares only about one thing: payment.

And so, despite the fact that Kirstine was trying to do what she could with mending and sewing for barter, the couple were forced to look on helplessly as Callan snatched their livestock and threatened to do worse the following month if they didna' settle their debt. Time for payback, MacKinty, only not the kind yer expecting. 'Tis a night of reckoning.

"Hey, Donal. Give me a hand here with Dewey. His eye's all runny, but he will not let me near it," the robust voice of Brodie halted my thoughts, returning me to the present moment. "Och, yer head is so oft in yon clouds 'tis a wonder yer feet are still planted on the ground, ye fool."

"Well, at least I have a mind that has the power to roam, ye ken. Yers is fixed on three things: food, drink, and reiving. If ye'd had a dash of flair about ye, maybe it'd be four things, but even if ye contemplated the fairer gender, there be no lady who'd go within a loch's distance of a stinking, dirt-ridden, sour-breathed muttonhead such as yerself," I retorted.

And before my final words were out, Brodie—despite his wide girth and size—turned and launched himself in one quick action, burying his shoulder into my belly, knocking us both to the ground. Outweighed by two-stone, I ken I had no chance to lift Brodie off my chest, so I opted to slither and slide out from beneath him, grabbing his wrist and bending the man's elbow up so far that it was near the center of his back. Planting my knee into his shoulder blade, I twisted and raised the wrist till I had him yelping for mercy.

My victory was interrupted by the "voice of reason" in our group, "Och, fine, then. While ye two dimwits are tussling about, we're wasting valuable preparation time. Git up now. I guess it'll be up to me to see about Dewey's eye." Owen spoke these words as he impatiently made his way over to the sturdy horse.

Although Dewey was but fourteen hands, he was a giant in terms of stamina and maneuverability. The hobbler could navigate any obstacle—steep hillsides, muddied bogs, rocky streams—with a confidence that transferred seamlessly to his rider. And although not shaggy now in late August, he would, by the winter months, be covered in a thick coat, a veritable blanket protecting him against the worst weather the Highlands could muster. Something troubling his eye was a major concern, especially for a creature so dependent upon the precise night vision that we reivers rely on when either pursuing or being pursued.

As Brodie stood slowly, using one hand to push himself off the ground and the other placed palm-side down against his bruised back, he eyed me. "Just ye wait, ye. Ye may have slithered out of my grasp this time, but ye'll see…"

"Well, I'll leave ye to your planning then and Owen to his doctoring. Keep an ear out for young Ross, will ye? He should be upon us within the hour," and with those words I moved away from our jesting and banter to be by myself and clear my mind for what lay ahead.

We would ride tonight—Brodie, Owen, Ross, and I—under the cover of night to the MacKinty land to settle the score. But we still had over an hour before needing to set out, so I, restless as ever, absented myself from their singing and camaraderie, walking deeper into the thicket.

I welcomed the shadows that embraced me, breathing deep of the scent of seasonal change in the air. The overripe smell of vegetation in these late days of August would soon be surrendering to the ashen scent of the fallen leaves of September. Not having any familiarity with motherly love, as mine own had died when I was but a wee bairn, Nature assumed that mantle for me. She was my instructor, my healer, my guide, and my center. I sought her counsel and found her voice amid the silence of my surroundings. This venture into the woods was a welcome retreat into the stillness that united us both.

There was no moon this eve, so I moved forward by relying on sound and touch. From trunk to trunk, I reached with my hands upon the corrugated bark of each tree as I listened to my steps land upon the soft mulch. Occasionally, I would hear the crack of a twig snap beneath my feet, but other than that momentary intrusion, the forest was remarkably quiet.

It was in this manner that I came upon a felled tree, next to which something seemed to shimmer with light. As I bent lower to the ground, I could see strands of red and gold silk, and without thinking further, my hand of its own volition was drawn to touch and feel those silky strands. Not quite simultaneously but close to it, the contents beside the trunk shifted, and the red and gold strings tumbled downward, revealing to me the face of an angel, one whose look of contentment was belied by tear-stained tracks beneath each eye.

With an abrupt intake of breath, I immediately came to realize that this celestial creature before me was not of the heavens but of the land, the land of the McElroys. She was none other than Mary McElroy, daughter of the Laird

McElroy. I had heard tales of her beauty and her wild spirit, but I myself had never met her before. As I stood there marveling at the perfection of her features—the curtain-fringed eyelashes, the delicate upturned nose, the strong set of her chin—I was awash in the strangest combination of tenderness and desire. What *was* she doing here? I wondered. And why in this place? Was she running away? Clearly, whatever prompted her to be here in this location was accompanied by some degree of anguish. Perhaps she lost her way?

Only by waking her would I find the answers to these questions, and I ken that I didna' want to do that. The last thing I wanted was to frighten her by my presence or disturb this serenity she had found in sleep. Even if she had voluntarily run away, I pondered, I couldna' just leave her here to the elements. After all, she canna be any more than sixteen or seventeen, and what young lady—wealthy or no—would be able to fend for herself out here in the woods? No, the way I saw it, I couldna' leave her here in this place; I would carry her back toward her property, place her gently on the grounds there, and slink back into the woods. As long as I ran during my return, I would still be able to keep my appointment with my fellows for the evening's 'activities'.

And so with the gentlest of movements, I slipped one arm round her back, the other beneath her head, and lifted her up to rest upon my chest. With every step, I inhaled the scent of pine that kissed her red-gold hair, finding myself intoxicated with her very spirit.

Mary – Real or Imagined?

It started with a faint tingling in my nose. Teetering between dreaming and consciousness, I scrunched my face and shook my head just to stop the sensation. This sideways movement, however, brought me no relief, so one hand, then the other, moved to my face as I attempted to snuff out the sensation. Not that it was an unpleasant vibration; rather just one that commanded my immediate attention. With such abrupt movements, I opened my salt-crusted eyes, feeling the disorientation one often has after a night of frustration and tears. Despite the heaviness of that memory, I was surprisingly alert as the tingling extended into the very marrow of my bones. The scent of moss and leaves hung in the air, though I found myself outside the forest and on the stone path in front of Undlay.

As I pushed myself up from the ground, I found my legs unsteady and wobbly, so I began searching the recesses of my mind in order to recall the events of the past few hours.

The game—the hiding—my subsequent wandering off-track—these were the sketchy remnants that I stitched together. And of course, my surrender—that I remember most deeply—mainly because I've always hated to concede. But yes, it was at that moment, the moment I realized I was but a foolish girl—a mere pawn to be manipulated by the greater pieces on life's chessboard—it was then that I simply quit. I gave up the fight. I relinquished my will. And I despised myself for making such a cowardly choice.

But it was in that vulnerable state of surrender when a most miraculous visitation occurred! When I consider the vague outline of that encounter, I canna ignore the accompanying warmth that emanates right now from the center of my body to its farthest reaches. If I had a glass before me, I'd wager that my whole being were aglow with light. I ken I was touched by someone or something, but what was it? Or…who was it?

I do remember the tenderness beneath a calloused hand, the surge of muscle, the safe cocoon that encircled me as I nestled within cradled arms. Even now, I inhale the leathery scent of his gear and feel the texture of his cloth against my cheek, the coppery smell of his sweat mingled with earth and woods. Enveloped and protected by the breadth of his shoulders, I could hear the determined beat of a heart that pulsed with confidence and conviction. And as for me? All I could feel was pure contentment and the sensation of being totally safe.

Was it magic? If so, what power brought me here? Was it real? If real, then who was this protector, this savior of mine? With these questions circling and swirling in my head, I dusted my skirt free of the twigs and brambles of the forest and walked forward onto the path that led to the castle door, my step as light and airy as the thoughts which lifted my heart into the misty haze of love.

The Return to Undlay

"Chchtt, chchtt," Annag sounded from the window above, as Mary swung her head about, searching for the sound. "Here, Mary! Look up, ye. Up here." From the carved-out window two stories above, Annag stretched her whisper to a yell that pulsed with urgency. "Do not go through the front now. Meet me nigh the west tower and come in through there!"

Mary scurried off the stone path, moving lower down the hill, approaching the tower that stood closest to the loch. The smell of the water lifted off the surface, infusing with moisture the air that surrounded the castle. Traveling in a semi-circle around the exterior of the tower, Mary came to the door just as it began to creak with complaint at its opening.

"Sssshhh," implored Annag, "ye're supposed to be in yer room, lying abed. That's what I told your Ma when we come back from the hiding game without ye. Where have ye been, Mary? Ye had me so scairt. I was afeard they were going to send out the hounds for ye and that they were going to flog me raw once they found out I was lying as to yer whereabouts."

Because Mary's eyes appeared unfocused and her head tilted sideways in bewilderment, Annag grabbed her shoulders and shook the girl, willing ripples of reality to penetrate her senses.

"Do ye hear me now? Mary, are ye in there at all?"

"Annag, yes. Stop. I'm here. Dinna fash. What did ye tell the others?" The girls began to make their way up the twisting steps, so narrow they could not stand two abreast.

"Well, I pulled yer mother aside and told her we were playing with the younger ones, ye ken, when ye were taken with your courses verra suddenly and verra bad. I told her I brought ye directly to yer room, and that ye were resting a spell since yer cramps come powerful strong. What she told yer Da', I do not ken. All I ken is I bought ye enough time to skip the meal without anyone being alarmed. And now that I see ye, I feel I'm ready to pass out from relief that yer safe, and I'll not be whipped!" After this pronouncement, Annag leaned up against the stone wall of the staircase, lifting her eyes up to the sky.

From the step below, Mary looked up at her friend with eyes that shone with gratitude. She knew that Annag had not only saved her from her father's wrath, but that she had also cleverly managed to free Mary from having to sit with George Campbell. For that, Mary was utterly indebted to the girl, and she reached out to clasp Annag's right hand with both of her own. "Annag, ye're so good to me, so dear to me. I've much to tell ye about this evening. But quickly, let's hurry to my room where I can try to put into words something that I'm not sure can be told."

With that promise, the two finished climbing the steps and reached the long corridor which connected the tower with the main castle where the bed chambers were. Wall sconces illuminated their way, both on the stairs and in the corridor, casting a softening glow upon the stone passage. The smell from the loch dissipated somewhat as they walked deeper along the connecting hallway, and after they passed the door for the younger children's room, they next came upon the one that led into Mary's quarters.

As she closed the portal behind them, Annag moved toward the hearth. Seizing the nearby poker to stir up the embers, Annag next placed two small pieces of firewood upon the red-orange mound. Mary, still not totally grounded in reality, gently sat down upon her quilted bed, her hands folded in her lap and her eyes gazing faraway.

She began, "I'm not sure of anything, Annag. I ken I ran into the forest. I had a fine place to hide, but I was so mad over so many things that happened today, and I dunno. I think I got lost. Crazy that I should get lost in a wood that I ken so well, right? But I did. Maybe it was the darkness. Maybe it was my own distractions. Maybe I was too busy being mad that I wasna' aware of how deeply I had gone into the shadows. All I ken is that I felt so lost that I just gave up. I curled up like a puny bairn and cried myself to sleep.

"Cried because I'm a fool for thinking that I would be able to make choices for myself based on what I want. *Am* I a fool, Annag? Am I wrong to want to scream out, 'I do not want to be bound to Georgie Campbell' or that 'I do not want to be sewing and mending and cooking when there's so much out *there* that's more exciting?' Tell me, Annag. Yer older, ye've been around longer and seen more things than I have. Am I wrong?"

"Well, I dunno about some of the things that ye be desiring, Mary, as I'm kinda content with a few of the tasks ye be mentioning, like baking and mending. I find there is great pride in doing those things and doing them well. But I can tell ye, yer not crazy for wanting to make yer own choice when it comes to marrying. Ye see, it's actually better to be a girl in my station than to be one in yers. We have a bit more, how shall I say, 'love choice' than ye do, my lass. We can let our preference be known when it comes to wedding.

"Och, sure we want our husband to be able to provide for us and to give us shelter and hopes for a solid future, but it's nigh about estates and lands and titles and such. So, no, I do not think yer wrong for feeling like a wee mouse cornered by hungry cats. It's just that ye are quite a sumptuous prize to be offered for the taking. But for that, though, ye may be grateful. Ye'll not be given to just any man, but only to a true laird. So one day, Mary, ye'll be the great lady of some fine estate, and then ye can set the tune to whatever music ye wish to hear, ye ken?"

"Oh, Annag. I canna wait that long. And in order to get to that point, I would have to bond myself to someone I canna abide. What do I do with myself when I'm forced to make my heart go dead? Especially when I ken what it feels like to be aflame with passion and desire?"

"Passion and desire? Wait, when did ye start feeling *that*, Mary? What have ye not told me about this eve?" Annag's eyes scrutinized Mary with suspicion.

Mary twisted her hands in her lap, knotting and unknotting them as she struggled to find words to explain the inexplicable. "Well, as I said before, I'm not quite certain of all the details, cause, ye see, so much 'tis cloudy and dreamlike. But I ken I was lost and I wrapped my shawl about me and lay down in the wood, sobbing myself to sleep. And then, someone—or something—came to me. I could feel it even before I was lifted up.

"I thought maybe it was something from the otherworld, like a fairy spirit or something, but then I could smell the coppery, thick scent of a man. I still wasna' sure if it was earthly or no. Perhaps it was *Ghillie Dubh*, the male woodsman, ye ken? The one who comes to the rescue of children who venture into and lose themselves in his leafy kingdom, but I do not think it was he. No, it couldna' be, because I could feel a fire starting to spark deep in my loins when I was enveloped by his arms, and I do not think any fairy spirit could create such powerful yearning deep inside a person, right, Annag?"

"Well, did ye get a look at him? Maybe a quick sideways glance or something? A fast lifting of one of yer eyelids perhaps?"

"No, I didna'. I was afeard that if I opened them then the magic—if 'twere magic—would vanish, and that warm feeling inside me would grow cold again. I didna' want that sensation to go away; it was heating me up from within. The more I breathed in my guardian's presence, the more I surrendered myself to him, and though we were only connected as one for that brief journey through the forest, I think I ken now what it means to be filled with wanting." Seated on the bed beside Mary and entranced by the story, Annag stared at the hearth in silence. Mary continued, "So, yes, Annag, now that I ken what is possible for a woman to feel deep inside herself, I canna settle for anything less. I need time, time to delay any discussions between the Campbells and my family, time to find this forest-man, and time to see, once I do find him, if he feels the same burning for me as I do for him. The short of it is, I'll not have George Campbell touch me, hold me, carry me, take me anywhere—not when I've come to learn such sensations are possible."

Annag gently shook her head from side to side as she considered Mary's declaration. After a gap of silence, she reached to take hold of Mary's hands and began, "These are bold words, Mary, especially when yer not even sure of what's real and what's not. What if yer forest-man turns out to be nae more than a fairy spirit, *Ghillie Dubh* or no? Then where are ye? Ye could be searching for nothing more than an illusion, a dream, and all the while be giving up yer chance to be the richest, most powerful lady in the glen. Go slowly on this one, Mary. Keep Georgie at bay only; do not push him away outright, just in case your rescuer is but the wishful imaginings of a spirited young lassie, such as yerself."

Thrusting aside her friend's hands, Mary rejected Annag's advice. "But do ye not see, Annag? Whether he is real or not, I canna pretend I never had these yearnings, these desires! I feel naught but disgust and revulsion round George, wealth and all. To deny the emotions I had this eve is to deny my verra being and to become but a shell of a person. I tell ye, Annag, I'll not be long for this world if I have to live a life without passion in it."

Resolved to this commitment, Mary stood from the bed and began pacing back and forth in front of the fire. "First, I must try to find my forest protector. I'll make it a point to venture into the woods throughout the days to come. I'll try different hours, being sure to always include the evening. I'll just have to make excuses about my whereabouts at times—or I'll just sneak out and have you cover for me." At this point, Annag gasped in protest, but Mary persisted, "And if that doesna work, I ken what I'll do. I'll make that journey through the glen to the shack by the loch."

While Annag, in shock, covered her gaping mouth with her hand, Mary finished, "I'll seek counsel from Hilda."

Donal – Anticipation

I wanted to linger. Just one last, long moment to gaze upon the beauty that lay before me. Taking a backward step away from her, I kept my eyes fixed on her features and found myself fighting the pull to have her back in my arms. I ken that I must leave, but I wanted to carry this vision with me, tonight and always. Cupping both of my hands to my face, I inhaled the traces of pine with which she had anointed me. And with a final intake of breath, I turned and ran into the shadows of the forest.

Accompanied by a full chorus of night creatures, my footfall was muffled and secondary to the sounds that surrounded me. In the distance, the deep-throated roar of a stag provided the backdrop to the more immediate scruffling and sniffing sounds coming from the hedgehogs nearby, their rumaging splintered from time to time with the high-pitched "twit" and "too-aaon" from a pair of tawny owls above.

My legs carried me back to the designated tryst where Brodie, Owen, and, by now, Ross were waiting upon me. Thrill pulsed in my veins, a strange combination of both unfulfilled desire and the promise of upcoming risk. My nerves were taut and my senses sharp, thinking about what just happened and knowing what lay ahead. With my mind racing as fast as my feet, I etched these lines in my head:

Swiftly forms the globe of blood
That follows the first pain.
A thistle's alarum for the danger to come
From no army, no soldier's tread
But from hair red-gold and eyes of emerald
That pierce my heart instead.

Hmmm. It'd be needing a tune, I thought, and once we've settled our score tonight with MacKinty, I'll return to these verses. Almost immediately after pondering this idea, I began to hear the braying of horses and realized that I was close.

"Well, that was one long woodland ramble, Donal. We thought ye'd changed yer mind about tonight's business, ye ken," Brodie announced once he saw me emerging from the thicket. Sitting atop Dewey with his lance in hand and cutting sword in its sheath, he looked at me quizzically, awaiting an explanation for my delay, an explanation that was not forthcoming.

Instead, I moved over to Ross, slapping his chestnut-colored mount, Bran, "Welcome, my friend, last I recall we were waiting on ye for a bit there. All is well with the Gregor clan, I trust?"

"Aye, sure. I just had a time of it getting free," he explained. Ross was the youngest of our four, and while he was most ardent to be part of our raiding expeditions, he was truly the most jumpy when it came to the actual event. He had two older brothers who were slaves to their whiskey, and so most of the chores and responsibilities of the homestead fell onto Ross to complete. His bright red hair stuck out straight in varied directions off his head, giving him the look of being perpetually scattered. Once in the saddle though and thrown into the action, he was a brae fighter, always looking to prove his worth to us all.

"I had felled two trees nigh yesterday and still had more chopping to do. I didna realize we had run so low until Sara told me such. But I was able to put a good number of logs by the hearthside before saddling up and heading here."

Never one to shirk his duties, Ross worked hard to keep his two sisters, Sara and Nora, supplied with food and other necessities while trying to prevent his good-for-nothing brothers from bringing the land to ruin with their drinking and gambling. Both of Ross' parents had died from the fever five years ago, and the little money that they had put aside had already been squandered by Derek and Angus.

I made my way over to my horse, Cerwyn, picked up my lance, knowing I already had my dagger and pistol with me. Stepping into the stirrup with my left foot, I swung my right over Cerwyn's back and turned him round to face the group. In conjunction with that movement, Owen asked, "I ken which way we will be approaching MacKinty lands, but have ye given any thought, Donal, as to which way we'll be leaving them?"

Raising his eyebrows and lifting his voice to match the question, Owen continually proved he was a methodical planner. He always liked to have things drawn up and organized in his own mind beforehand, and it irked him when we repeatedly had to make adjustments on the fly. But that is the nature of reiving; ye had to be ready to switch and turn and change as quick as the weather.

Smallest in stature among us, Owen was (next to me), however, unlimited in his desire for adventure. Maybe that was because adventure was so foreign to him in his everyday existence. As the third son of the village preacher, Owen had a biblical text for every occurrence so that his life was never upended by surprises. All was according to God's plan. The passing of Ross' parents, the lightning strike on the Gilchrist pasture, the razing of the Citadel of Inverness in '62, everything was orchestrated by the divine puppeteer in the clouds who presided over and manipulated his creatures in order to fit some highly orchestrated and measurable performance, to which only He—and Owen himself--were privy. His wispy blonde hair, bound with a leather strap that encircled his forehead, stayed affixed to his skull as solidly as did his opinions.

But there was a discernible wild side to Owen, evidenced by his willingness and enthusiasm to join us on these excursions. I believe, on some level, he likened himself to a Medieval crusader plundering the Moors, quoting his bible along the way for justification.

"Of course, I've got the leaving path in my head, so dinna fash. But no matter which way I *think* we may return, just ken that ye and Ross will stay with me while Brodie will lay wait in ambush if need be."

With a playful grin and a hand beating his chest, Brodie announced, "'Tis what I do best, is that not right, Donal? Remember the run-in we had last autumn with the Cunninghams? We had nigh about fifty cattle, and Gavin Cunningham himself with his two boys come in pursuit of us. Springing out of the underbrush, I led the old man and his horse into the millpond bog and then swung back and unsaddled both Roddy and Lennox with only my lance. That gave us two fine steeds to go with our fifty head that we brought to market that time, aye? Quite a profitable night, if I do say so myself."

Brodie nodded his head in affirmation, beaming with pride as he recounted the tale. As our most imposing figure, Brodie offered a veritable wall of protection for each of us as we ventured into danger. Bombast' had a presence that couldna' be ignored. Though he wouldna' \

know, the softness in his heart was just as profound as his physical brawn, and I can remember catching him brimful of tears just gazing at the beauty of the mountaintops blanketed in white after the season's first snowfall. His brusque manner belied the tenderness hidden within.

Brodie's curly brown hair hung down to his shoulders, and his face was covered in a thick beard of red. Aside from the width of his enormous shoulders, he commanded even more attention from his most powerful asset: a pair of forearms that resembled legs more than arms. With the brute force that emanated from them, he could wield a lance, a longbow, a claymore, anything really, as if 'twere a mere twig.

"Didna' forget to explain how ye lost yer way there for a bit though, hefty friend," challenged Owen. "Ye didna' catch up to us till after dawn the next day, remember that?" Owen needled Brodie with the factual recollection of events, something of course Owen would recall precisely.

"Och, what do *ye* ken? I had to stop and water the steeds, that's what caused my delay, ye fool. Why don't ye keep yer facts and details to yerself? Instead of bragging about defeating legions of demons in yer spiritual battles, talk to me when ye can overcome an earthly fight that's three-on-one, aye?"

This playful banter was typical of the verbal exchanges we had on the nights when we rode out. It was an indication that we were impatient, restive, and intent to get underway. As we maneuvered our horses to fall in line, Owen shouted, "*Be strong and do not give up, for your work will be rewarded.* Second Chronicles, lads!"

With a nod to all three, I added, "Onward."

The Raid – Litchfield

A slight wind stirred the air, spurring the mist to shift with movement. Donal led his band in silent formation as they traversed the hills, keeping the burn to their left so that the horses' feet could plant firmly upon more solid ground. Being only late August, the livestock remained in the fells, not yet needing to be transferred to their winter grazing grounds, a change that would only be made once the summer pasture turned coarse and dry, marked by clatches and clods of dried mud.

Having to lift the cattle from this location would be a more dangerous feat than if they were in their wintering spot, as the summer area was closer to the MacKinty estate and the odds of being caught much higher. But if the crew moved with alacrity and stealth, the plan should go smoothly. As the narrow path widened, Ross pulled up alongside Donal, the boy's eyes glistening with anticipation. "Donal, d'ye want I should ride a bit further ahead to see if there be any watch tonight?"

"Aye, lad, keep the stream on yer left, and stay to the rocks near the two split pines that mark the beginning of the drookit bog. Then report back to me as fast as ye can," Donal directed.

With a distinct slap of the reins, Ross willed Bran to take the lead in order to scout the region, pleased to be given such an important task. The hobbler moved nimbly over the terrain, streams of vapor jetting from his nostrils as his rider compelled him to increase his speed. Avoiding the burn and noting the two split trees, Ross guided the animal over the rocky boulders, careful to avoid the marsh.

Ascending to the peak of the hill, Ross slowed Bran to a halt as he tried to ascertain what lay before him. The glowing embers of a small fire cast its light upon the horizontal body of the lone guardian of the watch. Pausing to wait a few minutes, Ross needed to be sure that the man had no companions with him this evening, no one who was perhaps gathering more twigs and wood for the slowly dying fire.

Ross then surveyed the landscape that opened before him. The cattle stood together in small groups, foraging with their snouts pressed to the ground. A few bold ones had crossed the burn to the farther pasture, satisfying their wish for fresher, finer grass. The whole scene reminded Ross of the idyllic settings his sister Nora captured in her artwork. Both her sketches and this vision before him were marked by a hushed sense of serenity and contentment— something he could never find within the recesses of his own mind or heart. Having gained the information he sought, he clicked his tongue, directing Bran back to his crew.

Equipped with Ross's scouting report, the four riders bounded down the ridge above the grazing field, conscious of slowing down their pace as they approached their prize. Suddenness would alert the watch and alarm the beasts, so speed was sacrificed for secrecy. Donal instructed Ross to take care of the lone sentinel while he directed Owen to seize two or three chickens from the barnyard area.

In the meantime, Brodie and Donal would corral the cattle into a tight pack and begin their trek back home. It wouldn't be an easy task, moving these creatures across rough ground through the night, but the promise of profit and retribution, along with the tantalizing audacity of the whole proposition, superseded all hesitation and doubt.

With scarcely a sound, Donal began to assemble and lead twenty-five cattle and two goats back up the ridge, leaving Brodie to secure the rear. From this position near the back, Brodie swung about intensely when he heard galloping, but his tension eased when he recognized Bran.

"How'd it go, lad?" Brodie's voice barely above a whisper, his words sparse.

"'Twas some sight, Brodie, I'll tell ye," Ross responded, his red hair alive and on edge with palpable excitement as he turned his head from side-to-side. "The oaf nearly shot me with his pistol when he heard me sneaking up behind him. I swear I made no sound; I was verra careful about that, so he must've smelled me or something, I dunno. But when he reached for his weapon, I clunked him on his pate with the hilt of my sword."

The words came tumbling from Ross' mouth like the current of a river swollen with water from the mountains' melted snow. "Knocked him out cold,

I did. I do not think he'll be coming round any time soon, neither." As he finished these words delivered in fervent undertones, Ross sat more stately on his mount, flush with self-satisfaction and longing for a sign of approval.

"Ye done just fine, boy. Now, shut yer trap and move ahead to middle of the pack. We've got to cross the ridge and get back before ol' MacKinty calls for a hot trod." Brodie smiled to himself in amusement as he watched the young rider move ahead to the center of the herd.

Not long after Ross' reappearance, Owen pulled up alongside Brodie, his saddlebags full but his confidence shaken. "God save us, Brodie. To think I nearly scuttled everything because of some foolish rooster!" As he directed Oswallt in step with Dewey, Owen continued, "I went over to the henhouse near the barn, as Donal told me and found the group of them setting on a perch, seemingly taking their leisure. I picked out two of the plumpest, and as I went to reach for the neck of one of them, in comes this rooster, feathers aflying, squawking 'ooo-ooo'. You'd a thought I was Peter denying the good Lord the way he was bringing attention to me! Anyway, next thing I ken, every one of those hens starts running for cover."

Halting only long enough to take a breath, Owen continued, "So, as now I thought, I've got to silence this bugger—which wasna' easy—look at what he did to me!" and with this, he displayed the bloody-pecked fingers of his right hand. "Och, sure now I looked like the village fool, spinning in circles and bumping into walls as I pounced and twisted the neck of him and two others. But," slapping a saddlebag as he said this, "my pouches are full of quarry, and Donal will be pleased no doubt, for *Blessed is the man who remains steadfast under trial*, aye? That's James, chapter one, ye ken."

"Go on, ye may not be a village fool but ye are a Bible-thumpin' eedgit. Ride on ahead and do a better job keeping these animals in check than ye did with the feathery ones, man!" And after issuing these parting words to Owen, Brodie looked back over his shoulder to the land they were leaving behind. Seeing an empty landscape and no pursuers on their trail, he settled into his final mile of herding until it would be time for him to break away and lay in ambush in order to greet any potential visitors.

Donal – Man and Beast

The shrill sound of a whistle shattered the tranquility that had enfolded me. Immediately, I spun Cerwyn about with a squeeze from my legs and a shift in my seat. The hot trod must be underway, I surmised, and Brodie in need of assistance.

Cerwyn masterfully picked his way down the steep, slippery hillside, requiring verra little time for me to pick out Ross in the distance. Without the need for secrecy any longer, I shouted to him, "Take the point, will ye? And instead of returning to Undlay Bay Woods, lead the herd directly to Drummondshire."

"Aye," Ross confirmed, urging Bran to surge to the front.

Opting for a different path than the one we followed with the cattle, I could cut my return time to Brodie in half just by moving away from the rocks and closer to the grassy tussocks that edged the marsh. I knew these lands better than the scars etched on my body, and with the trust that flowed between me and Cerwyn, I believed he would feel my confidence and ignore the danger. Downhill we sped, the sucking sound of the water upon his hooves traveling up to my ears. The creature's agility and sheer athleticism were a marvel as we clung together on the outer rim that surrounded the bog and willow scrub.

Fearful to take my eyes off the next two feet in front of us, I relied on my sense of hearing and detected the braying of at least two horses coming from the ridge above. Not daring to look up, I wager'd that the horses were without riders; otherwise, they'd not be making such sounds. Let's hope that means Brodie has already disposed of—or at least detained—their passengers. Just a bit more stretch here to go before I'd be able to ascend once again to the safer terrain above. Bits of muck and mud kicked up onto my boots and covered Cerwyn's side and belly with grime, but we were nearly there. With a tug on the reins and an adjustment of my weight, we moved upward to the location earlier established as Brodie's watch-point.

My approaching gallop elicited a softer whistle from Brodie this time, and with the benefit of that sound, I ken where to find him. Sure enough, I saw the two MacKinty boys, each captured and affixed with rope on either side of a tree, beside which stood my partner. With spittle dangling from the red, wiry hairs that surrounded his lips and chin, Brodie explained, "Donal, these fellows will do nae harm now, and I'll snag those two fine stallions by the stream, but ye must go and stop MacKinty himself. He picked up Laird Campbell and his son George on the trod, and they're planning to outrun ye and the herd to Undlay Bay Woods and seize the plunder from us."

"Aye, well, we'll be making a slight change then in travel plans," and I gestured with an inclination of my head for Brodie to come closer so that I could reveal to him how Ross was driving the livestock straight to the market at Drummondshire. And with that disclosure, I was off again, Cerwyn's hooves clacking on solid ground.

I praised God for the wonder of the animal beneath me. Such a short, stout fellow—my feet dangled well below his belly—and yet he was unlimited in his stamina and in his craving for action. Rather than cut back through the bog, I spurred Cerwyn to greater speeds, knowing that we'd soon overtake the three stalkers because of the frailty of their own horses. If I could leap beyond them and circle back, I would lead them into the treacherous moss near the place where the two burns intersect. And if I could do that, Mother Nature would take care of the rest.

My ears were filled with the rhythmic pounding of Cerwyn's hooves, and my thoughts ran with designs of revenge. I must say I was quite surprised that MacKinty was able to convince the Campbells (or anyone, for that matter) to join him in this hunt. The old man was nigh near hated in these parts. He'd offended almost every clan in this region of the Highlands, mainly due to his greed, his disloyalty, and his corruption.

The Campbells were no great prize either, so maybe they were planning to unite forces and blanket the entire region with their devious machinations until they strangled and suffocated the will of the people. An oath given by a Campbell or a MacKinty was as fickle as a young child's interest and as empty as a dead man's eyes.

Up ahead, I could see a point of light, jostling up and down in the air. Ah, sure, it was the fiery turf affixed to the tip of a lance held by one of the three sots moving slowly and carefully on their large mounts. The hot trod. Realizing that we were rapidly coming upon the two streams, I made my move.

Shouting the Donn battle cry, "*Dh'aindeoin co theireadh* [Gainsay, who dares?]," I invaded them from behind, and in the ensuing chaos, Laird Campbell's mount got spooked and reared. Upon landing, it lost its footing on a rough-edged boulder, sending horse and rider to the earth.

"Aaoooow, no!" shrieked the Campbell sire, whose wrist had snapped and was pointed directly inward toward the man's belly. Supporting the arm at the elbow, he groaned in agony, causing George to dismount and come to his aid.

"Donal Donn, ye bastard," gritted MacKinty through clenched teeth. "Ye come in the night and steal my property? Ye're a coward, ye are. And now ye're mine, ye no-good blackguard." With that, he reached into his belt and withdrew his pistol which he then pointed directly at me.

But Cerwyn and I had not broken stride, and we glided past the other two faster than a phantom in a graveyard on Samhain. One shot was discharged, but the bullet was so far off target that it penetrated a distant tree trunk quite far from me.

I glanced back over my shoulder to see George clambering up his horse, hoping to join MacKinty who trailed me. Their horses continued to struggle with the uneven, rugged territory, but despite their awkwardness, they began to accelerate to the speed which I had hoped they would reach. Moving at this kind of pace, the riders would find it nearly impossible to halt forward progress, and soon they would both inevitably find themselves mired in the muck.

Once I came upon the crossing burns, I pulled Cerwyn hard to the left and then stopped to watch the ensuing drubbing. In these parts, a mossy area near the banks of two streams is not always a patch of soft, puddled green paddies, but rather a flimsy mask that conceals a deep, black pool of cloying, sucking mud. And in the quick movements that followed, that is what embraced my two pursuers.

MacKinty's horse went down first, his front legs embedded in the grime, while the man himself teetered in his seat before tumbling to the side and splashing into the ooze. Campbell, upon witnessing this, tried to pull the reins back on his horse, but his response came too late. Horse and man were suspended—upright and unmoving—as the swamp gripped them and held them fast in place.

Tipping my finger to my brow, I saluted the two sodden buffoons and then steered Cerwyn in the direction of Drummondshire.

**

It never comes as a proclamation; nae, it begins more like a hint and then a gentle whisper: thin bands of red and purple stripes in the eastern sky, and then, a sliver of gold flares up above the loch's edge over the distant horizon. The slivers grow and round out, spreading brilliance in outward directions that emanate from the central sphere. The colors begin to dance and change from red and purple to rose and pink, till the whole sky erupts with light, sending glittering sparkles that seem to pulse on the surface of the loch. I never tire of seeing the sun rise. An event so commonplace and expected that most forget to pay it any mind, yet for me 'tis so majestic and wondrous that it becomes a daily reminder of the beauty man can never generate. 'Tis a revelation of God himself.

Beneath this heavenly vault, I was drawing closer to the rear of the herd and could perceive the wide back of Brodie from this vantage point. The animals were gathered together more closely so that both Owen and Ross were also within view.

"Greetings, lads," I called out over the gap between us, causing each of them to pause and glance around.

"Ay, yer back, and none the worse for wear, I see," Owen responded. "Ross told me ye altered our return route so's I wondered if 'twere because ye'd come up against some trouble from MacKinty and his crew. Brodie explained how he was able to split their group in twain, but we werena' sure how ye were going to manage the other three on yer own. How'd ye do it, man?" Owen posed this question while leaning so far forward in his saddle that the fellow seemed about ready to fall face forward right over Oswallt's head.

"I'll tell ye once we sit down later and share a toast and the profits of this outing. For now, just give me two of yer saddlebags there, and Ross, bind together those goats yonder. I've still got some business to be about," and before these words were fully spoken, both men were busy fulfilling my requests.

As Owen handed me both pouches and Ross tethered the goats together, Brodie pointed to the two stallions he had in tow. "These should fetch us some fine coin at the market, do ye not think, my friend? Such bonnie coats on them and such size! Not much good though for the likes of us," he chuckled knowingly at this, "but I'm sure they'll be quite the prize for one of the lairds in the region, eh?"

Brodie may have been puffed up with the swell of his own glory, but his eyes betrayed a tinge of sorrow, so I felt compelled to offer, "Why don't ye keep maybe one of the two for yerself perhaps? I ken it'll be of no use to ye on nightly jaunts such as the one we've just had, but it'd sure look quite impressive if ye'd be riding one of these up the path to the Chisholm lands on yer way to courting Lorna. Now what lassie wouldna' be taken away with a vision such as that? She may even forget how ye smell like the hogs in her barnyard for a wee bit if ye come riding along in such style." With a wink and an elbow nudge into his oversized trunk, I goaded Brodie into agitation.

"I'll not be courting Lorna, nor any lass for that matter," he declared, then added after further consideration, "but I wouldna' mind having this fellow on my property for sure. Would lend a little dignity and refinement to the Munro stable, he would."

"Well then, that's settled. Take care of the exchange of goods, men, and we'll celebrate our success back at the forest of Undlay."

As they kept moving north, I turned to the west toward Strathmore and the Donough homestead where I would leave behind the goats and the contents of the saddlebags for William and Kirstine, along with the coins in my sporran, (coins that would soon be replenished in a few hours' time with the profits from our outing). With the sun creeping higher in the sky and my own riding pace more deliberate, I turned my mind to finding a worthy melody that would match the verses that resided within my heart.

Mary – A Leap of Faith

After a night of tossing amidst fitful dreams, I finally gave up trying to find the peace of slumber some time before dawn. I ken that I'd be able to escape further scrutiny regarding last night's absence as long I dressed quickly and left the castle before the servants were stirring. The early morning air was touched with the hint of autumn, as it was brisk and chill in my chamber. Already the lethargy that often accompanies a summer day was being replaced by the sense of urgency one feels when days are growing shorter.

Putting on my skirts over my shift and lacing up my bodice, I reached for my woolen shawl and pulled it tightly round my shoulders, making my way toward my chamber door and the hallway that led to the staircase. Upon touching the final step, I began to move more cautiously as I drew closer to the great hall and the kitchen for fear of being noticed.

I detected no pleasant aromas coming from the kitchen area; perhaps Annag's mother, Fiona, had not yet begun the breakfast fare. From the subtle thudding I heard, it seemed as if she were just starting to kindle the fire in the huge hearth, and I felt relieved that I would be able to avoid having conversation with her or Annag. My father had a reputation for being an early riser—*Rise when the day draws, bed when the nicht fa's, Mary*—but even he did not to appear to be in the great hall or anywhere near his private hall, which branched off from the larger one. Maybe last night's dinner went longer than expected, and by stealing away some of his precious hours of rest, he chose to go against his precept and make up for it on the other end. In any case, I slipped with ease past the entrances to both rooms and scurried toward the courtyard.

The normal hustle and bustle of the open square had not yet begun. No servants were carrying water, no dogs were running about, and the workshops against the walls were yet empty and still. It was almost as if everything were in a state of suspension—kind of how I felt about my life right now. I stood at the edge of a cliff and felt myself frozen in place there. I ken that I couldna' cling to that ledge forever. I'd need to leap from that precipice soon, very soon, but I wanted, *I needed*, to know what I was falling into.

To freefall into the clutches of George Campbell would be akin to death, but surrendering myself into the arms of my "forest-man," well, that would be sheer exhilaration. A life that would bring me to a level of intensity and excitement such as I'd never known before. And so, rather than passively wait to be thrust over the edge by circumstances, I've decided to seize my future by searching for what could be biding there once I leapt.

The best place to begin is the scene of the crime, is that not what the constable always says? All the clues one ever needs are usually right in front of ye, so in my case, that means I need to head back into the woods right now.

With the keeper still in his room, I pushed open the yett—the metal gateway—and turned the knob of the great wooden door. Free from the confines of the castle and my life therein, I allowed the downward slope of the hill usher me into a run, making my way toward the stables where I found Devin already at work mucking out the stalls. He heard me enter and was startled. Looking over at me with eyes still puffy from sleep, he spoke in a gravelly voice, "O, dearie, ye've come so early." He cleared his throat and continued huskily, "I ken I said we'd ride out this day, but I figured it wouldna' be for a few hours yet. I still be needing to clean here and replenish the hay before harnessing up any horses for hunting."

"Och, no, Devin. I am not here for that at this hour. It's just that I couldna' sleep, and since I didna' feel so well last night, I thought I'd recover faster if I could take a good long ride before breakfast, ye ken. I think the fresh air will help ease the waves I be feeling in my stomach." I offered this explanation as it seemed closest to the truth. For sure, my stomach was queasy, and the crisp air would, no doubt, do me good. But Devin need not ken that I was going on a different sort of hunt.

"Aye, sure. Why not take Maebh today? She's been fed already and seems impatient to be out and about. Ye ken where her bridle is," he said this as he nodded over his shoulder toward the mare's stall and hunched down to continue his cleaning.

"Thank ye, kindly, sir," I said cheerfully, placing both of my hands on either side of Devin's head and kissing his bald crown before making my way toward my mount. Once Maebh was saddled, I swung my leg over her back and clicked her into action. It wasna' long before we entered the forest which was dappled with streaks of yellow from the rising sun.

Now if I could only remember my way, I thought. There were some landmarks I recognized that I had passed during last night's hiding game, but once those were gone, I had no idea which way to go. There were no tracks I could follow, and my own recollection of events was marred by the overindulgence I had given to my emotions. And what am I looking for anyway? Am I thinking that he'd still be here? Then that *would* make him a leafy spirit of sorts, and I do not want him to be that. I want him to be real, to be a man of flesh and blood, a lover, I daresay—I couldna' help laughing at myself for *that* thought! One embrace, Mary, and ye've got yerself wishing for this stranger to become yer lover! That's a bit much, no, for a reasonable girl such as yerself?

But I'm sick of being reasonable and practical. It's dull and it's predictable and it's tiresome. I didna' want safe anymore; I wanted to feel that sensation of letting myself go, of leaping off that ledge, and embracing the exhilaration that comes with falling. I wanted to exist in the realm of possibility. And the allure of that mystery is what keeps me riding further on.

Keeping the Wolf at Bay

He rode with haste, not pausing to stop to tend to his mud-splattered appearance or his fatigued horse. His mind was fixed on one thing: justice. He stewed in a rage that was bubbling and boiling within himself, impatient to get to his destination where he could release the dam and let his anger sweep away his enemies in its destructive current.

Dismounting in front of the stables, he flicked the reins in Devin's direction and snidely commanded, "Clean her." Stomping away in arrogance, George Campbell marched up the hill toward the entrance to Undlay. He was unconcerned with how many shoulders he jostled and how many bodies he thrust aside; they were all expendable, mere inconveniences in his way who deserved to be crushed. They needed to be shown their insignificance. He did not see the looks on their faces as he trampled them—he didn't care enough to glimpse—looks infused with hostility and contempt. Some even spit upon the footprints he had left in his wake.

Not tarrying long enough to be announced or introduced, George burst through the double doors of Laird McElroy's private hall, interrupting the nobleman as he was reviewing his ledgers.

"Well, good day to *ye*, George Campbell. And what cause do ye have to come barging into my chamber looking as if ye've had a tussle with Satan himself? What's so urgent that ye had to pounce on me before I've even finished my parritch?" There was a distinct note of annoyance in Teague McElroy's voice, made more emphatic by the abrupt slamming of his papers to the table.

"Laird, Donn is at it again. That vile criminal is turning the countryside into his own hunting grounds. Less than a fortnight ago, he lifted 100 cattle from Cunningham lands, and last evening he ravaged the MacKinty estate. He made away with at least another 100 or so, and, what's worse, he attacked my

Da', maiming him in the process. I demand justice from ye, the laird of this region and the man appointed by his Majesty to maintain the law."

Although George believed in his heart he was making his demand with the conviction and determination of a great hero, his words, in truth, sounded whiny and petulant, more like that of a spoiled child who is crying because some other toddler has a bauble he covets.

Teague McElroy surveyed the man who stood before him and privately thought, *Thank ye, Jesus, that this is not my own son. If I'd a been cursed with a muckle-mouthed twit such as he, I'd have left him in the woods when he was a wee bairn for the fairies to snatch away. His disappearance would have been cause for celebration.*

But as he made these observations, McElroy also knew that he couldn't risk alienating the Campbells and thereby ignite a possible blood-feud between the two clans. The Campbells may have had less land than the McElroys, but they actually had greater wealth, thanks to the booming wool trade and to some fine nautical investments Campbell had made in overseas trade. In addition to the disparity in land, the two families were also on opposite ends of the pole when it came to political favor.

Fortunately for Teague, the McElroys were now reaping the benefits of being Royalists, and because of their devotion to the crown, Charles II had given Teague dominion over the county to rule in the name of the monarchy as he saw fit. The Campbells could not ingratiate themselves with the current king as they had been staunch supporters of Parliament and practicing Covenanters to boot. So while the Campbells had their fortunes and their titles, they still had to figuratively bow before the McElroy clan in matters of jurisdiction.

It alarmed Teague, however, that this recent raid had taken place on MacKinty lands. A bond forged between those two clans could spell trouble for his own. It was this prospect that compelled him to appear interested and engaged in listening to George's rantings and exaggerations (200 cattle in three weeks, truly?). Teague's momentary pause served only to foment the anger within the petitioner as George impatiently shifted his weight from one leg to the other, exhalations through his nostrils becoming more rapid and more audible.

"Och, ye ken what, George? I'm glad ye came to me first thing this morning. I was meaning to announce this last evening, but ye left so early from our dinner that I didna' have a chance." As Teague said this, he pushed out the adjacent seat, motioning for George to join him at the table.

Once George was settled, McElroy reached toward him with his left hand, pounding it on the table. "We've been needing to create a watch again. Lawlessness has swept over our lands again. Now more than ever, we must work together to maintain our property and our wealth. Ye, George, can be in charge of instituting a watch. I'll give ye some of my men to be under yer direction, and ye can have them guard over the grazing fields ye think are most liable to plunder."

George seemed to sit taller in his chair, and his lips began to curl into a demonic smile at the thought of being handed power over others. As those thin lips parted, brown chicken pellets that masqueraded as teeth came into view, and McElroy recoiled a bit at the sight of them before he continued, "We're coming upon the prime season for this kind of thievery, George, and ye can be the savior of our glen. From September to February, ye'll be the guardian of these lands, keeping our neighboring clans safe from the likes of such ruffians as Donal Donn and company. And if ye seize any of these bandits, ye bring them to me, and we'll have them dangling from the noose upon Craigmonie Hill. Now, go on home, clean up, and present yerself here in the afternoon. I'll have the men assembled for ye when ye arrive."

Like a cook who spoons a final dollop of blackberry jam into his dough, McElroy couldn't resist adding one further comment to sweeten the pact, "And ye ken, George, any actions ye take to protect his Majesty's lands and property will go far in bringing royal favor upon ye and the entire Campbell clan." With these words, McElroy gestured to the enormous ruby ring he was wearing on the fourth finger of his right hand, and George's beady eyes lingered on the jewel with the hunger of a wolf detecting the scent of prey in the air.

A little bit of saliva dribbled from George's bottom lip, traveling downward unimpeded because of his sunken chin, until a small puddle was left behind on the table. Without even attempting to politely wipe it away, George glanced at it, stood up, and announced, "I will round up these men and give them their orders," his eyes alighting once again upon the ring before he turned on his heel and stomped out.

Alone at the table, McElroy shook his head back and forth and raised his eyes to the high ceiling above. He thought to himself, *Playing tyrant over a few men may appease this brute for the time being, but it will take much more than that to fully quench the man's growing thirst for power.* Shifting his sight downward to stare at the glob of spit, he shuddered to think his own daughter might have to serve as that elixir.

***

"What? Are ye not done yet?" George raised his hands in exasperation, slapping them with displeasure on either side of his legs. Rather than turning about to make eye contact with his haughty visitor, Devin simply finished one more stroke with the brush down the horse's back and then moved toward the post to unfasten the cross ties that held the animal in place.

"Dumb beast doesna' deserve the attention. Fails me every turn. Doesna' need to look any better than the stinking hogs in the pen, serves her right." At this, George forcibly grabbed the reins from Devin's hand before the groom could even offer them to him.

The horse bristled at the voice of her unforgiving master, and Devin could only wonder why it was that the good Lord gave man dominion over the animals of the earth when most animals were far superior to men anyway, especially dullards like George Campbell. Listening to Campbell's complaints was like having a dirk twisted in the stomach; the longer Devin had to suppress his opinion of this fool, the deeper the searing pain inside his gut.

"I had those thieves in my clutches, ye ken? I dodged their bullets and was able to close in on their leader, that is until this one" and at this he shoved the hind legs of the mare, "decides she doesna' want to listen to commands any more. Refuses to speed up, she does. Only maintains the same gallop. Has no spunk in her, no will to go faster. She's only good for being put out to pasture this one, or even better, sold away to some unsuspecting fool who wouldna' realize his own hound dog is faster than this mound of sludge."

It pained Devin to think that a fine mare such as the one before him was at the mercy of a despicable man like Campbell. At times, the world did indeed seem to be upside down.

Campbell's words infected the air, their bitterness carrying across the distance to where Mary, forlorn and on foot, was leading Maebh back to the stables. Upon hearing such venom and recognizing its source, she abruptly turned the horse and started to run in the direction of Aidan and Deirdre who were taking turns rolling on their sides down the green hill. Mary's movements, however, were not swift enough, and George intercepted her by summoning her over to the stalls.

"Mary, wait! I've some good news to tell ye," he called to her in a voice inflated with self-importance.

Ensnared by his demand and unable to escape, she plodded reluctantly toward him as he made this announcement within earshot of the groom.

"Ye'll be seeing a bit more of me now round Undlay for the next few months. Yer father appointed me to be leader of the watch in this region. I'm going to be the protector of these lands from now till Candlemas." He placed his hands on his hips in triumph.

Making the sign of the cross, she answered, "Blessed Saint Margaret, save us. Ye, Georgie Campbell, in charge of the guard? We must be in sorry shape if father had to choose ye as a leader of men. Has every other able-bodied male come down with the pox or something of the like?" Devin couldn't help smirking silently after hearing her response and watching her move past George without stopping.

But George took her words for teasing and not for the loathing intended, so he answered smugly, "Ye ken, Mary, how much ye think of me. I ken it too. I'm just telling ye that instead of having to spend so much of yer time in yer head, ye now have the real thing—me, in the flesh. I'll be setting up base camp in the grazing fields off Undlay."

Not wanting to sound interested but curious nonetheless, Mary had to ask, "Why? What need do we have for a 'base camp' as ye say?"

Pleased to have been given the chance to lengthen their encounter and to bolster his own standing in her eyes, he began. "Reiving parties have started plundering the countryside again. They've hit two estates back-to-back. Just last night, a crew led by Donal Donn lifted 100 MacKinty cattle. I joined Callan in pursuit and unseated two of the scoundrels, beating them to a pulp with my own fists, but Donn, their leader, started shooting at me. I managed to avert the bullets and chased him over the hillside, but Miss Listless over there, had no staying power, so I had to surrender the chase—last night anyhow.

"But now yer Da' is placing me in command of a crew of men, and we'll set up watches throughout the area in order to bring to justice outlaws like Donn and his boys. So dinna' fash about me, Mary, yer safe and secure under my guardianship." His thin moustache seemed to extend from one side of his face to the other, and his lips parted a bit as they seemed to run in opposite directions trying to escape the foul breath emitting from his mouth.

"I wager I'm supposed to be impressed by all this, George Campbell? I'm not sure I'm feeling verra safe if ye've been named the savior of this glen. I think I'm more secure in the notion that my father must be daft and heading into the 'mere oblivion and second childishness' of old age by making such a decision as this." With that, Mary flipped her head and swung her hair in defiance, continuing on her way past him and Devin toward the water trough.

Nonplussed, George straddled his horse and yelled to her, "I'd not be so rude to me, Mary, if ye ken what's good for ye. Willna' be long before I'll be the *only* one enforcing the law around here." And with that warning, George struck his horse fiercely with his riding crop and galloped away.

When Mary finished tending to Maebh, she wandered over to the corral where Devin was using carrots to lure one of the horses into the open ring. The stallion had been injured in a bad fall and was reluctant to do anything other than exist in his stall, eating and drinking sparingly. Its front legs had been twisted in the spill, but thanks to Devin's care, no signs of physical damage remained—only the mental wounds still lingered. Linking her arms over the top rail and standing on the bottom, Mary asked the groom, "What did ye think about all that?"

Pretending he didn't understand her meaning, he responded, "All what?"

"Ye ken. What George Campbell said, about the watch and the reivers and such," she offered leadingly.

The horse began to take bigger steps as Devin continued to draw him forward with the lure of treasures in his hands and additional ones in his pockets.

"Well, let's just say I question the truth of the man's story. I believe yer father *may* have given him this responsibility, but I do not think it's because of the fellow's valorous deeds." Devin had the horse moving more confidently and assuredly at this point.

"Go on," Mary pleaded.

Not wanting to do anything to mar the animal's steady progress, Devin spoke in a voice that was measured and slow. "It's just that I've heard of Donal Donn before, and while it's true he's a firebrand and a bit of a rebel, he's no murderer. He's a man's man. He'd fight ye with his fists till he had no strength to lift his arms, but he'd not shoot at someone with a gun. It's not his style. So let's just say, George's story sounds more like the kind of yarn spun out of pure imagination than truth so's himself could look brae and daring.

"Besides," the groom continued, "I ken the Donn clan for many years. There's a story that goes way back, of the bad blood between the Campbells and the Donns. Even still, I do not think that bygone times would drive Donal to shoot at George, but I do believe it may explain the vengeance the Campbells still harbor toward the Donns and why George is so hell-bent on destroying the man and his crew."

Intrigued, Mary shifted her position so that she was sitting rather than standing on the railing. The horse now was cantering fluidly in the ring, allowing Devin to be a stationary observer.

The groom's eyes followed the horse's current movements while his story told of events from years past.

"A long time ago, the Campbells went to visit the Donns during the terrible winter of 1598. 'Twere about twenty of them who were hosted and welcomed by the Donn clan. The Campbells stayed for nigh on two weeks, and after they had eaten their bread and drunk their whiskey, the laird of the Campbells gave the command. In the dark of night after an evening of feasting, the Campbells, greedy for land and riches, put all to the sword.

"Thirty-eight Donn clansmen were stabbed in their beds before they could even arm themselves. The people who tried to escape—women and children mostly—were caught in a blizzard in the mountains and froze to death right there in the countryside. A few managed to reach houses in the next village, and those survivors are the ancestors of your current rogue, Donal. I think the fact that the Campbells couldna' wipe out the clan entirely has always been a thorn in their side, so maybe that explains why George here is so driven to get Donn. He wants to be proclaimed the hero and savior of the Campbell clan."

Mary was still visibly confused. "Yes, but if the tale's true, does that not give Donal even more reason to try to murder George after all?"

"Ye'd think so, right? But no, that's not the way of the Donn clan. They'll not forget the injury done to them, but they'll retaliate in ways other than murder. Their bloodline is pure and honorable; they do not ever wish to be equated with the likes of the Campbells who continually resort to underhand methods to get what they want. The Donns will have their vengeance—of that ye can be sure—but it'll come when they force the Campbell clan to destroy itself, while their own hands remain unstained by blood." Devin, gazing with pleasure upon the horse who was frolicking in his newfound freedom of movement, put the leftover carrot back into his pocket.

"But then," Mary asked, her green eyes wide with vulnerability, "why would my father wish to hand me over to a family whose history is so abominable?"

"Well, times do change, lass. Sometimes alliances must be formed despite what enmity existed in the past. Personal reluctance must be overcome for the greater good of the clan; its safety and longevity supersede individual doubts or misgivings. It's not always sincerity but survival that rules decision-making, Mary. But yer Da' is a smart man. He'll not trust the Campbells nor George too far. I'm thinking he's just getting what he wants from them, and when he has them moving in the direction he needs them to go, he'll pull away the bait and have them eating from his hand without any object in there at all."

Mary sat in silence, grasping Devin's meaning and her role in this plan.

"Listen to me, Mary. Your father willna' let ye be snatched away by the likes of George Campbell. Animals like him have a way of laming themselves before they can ever capture the prize." Lesson over, Devin moved toward the horse in the corral, caressing and congratulating him on rediscovering the joy of emancipation.

By the Shores of Loch Ness

On the sandy beach in front of the loch, Mary sat motionless on a large rock while Annag stood plaiting Mary's long tresses. While the waves gently rippled onto the coastline and the sun descended deeper in the sky, the bond between the two girls mirrored the relaxed, tranquil setting that enveloped them. Annag's fingers moved carefully and skillfully, in and out, as she slowly twisted Mary's silken threads into a thick braid that was as wide and full as the ropes that tethered the boats to the dock. Neither of them was operating in the present, Annag's eyes were fixed on the horizon and thinking of the future and Mary's on the liquid tendrils at her feet, thinking of the past.

After being lost in time, Annag stepped out from the silence and murmured softly, "Mary? What do ye think of Hamlin Balfour?"

"Hamlin? Not verra much. He's the blacksmith's apprentice and sometime farrier, is he not?" Mary answered in a slow cadence, taking a pause between each statement so as not to upset the stillness.

"Aye, well, he's a fine man, comes from a good family, the Balfours of Drummondshire. I see him, ye ken, from time to time when I'm crossing the courtyard past the workshops. First, we just nodded to each other, then about two weeks ago, we started saying *good morning* and *good day* and such. I have to confess to ye, I've kinda been making it a point to walk by his stall when I'm headed to do the laundering."

Annag giggled as she tied the ribbon at the bottom of Mary's plaited hair, and then switched positions with her. Settling herself upon the rock, Annag unfastened her bun and handed Mary the comb that was lying on the seashells and pebbles that they had gathered to make a ledge.

Annag continued, "Two days ago, he motions to me to step nearer, seeming like he wants to show me something. So with the basket on my hip, I moved closer to his workshop, thinking he's going to show me some sword or lance or chain he's made, but instead he holds up a verra intricately designed key, flipping it over back-n-forth in the palm of his enormous hand. Now, of course I'm verra confused at this point, and before I can ask him what it's about, he says, 'How do I unlock the secret of who ye are, Annag?' I nearly dropped my washing, ye ken! Have ye ever heard anything so romantic, Mary?

"Well, I was too flustered then to respond, but today, after our nods and 'g'days', I stepped over to him and whispered, 'Secrets canna' be revealed without trust, ye ken. Can I trust that ye'll walk with me at sundown by the loch tonight?' I couldna' believe I was so bold, Mary! But I was, and now I'm all spun-up inside because the time is drawing near. O, can you fix my hair with a pair of thin braids on either side so that the rest falls down natural?" Annag gestured with her hands as she described her request.

Mary nodded unseen from behind Annag's head, so she added, "Aye. 'Tis so exciting, Annag. Where is he meeting ye?"

"By the watergate. I figure we can walk along the water's edge till we reach the wooded area, and then if we turn back from there, I'd still return in time before dinner is served. Just enough space to see if Hamlin is worth listening to. Ye ken, like is he interesting enough for me to someday let him use his key in my lock?"

At that, Mary struck Annag on her shoulder with the comb. "Shame on ye, Annag Carmichael! Yer as wild as those French women at court. Next thing, ye ken, ye'll be using yer tongue for kissing!"

The styling was momentarily suspended while the two continued to snicker at their divergent perspectives on the situation. Then Annag inquired, "And what about ye, Mary? Any news about yer 'forest friend'?"

"Nae. It's been three days now, and I've not heard or seen anything in the forest that relates to that night. At this point, the trail is getting verra cold, as they say, and the chances of me stumbling upon him becoming more and more distant." Finishing one side of the braid, Mary turned Annag's shoulder a bit so that she could begin working on the other side of her friend's chestnut-brown hair.

"Ye ken, Mary, I'm not too keen on ye going in and out of the forest on yer own. Did ye hear the news that the tinker brought? The servants have not stopped talking about it!"

"No, what did he tell?"

"There's been fierce trouble throughout the neighboring counties, Mary, with thieves and evildoers about, and I'm not talking about just robbing. The tinker said that one band of outlaws not only made away with livestock and revenue, but they burned four houses, two of them with the people still inside! And, what's worse, they kidnapped one of the daughters in the family as well, for the people found her beaten and ravaged beside Loch Ness a full day's ride from her home. It's not safe, Mary, for ye to be ambling about the woods at all hours of the day and night with rogues like them lurking round!" Annag's voice raised in urgency as she delivered this warning to her friend.

"Saints preserve us," Mary made the sign of the cross. "The poor girl! And those families. But dinna fash. I will not be needing to go searching in the forest for quite some time, or maybe even ever again..."

At these words, Annag quickly spun around to face Mary. "Ye mean, ye've given up and put your *Ghillie Dubh* to rest? That's the most sense I've heard from ye in three days!"

"Och, no, I'm not giving up. Not yet. I am just recognizing that my methods are not working. I've got one option left, and I'm going to explore it tomorrow."

Seizing Mary's wrist, Annag pleaded, "Do not go dabbling into the spirit world, Mary. Ye'll be stirring up all kinds of trouble. Once ye awaken demons ye canna' lullaby them back into slumber."

Flippantly, Mary countered, "Well, I do not think Shannon is having too much trouble with visions tormenting her, is she? From what I hear, she and Malcolm are already handfast and living together, and after the turn of the year, they may be welcoming the first of many little Gordons into the world." With an added dash of confidence, Mary set forth her philosophy, "The world of mist and shadows doesna' always end in darkness, Annag. Sometimes ye have to tiptoe through the danger if it offers ye a shortcut to fulfillment."

Tying a small ribbon around the second braid, Mary tapped Annag on the head to signal that she was done. Handing her the comb, Mary, with a sly, knowing grin, made it a point to say, "Ye, too, Annag. Be careful where *ye* walk tonight." With a mischievous wink, she turned toward Undlay, leaving her friend to ponder her upcoming lakeside stroll.

Donal – A Ceilidh

A few miles north of Undlay Castle, on a steep hill that overlooks Loch Ness, is the house I call my own. It is not verra much to look at really—wood framing, thatched roof, walls of stone that stretch nigh to my hip, and blocks of sod on top of the stone that stack up level with the roof. Aye, for sure 'tis no palace, but it affords me all the privacy I need and the freedom to come and go as I please without having to answer to no one.

I keep a peat fire going in the small indoor hearth on days that are cold and dank, but more often than not I find myself on the outside of those stone walls. Confinement never agreed with me, physical or mental, so long as it isna' pouring, hailing, or snowing, I'll be out here breathing the air that wafts up from the lake and swirls among these hills.

Three goats nuzzle the ground, searching for their daily meal, and Cerwyn is with them, busy grazing on the adjacent field and looking about as unassuming and unremarkable as one could ever imagine. Saddle him up though when there's a hint of adventure in the wind, and he magically transforms into the exalted Bucephalus of Alexander. Astonishing really, especially if ye could see him right now losing a battle with a particularly stubborn leafy portion of a bush that's refusing to surrender to his champing teeth.

With the profit we made off the MacKinty stock, I bartered for two hens and a rooster and am now currently finishing up building a small hatch and perch for the jittery creatures. A little frenzy does me no harm in light of the contentment they'll bring once their bounty of eggs comes due. And so, as I fit into place the lengthy rod that will serve as their perch, I begin humming a tune aloud, a melody that sprang from my need to recapture the mystical experience from a few nights before. My fingers itch for the strings of my harp, as they start to pluck the air in silent song. With the peat already stacked and drying and my other chores complete, I duck my head down as I enter the door and move toward the small footlocker that serves as both storage place and table.

"Aaahh, there's milady," I say with tenderness, lifting the small harp up to me as if she were the Grail itself. And she is this to me, truly—providing me with a kind of sacred nourishment for my soul. I never took to meeting houses and churches and such. Religion was too stuffy a practice for me—standing, sitting, kneeling when ye're told. Singing songs drained of feeling and having to listen to some off-key worshipper who wants to prove his prayer more worthy by drowning out all others with his volume.

Nae, the sanctity of faith doesna' exist on a page. It's found in the breezes that blow through the heather, in the white glow of a full moon shining on the forest floor, and, of course, in the sounds that ascend from these strings to the heavens. I often turn to milady when my mind makes no sense and is running as wild as a fawn skittering to safety. With each caress of my fingers upon the strings, she calms those impulses and pulls them together into something more fluid, more coherent, and I need her now to help me sift through the enchantment I am under.

Returning to the open area in front of my home, my mind races with thoughts of Mary McElroy. At the edge of the cliff, I sit down and shift a rock into place to lean against while I absorb the full vista of the lake below. Like the waves that churn beneath the water's surface, the memory of her beauty pulsates within me, and my fingers find a tune to accompany the words that unleash this longing.

Is she thinking now of me, as I am tonight of her?
My arms tremble with the emptiness of what's lost.
When I held her to my heart, there was meaning in my world,
But now I wander and feel abandoned deep within.
I draw breath, but it fortifies only sorrow.
I take food, but it doesna' ease the hunger.
Will she come to me again and give me back my life?
Or will I wither like the sedge gone cold and dead?

I must find a way to see her again. To speak with her. To smile with her. Would she permit that? Would she unfold herself to me? Our chance encounter imprinted timelessness, for she now exists in my past, present, and future.

Abiding in all three, she is as alive and as real as the delicate white petals of the wood sorrel at my side, despite the miles that distance us.

My attempts to reconnect have been futile. A handful of visits, but no treasure to claim, only a single ribbon left abandoned on the wooded trail. A trinket that provided the slimmest thread of connection. Beyond that, the forest remained silent, concealing its secrets. And so I offered my verses as prayer, binding it with the lone strand and leaving it behind in a hollowed-out trunk as an oblation to the Lord above. Will He heed my call?

The sound of hoofbeats interrupt my supplications, jarring me back to real time. The boys are coming by, a *ceilidh*—small gathering—of sorts, and based on the direction of the sound, I'm guessing 'tis Brodie approaching from the west. Although the moisture in the air has thickened, I still prefer an outdoor wood fire to the smoky peat one inside, so with one hand, I tuck my harp toward my body and push up off the ground with the other, making my way over to the circle of stones where some fresh wood is piled.

I do believe that miracles are all around us. Take starting a fire, for example. Think about it: darkness to light, chill to warmth, fear to safety, emptiness to vitality. Is that not a miracle? With a pile of tinder atop the logs, I take from my pouch the flint and steel and a piece of hoof fungus and begin snapping the two together until a spark catches the kindling. That is the onset of wonder. Taking that tiny hint of what's to come, I place it ever so delicately into the tinder, cradle it toward my lips, and blow verra softly upon the dried mixture of brambles and grass. There is that tentative moment where hope is held in abeyance, and then, a small flame begins to materialize. Laying the growing flare carefully upon the wood, I witness this wondrous marvel come to fruition. The whole performance makes me feel like a conjurer bewitching what's dead into life.

The larger logs were just being licked when Brodie dismounted, carrying in his hand two skinned hares. "Brought ye a little snack for tonight, my friend. I caught three of them today and made a fine stew earlier for myself and Ma back at the house. These two are for ye." And as he made his way toward the fire, I was already assembling the sticks together that we'd use for roasting the meal.

"I had not planned on feeding the crew, so I thank ye for turning me into a better host," I said with sincerity. "I thought we'd be sharing only liquid refreshment this eve." I nodded toward the door of my house where beside it sat two jugs of whiskey.

"Oh, that'd be a fine meal in and of itself, of that I'm sure," Brodie's eyes glistened in anticipation, he grabbed one of the jugs and sat next to me by the fire.

"How's yer mother doing these days?" I asked casually, trying to mask my concern. Not wanting to sound as if I was prying deeply into areas that are too private to discuss aloud, I busied myself with monitoring the fire, pretending to be intent on not crisping the meat too quickly. Quiet enveloped us for a bit, a comfortable stillness, the kind where a man can formulate his thoughts without his listener trying to rush him to do so.

"Ah, not so good these days, not so good."

Again, I waited, letting the night creatures fill in the gaps in our own conversation. After a time, I asked, "Still dealing with the cough, eh?"

Another pause. Only crackles and snaps from the fire punctuated the air. Then, after a deep exhalation, Brodie resumed, "Aye, and 'tis getting no better. When I first told ye, it didna' seem to be anything more than the usual kind of sickness that comes round from time to time—fever, nose running, coughing—nothing that a few days rest wouldna' cure. But this," he paused at this point to look above to the heavens, "this has been going on now for nearly the whole spring and summer season. Sometimes she gets to coughing and canna stop till she vomits out her insides. She canna move around nae more, she canna laugh, sneeze, or shift position without screeching in pain. I'm not sure, but I think she may have split a rib from the hacking. It grieves me to see her wasting away right before me." There was a watery film covering his eyes which didna' spill, so long as he continued to gaze upward.

"At Drummondshire after the raid, I picked up some jars of fresh honey, thinking that might soothe her troubles and calm the spasms a bit. It made verra little difference though, so I'm believing she'll need stronger medicine than what I can provide."

His words hung in the air for a few moments, both of us helpless—he for failing to heal his Ma and me for having no other solutions to offer.

"There was blood in it today," he said in a detached sort of way. "In her spit. I saw it. In the bowl by her bedside." Again I was silent. "I'm setting out tomorrow to seek out a true healer. I'll not let her go this way." With that announcement, he took a long swig of whiskey, and passing the flask over to me, he changed the subject.

"Anyways, did ye hear what the Cameron boys did in Avochmore? Well, they say it was the Camerons, but it's not for certain."

Taking a sip and letting the warmth of the liquor trickle down my throat, I answered, "Nae, I didna', but they always were a miserable group of crooks, so I can surely believe they're capable of the worst. What's happened?"

"Blake and his crew burned down four homesteads, among them the Barclays of Avochmore. Ruined Kendrew's daughter in the process too, using her to satisfy their own vile urges and then abandoning her by the shores of Loch Ness. Villagers are up in arms, and I do not blame them at all. If I could get my own hands on Blake, I'd fasten my grip round his neck so tight that his eyes would come bursting out of their sockets. As for the rest of them, for what they did to Edina, I'd take my blade to them, leaving them all *bullocks*."

I, too, felt horror at the news. 'Tis one thing to go about lifting cattle and such, but 'tis quite another to utterly destroy things just for greed and enjoyment. "Nothing redeeming at all about the Camerons. Destruction for the sake of fun. Harming innocents to satisfy their own lurid desires. Edina's father and brothers will not rest, I'm sure, till they have their revenge, but poor girl, she'll never erase from her memory what's been done to her. Nae, that'll haunt her mind forever."

"Aye, I'm with ye, my friend, when it comes to crossing certain boundaries. There'll be some who call us rogues and outlaws, but we're no such thing. There's always a reason, ye ken, behind every one of our raids, and we steer clear of involving anyone other than the person who needs to be taught the lesson. Burning homes, violating women, that's just savagery, and if the villagers asked me, I'd join in the search for those men and gladly be the one to tighten the nooses." Brodie was getting worked up as he built to that final comment, so I felt the need to point out to him one further detail.

"Ye see how filled with fury *ye* are over this? Now imagine what the Barclay men must be feeling? I know yer itching to play hangman, but that privilege should go to her kin."

"Agreed. No argument from me on that account. I'll just say then that I'd be quite content to witness the whole group of them scoundrels dancing at the end of the hemp."

"Who's dancing?" came the question from the young man who was walking up toward the fireside. Owen must've already hobbled Oswallt in the area behind the house where Dewey and Cerwyn were biding. "'*Let them praise his name with dancing*' Psalms, aye? Did I miss out on a celebration somewhere?" The earnestness of his inquiry was matched by the enthusiasm he showed toward the contents of his satchel. "I brought ye something, Donal. Ye'll see 'tis better than what I brought ye last time!" At that, he reached into his pouch and tossed a small book at me, a translation of Petrarch's *Triumphs*, I could see printed on its cover.

Standing to my feet, I walked over to Owen. Clapping him on the top of his shoulder, I said, "Thank ye, man. 'Tis much better than last month's psalmody, though reading it did do wonders for my imperiled soul! Petrarch will help get me to the same place—sin to redemption—but it'll be a much more enjoyable journey for sure. Yer not studying Petrarch in yer classes now, are ye?" I asked as I handed Owen the flask and walked over by the house to retrieve the second. Brodie, meantime, removed the meat from the fire, placing it off to the side in order to cool and then slid over to his right making room for Owen.

"Aaaahhh, *uisge-beathe*, the water of life," Owen remarked as he lifted the bottle in a toast before bringing it to his lips. "Och, no. We're in Vergil, right now. Da' likes me to be in charge of all the Latin lessons, and we're now in the middle of Book 2 of the *Aeneid* right now."

"Yer speaking worlds above my head, ye two. Petrarch? Vergil? We Munros only study the catechism, not these high-faluting Italians," Brodie uttered in dismissal.

"O, ye'd like Vergil, ye would, Brodie," Owen suggested. "'Tis all about war and honor and fate and such, ye ken."

"I ken the story, ye fool, I just didna' *read* it is all. A warrior devoted to family, refugee of Troy, founder of Rome, I ken all about Aeneas and his travels. I just didna' care to plod through all that gibberish on the page," Brodie responded irritably.

"Well, sorry then, man." Owen sidled over and found a place near the fire. Joining us on the ground, he explained further, "We're at the part where Aeneas is retelling the fall of Troy, and he has this dream, this vision appears to him. 'Tis the ghost of Hector warning Aeneas to flee the city. 'Tis a really good part, and the students are spellbound with the translating we're doing.

Even I'm kind of fascinated by it myself, despite having read it over seven times already. I mean, imagine getting a message from the dead?

"Hector, he appears all bloody and covered in dust, his feet swollen and pierced by the thongs. He's not in all his military glory, nae, he's rendered in his most tragic moment. Hair matted with blood, body bearing the wounds from being dragged by chariot round the city walls. 'Tis a most chilling passage."

These last words floated above us, suspended in the air, while the crackle of the flames was the only sound that accompanied the slicing of my dirk as I carved up the meat. Doling out sections among the three of us and reserving a portion for Ross, we turned our attention to the succulent meal before us, each man lost in his own thoughts. After some time, Owen broke the silence with a pointed question: "So…do ye think the dead come back?"

Before Brodie or I could respond, a voice from behind us took the liberty of answering. "Aye," Ross answered from atop his horse. "That I do. Hallo, boys, and what's all this business about the dead?" He spoke with the intent of injecting a little lightheartedness into the conversation, but the rest of us had already descended into a much more somber mood. Ross brought Bran round back, and then returned to settle beside the fire with us.

"I'll tell ye," he continued as he flopped upon the ground next to us, "Nora swears she feels spirits all round her when she's sketching, and Sara says she hears Ma and Da' sometimes, their voices reaching to her in her sleep." Inserting himself immediately into the conversation was Ross' way of distracting us from noticing his appearance. Despite the darkness and the uneven light coming from the fire, each of us caught glimpses of his battered face.

The boy must've had a fairly awful beating, I thought, most likely at least a day old, judging from the purple rings and overall swelling around both eyes that left them looking like slits. None of us spoke a word of it though, figuring it'd be his choice to talk about it, when and if he wanted. So instead we played the game with him and stuck to the topic of the dead visiting the living.

"Of course I believe in spirits," Brodie piped up. "My favorite one comes and visits me nearly every night in my room. The Lady of Loch Needs. She drifts up from the loch and into my room. I ken she's come into my dreams when I feel the moisture in the sheets in the morning. Now that's a ghost I'm willing to have haunting me every time I lay down to sleep. She causes a bit of a mess, but she's captivating when she comes."

"Och, Brodie, go on! Yer ghost'll be the closest ye'll ever get to a real woman. Nothing made of flesh and blood for ye, ye ox. Just a mere vision," Ross shot back.

"Truly, though," Owen attempted to steer the conversation away from bawdiness, "do ye believe in the dead coming back, Donal? What're yer thoughts?" Owen asked with a sincerity that restored seriousness again.

I waited a moment before answering, debating whether to push aside these thoughts of the spiritual world to return to the kind of playful banter we were more accustomed to. But it was a night of shadows, so I chose to venture deeper into the darkness. "I do, Owen. Aye. And I think they can come in all kinds of forms and shapes. I remember a story my Da' used to tell, goes back to the massacre of '98. He was but a young lad then, only five or six, but the memory of that night and the day that followed stayed with him for the rest of his life." I shifted my position a bit, settling in for the telling of a tale. With the flames reaching to the sky, sending a spark or two upward, I held their attention in the fire's glow and began.

"On the night of the slaughtering, his Ma was in his room with him and his younger brother who was on the mend from fever, so she wasna' in the bedchamber with his father when the shouts and screams pierced the night. It was all confusion and tumult as people were grabbing what they could and running for the door. A few brae—and ultimately foolish—souls made their way toward the Great Hall to discover the source of the commotion, but his Ma must've known something was terribly amiss, for she left her husband to his own devices while she huddled up the two boys and raced into the frigid darkness. All three of them ran as fast as they could as a group bound together, but they couldna' make much progress on account of the wind and driving snow.

"Eventually, they stopped under a large crag that provided a wee break from the wind but could do naught to lessen the cold. Wrapping the plaid around the three of them, she pulled them to her breast as they lay shivering together in the snow beside the rock."

My gaze penetrated further into the rippling flames as if the fire projected the image I was relating. "But my Da', he couldna' close his eyes even though the other two had done so, for when he tried, the icy blasts of wind mimicked the high-pitched screams he'd heard earlier. And with his eyes open, he witnessed the strangest of sights. A large red stag, seemingly unaffected by the conditions, came toward them, then trotted a few steps away, and then came back again. The creature did this many times—come forward, trot away, come forward, till finally, my Da' shook his mother awake and told her to watch with him. With frost lining his lashes, he looked pleadingly at her, and whispered, 'I think he's trying to tell us something. I think he's wanting us to follow.'

"Of course his Ma thought it was a verra poor idea to go back out into the wilderness chasing a mere animal, but deep down, she also ken that if they remained where they were beneath the bluff, they were likely to slumber into death."

I paused at the gravity of the words and took a long swallow of whiskey before clearing my throat and resuming the tale. "So they awakened his brother and began following the beast. Every couple of steps, the animal would turn back and fix its eyes on my Da', making certain they were still trailing. Up the side of the mountain they went, tears streaming down their faces from the wind, fingers and toes numbing with the chill. After a time, the stag halted its movement, and right before them was a small cave, a sheltered place to wait out the storm.

"And as they moved into the opening, my Da' turned back to seek out the stag. They locked eyes with one another. My Da' swore that it nodded its head at him in approval before vanishing back into the woods. Till the day he died, he believed that deer was the spirit of his own father who'd been butchered in the assault and that his Da' was the one leading them to safety and passing on the role of protector to his young son.

"By morning, the cold persisted, but the snow had stopped, and the three of them made their way to the neighboring village where they were taken in and cared for. From that stormy night to the day we placed his body beneath the stone in St. Columba's graveyard, my Da' paid homage to Cernunnos, the horned one. So aye, I do believe in the dead coming back to us, but not always in the form that we expect."

The four of us sat in silence, watching the dwindling flames and pondering our own connection to the world beyond. Brodie reached behind his head to lift another piece of firewood, his huge forearm pulsing as he gripped it with one massive hand and placed it atop the others. Just like our quieted conversation, the new log seemed to do nothing for a few moments till the corners caught and began to burn, much like Owen who had been silent but then grew alight with speculation once again.

"I've not seen any spirits or visions myself, but I ken my Ma has visitations almost every winter solstice when Sowans Nicht is nigh. It was then that wee Isobel was born, poor mite," he blessed himself as he spoke her name. "Isobel was Ma's dream come true—what after having three bickering, fen-smelling boys—for she had been yearning for a girl for so long. But I suppose it wasna' meant to be…couldna' thrive, *wee yin*, lasted but two sunrises before the angels swept her back to heaven. And she was such a bonnie thing, tiniest fingers and toes, but her skin never glowed pink, only a pure white, with tinges of blue coursing under the surface." Owen shook his head to rid himself of the injustice of it all, the unfairness of an innocent babe being denied the spark of life.

"Da' had an awful time removing the baby from my mother's arms. She kept believing she could stir life into Isobel if she held her tight enough to her own beating heart. Kind of infusing the child with her own strength to stop the ebbing of it in the babe's. But it didna' happen. Anyways, when the solstice is coming on, Ma grows solemn, and for two nights wanders through house and round the property, swearing she hears a bairn crying.

"My father explained it once to us boys, and I remember the time I stayed awake to watch her—ye never seen a person more determined and more heartbroken at the same time. Lines of tears tumbling down her cheeks and her movements all frantic and such, like she's running out of time, ye ken? So affixed was she on the sound she was hearing, I suppose. Da' said we need to pray for peace to come into Ma's soul. He says she blames herself for Isobel going cold and stiff, and that the cries she hears are just coming from her own mind, not from any ghost.

"But it's so real, ye ken? At least to my Ma, and though I couldna' hear anything, if ye'd seen her, ye'd believe it was truly a haunting for certain." Owen's eyes had a faraway look in them, and ye could tell it was an occurrence he'd been considering for quite some time.

First to react, Brodie commented, "Ye boys are inviting a chill into my bones with all this talk about visitations and death and spirits and such. And beyond these ghostly matters, I'm shivering just thinking about the wintry days that ye both just described that I ken are ahead of us here in the weeks to come." Brodie folded his arms and shook his shoulders as he said this.

"Aye, days are growing shorter already," Ross agreed. "The changes do come upon us fast, ye ken. Always have to be one step ahead, I suppose. And damned be those who are caught unawares," he added invitingly, "like the four who were stopped by the Tyne."

Spontaneously, the song came to my mind, and after I offered up the first verse, the rest of the crew joined in.

A frosty eve they set out riding
Just the four that crossed the border
And they found five more lads willing
To make haste and cause disorder.

So they rode far past Durham,
Into the woods near Walsingham
Where they grabbed the local parson
A bonnie ransom soon in their hands.

But the winds they were a' blowing
And their faces rimed with ice
Winter's chill had begun to claim 'em
Leaving their judgment imprecise.

The alarum had been sounded
With the bailiff on his way.
But the waters of the River Tyne
Were overflooding all that day.

'Twere no fords 'round fit for crossing
And the bridge was barred and chained.
So they set their horses loose there
And by foot they made their way.

'Twas not long before they heard 'em
Hounds pursuing them in their tracks.
Two were killed and two held captive,
But t'other five though made it back.

No ransom would they be splitting
No profit would they be making
But sure 'twas better than doing a jig
At the end o' the rope for hanging.

And with those final lines, our singing grew louder as we toasted the five who managed to survive their foolhardy raid and avoid their appointment with death.

"Well, let that be a lesson to us all, friends, that we be wise to the elements before we take to our business ventures," I announced as we passed the evening in good fellowship. Clearing my throat, I continued, "Speaking of that, we need to lay low for a time as the Camerons have worked the neighboring towns into a frenzy with their foul deeds. Willna' be safe to go out riding for a bit. Though I do want to suggest visiting the Campbells on our next outing. Brodie, tell these fellows what's been going on of late, will ye?"

Pushing himself up from his prone position, Brodie sat tall and leaned forward with intensity while he shared with Owen and Ross what he had told me just a little while before.

When Brodie finished, Ross eagerly leapt into the discussion by updating us with the latest he had heard. "Ye ken," he explained, "even before the Cameron raid, I heard news that a watch had been set over our local lands, thanks to the success of our last excursion and our treatment of Georgie Campbell."

"Truly?" I inquired. "And how did you come to learn this?"

"Well, the information came at a price," Ross explained, pointing to his face as he said it.

"Och, no!" Brodie exploded, "Do not tell me ye let Campbell lay that beating on ye, boy?" he shouted in disappointment. "If that be true, then ye best be telling me the Campbells are digging a grave for their rat-faced son this verra minute!"

Ross pushed back into Brodie's chest with both arms, offended at such a suggestion. "Get out, Brodie. Do ye not have more faith in me than that? Surely, I can handle a squawking chicken like Georgie without suffering a scratch upon myself! No, this look comes courtesy of my brother, Angus. But the good news is, I laid him out cold for a few hours. Had to drag him from the front yard to the porch of the house where he just wallowed and moaned for a time. So I'm not the one who got the worst this time. Still hurts a bit though," Ross winced as he touched the area around his eyes, "but his pain is my salve. Angus was the one who told me about the watch because he is now part of it. And *why* he's part of it is the reason I had to crush him with my fists."

"Thankfully, he's no idea that yer in our raiding crew, so we do not need to panic right away," I responded. "In truth, this is actually a blessing for us because ye can find out who's on duty and where, and then we'd be able to choose when it'd be best to strike according to that information. But, go on. How did he get to be part of this whole undertaking?" I questioned him.

"Well, ye see, that was the reason for the fight, ye ken," Ross explained, his red hair springing all round like the dancing firelight. "He was playing cards with Campbell the night before and dug himself into a verra deep hole, so deep that he kept doubling the wager, attempting to get himself out. The dumb ass eventually staked a portion of our land—and lost! Now two acres of decent farmland on our property belongs to the Campbells, but at least Angus had some semblance of a conscience because he begged George to strike a deal with him that if he works for George for twelve-month and a day, then the land would revert back to us and the debt forgiven."

His anger palpable, Ross concluded, "Now ye ken the reason for the fight. Years to build a homestead and one night for a fool to destroy it. I still canna control my fury. Whenever I think about it, I just want to drag him down to the water's edge and force his head under till he sinks to the muck at the bottom where he belongs." The slits that stood for Ross' eyes grew even narrower—if that 'twere even possible—and his teeth clenched tight as he described his brother's departure from this world.

"Angus begins his watch tomorrow night, and I'm sure I'll be able to get more information from him as the days go on. So yer right, Donal, 'twould be a good idea to hold off raiding till we can figure things out to our advantage," Ross concluded.

Then he stood up verra slowly, a testament to the aches he was still having, I'm sure. "I best be going now," he said. "Nora and Sara asked me to take care of fixing the railing on the porch. We snapped it during the scuffle. I'll not fix it tonight, but I'll not want them to think I'm out drinking and carousing till the wee hours of the morning when there's work to be done at home at sunup."

"Wait, I'll ride with ye, Ross. I've got my students to deal with in the morn, and they'll be looking for me to carry them through the fall of Troy. Like

Anchises on Aeneas' shoulders, they'll be riding on the strength of my knowledge as they sift through the carnage of their own feeble translations," Owen proudly declared as he scampered to catch up with Ross.

Abruptly, Ross turned back around to face the fire and pulled an object out of his pouch. "I almost did it again, Donal. I've been carrying this round for a while now, and I keep forgetting to give it to ye. I had an extra one lying in the barn, and I ken ye were looking for one to hang above yer door." At this, he extended to me the gift of a horseshoe.

"Much obliged, Ross," I said, and after standing, I took the shoe with one hand and clasped his hand with the other. "Thank ye."

"That's complete then." Owen chuckled to himself at his own keen sense of biblical humor, proclaiming, "Come, Melchior, let's be on our way. Gaspar, I take it ye'll depart to yer own country by a different route, eh? We came bearing gifts and now we'll be making our way homeward."

Brodie and I shared a good laugh at Owen's farfetched suggestion, and as the two strode away, I examined the horseshoe in my hand that Ross had just given me. I couldna' help thinking to myself how well this would look above my portal, hanging upright in a proper tribute to Cernunnos. Mirroring the crescent shape atop the head of the horned one, the charm assures its holder of both good luck and the promise of fecundity. With a break from reiving for the next few weeks, maybe it'd be a good time to look into fulfilling that promise.

Trying to conceal the excitement that I felt inside of me, I asked casually, "Brodie, what do ye ken of Laird McElroy's daughter, the one they call Mary?"

Mary – The Threads of Fate

About once a week, I visit the widows and children who are cottars on my father's land. It started just a year before when I was riding and come upon two little ones gathering up acorns to be split, shelled, leeched, and made into meal. Without a man to provide, the families were forced to come up with creative ways to fill their bellies when the harvest was meager or provisions low.

Never wanting for anything in my own life, I remember the shock I felt at confronting such stark deprivation. And to see that kind of hardship on the faces of innocent children seemed about the unfairest thing in the whole world to me. A brief conversation with my Da' ripped away the veil of privilege from my eyes, and I started to see the harsh truth that was all around me. It was a universe of pure chance—ye either fell on the side of those who had the freedom to daydream and plan a rosy future or ye were forced to battle everyday for yer wretched existence with yer reward being the right to do it all over again with the next sunrise.

I took to the habit of visiting these families who were tethered to enduring and always marveled at their ability to find joy in the simplest of things. A pint of fresh goat milk, a handful of newly picked wildflowers, a gift of a jousting knight Devin had carved for me. Offerings so small they shouldna' make much difference shifted their world from bleak to bright at least for a brief moment. Most treasured for me, however, were the talks I'd have with the widows themselves.

Sitting at table with them and listening to their stories, I began to understand there was a verra small dividing line between comfort and hardship, the latter ensuing because of the absence of a husband or father. 'Tis true, the women were brae and resilient despite the cruelty of fate, but I couldna' help thinking how impossible it was for a woman to be given the chance to provide for her family on the same level as her male partner. Sewing and embroidering, cooking and cleaning, caring for little ones: that doesna' translate into profit.

No material wealth comes out of such pursuits, and so these families teetered between survival and surrender. I couldna' contain an overwhelming sadness and a deep sense of frustration that prosperity was only theirs if a man took their hand—literally—to bring them to a land of milk and honey.

Thinking of the injustice of it all did nothing to allay my shame for filling up my basket today for someone other than those women. Consoling myself with the promise that I'd be making those visits to them tomorrow, I tried to quell my pangs of guilt.

I had no trouble leaving Undlay this morning; my family was accustomed to my goodwill visits, my Ma even encouraging me to make myself known throughout the land as a lady who cared for her tenants. She said that'd go far in determining what kind of opinion the people held of me, and their opinion mattered much, especially in a region continually marked by strife and conflict where securing allegiance often meant the difference between thriving or perishing.

My mother didna' ken I had no great interest in cultivating a reputation; no, I was simply drawn to their methods of self-sufficiency and independence, any approach that didna' require a piece of jewelry being placed on a finger.

So I comforted myself in the knowledge that tomorrow I'd tend to that, while this day I turned toward the east, making my path through the brush and down the hill that led to the lone shack by the loch. The sky seemed to scowl at the foolish and vain pursuits of those who moved below, and I was dismayed by the rain that pelted my hair and face. Placing the basket down briefly, I used both hands to lift the hood from my cloak and place it firmly over my head. The extra material provided a kind of ledge that kept my eyes dry, and I was able to see the untrodden passage, thick with vegetation, before me.

Years ago, Annag and I would sometimes climb down from Tannock Hill, just far enough to behold the humble dwelling, but we didna' have the courage to venture any closer than that. We had heard so many frightening stories about Hilda—an especially terrifying one asserted how she was a female vampire who remained youthful by drinking the blood of wayward children who had lost their way in her woods, never to return.

Another more intricate story claimed she was the spirit of King Monie's sister and that she had hidden in an enchanted cave when her brother and his Viking invaders were defeated by the inhabitants of Undlay. In the cave, she committed herself to the Evil One, transforming from a lovely princess into *baobhan sith*—a female demon. To this day, villagers who've kept watch in the woods report that they've seen the Devil riding in his chariot—horses snorting flames of fire—in haste to reunite with Hilda. Some say they've even witnessed the two walking out upon the surface of the loch, calling to the spirits of the fallen Vikings whose bodies were cast into its murky depths.

I hadna' realized how my pace had slowed as I was recalling those whispered accounts of the woman I was actively choosing to go see. The thumping of my heart grew louder and my breath shallower, contradicting my slower movements. I was letting my mind scatter into these dark places rather than focus on my mission. After all, many a person has sought out Hilda before, from seeking a cure for an ailing cow to securing a potion for an ailing heart. Besides, I'm not asking for much here, at all. Just a wee bit of help in locating an elusive woodsman, right?

The rain softened to a mist as Hilda's hovel seemed to rise up out of the clouds that had formed by the loch's edge. Encircled by sallow trees, the dark turf hut was simple in construction, its edges enveloped by the leaves that drooped with moisture from the tree's branches. A sudden rustling of those leaves froze me in my tracks as my attention was fixed upon the door which quickly opened and closed. A large, imposing figure dominated the entrance way, casting his eyes about in both directions before fastening his bonnet upon his wild, untamed hair. He moved with astonishing speed to the side of the shack where his horse was waiting. In one fluid motion, he mounted and was on his way, riding as if being pursued by a colony of agitated bees.

I moved away from the tree behind which I was hiding and began to absorb the immediate surroundings of her home. In the area where the man's horse had been was a red fox with three kits, curled up near her belly. A little further apace was a grazing goat, and under the small awning to the right of the door were two chestnut-brown pine martins who lifted and stretched their necks at length at my approach. With tentative steps, I drew closer to the door, not wanting to alarm the menagerie of creatures who had gravitated to this peculiar sanctuary. Only by getting nearer did I catch a glimpse of a doe and her two fawns who had stopped their foraging to examine me with curiosity.

My free hand extended out from my cloak as I readied myself to knock, but before I could do so, the door opened of its own, and a soft voice called out, "I felt ye coming, lass. Do not be afeard."

Swallowing the blockage in my throat, I stepped across the threshold to see the alleged witch of Loch Ness. I tried to take in her appearance with one long look and was startled by how ordinary the woman seemed—no warts, no crooked nose, no scraggly hair. She was seated upon a stool in front of a glowing peat fire, and in her lap was a rabbit she was soothing with her petting.

"Come closer, lass. I'll not be seeing so well these days," she said as she gestured to the empty chair that was situated on the other side of the fire. Her eyes, indeed, had a filmy sort of covering over them, like a sheet of thin gauze laying atop each one. Beneath the veil, however, were a pair of blue piercing eyes that seemed to possess a vision not confined to apprehending only earthly objects.

I still had not found my voice as yet, so she continued, "This here is Gunnar. Been with me since last winter. Attacked by a wolf or some other creature as ye can tell." With this, her hand moved gently to caress the stump where his second ear should have been. "So I do his hearing for him and keep him out of harm's way, and he does some seeing for me, leaping and guiding me to the things I canna seem to find."

As I watched her hand move calmly and leisurely across his rich white fur, my eyes grew involuntarily wide when I detected the extra growth sprouting off her thumb. Disguising my gasp as a deep inhalation, I murmured, "I brought ye some jam and some bannocks, if I could ask a favor of ye—"

Before I could form the words of my request, she observed, "Always seems worlds away, but it's closer than ye think." Softly placing her companion on the ground, she stood and waited for the creature to hop over to the object she desired.

She must be able to see his coat more clearly than other things, I thought to myself, as I watched her pick up her drop spindle and distaff and return to her comment that had left me puzzled. "Love, that is," she finished.

She made her way back to her stool and reached into the basket of wool that rested beside it. Grasping a clump of it, she started to pull and separate it into thinner strips. "Ye must think of yer intention. Fix yer mind and yer will upon what it is ye wish to have."

With those words, the old woman began to draft the fiber out thin, getting it ready to join up to the spindle. Twisting the stick in the same direction and keeping a tight pinch on the fiber, she began to sing a melody that I had not ever heard before, the words Germanic and, judging from the beauty contained in her voice, something very sad and ancient.

Captivated by the rhythm of her hands, the spindle, and the music, I allowed myself to summon what it would feel like to be in the arms of my protector again. As the energy passed from her hand into the wool, I felt my own spirit lifting out and away from my body into the air of the song. I dunno how long this went on; well, however long the song was, I suppose, but I do ken that I was filled with a deep sense of assurance that my wish was manifesting into reality just as the fluffy fiber was transforming into thread. When the tune ended, she reached both of her hands out to me, so I crossed the small room and walked over to her, kneeling in front of her like a petitioner waiting for a response to her prayer. Still enveloped in something of a faraway trance, she spoke these words:

Hearts filled, but later broken.
Words exchanged, but canna be spoken.
Searching about, but not lookin'
In the secret place resides yer token.
Fires of passion need no stokin'
But sorrow shall this love be cloaked in.

The warmth of her clasp around my cold, trembling fingers was accentuated the moment she let go, and I felt the chill seize me anew. I didna' ken what to say or do, so I remained kneeling there for a few moments, suspended in time. I waited.

With her eyes and voice now closed to me, I took the hint that my audience had concluded. Not wanting to disrupt her stony silence, I rose from the ground verra quietly and walked back over to where my basket lay. Removing its contents, I placed my offering on the empty square table behind me and made my way toward the door. With one foot on the other side of the threshold, I turned back for a final look, the only perceptible movement was Hilda's hand stroking the ball of white fur that had resumed its position on her lap.

As each step brought me further away from the shack, I willed myself to commit her cryptic prophecy to memory. Some of it seemed clear—although ominous—and other parts shrouded in mystery. My feet sunk into the wet soil as I clambered up Tannock Hill amidst the steady rain. I couldna' devote too much consideration to her sorrow-laden pronouncements about the sadness of love and hearts being broken. After all, any venture incurs risk, and I was willing to accept those conditions for the chance to be in a romance that burned with no other agent than its own passion.

I wasna' sure what she meant by exchanging words but not speaking them. How else would I communicate with him if not by talking? Maybe we'd never have to utter a sound because we'd know each other so well? *Och, I dunno about this part at all*, I thought, as I slapped my empty basket against the side of my leg in frustration, noting how my ascent was becoming more slippery with every step.

I did ken, though, how I'd been searching but obviously not looking in the right places. By going into the forest and trying to find the location where we had met that eve, I'd clearly been following a mistaken trail. "In the secret place resides yer token"? What "secret place"? I have only one "secret place" and that'd be the hollowed-out trunk where I had planned to hide the night of the game but never made it there. As I stood at the crest of the hill with the rain falling, I decided on my course of action. I'd go directly to that spot to see if, in fact, there was some clue waiting for me there. Firm in my resolve, I headed in the direction of Undlay and the woods that lay beyond.

Donal – Reflections

I twisted the remaining ribbon round my finger, staring at its splash of color against the dirt beneath my feet. I had found a small covert which gave me a bit of shelter from the raindrops, and I sat on a stump inside it, coiling and recoiling the strand as my thoughts twisted and turned in my mind.

Just a little while ago, I left my third set of verses, tied with a portion of the ribbon, beneath the small canvas I had placed in the hollowed-out trunk just a ways in the distance. Shaking my head, I returned to the thought I'd been mulling over since last evening. Who'd imagine that Brodie would ken anything about Mary McElroy? He of all people? A fellow who seemed to be ignorant of all comings and goings unless it pertained to satisfying his own appetite for food and drink? And yet, he's the one who's brought me here to this place, all because he remembered a minor occurrence some two or three years before.

'Twas a lucky thing, then, that I ventured to talk with him last night about her. Turns out he ken more about Mary McElroy than I did myself! He'd had dealings before with Teague McElroy and was aware that the man had his hands full with his spirited daughter. On one occasion when Brodie had gone to McElroy to discuss sheep breeding, they were interrupted by his wife who was asking if Mary had been given permission by Teague to skip the ladies' sewing hour because she was nowhere to be found, once again. Only on his ride home through the forest did Brodie come upon the mischievous lass— with bunches of flowers that she had strewn around the edges of yon tree trunk.

Climbing inside, she seemed to pretend she was in her own skiff, sailing forth to *sithiche*--fairyland--among the flower sprites she'd gathered about her. Granted, that were two or three years ago, and she was just a wee lass then, but for most of us, we never outgrow the charm of those magical places borne of our youthful imagination—even if just to revisit them when we've lost the enchantment of being alive as we grow older.

And so, I spin this thread round and round, hoping that she will someday return to this spot and let my words of love cast their own spell upon her.

Mary – Kindred Spirits

Containing myself no longer, I broke into a full run, ignoring the branches that thwapped against me with their wet and soggy leaves. Despite having waited my whole life for love to come to me, I sprinted as if I had no time to waste, like whatever "token" was there was going to vanish if I didna' retrieve it at once.

As the place came into view, I felt my spirits sag just like the leaves that drooped with dampness. There was nothing unusual about it; no difference from yesterday or the day before or the day before that. I had hoped that the area would have been transformed in a way that bespoke of my protector's identity, but it was as it had always been. No longer running, I could hear my own short, panting breath drown out all the other sounds of the glade. Marked by disappointment, I slogged my way over to the tree, wondering if I had misunderstood Hilda's message. As I sat down upon its edge to ponder this further, my eye was caught by a piece of canvas that lay inside the opening.

Hesitantly, I reached inside, afeard to hope that beneath it may be traces of what I'd been wishing for. The tips of my fingers tingled as they touched the cloth and lifted it aside. With a sharp intake of breath, I marveled at the three small scrolls before me, each bound with a piece of ribbon—the same color as the one I had lost on the eve of my encounter. Untying the thread on the first one, I unfurled paper and read about "a thistle's alarum" and "hair red-gold" and "eyes of emerald."

One part of me wanted to linger over these words and let them wash over me, but I couldna' wait a moment longer, and with my heart racing I reached for the second. Liberating the paper from its fastener, I trembled at the words of the question, "Will she come to me again and give me back my life?" Fighting back the urge to shout a resounding "yes" to no one at all, I dipped my hand back into the opening to pull out the third. Reveling in the confirmation of my dream, I was silent no longer and read the following words aloud:

An ember still holds within
The promise of what once was
And what can still be.
A mere glow in this moment
Can return to full flame

But another voice joined in with my own, reciting the final line:

When ye give yerself over to me.

I held my body rigid in complete stillness, lifting only my eyes off the paper and up toward the direction of the sound. In front of me was an arresting sight—a tall, striking man whose presence energized the sylvan setting. Blue and gray plaid surrounded his body, and a pair of powerful hands held a bonnet that he gently fingered as looked upon me in earnest. Startled I was, but not afeard. Like the rippling waters of a springtime creek, my emotions surged inside me—not with cold but with a warmth that bubbled from the center of my body to its farthest points. Thick, wavy hair of ebony fell untied to his shoulders and glistened with droplets of moisture, casting him in an otherworldly type of shine. Pretending a boldness that I didna' have, I held his gaze for a few timeless seconds before surrendering to the power of those jet-black pools that conquered me with their depth.

Clinging to the hope that I'd not be wrong, I asked, "Ye *are* real, then?"

"Aye. I am," he answered, later adding, "Mary."

When he spoke my name, he dwelt upon the sound of it, almost as if he were singing out each of the letters. He didna' smile nor scowl; he just simply stood there, absorbing every inch of my person with his eyes. Clearly, he was aware of my identity, but I was at a loss as to his. He may have claimed to be of flesh and blood, but there was something ethereal about him as if he had arisen from the mist and woods and was one with them in spirit. Those dancing eyes beckoned me with the promise of thrill and adventure, and I could feel myself being swept away by his bearing. There was a ruggedness about his person that became more apparent when contrasted with the soothing, lyrical tone of his voice, kind of like hard oat scones that are softened with a bit of drizzled warm honey.

The distance between us remained constant. I think we were both afeard that moving too quickly to close the gap would scatter the other one away, as a tortoiseshell butterfly takes to the air to escape a child's grasp. The rain continued to fall, cascading down my cloak, so I clutched the three papers together, felt for the inner folds of my coat, and tucked them safely inside, without ever turning my eyes away from his.

"How do ye ken who I am?" I asked him pointedly, tilting my head as if in challenge.

Instead of answering, he inquired, "Do ye have any recollection of me at all?" And he raised his chin a bit at this as if turning the tables back on me.

"Aye," I said softly, finally breaking the spell of his gaze as I looked down upon the empty hands in my lap.

"I found ye," he started, "not too far from this verra place. Do ye mind if I step a bit closer to ye now? I'll not hurt ye," he spoke with such melody that I felt my own spirits lifting and being carried away, by words this time instead of his arms like last.

After I nodded silently, he moved nearer to me with a kind of fluidity and smoothness to his step that resembled that of the creatures of the forest. Bending down upon one knee to bring himself eye level with me, he spoke, "I'm Donal Donn of Bohuntin. Would ye be willing to walk a few paces with me now to the shelter over yon? There's some cover there that'll keep us from the rain."

Without speaking, I proffered my hand to him, knowing that I was drowning more deeply with each passing moment. I was dangerously close to completely falling under his charm. Is it possible to hold a hand of muscle and sinew and yet feel as if yer gliding with a spirit? Despite his height and his physical strength, he moved with such ease and grace that it seemed as if he were floating not treading upon the earth. Stooping lower to the ground, he pulled back the branches that enclosed the covert and ushered me into a place that was snug and protected from the showers that fell outside of it.

Unfastening the portion of the plaid that had been wrapped around his shoulders, he lay the fabric on the soil and made a place for me to sit. Across from that, he faced me, his knees nearly at his chin as he took his seat upon a tree stump.

"I've ken yer family for many years, Mary. My Da' always talked about the bravery of yer father when he refused to sign the Covenant in '38—not because he didna' believe in preserving Scotland's ways, but because he believed more in practicing religion however one pleased to. We heard only good things about Teague McElroy, and I ken he had two fine sons and two bonnie daughters. When I came upon ye that night, ye were asleep, but it looked like ye'd been sorely troubled, lass. Were ye running away from something or from someone?" He asked me this with such complete sincerity that I believed I could open my mind to him without fear of being judged.

But I could not do it. I was still guarded with him. So I tried to make light of the whole event, brushing aside his question with feigned nonchalance. "I was just having a wee cry for myself that night before I got lost in the woods." Here, I shook my head dismissively, inserting a small chuckle to emphasize the insignificance of those tears I had shed.

When he continued to study me with great intensity, I swallowed that laughter abruptly. I didna' want this man to think I was some spoiled child who reverted to tantrums when her vanity was wounded. I decided then that I would not hide who I was--even if he thought me a fool, even if he could not understand my vexations at having so little power over my own life. And almost like an affirmation of that decision, he said in a most tender voice, "Go on."

He looked at me so deeply, with such gentleness in his eyes, that my words tumbled over themselves, and I told him about the hunt and Robby and my chores and my desire for adventure, the kind that extended way beyond the walls of Undlay Castle. I spoke about paths I could follow of my own choosing, not ones that were already designed by someone else. I explained how I was being pushed along these roads through no power of my own, and I exploded with the injustice of my parents forcing me onto a course of their own creation by thrusting me into a union with George Campbell.

"And I loathe him with the kind of disgust ye feel when ye see maggots crawling upon a carcass. I canna abide being anywhere near him--he's ugly and mean and petty and dumb. Just because he's a Campbell, he's a good partner for marriage? Och!" I could feel my face flushing red with rage as I finished, "I'd rather be sent to the pricker and later burnt alive than to have George Campbell's breath upon my body!"

I had not dreamed of speaking so freely to a man I'd known for all of a few minutes, and yet I'd always been a person who, when the floodgates opened, couldna' control the flow of words coming through. I thought I'd shocked him into horror, but instead he leaned closer to me, and once again, went down upon one knee, our bodies now nearly touching.

"Ye're no witch, Mary," he said with conviction. "I'm sure ye understand the job of the pricker, aye? Only if he plunges the needle into yer flesh without ye feeling pain can he declare ye a sorceress. And ye, my lass, are all feeling and passion. May I?" And as he asked me this question, he reached one hand toward my face and with his finger started to trace the outline of my lips.

Deep inside of me, a fire started to swell, and I found myself leaning forward to close the gap between us. For most of the conversation, I had been striving to resist the pull that was drawing me into him, but with his touch upon my mouth, I could resist no longer. Instead of allowing me to plunge further with abandon, he placed his hands on either side of my face and transfixed me with his gaze.

"We burn with the same flame, Mary McElroy. Ye've saved me from withering and wasting away in this world so absent of feeling and light. I've yearned to be with ye, to speak with ye, and when the longing grew too great, I let my words explode on the page. The writing canna replace the heat that's running through my hands when I caress yer face, but it helps me deal with the absence of it by allowing my imagination to conceive of it and to live it in my mind. Maybe that could work for ye, as well. If yer voice is not heard, let yer words on the page do the speaking. Sometimes just getting it out of yer heart and into the world makes things easier to handle."

He dropped his hands to his sides but continued to hold me captive with his penetrating look. "I canna tell ye what yer father's plans are for ye and George Campbell, but I *can* tell you this: I'll not let Campbell take away from me the girl who's bewitched my soul. Nae, the only burning ye'll do, Mary, will come when ye feel the heat of my desire."

With a final lingering look, he pushed himself away from me, and I wondered if he had distanced himself from me because he—as I—felt that we were moving dangerously from desire to action. Although I should have been grateful for his restraint, I longed to feel his lips upon my own and wished that he had joined himself to me in the shared intimacy of a single kiss. I hoped his emotions were fluttering inside as much as my own, but I couldna' deny a slight disappointment at seeing how serene and relaxed he seemed to be as he returned to his seat across from me.

My heart skipped in my chest when he asked, "When can I see ye again? I must go now, but I canna leave without knowing when we will meet once more…" His voice did not tremble, nor was there any discernible forwardness in his request, only an underlying sense of longing matched by my own sadness that any amount of time in his absence was simply too much to bear.

"I'm to go visiting among the tenants tomorrow in the early morn. That'll bring me back to Undlay sometime around mid-day," I answered swiftly and then watched his dark eyes look upward as if formulating some kind of plan.

"Do ye ken the place near the shoreline where the two alder trees lay criss-crossed in the water? The ones that fell in last winter's storm? Nearby, there's a rowan tree above whose leaves are turning redder with each passing day. Ye'll not miss it. I'll be waiting for ye there, *mo ghradh*." He spoke these words with such warmth that I wished to magically leap the gap of time and make it tomorrow immediately. But since I lacked the power to shift the universe to my own liking, I instead savored the final moments I had to watch him bow in deference to me, place his bonnet atop his black mane, and glide off into the mist.

Alone now, I could take a deep gulp of moist air to try and process all that had just transpired. He is real. I'm not crazy--do I dare tell Annag? I was afeard though that speaking of him to another would diminish the intensity of our encounter, but I also ken that, with my heart bursting like this, it'd be near impossible to keep it contained within. I'd have to swear her to secrecy, of course, as any hint of my knowing Donal, let alone meeting with him, would send my Da' into fits over my undermining his marital plans for me. I dunno why I felt so confident that I had a found a new ally. I guess it was because I trusted in Donal's word; he'd not let the union with Campbell be made, and I believed in his promise. Without even knowing much about him, I'd put my safety in his hands. Funny, I could have all the wealth and comfort a girl could ever want by becoming Lady Campbell, and yet I'd choose to set up house in a forest alcove if 'twere furnished with this man's love.

Oh, why canna it be tomorrow now? I thought, as I began to remove the three sets of poems from the inner folds of my cloak. Hoping to hasten the hours along, I flung myself into the content of his verse, relishing each line, each word, that fastened his soul to my own. Although the rain continued to fall beyond the sheltered bower, I paid it no mind. No storm out there could ever douse the flame we had just kindled within.

A Coming of Age

When Mary stepped out from the forest into the open field, she wasn't greeted with a parting of the clouds or brilliant sunshine as the lightness of her stride would have indicated. No, gray skies continued to envelop the glen, her clothing was soggy and rain-soaked, and her toes sloshed inside her shoes with each step, but Mary was oblivious to it all. Floating somewhere above the physical world, she was thinking only of how, in the brief expanse of a few hours, her life had shifted momentously.

Just a week ago when faced with the prospect of being tethered to George Campbell as his wife, she had knelt before God asking Him to grant her an early death, but now she reversed that prayer, beseeching Him to grant her endless days and countless years to come. The rain showers became sacramental, in a way, consecrating her on this new journey which featured the commingling of tenderness and passion. Wrapping herself in the promise of such delight, she was thoroughly unaware of the approaching rider until he pulled up alongside her and announced, "Ye best git yerself off to the side, Miss McElroy."

Taken by surprise, Mary gasped with alarm when she heard the voice and beheld the beady, black eyes of George Campbell. Immediately, her spirits, like the elements, descended into gloom. "I've got some vicious rogues to deliver to yer father, and ye'll not be wanting to tempt them with yer bedraggled look. They might mistake ye for someone belonging to their own class, someone desperate for money whichever way she can make it, even if it meant pulling up her own skirts to be of service." He chuckled to himself as he said this, a fiendish smile curling upon his lips.

With her stomach knotted up inside her, Mary spewed words of venom. "How dare ye speak to me that way, George Campbell! Ye are the most despicable creature in the entire province. 'Tis a shame for us all that ye were ever born; ye coulda' saved the rest of the world from suffering through yer presence."

Mary took advantage of this opportunity to release the feelings she had been holding back for some time. "I dunno who ye think ye're entertaining with such base comments. There's nothing the least bit funny about yer humor, and I certainly do not need the likes of ye to protect me from any 'vicious rogues' ye might be bringing to my father. They're villains, no doubt, but ye, beneath those fancy clothes and lands and title, are a far worse brute for the hypocrisy of it all!"

In an instant, George aggressively yanked the reins of his horse to charge directly toward Mary, pushing her back toward the forest again. Leaning down menacingly within inches of her face, he spoke through clenched teeth. "Now ye listen to me, Mary, I'll not take any fresh talk from ye any more. Yer lucky I even lower myself to speak to ye, ye with yer slovenly look and wayward behavior. Remember, 'tis my choice whether or not to give ye the Campbell name and make a lady out of ye. The more disagreeable ye are to me the more I think I'll just skip the name giving and take what I want from ye some dark night when no one is about--and do not think I won't.

"I'll have ye ken that ye and yer family have *me* to thank for ridding the land of two Cameron villains; *I* found them, *I* pursued them, and *I* captured them, and yer father will have his chance to wield his justice thanks to me. No doubt he'll be indebted to me for such fine service and will want to bestow favor upon me. So ye'd best keep yer tongue in that mouth of yers--unless of course yer going to use it to show me how contrite ye are later on by meeting me in the forest when I'm on my way home." With lust in his eye and the threat of violence in his voice, George snapped the reins and dashed off to meet with Teague McElroy.

Mary stood there silently considering this exchange with Campbell. Her mood plummeted as her faith in a possible future with Donal crumbled, leaving her hollow inside. Would George's success hasten her father's decision to marry her off to him? How could Donal, as he had promised, prevent this from happening? Would Donal speak to her father on her behalf; would he ask for her hand? And although Donal had spoken kindly about his respect for her father, would her Da' feel the same about Donal and his clan? With these questions plaguing her, Mary heard additional hoofbeats and turned about in time to see Ollie MacCain, the tanner from the castle, returning from the watch and drawing nearer.

"Ollie, what's the news? George Campbell just sped by and declared that he was responsible for capturing some outlaws. Did he really do so? What happened on the watch?" Mary waited earnestly for his reply, praying that there was more to the story than the version that George had just recounted.

Removing his bonnet and using the back of his hand to wipe away the wetness from his bushy eyebrows, Ollie commanded his horse to stop in order to give Mary the details of the arrest. "Ye'd be mighty proud of ye younger brother, Miss Mary, ye would. It was he who brought Blake Cameron to his knees. Without even a weapon on his person, Robby's the one who's making Cameron atone for his crimes. Had naught to do with Campbell at all—fawn-hearted fool, the man is," Ollie added with a lift of his head, "though if ye hear the story from that one, he'd tell ye he brought in both ruffians and the devil himself to boot!" When he finished this comment, Ollie drew his lips into a frown, closed his eyes, and shook his head in disgust.

"Robby? Truly?" Mary asked with a combination of surprise and admiration.

Her question invited Ollie to continue, "Aye, so Robby was given the watch when the night hours are the blackest, and the two of us—Bryston and I—were sleeping under the canvas a ways off. Well, I guess Robby heard something amiss, something like multiple horses moving fast, like on a raid. So he gives the bale warning, lighting up two bundles of hay to signify that the thieves were about, and I suppose Campbell saw the fires from the comfort of his estate and tried to get in on the action. I wasna' sleeping well anyway, and I smelled the smoke and roused Bryston and we mounted to follow Robby." Ollie's speech quickened to match the excitement of the story.

"I couldna see verra well, but I could hear yer brother thundering away on Hubert, but then his horse whinnied and must've been harmed, because Robby was thrown, and of course that made Blake turn about with the intent to send yer brother to the angels. I spun back to help, but it all happened so fast, and there was no need for me to interfere, as ye'll soon learn. Och sure, Blake had a great advantage, being on horseback and Robby on foot.

"Cameron took a backhanded cut at the boy's head and face, slashing downward, but Robby grabbed hold of Blake's leg and wouldna' let go, even while dodging the slashes, till he tumbled Cameron out of his seat. Once they were on the ground, Robby pinned Blake beneath him, but the scoundrel sliced into the boy's thigh, and Robby let out a terrible howl, a sound that invigorated and enraged yer brother even further! He lifted Blake's shoulders off the dirt and rammed the man's head against the large rock that lay beneath them both.

"Took only two times before Blake was stilled—allowing Robby to fetch the rope off Hubert and bind the man's hands and feet together. Bryston and I had a bit of luck corralling one of the other Camerons—Blake's brother, Drew—but the rest of them rode away. Course when all the fighting and seizing and capturing was over, *then* Campbell comes out of the shadows, claiming to have been part of the chase…but we—Robby, Bryston, and I—ken that he was cowering in the bushes waiting for the tumult to die down before making his appearance."

Mary stared at the ground in disbelief and awe, recognizing for the first time how much her brother really meant to her. Listening to Ollie's explanation of the danger Robby faced made her heart expand with concern and love. And hearing of his heroism made her glow with wonder at his bravery.

Ollie broke her into her thoughts, announcing with a smile, "He and Bryston'll be coming along shortly with the prisoners in tow." After a moment's hesitation, he added with gravity, "But he'll be needing tending to, Miss Mary."

"Of course. Thank you, Ollie. I'll take care of whatever is necessary, ye can be sure," Mary answered without hesitation, and Oliver bid her farewell and made his way to Undlay.

Rather than continue toward the castle, Mary retraced her steps in anticipation of seeing her brother. When two riders on horseback emerged from the forest, she felt awash with pride at the sight of the boy she had incessantly teased and insulted throughout most of her life. Now he sat tall and dignified in the saddle, a big change from the child who bubbled with excitement over his first successful hunt just a few days ago. That bright-eyed youth who relished his individual conquest over an animal had transformed into a man who was now the savior of his people.

Mary – Of Crime and Punishment

Even from a distance, I could see the bloodstained rag that encircled my brother's leg, and I fought hard to hold back the tears that started to well up in my eyes. Blinking furiously, I marched on with false courage toward the two riders headed in my direction.

The bandage was thoroughly drenched in rusty-red, a bit of a blessing since that meant the bleeding must have slowed. But sitting for hours on horseback was clearly taking its toll on poor Robby, for he winced in pain with each contact Hubert made with the ground. Underneath Robby's grimace were gashes and cuts, one that formed a red trench, extending from his left ear and across his whole cheek. Other smaller nicks and scratches were engraved upon his face so that he gave the appearance of a child who had feasted upon ripe berries and left evidence of his raid behind—only this were child's play nae more. My brother had grown into a man seemingly overnight, and his confrontation with death had catapulted him far beyond me in terms of experience and wisdom. It was I who now felt inadequate and childish.

"Hallo, brother," I tried to sound cheery. "Bryston," I nodded at Robby's companion. "I tell ye, I'm verra relieved to see ye with my own eyes. I heard all about the skirmish from Ollie just now," and I waved my hand back toward the path where the tanner and I had just spoken.

"Mary," Robby spoke with difficulty, "it'd be better if ye were on yer way. Go on ahead and tell Da' to have the guard to meet us at the dungeon." With his lips cracked and swollen, my brother had to swallow a few times just to loosen his tongue enough to form these words. Although he continued to remain erect and put on a brae front, Robby's shoulders drooped with fatigue and pain every time he exhaled, and I had to restrain myself from wanting to wrap him in a comforting hug as I once did on stormy nights when he'd patter down the hallway and tap on my chamber door for admittance.

Neither Bryston nor my brother had stopped their horse's forward progress, but their pace was verra slow and deliberate. From the corner of my eye, I could now discern the reason for both their slackened pace and Robby's concern for me. Rope dangled from the back of each horse, and at the end of each was tied one of the Cameron thugs. With feet and hands bound, they could move only with mincing steps, their long, tattered coats dragging upon the dirt. The one with Robby seemed to have no awareness of what was happening, for he didna' look up at all and seemed capable of only the smallest degree of mental acuity, the simple kind that required merely putting one foot in front of the other.

Behind Bryston was the more spirited prisoner—his thin, blonde hair hung down his face, covering his eyes in yellow strands that seemed dipped in grease. He whipped his head up to the side to clear the strings away long enough to swallow me with his leer. I found myself taking a step back from the palpable flow of evil exuding from the man. My fear increased tenfold when he thrust his slimy pink tongue between his lips and began making quick lapping motions in my direction, all the while his glare locked upon me.

Forcibly closing my own eyes, I turned and darted back toward the front of Hubert and assured Robby, "I'll deliver yer message for ye, brother. And when yer done depositing yer cargo, meet me by the kitchen hearth, and I'll see to replacing those bandages for ye." Like a red squirrel bolting from a raptor's talons, I dashed home to erase this brush with malice and make ready the way for Robby's arrival.

***

I heard the tapping sound of each footfall as I ran across the drawbridge and through the arched gateway of Undlay. Nodding to the keeper, I slowed my pace a bit as I cut through the hum of activity that vibrated in the courtyard. A too-lengthy glance over at the smithy—just to catch a glimpse of Annag's Hamlin—resulted in my smashing into a bouquet of pheasants who flitted and scamped about in response.

Rushing up the staircase two steps at a time, I arrived at the landing and then strode past the kitchen on my way to my father's private hall. Despite having to probably cross paths with George once again, I wanted to fulfill my promise to my brother and, while I was at it, set the record straight about the details of the arrest. I was intercepted, however, by the sound of my mother's voice coming from the kitchen, ensnaring me in place. "Mary, is that ye I hear? Come talk to me, lass."

My mother was a dainty woman, small in stature but commanding in will. Unlike myself who was constantly tripping or falling or crashing into things, she had an elegance and grace that infused her every movement. She never seemed to be rushed or unbalanced, even in the most trying circumstances. I remember the day a few winters ago when Robby had gone missing, and Devin found the lad shivering and nigh dead from the cold, having fallen through the thin sheet of ice that had formed on the loch's surface.

I had shrieked in horror as Devin presented the drenched bundle that was my brother, his face white as alabaster, his lips purple and unmoving. But with the calmness ye see enveloping the meadow at sunrise on a still summer morning, my mother readied a place before the grand hearth, replaced the wet blanket with a dry one, pried open those frozen lips, and poured down a measure of whiskey into the boy's chilled bones. Nae, unlike the birds I'd just recently trampled, there is nothing I've ever seen that could ruffle my mother's feathers.

"Good day, mother," I said, trying to sound dutiful—and not impatient as I truly was.

Finishing first with Fiona, she said, "Aye, that'll do. Plan for at least two to three extra places at table this eve," and then turning her attention to me, she asked, "And how did the visiting go today, Mary? Did ye bring the extra wool with ye to Mrs. Nairn?"

"Och, no," I answered, attempting to quickly concoct a believable excuse. "I didna' get as far as Mrs. Nairn this day as I was relishing the stories I heard from Mrs. Ruadh and lost all track of time. I'll have to share with ye sometime the history of how the Campbells nigh ruined her husband's business, stealing his catch, pilfering his nets, even going so far as to scuttle his boat!"

Although that tale was not revealed to me today, it was a true one nonetheless, and I figured sharing it now with my mother might serve me well if the topic of my marrying into that family came up again in the near future as surely it would. I continued, "So I'll be heading back out again in the morn tomorrow, and that's when I'll spend time with Mrs. Nairn and Mrs. MacAra." I was struggling to sound light and cheery when all I really wanted was to be on my way.

As these words were delivered, the thick door to my Da's private hall cracked open, and I caught his words mid-sentence, "...so we'll need all of this concluded before the harvest celebration. They'll be no dark cloud hovering over the festivities. No hearing, no trial. I'll be wanting to send a message." With purposeful stride that matched the conviction in his voice, my father moved so quickly down the hall that even when I called out to him, he didna' slow down nor stop.

"Father, Robby's a coming, with two criminals in tow. He asked me to tell ye to have the guard meet him at the dungeon." I panted these words out in stilted fashion as I tried to catch up with him, but I couldna' get past George who was trailing my Da' so closely.

I heard him respond, "Aye, Mary. I'm on my way now to meet him. Thank ye, lass. Go tend to yer mother." Though his tone was dismissive, I was not hurt nor disappointed by his command. At times like these, I ken there were certain roles relegated to the genders, and mine meant that I couldna' be witness to the actual jailing of a prisoner in our dungeon...but that didna' mean I couldna' do other things behind the scenes to help my brother's cause. And so, I stole into my father's chamber, sat at his desk, took a piece of parchment, and, as Donal said, let my writing be my voice.

Dear Father,

I'm sure ye heard a story from George Campbell today about the arrest of Blake and Drew Cameron. I wanted to tell ye that George's words are not true, for I've heard from a reliable source...

***

There. That being done, I returned to the kitchen and asked Fiona if she could gather together for me a few clean rags and some boiling water in order to care for Robby's wounds. While Fiona was busy with that, I thought I'd sneak down toward the dungeon to see if Robby and Bryston had finished depositing the cargo inside.

I'd not often ventured into this part of the castle. The twisting staircase generally remained in darkness, the torches only lit when a guard had a tenant to mind, and it had been quite some time since we'd had a prisoner or prisoners—at least as far as I ken. In the old days, Devin told me that the entranceway was nearly always lit because of the lawlessness that ran rampant in the region. Father, as laird of the glen, assumed the mantle of constable, jailer, magistrate, and executioner. The security of the land and its people was in his hands, and now that trouble was stirring anew, he needed to exert his authority once again.

The narrow confines of the staircase, coupled with the darkness and foul stench, seemed to close in on me, and I needed to place both of my arms on either wall in order to steady myself as I went deeper into the bowels of the tower. The prison sat at the lowest point of the castle, the least desirable part of the whole structure. At times, it seemed as if the room were perched right upon the loch itself because on stormy days water would strangely bubble up from beneath the dirt floor of the dungeon, bringing with it the smell of decayed fish and corpses, the detritus that was rejected even by the sea monster of Ness.

I could feel the coldness increasing beneath my feet as I touched each slab of slate that brought me downward to the bottom of the staircase, but before I could get to the end, I heard voices further off. Trying to block out the smell of urine and feces that was filtered from the castle privies into the dungeon, I strained to hear the conversation.

"Give them nothing for now, and keep them bound, hand and foot," I heard my father say, and another voice followed in response, "Yes, my Laird," and then I detected a loud shove or push followed by a thud. Taking the final two steps ever so slowly, I craned my neck round to get a glimpse of the entrance to the prison, hoping to remain unseen while doing so. It was no easy feat to stay hidden yet satisfy my curiosity. A dangerous balancing act it was, with no reason for assuming such a risk other than my own inquisitiveness and concern. The thick stone walls on either side of the entranceway were joined together by an iron door with criss-crossed strips of metal. This lattice door, marked with empty square spaces, betrayed nothing of its contents beyond; darkness enveloped all that lay within.

Beholding a sight such as this reaffirmed my belief in those ancient legends that were associated with Undlay and the rumor of the contents of the vaulted cells hollowed into its very rock. According to the tale, one chamber contained an abundant treasure of gold but the other a fearful pestilence—the kind which, if released, would stalk and kill every person in the land, after having first slain the hand that unlocked the chamber door. That threat has been enough to quell even the greediest of men, thus the chambers remain unexplored. Standing here, feeling the chill in my bones, and breathing in the fetid smell of decay, I could certainly believe a plague was buried within and yearning for release.

Again, my father's voice, "See to yer wounds, son. Ye've done well." At this utterance, I backed up into the recesses of the staircase, careful to make no noise in my retreat. I had safely made it to the top when I heard a slow and deliberate footfall ascending and growing in loudness. It seemed to me that Robby most probably was taking each stair with the same single leg, probably to take the pressure off the wounded one. Wiping my soiled palms on the sides of my skirt and smoothing my hair into place, I wished to give the appearance that I had been waiting for him here in order to bring him to the kitchen to clean his wounds.

When he placed his left leg on the step, he had to manually lift his other to meet it, but his eyes must have traveled far enough in front of him to see my feet before him, and he glanced up at me with relief, one that bespoke of his desire to relinquish manly pretense and revert to simply being my younger brother once again.

"Okay now, let me lend ye a hand here. Fiona's got everything ready for us in the kitchen," I raised my shoulder a bit higher to pin it beneath his armpit and latched his arm around my other shoulder to bear some of his weight. We made steady but slow progress through the hallways of the castle, and I tried to move fluidly with him so as to avoid any jarring stops or starts.

I broke the silence. "So who'd ye think ye are? William Wallace? Going after Blake and his rogues with no back-up at all. Couldna' wait for Bryston and the rest to come and help ye? Even Wallace was nigh on twenty-seven years before he defeated the English at Stirling Bridge, and ye're not even sixteen!" If I had a free hand, I'd have tousled his hair at this remark.

Trying to lean on me a little less in order to match the bravado of his words, Robby replied, "Age has naught to do with it, Mary. Ye either have it or ye don't—that impulse to jump into action without hesitation, no time wasted on considering the danger ye're in or the circumstances. Ye just act. That's all I did. I had no care for what would become of me. I ken one thing only—that if I didna' jump on Hubert and immediately go after that scoundrel, he'd ride away without having to pay for what he did to Edina Barclay. And that wouldna' be right."

The profound meaning of his words struck me, as he had whittled down the essence of a hero into a few simple statements. Heroes just act; they don't consider their own welfare. The cause of justice and the pursuit of what is right supplants individual needs or concerns. That's what heroes do.

We stopped for a bit so that Robby could muster his strength before we were about to enter the more populated area of the kitchen. I knew that this pause was to replace the grimacing and the wincing he had done throughout our walk with a bold fearlessness he could present to the world, and I was more than willing to be a partner in this performance. Ushering him in through the doorway of the kitchen, I brought him to the chair that was placed near the great hearth where the pot of water had been boiling.

I had seen one of the castle's healers do this before—submerge the rags into the bubbling water, then ladle them out, and place them upon a clean fabric on the counter to cool. While that was happening, I began to unravel the rust-colored bandage that was tied around Robby's right leg. He took a sharp intake of breath when I released the binding, and I could see fresh blood begin to flow. This was not good, I thought to myself, but I couldna' wear my feelings openly before Robby.

Reaching quickly into the pile of dry rags, I pulled out a lengthy one and held it in place atop the wound, hoping to stanch the ooze. "I'll give ye a new dressing for this leg, but ye're going to need to do a better job of it in yer chamber when ye can remove yer clothing and wash the whole area." I said this with earnestness in my voice, but when I looked up at him, his eyes were looking into the distance and his mind preoccupied with other things. "Did ye hear me, brother?" I asked with urgency.

After a brief shake of his head, he said absently, "Aye."

People were coming in and out of the kitchen, making preparations for the evening meal, but they paid us no mind. I continued to remain in that position, applying pressure to his injured leg and periodically checking the rag to see if the blood was still pouring. Once it slowed to a trickle, I took a fresh piece of cloth and bound the spot again as it was before. "Now remember," I repeated with emphasis, "I've not really gotten in there at all, so ye've got to use the water basin and rags I'll be bringing ye to clean it yerself, okay?"

He nodded in agreement, and I stood and picked up one of the cooled, boiled rags and began dabbing the cuts and scratches on his face, careful to avoid the deepest slice across his cheek. I'd decided it'd be best to start gently with the little scrapes first and then build to tending to the largest gash. This method proved to be an accomodating one as it eased Robby into further conversation.

At this point, Annag entered through the doorway, her eyes wide with curiosity and worry. Robby's back was toward her, but I could tell that she ken the identity of my patient for her neck extended toward me, and she silently mouthed the question, "What happened?" With the slightest of gestures, I conveyed to her the need to remain quiet, so she busied herself with chopping some of the ingredients for the night's meal while remaining within earshot.

With an edge in his voice, he began, "Ye ken what he said about me the night the watch was assembled?" Beginning mid-thought as he did, I couldna' say I was sure who the "he" was, but I wasna' going to interrupt Robby's need to heal his other, less visible wounds.

"Out loud, he says, 'Six and a half? That's what I've been given? Six and a half men to conduct a watch? To secure a whole region?' All the while, he's looking straight at me as if the other men couldna' figure out his meaning. I knew right then that, though I'd no hair sprouting yet on my chin, I was more of a man than that whining, overindulged brat." I continued to move the cloth delicately over his forehead and chin, and with such proximity to his face, I found myself subsumed in the thunderous emotions that flickered across it with each additional remark.

"And I tried to talk to Da' about it, about how I'd been insulted before all the men and how Campbell himself had never done anything to be given charge over anyone—the only thing I've ever witnessed him do is prey upon the weak and insert himself into everyone else's business. But father didna' even try to explain or defend his reason for giving Campbell the position.

"No, instead he turns it on me, saying it'll make a man of me to be forced to serve under a person I didna' respect. He says it makes ye learn at a young age what ye can accept and what ye canna live with." He paused here for a moment, as if to wonder what he had gained from his experiences over the last few hours, and this allowed me a chance to gather myself before going after the deep red slice that traversed his cheek.

"And ye ken," he stopped abruptly to flinch in pain because I had started to clean the trench. After a deep inhale, he finished his observation. "Da' was right. It *has* made me grow up and understand some things about myself and about others. First, what I did last night, I'd do a thousand times over if it meant clearing the glen of devils like the Camerons. I do not care about the cuts and the fighting, so long as what's right is done. Even if I'd died trying, I'd be able to rest in my grave knowing I took my last breath defending my people and my land.

"Second, I realize now that it doesna' take years or wealth to make a man. I told ye before about the age thing, and now I'll tell ye about true riches. Fellows like Ollie and Bryston have hearts in their chests that beat the same as my own. No matter how tattered their clothes or how humble their homestead, I'd pledge my loyalty to them as I would a king, for their entire being is tied into mine.

"And finally," he furrowed his brow and announced, "I've come to see that there's verra little difference between the prisoners we threw in the dungeon and the one I'm forced to report to. They cheat, they lie, they care only for themselves, and when ye give them any kind of power, they use it to trample those beneath. Six and a half men? What gall. And ye ken where he was during the whole tumult? Hiding in the bushes he was, till we'd taken command of the brothers. Then he comes onto the scene, sword raised but unbloodied. Och," he repeated in disgust.

By now, I had completed whatever mending I could do for the time being and reminded Robby again of what he needed to take care of once he returned to his private chamber. As he raised himself up off the chair, he tilted to one side, taking the weight off the bandaged leg. The need to protect and care for this younger brother of mine reasserted itself, and I declared aloud as he was shuffling out of the kitchen, "Yer no half-man and never were, Robby McElroy. Ye've done more for the Barclay family and for the whole countryside in one day than that louse with his pathetic wisp of a moustache will do in his lifetime. But no matter all this talk of manhood, yer still my younger brother, and I'm commanding ye to heed my instructions and go clean out that wound!"

Acknowledging my directive with a brief wave of his hand, Robby turned the corner and disappeared from view. I stood there watching the vacated space but wasna' really looking at anything other than the thoughts that wafted and drifted round my head. The time had arrived; a threshold had been crossed by us both. We were children no longer. Transformed by his confrontation with violence, Robby responded in a manner he had wished for when he was a wee lad battling imaginary dragons.

How comforting to know that he had grown into the man he had envisioned he would one day be. And what of me on this day? I too was transformed, shedding my youthful notion that love would even out life's hard edges, that 'twould offer to its passengers an idyllic boat ride upon calm seas. Instead, I was knowingly embarking upon a voyage marked by currents and conflicts that would, most assuredly, capsize my prior way of life. Although I wasna' staring down a knife readied to send me from this realm to the next, I had leapt into action with no concern for the risk. And like Robby, I wouldna' dwell on the consequences but only on the compulsion to act. In matters such as these, following yer heart is all ye ken; truth is what the soul yearns for.

Annag moved close enough to me to brush against my shoulder and whisper, "Talk to me, Mary. Who did that to Robby? I've heard rumblings that the Avochmore killers have been brought here to Undlay? Is it true?" She continually looked side-to-side and over her shoulder to make certain no one had overheard the questions she shot at me. With the chopped vegetables enfolded in her apron, she made her way past me toward the largest kettle centered in the hearth.

Knowing Annag would pass by me again once she deposited the ingredients into the stew, I held my position and just continued to sort the bandages, pulling the used ones apart from the fresh, till she did.

"'Twas Blake Cameron who did that to him," I nodded in the direction my brother had just taken, "but Robby wrestled and captured him, and Ollie and Bryston arrested Cameron's brother, Drew. Both are now locked up in the dungeon below," I whispered back hurriedly. Even as I retold the details, I felt a quickening of my breath as if the episode were occurring right then, before my verra eyes.

"Blessed Mother Mary!" Annag declared with a sharp intake of breath. "Will he mend? Robby? I canna believe he had to tangle with those men, and he just getting started on the watch. What an initiation for the boy!" Annag worked beside me, and I, like Penelope with her tapestry, began folding and then unfolding the same cloths in order to lengthen the time we'd have to talk.

"Aye, he's done a verra brae thing for us all, putting those two under lock and key. Speaking of keys..." and I offered her a mischievous look at this point. "Whatever became of yer meeting with yer key-holding smithy?" I was close enough to her to give her a little nudge with my elbow as I teased her about Hamlin. It seemed like weeks ago, but it was just last evening when they were to have taken their loch-side walk.

Annag gave me a sidelong glance, and I could see her eyes dancing a bit as she began, "Well…he's no verra much for words, that I can tell ye—which is strange as it was *he* who spoke first to me—but no mind. Anyways, I did all the talking mostly, and he did all the listening mostly, which means I didna' learn verra much about him that I didna' ken before our little walk. I kept chattering on, even after we stopped to sit for a wee bit, but I could sense he was content just to be together and gaze at the water in silence.

"So he's either verra shy or verra dull, but I did manage to hold my speech for enough time to call his bluff and see if he'd try to fill in the gaps of quiet. But instead of putting his voice to work, he reached across my lap and covered my hand with his massive one. I could feel the weight of it upon me, and it thrilled me to see its thickness and touch its roughness."

She lowered her voice, confessing, "I find myself wishing to feel those calloused hands not just caressing my own but running up and down the more delicate and sensitive parts of my body." She tried to restrain a giggle from spilling out and finished, "Let him stay silent as a salmon. I'd be more than pleased if he let his body do his communicating for him!" She winked at me conspiratorially and tapped the pile of cloths to signal that she had to move on to her other chores before dinner could be served.

Filling a basin with more steamed water and grabbing a handful of my expertly folded bandages, I left the kitchen and made my way to Robby's room, knocked, and left those items beside his door for him to care for his leg wound. Continuing down the hall toward my own chamber, I realized that I was kind of grateful that the capture and imprisonment of the Camerons had distracted Annag from asking me about my own adventures this day.

Pushing open the door to my own room, I promised myself that I'd fill her in later on this evening about Hilda and her message and my meeting with Donal. But for now, I had yet another task to accomplish afore readying myself for dinner. Walking over to the books I had collected from my days of being tutored, I found some paper, a bit of ink, and a quill, and for the second time that day, once again let my writing be my voice. Enveloped in the silence, I listened to the rumblings within my heart, and the blank sheet before me soon became filled with all that had been locked inside.

Annag was right; there were other ways to communicate aside from just speech—and the more I wrote about Donal, the more I wished he would begin using Hamlin's physical form of communicating in the days and weeks to come.

Mary – Imminent Danger

"Farewell, Mrs. MacAra," I called out to the woman in the doorway, and as she waved back at me, I turned Arwen about and departed from the small cottage. I ken it was wrong of me to be wishing to be done with these visits this morning, but I couldna' prevent myself from thinking about Donal and our plan to meet later that day. The blue skies above were a welcome change from yesterday's steady rain, and I started to wonder if that meant we could maybe spend even more time together than we were able to do the day before.

This morning, I had picked out my most favorite shawl—a deep green one—and freshened my hair with rose water. Now with the reins in one hand, I grabbed a handful of my tresses and brought them to my nose to see if the fragrance was still there. Faint traces of it wafted up, and I fluttered inside thinking how close he'd have to come beside me in order to catch the scent. Just the image of that lifted my spirits into the clouds that bounced along above me, and I found myself thinking about nothing other than his touch upon my lips once more.

It was a quick jaunt from Mrs. MacAra's home to Mrs. Nairn's, and I ken the way well enough that my mind could wander without fear of losing the trail. I thought of what Donal would say when I told him about the jailing of the Camerons. We had not had the chance, in our brief encounter, to discuss what had been happening in the glen the last few weeks. Had he heard about the burnings and about Edina? He said he was aware of the children of Teague McElroy, but I could not wait to see his reaction when I told him about Robby's role in the capture of Blake.

And, I wanted to share with him how George Campbell was trying to take credit for the arrests. I'm sure news like that would reinforce Donal's determination to liberate me from my betrothal to that scoundrel. Most of all, I couldna' wait to tell him how I had taken his advice and had begun to write my way through my troubles, and how it had given me a platform when I normally had none.

I was sifting through all of this in my head when I heard the beginnings of a yelp or scream that was almost immediately silenced. Arwen heard it too, and she stopped in her tracks and lifted her head as if to detect where the sound had come from. Her nostrils pulsed in and out as we remained perfectly still for a few moments, so quiet that I could hear the weakened droning of left-over summer insects skittering about us both. Then, there it was again. The same squeal and then an abrupt halting of it. This time, I could tell it was coming from the west, and although I could hear the thumping in my chest keeping pace with the fear that coursed in my blood, I yanked Arwen in the direction of the sound, not knowing what we were riding into but accepting I couldna' ride away from it either.

I reached down the side of my leg to make certain that my dirk was tucked into the pocket that had been sewn on the underside of my skirt and felt a surge of reassurance when my fingers made contact with the blade. As we drew closer to the fields tilled by the Nairn clan, I noticed an unnatural movement in the tall, purple heather that grew on the outer edge of the plowed meadow. In the distance, a horse had been turned out, one that looked familiar to me. Was it? No, he'd have no reason to call upon Mrs. Nairn, would he?

Drawing as close as we could to the wild growth, I dismounted and moved toward the place where the plants were moving unnaturally against the direction that the wind was blowing. I could discern the outline of a man, straddling something that writhed and wriggled beneath him. Without waiting a moment longer, I pulled out my knife and shouted with the most commanding tone I could muster, "Ye there! What are ye doing to that creature?"

Like an unshriven soul seized for judgement before it can ask for grace, the man abruptly jumped to his feet and turned to face me, his hands raised in counterfeit innocence. I looked with disgust upon the face of George Campbell, but then immediately turned my attention to the "creature" with whom he'd been wrestling.

It was the youngest daughter of Mrs. Nairn, her face stained with streaks of dirt mingled with tears, her bodice half-undone. Brandishing my blade in his direction, I spoke with loathing, "Git away from Meggie right now, ye lech, or I'll slice yer *knob* into ribbons." I could feel the spit coming through my teeth as I made my way closer to the stunned girl.

113

"Ye've got it all wrong, Mary," he pleaded, his voice unctuous and smarmy. "She's the one who lured me in here, telling me she'd do anything to get some extra coins for her family as she herself didna' want to do the farm work nae more. I was trying to tell her that I wanted no part of that kind of game, but she wouldna' be denied and ripped open her clothes in order to get money from me. When I refused to pay, she started screaming and saying that she'd make everyone believe I was up to no good with her." George's quick-thinking lie may have convinced other less skeptical witnesses of his innocence, but 'twould do no such thing for me.

"Git yer *reekbeek*, pathetic self out of my sight, and do not ever come within a stone's throw of this homestead or this child ever again!" My voice dropped into its lowest register, the revulsion palpable. "And if I find out that ye've broken my behest, on my father's word, I'll have the entire glen hunt ye down so I can cut off yer *baws* and boil them before yer eyes. Now git!"

The unequivocal conviction in my voice muted any further attempts by George to deflect his culpability onto Meggie, and he stomped off in a huff as if he were the affronted victim. Without even waiting for him to ride away, I hurried over to the young girl who was struggling with the simple task of adjusting her clothes, her hands trembling too much to get the laces right.

"Miss Mary," she said in between halting breaths, "please, please do not tell my Ma about what ye've seen. I shouldna' have been here in the first place, as I was supposed to be by the barn skirting the fleece from the sheep Michael had shorn. But I wanted to check up on Shona and her pups, and then when Mr. Campbell said that the smallest of them had wandered away from the litter and was lost in the heather, I ran in to find him without thinking."

She clutched my hand with both of her own and tugged it toward her as if drawing me into her desperation. Her enormous light-brown eyes were wide with sincerity, and although no tears were spilling over from them at the moment, her emotions were at a pitch.

Kneeling upon the ground, I wrapped her in my embrace, and tucking her head beneath my chin, I began gently stroking her tousled hair. "Dinna fash, Meggie. I'll not say anything to yer mother today, but I ken what I saw and that makes it verra hard for me to say that I can keep my promise to ye forever." Placing my hands on her shoulders, I pulled her away from me so that I could look directly into her eyes. "Is this the first time he's tried to get ye alone? Tell me truly."

Meggie shifted her gaze to the ground and silently shook her head from side-to-side. I saw a tiny globe of water fall upon her skirt, followed by a second and a third as her tears tumbled forth.

"When? When, Meggie? What did he say to ye? Did he ever touch ye before today?" I persisted but was careful to cushion my words with softness.

Wiping her nose with the back of her hand, she inhaled to stop it from running, and with her eyes still fixed on the dirt, she explained. "It started in spring. He'd come by to check up on things, saying he was doing Laird McElroy's bidding. In the beginning, he'd stay upon his horse and just talk to me while I was busy doing my chores in the field. I'd silently pray to St. Triduana to make him vanish from my sight. I never uttered more than a yes or no to him, so I didna' understand why he kept wanting to seek me out. I couldna' tell Michael about it because he'd do something extreme-like and get himself and both of us in trouble, and I couldna' tell mother because she had her hands full with Jeremiah being ill, his sickness coming on so soon after Da's passing."

She paused here to look up at me as if asking for approval of her reasons for hiding all this. I tried to convey my assent by tapping her hand in consolation.

"So at the start, it was just talking, and although I didna' like it, really it was no harm. But two times before today, he snuck up behind me—like *Cu Sith*—and reached round my waist to stop me in my tracks. I'd yelped in surprise, but that just made him smile that crinkly grin of his, and he'd look all hungry like an underfed wolf. Both times I'd dropped my milk pail—thank the Lord it was empty—and he turned it upside down and sat upon it." Meggie shut down at this point and was unwilling to continue. She bit her bottom lip so intently I thought she was going to draw forth blood.

"It's okay, Meggie, it's okay. Ye can tell me what happened next. It's not yer fault. Do ye hear me? It's not yer fault." I hoped my words would offer her the forgiveness she sought so that she could purge herself of this man's poison.

"O, but 'tis my fault. 'Tis," she covered her face with both of her hands, trying to conceal the shame she wished to shroud. "He asked me to sit on his lap for a bit. Said it could be like going for a ride on his fine mare. He offered me a shiny silver merk to do it. And when I saw the coin glistening in the sun like that and knew what it'd mean for my family, I took it and did what he asked." Her small shoulders crumpled, her arms knotted around her knees, her weeping set free unabated.

"Meggie, stop. 'Tis all right. Believe me, ye've not done wrong here. Ye simply made a choice—one that no adult should've ever forced ye to make. Ye chose yer family—little Jeremiah's health, yer brother's safety, and yer mother's welfare—over yerself. Ye're not the wicked or sinful one here." I cupped her face with both of my hands and felt my own eyes begin to well up with emotion when I said, "Ye're like the holy martyrs who sacrificed themselves in order to save others. That's who ye truly are, Meggie Nairn."

At this, she cracked a fleeting smile and finished the remainder of her story. "Och, well, Miss Mary, I dunno about that holy comparison ye're making of me, but I can tell ye that after the second time of taking the silver and sitting atop Mr. Campbell's fits and gyrations, I wouldna' do it again for all the treasure in the world. It made me feel so dirty inside, even though I didna' really understand what it was all about and what thrill he was getting out of it to make him want to keep asking me for more.

"But today when he told me about Shona's little pup being lost in the heather, I didna' think twice about rushing in, and once he had me in there all to himself, I ken that whatever was going to happen would be worse than any horsey ride. When I tried to scream, he covered my mouth with his fish-smelling hand, and I tried to get myself to vomit into his spindly fingers. But I couldna', and his hand was so tight around my mouth and it covered so much of my face that I couldna' even bring breath into my nose. Before ye came, I was about ready to pass out—I think I may have even done so a bit because I didna' remember him undoing my laces at all. But thanks to heaven, ye came!" Meggie encircled my waist with her arms, bowing her head to me in gratitude.

Despite the day's warmth, a chill rippled through my body when I considered what may have happened had I not come by the field when I did. At least now that I was armed with this knowledge, I could use it against Campbell and ensure that he'd never trouble this child—or any other one—again.

"Come here, love," I said as I lifted Meggie to a standing position. "Let's get some water from the spring to clear up that beautiful face of yours, and then ye can show me Shona and her new litter."

As I placed my arm around her shoulders and we began to leave behind the crushed heather, I marveled at the resilience of youth when I saw the gleam return to her eyes at the mention of the little whelps.

Donal – Charm of Protection

Sprung from this source
Ye reach out to my soul.
As the current drives me
Farther from shore,
Frothy waves crash 'round me,
Surges batter all my bones,
Raging waters force me under.
Time is fading, life is lost.
But the bending branch above me
Beckons my spirit one last time
To clasp onto yer outstretched hand
And defy the course of fate.

From my outstretched position lying on the grass, I looked up to see the mid-day autumn sunshine flashing off the clusters of brilliant red berries set against the feathery green foliage. The speckled dabbling of light shifted with the swaying branches as swirls of wind gently dipped and raised the limbs above me. Inhaling the fragrant air, I closed my eyes to listen to the chorus of redwings who, in between pecks and gulps of fruit, squeaked and chirped with joy at the abundance of the moment. Were it not for the anticipation I felt at the prospect of seeing Mary, I could have easily just glided right into a contented slumber. Reaching my arms to full extension above my head and lengthening my legs as well, I stretched my body in both directions, savoring the beauty of the day, made even more enticing by the thought of sharing it with her.

Like the birds pecking aloft, I needed to immerse myself in this present moment; I had to remain anchored here, for when I thought about the days beyond, the horizon of the future filled with gathering clouds. I had not much to offer the lass—no title, no sprawling lands, no real riches by the world's standards. But no matter, I'd make her my queen of the valley and clothe her in gowns of splendor, woven with threads of passion. What care she for the trinkets and baubles of the passing world when our gift to one another would be unbounded love, invulnerable to Time's fell hand? She ignited in me a sensation I've not felt before.

Sure, there've been interludes and affairs in the past where the stirring of desire streamed through my body, but this bond with her went much deeper. It was a power that could not be ignored or restrained; it existed through the force of its own will, never to be contained or limited from expression. Defying logic and rules, it had taken dominion over my being, silencing those doubts and worries about the future till they melted away and vanished like puddles on a sunny day. There was something mystical about its power, as if it could shatter every link in the chain of Time, destroying the bindings that shackle a person to a finite earthly experience.

No, something greater was operating here, and although it sounded somewhat crazy, I believed this need for her went beyond this realm. So I brushed aside the fear that a union like ours should never be and instead surrendered to the force that had subsumed both me and circumstance.

Beneath my body, I felt a vibration in the earth and cocked my ear to listen. Aye, 'twas the pounding of approaching hoofbeats, and I lost my breath over desire to see her again. Standing up, I scanned the landscape and saw her rising and falling as she made her way over the rolling hills to me. She and her horse moved as one, elegance and grace in the fluidity of their pairing. She held the reins in one hand, and with the other, she was balancing something upon her lap. As she drew closer, I could see a white fur-ball topped off by an entirely black head with ears that bounced and flapped with each gallop. A little collie pup, was it? Protectively guarding her prized passenger, Mary maneuvered the horse over the rocky mounds, slowing its speed as she came nearer to me.

Her unbound hair flew behind her, auburn waves that rippled and sparkled under the sun's caress, and she looked upon me with with unadulterated joy. "Well, now, who do we have here, milady?" I asked as I came to the side of the horse and reached my hands up toward Mary's bundle.

With a tinkling in her voice like the softess of a bell, she giggled, "This here is Thor, a gift from Meggie Nairn whose house I'm just returning from," and after petting the top of the pup's head, she reached under his belly and passed her companion over to me. Despite the whelp's size, there was a weightiness to him on account of his frolicking and squirming; he was a challenge to corral.

"A fair amount of spirit abides in this fellow, aye?" I declared and watched the pup spin round in circles in celebration of his newfound liberty. After he pranced over to the tree and took care of some business, he rolled on the grass belly-up, eyes closed, his head twisting back and forth seemingly trying to snag his ever-elusive tail. Mary and I shared an amused smile at his antics, and then I turned to lift her off her mount, placing my hands on either side of her slender waist.

"I'm so pleased to see ye, lass," I professed as I placed her on the ground before me, our bodies so close I could smell the rose fragrance coming from her hair. "Now tell me how ye were able to retrieve a Norse god all the way from Asgard on yer travels today through this local glen."

We began to walk together along the shoreline, the rocks and shale clicking and clacking beneath our feet as we stepped. Turning her head to look directly at me, she explained, "Well, Meggie showed me the litter of pups they'd welcomed a few months ago, but this one wouldna' let me alone. Jumping on my lap, nipping at my fingers, even pulling at my skirts in a kind of tugging game to get me going on my way, he just wouldna' stop. I took the tugging as a hint that I had overstayed my welcome because I had stolen Meggie's attention for too long a time, but when I stood to leave, he started leaping up at me, almost begging me to pick him up and cuddle him.

"Young Meggie noticed it too, and so she said she wanted to gift him to me for helping her out with a situation that had come up today, and while I refused at first because I didna' want to separate him from his mates, Meggie—and the pup himself—simply wouldna' be denied. A demanding kind of fellow—even for his size, don't ye think?"

Thor, who had been trailing us for a time, took this moment to sound an alarm with his high-pitched bark. Standing his ground, protecting us and his territory, he yelped at a swan—much grander in size than our defender—that glided by.

"O, 'tis fine, Thor," she spoke soothingly, "let it be, my *mo laochain*," and at her word, the pup resumed his trot but not without looking back three or four times at the interloper.

I remained quiet, just cherishing the time we were sharing when Mary stopped walking and touched my arm with a distinct shift in emotional intensity. "Donal, I must tell ye something verra private and verra horrible, something about today. A terrible thing happened—and has been happening—to Meggie at the hands of George Campbell. I came upon them in the meadow. He had her pinned on the ground and was trying to take away her innocence. Poor thing was doing all she could to get his filthy hands off her, but he had overpowered her with his size.

"Thank the Lord I heard her cry and was able to get him away from her, but she made me promise not to tell anyone, especially not her mother, yet I canna sit back and be idle when there's a cur like him sniffing about her maidenhood. Shall I tell my father? I believe I will, but I'm so scairt that if I tell him and he doesna' do anything severe enough to George because of clan politics, I'll never be able to respect father ever again."

I watched her expression change from sorrow to horror to frustration to worry, and then to cold determination when she avowed, "Truth is, I'd geld Campbell myself if I could."

"Mary, yer a courageous one, ready to take on anyone, regardless of size, strength, or rank," I said as I reached my hand to her face to soften her glower. "I'm fully aware of the kind of man—rather the kind of worm—Campbell is, and trust me, I'll take on yer vengeance from here, ye can be sure. Yer father wouldna' let this atrocity go unpunished, but if I handle it for him, he'll not risk the wrath of the entire Campbell clan—who would ultimately refute George's role in the transgression and smear Meggie's name throughout the glen.

"Beyond that, if I take care of things, yer father will not have to worry about an alliance being formed between the Campbells and McKintys should Callan's family believe the twisted lies George would tell."

I tried to maintain a semblance of calm in my voice and my demeanor, but inside, rage boiled within me when I envisioned what that scoundrel had attempted to do to the young lass. Already a plan was forming in my mind as to how I'd make him atone for his lewd and wicked ways, one that would ensure he'd not try anything like that ever again.

"Come, Mary, ye've done well to tell me what's happened, and ye can trust that I'll take care of the matter from here. For now, let's put it behind us and find some shade under yon tree," and with these words, I nodded my head in the direction of my former lounging place.

The three of us moved toward the leafy coverage, and as I edged past Cerwyn, I reached into a saddle pouch and took out a flagon of ale, some cheese, and an apple. "How sweet," Mary said, acknowledging my refreshments. "Ye brought this along for us?"

Thor's little nose twitched with the speed of hummingbird wings at the delectable smell of the cheese. With him perched between us, we sat together to enjoy our repast. "It's not much, but the ale is cold and the cheese is sharp," and with my fingers, I broke off a corner of it, crumbled it in my hand, and let Thor lap it up from my open palm.

I passed the flagon to Mary and was pleased when, despite the simplicity of my banquet, she didna' hesitate to take a fine, long gulp. A lock of her hair blew across her face, so I gently moved aside the wavy strand, tucking it behind her ear with the rest of her thick mane. "I heard about yer brother," I began. "How's he faring?"

"Ye heard? Already? 'Twas just yesterday," she responded as she brought a chunk of the cheese toward her lips.

Biting into the apple, I continued, "Aye. I heard he was the one responsible for nabbing Blake and that's no easy task—Blake's another scallywag cut of the same cloth as Campbell. Heard Robby gave him a good beating but took a few hits himself."

Delicately wiping the sides of her lips, she responded, "Aye, his face is a bit touched up with nicks and cuts and such—there's one verra deep gash across his cheek that he'll no doubt point to and use as bragging material in the years to come. But most grievous though is the slice in his leg that came from Blake's dagger. I couldna' really get a good look at it last evening, but 'twas bleeding pretty long and pretty regular for some hours after the fight." She added after a pause, "It worries me some."

When her eyes set upon the horizon and her gaze moved to the water in front of us, I covered my hand over hers. The touch brought her attention toward me, and I took that as my chance to taste her lips and absorb some of her sorrow. With a tilt of my head, I placed my mouth upon hers and felt the surge of desire running through us both. Slowly pulling my face from hers, I opened my eyes and looked deep into hers, losing myself in the flashes of light that sparkled within those emerald pools.

We seemed suspended there for a brief time until she placed her hand upon my cheek and drew me closer for another kiss. I longed to feel her body entwined with mine, but at that particular moment, our passion was halted by a little squeal from the creature who had been serving as a barrier between us.

"Come here, ye," Mary said playfully to the pup as she scooped him up and placed him on her other side, allowing our bodies no further impediment. I offered the apple to her and brought it to her mouth, and she cupped my hand along with the apple in both of hers. Focusing her gaze directly into my eyes, she took a taste of my offering, and when she was through, we placed the apple down, and I pulled her toward me as we lay together on our sides, arms enveloped around each other. I'm sure she could feel my arousal with each sensuous kiss we shared, and I grabbed a handful of her untethered hair and pulled back on it to caress her neck and chin, working my way back to her lips.

She responded to my touch and gave herself over to me—no pretense, no hesitation, no fear. While I ken how strongly I wanted to have all of her in my possession, I also realized that I didna' want a brief tumble in the grass but a lifetime of passion with this woman in my arms. I wanted to move slowly enough, deliberately enough, for both of us to linger over and savor every stage of our growing love.

Despite withdrawing my lips from hers, I remained by her side, bending my arm and resting my head on it as I continued to devour her with my eyes. We spoke no words; there was no need. The quiet spaces did not call to be filled, not when they were already overflowing with the pleasure of just being together. We remained like that for a while, enjoying the contentment of stillness, until eventually Mary returned again to the subject of her brother. "I *am* worried about Robby," she observed. "When I checked on him this morn, he told me he didna' sleep well overnight, and I could see he was running a fever. Once I get back to Undlay, I'm going to take a look at that leg of his, even if I have to force him to let me do so," she said decisively.

"There'll be no denying ye, Miss McElroy, when ye have yer mind set on something," I spoke in admiration of her resolve. Raising myself to a seated position, I let my fingers rummage through the twigs on the ground and found two decent-sized pieces to toy with. A low but steady snore came from our little playmate who had clearly found his own place of contentment in this shady spot. "I'm guessing the wee fellow's not capable yet of sounding thunderous, eh?" I asked Mary lightheartedly while removing from my pocket the remnants of a bright red ribbon.

Smiling at me, she answered in like manner. "No, he's still got some time before he'll be big and strong enough to assume the mantle of a god, I suppose." We both looked over at the sleeping pup who was oblivious to the ways of God and man, but I couldna' share the animal's blissful ignorance. I was all too aware of humanity's lust for power and his propensity for violence, so I reluctantly steered the conversation down again to heaviness and worry. Overcome by the need to protect Mary and shield her from danger, I had to revisit the capture of the Cameron brothers.

"I understand that when yer brother arrested Blake, Drew Cameron was captured as well. Do ye ken what's to become of them both?" I tried to sound casual when I asked this of her. She shifted her position to match my own so that we sat shoulder to shoulder as she moved her hair to one side and began twisting it into a braided rope.

"Right now, they're in the castle dungeon, but I heard my father tell George that they'll be making a swift judgment upon them, so swift that whatever is to come would be completed before the harvest festival which is to be held in less than a week's time. Because of their crimes, I'm thinking they'll be hanged before long." Speaking of execution and death cast a shadow upon her spirit as I watched her turn to Thor for comfort.

Cradling the pup in her arms, she bent forward to nuzzle his fur as if to shake the chill from the image she had just conjured. But I couldna' let the moment slip away, so I put my arm about her and lifted her chin to make her look at me instead of the pup. .

"Mary, if there's a hanging—and there will be—ye must tell Robby to take heed. The Camerons are savages. I've heard tell that they've done much worse things than robbing people and burning down homesteads. On one occasion, they flayed the skin off a man they believed had stolen from them, the brothers taking turns to see who removed the largest portion of skin intact. Another time they felt they'd been cheated at market when they didna' get a fair price for the cattle they'd stolen, so they went back at night and tied the man upside down by his feet and stuffed his mouth with manure till he choked to death on the dung.

"I do not mean to be frightening ye for no reason. I just need ye to understand my warning is not to be taken lightly. They'll not allow their kin to swing from the noose if they have any say in the matter. And their thirst for vengeance will only be quenched by spilling blood for blood. In their minds, yer brother is the one who's done them wrong, and their ways of evening up the score will be brutal." I paused here to let the magnitude of my speech penetrate deep into her understanding of the situation.

I ken I was speaking of a grim subject, but I had to continue, "Be sure ye tell him, and he can later explain this to all the others, that they should come to the killing site fully armed. They canna let their guard down. Just because they've arrested and placed those two in the prison doesna' mean that good has won out over evil. There should be no celebrating till those bodies are lifeless, and their souls are residing in hell where they belong."

Her eyes were wide with worry and fear; I could tell that she grasped the gravity of my message. When I beheld her vulnerability, I felt as if my heart were ripped from my chest and existed outside of my body. She had taken it; she possessed it. If anything should happen to Mary, I ken that I wouldna' have the life-blood to go on. She owned my very soul.

"Take this," I commanded gently and handed her the cross I had just fashioned out of rowan twigs and bound with a thread of her red ribbon. "Keep this with ye at all times, especially if ye attend the hanging. It'll keep evil at bay." Without any hesitation, she nodded in assent and took the amulet from me, turning it over in her hand. "And I have something else for ye today as well," I continued, attempting to restore our visit to its earlier, different kind of enchantment.

I turned a bit to the side in order to reach into my sporran, but from the corner of my eye, I watched to make certain she was putting the cross into her pocket for safekeeping. Removing a scrolled paper, again tied with red ribbon, I said, "I wrote this for ye last night when I was thinking about meeting with ye today. Read it later when we're apart, when ye need to have a memory of me and the power of my love."

And as I handed her the paper, I tilted my head once again to brush her lips with my own one last time before bidding farewell. Springing into action, Thor leapt up and stole my romantic thunder with a frantic licking of his own. Surely we mortals are at the mercy of the gods!

Donal – Judgement Day

I held the piece of wood steady so that Ross could hammer it into the posts on either side. He had already completed one section of the railing on his own, and I was now here to help him finish up the remaining three. The work was easy with two sets of hands to measure, level, and fasten, so we were not really looking to take a break when Nora opened the door and came out holding two cups of ale.

"'Tis fine work ye've done here, boys. Here's something to refresh ye both." She smiled, handing each one of us a draught. It took her some time to walk from the doorway to me and then to her brother. Her uneven step was the result of a childhood injury she had sustained when she fell from her horse and was trampled. Her left leg went askew just below the knee where it was twisted inward rather than straight, causing her to step-shuffle along as if she were constantly dragging some heavy, trailing object. A tiny thing, Nora seemed more fairy than woman, standing only as high as the bottom of my lowest rib. She did what she could to help round the house, but there were many things she was just too frail to undertake, so she often retreated to her world of art.

Ross told me that she was like an angel who had simply taken up residence with the Gregors, always finding what was best in each of her siblings, including the two sots, Angus and Derek. Straddling this world and the mystical one, Nora had an insight and a sensitivity that found full expression in her drawings. News of her talent spread throughout the region, and some of the wealthier families commissioned her to capture their likenesses on canvas. Because she only saw the good in others, the portraits were always admired and adored by their subjects. So the patrons were charmed, her work was in demand, and the Gregors benefited from the handsome income Nora would put down on the table after the completion of one of her projects.

"Thank you kindly, Nora," I said as I tipped my head to her in gratitude.

"'Tis nothing, Donal. I thank ye for helping Ross get this back together again so quickly. 'Tis nice to have this sitting place that's somewhat sheltered yet still outdoors and bathed with so much natural light. Will ye be staying to sup with us?" she asked me kindly.

"Truly appreciate the offer, Nora, but I'll be heading off soon as we've finished this. Next time, perhaps." I lifted my cup in silent toast to her.

"We'll hold ye to that then, won't we, Ross?" and with that, she turned and began plodding her way back to the door.

As we continued to assemble the railing, Ross asked, "How long before we go out riding again? I ken ye mentioned pausing for a few weeks, but now that the Camerons have been caught, maybe we can go sooner?" He pounded the nails into the post, speaking over the noise.

"Aye. I did want to talk to ye first before discussing it with Brodie and Owen, but yes, I did have something in mind that I'd like to get done—sooner rather than later, if possible. It involves the Campbells, George to be exact. But what can ye tell me about the watch? Have ye been able to get any more information from Angus about it?" Now that the section was finished, I walked over to the wood pile to measure and cut the next piece.

"Angus is not home, so we can talk freely. Off in town somewhere he is, hopefully not gambling away another portion of our land, for Jesus' sake." Ross's eyes narrowed, and he smoothed down that wild red hair of his as if calming his own anger in the process. "What do ye need to ken?"

Carrying the freshly cut piece to the next set of posts, I continued, "At what time is Campbell on guard?" I lifted the plank into place and waited for Ross to resume hammering.

"Angus says George always does the first turn. Doesna' want to be on duty after the witching hour when 'tis most likely there'll be some action. Typical," he responded with disgust.

"First watch? Not the best time of the night for us, but it'll have to do. I need to settle an account with him, and I'd like to take care of it this evening. Do ye think ye can join me?" I headed back to the heap for another wood piece.

"Aye," he said without hesitation. "And when we're through here, do ye want me to ride over to Owen's place? Will ye be wanting him too?" Checking the stability of the next set of posts, he frowned when he discovered one to be unsteady, which meant he'd have to anchor it better with rocks before we could proceed.

"Sure, and I'll take care of getting the message to Brodie. Let's meet at sundown in Undlay Woods. 'Tis really more of a personal debt I'm needing to settle with our friend Campbell, but having ye three along may convince him of the lengths I'm willing to go to show my desire to clean the slate between us. Good?" I asked after Ross had strengthened the post enough for us to affix the plank.

Seeing no movement in its position after jiggling it back and forth a few times, "Should be fine now," he said.

"Did Angus tell ye where they set up their base? Is it between the McElroy and McKinty lands?" Knowing the location would help me determine what equipment would be necessary.

Ross reached into his sporran to grab the final bunch of nails for this section of the railing. "Aye, he said there's a hill about a half-mile away from the ruins of the old broch that stands near the stone boundary and the high wooden barrier that denotes the beginning of the McKinty estate and the end of McElroy's. Campbell uses the high ground area to survey the landscape below." As this last piece was hammered into place, he announced, "Done," and settled his hands upon his hips to survey our work.

"We'll not be lifting cattle tonight, but I'll be needing ye to bring a good amount of rope anyway. O, and do ye have any of those spikes about a hand's length tall?"

"I do," he answered with interest.

"Good, bring those and a hammer as well." I turned away from him and made my way down the path toward where Cerwyn had been grazing in the shade while we worked. As I was departing, Ross shouted, "We'll not be doing home repairs for the Campbells this evening I hope?"

Speaking only with a wave of my hand in farewell, I left Ross to his curiosity while I smiled to myself and thought: the only one making reparation tonight will be George Campbell himself.

***

Under the cover of darkness, the four of us rode in single file with Ross leading the way since he had the best understanding of where Campbell's men would be stationed. Able to get further information from Angus when the prodigal brother stumbled his way home for dinner, Ross found out that the area by the broch was only used by the last set of guards during the final shift—which tonight would involve Angus and Ollie—or essentially Ollie since, if Angus even made it to his post on time, he'd likely be too far in his cups to do anything more than snore his way to sunrise. Campbell, along with Bryston, would be camped out about a half-mile from the broch, and as long as Owen was able to preoccupy Bryston with his false story of bandits being about, everything should work according to plan.

The air was dry, so was the ground from the day's sun, and we could hear every crackle and crunch of our horses' steps upon the earth. The absence of the moon wrapped our journey in a thick cloak of black velvet, giving us yet another advantage when it came to executing our mission. It was not long before we came upon the shoulder-high barrier that marked McKinty's property. A few paces more and we were right upon the broch.

"Hold here, Ross," I commanded our rider at the front. "Brodie, ye and Ross are going to remain here. Ross take those spikes ye brought and hammer them in through the top of that wood there. Someone's going to be taking a ride tonight on a wooden horse whose seat willna' be verra comfortable," I explained with a bit of a sinister laugh. "And Brodie," I reached into my satchel and took out two canvas bags and then guided Cerwyn alongside Dewey, "fill them with the heaviest boulders ye can find, aye?"

"O, ho! 'Twould be my pleasure to round up the weightiest ones I can lift. We wouldna' want our traveler to fall from his horse now, would we?" Brodie accepted the bags with the same enthusiasm as that of a child who is offered the first slice of a freshly baked pie.

"Owen, ye and I will continue on to Campbell's camp. Ross, we'll be back within the hour." The two of us turned the horses away from the broch, opting to follow a more wooded trail that would bring us beyond our destination. Because Campbell would be occupying a place from a high vantage point, a direct path from here to there would be readily detected and our mission thwarted. Instead, we'd carve our way through the forest, and then surprise them by approaching from the rear.

Since we were compelled to keep silent, I spent time in my own head with thoughts of Campbell's depravity. The image of him slithering his scrawny body up and down young Meggie's so enraged me that my hands ached for grasping Cerwyn's reins so tight. Tonight would be for Meggie's honor and for preserving the honor of all the other girls who would now be safe from

Campbell's lecherous ways. I had already discussed with Owen how he would go about distracting Bryston, and then, once Bryston was out of the way, Owen would return to assist me with the rest of the job. Didna' take much convincing to get Owen to buy in. As soon as I suggested how he'd be helping me reenact a Last Judgement of sorts, our preacher's son was thrilled to be called upon to help separate this goat from the sheep.

Leaving the forest behind, we came out into the meadow where we reversed direction and began moving toward the rear of their station. After a ways, I halted and nodded to Owen to go on ahead. Finding an overgrown area, I tucked myself and Cerwyn into the shadows and waited. The scheme was for Owen to tell Bryston and Campbell that he needed their help, he and his father being waylaid by two bandits who stole both the donation that the church was bringing to Widow March as well as his father's horse.

He'd explain how he managed to capture and tie up one thief, but the other got away with the money. Owen would then bring Bryston back in this direction, and because of the threat of the other thief still lurking about, George would surely opt to remain safe and secure at his post rather than ride into possible danger. At some point, Owen would confess the ruse to Bryston and, knowing the little regard the man had fer Campbell, there'd be no chance he'd do anything to obstruct us.

Sounds were approaching. Two men on horseback dashed across the clearing and passed me; it was time to commence with the weeping and gnashing of teeth.

***

It didna' take verra long for me to arrive at the base of the hill, and I slowed Cerwyn to a trot as we began our ascent. Whether Campbell heard me or not was of no concern to me because I had him trapped as tightly as an ice-bound traitor in Dante's hell. This was between him and me, and there'd be no one else around to save him from peering into the blackness of his wretched soul.

I was nearly at the crest of the hill before I heard him call out, "Who goes there?" in a thin voice, edged with worry. Standing beside his signal fire with a weapon in each hand, he tried to give the appearance of a prepared and formidable sentinel, but I wasna' fooled.

"George Campbell, 'tis I, coming to pay ye a visit. Thought maybe we two could have a bit of a chat regarding an account we have to settle," I said with feigned geniality.

"I have no cause to parley with a thief and criminal such as ye, Donn. Just let me catch ye reiving these lands again, and ye'll be joining yer lowlife brethren at the gallows. 'Twould please me beyond measure to place yer mutilated body parts on display all throughout the glen." Raising his sword and dagger aloft while he spoke, Campbell tried his best to assume an intimidating pose, but all I saw were the flimsy limbs of a run-down scarecrow.

"Och no, George. Tonight is not about my sins—though I'm aware of my own failings and do penance for those weaknesses, ye can be sure. No, this evening is about yers, and I'm afeard that yer transgressions require a more intense, shall we say, act of contrition." I dismounted from Cerwyn and began stepping toward my quarry, and as I did, his sword and dagger wobbled, the fearless guard plagued with a bad case of tremors.

"Approach no further, Donn, or I'll have to cut ye asunder right here," he forced these words from his mouth, but the threat was as hollow as a widow's cupboard in the depth of winter.

"Och, George, that's not a kindly thing to say to someone who wants to help redeem yer soul," and as these words hit the air, I sprang into action, kicking his right arm which then dropped the sword and then spinning about to grab his body and throw him to the ground. From there, it was easy to flip him over onto his belly—serpent that he was—and with my knee in the base of his back, I pressured his wrist till the dagger fell with a plink onto the rocky soil. Fastening the rope around his hands, I pushed his face into the dirt while he continued to remain on his stomach.

"How does that taste, eh, Campbell? Ever wonder what'd feel like to be buried alive? Beneath the dirt is the only place for worms such as ye. But that's not what I come for here tonight." I stood up, and digging my boot under his side, I lifted his body off the ground and demanded, "Git up."

Without the use of his hands, he had to roll onto his side and then re-assemble his legs properly so that he could raise up to one knee and then to a full standing position.

"What is it ye want from me, ye bastard?" he spoke contemptuously.

"I'm here on behalf of young Meggie Nairn and any other girls ye may have already tried to taint with yer vile touch."

"Ye've got it all wrong. That little bitch is the toxic one, like one of the lowlanders trying to get *blathaich mal* from me by making up lies about what I did to her, and I swear to Christ, I didna' even lay a hand on her. Truth is, she's the criminal here, trying to steal money from me so as not to spread those stories about me," he spit upon the ground for added emphasis.

"George, George, come now. The girl's no scheming wench and ye ken it. The first step to salvation is recognizing yer own sins. So tonight I'm holding up the mirror for ye." From behind us, the sound of a rider interrupted our conversation, and we both looked to see Owen emerging from the darkness.

"Look here, a churchman showing up just at the right time, well! Good evening, Owen Gilchrist, I've got a miserable transgressor with me who's in dire need of redemption—even if he doesna' truly accept that yet. Can ye share yer catechism with us and enlighten the fellow as to what happens on Judgement Day should his soul remain unshriven?" I was beginning to enjoy this unfolding drama, delighting in the impatience and discomfort stamped on Campbell's face.

Acquiescing to my request, Owen stepped onto the ground and answered, "By all means, Donal. Fire away with yer questions. I'll not turn my back on a repentant sinner."

Seething, Campbell broke in, "Who appointed ye God, Donn? Since when does Satan wear the robes of authority?"

"Ye ken, George, I do not think yer in any position to object to my authority—seeing as yer tied up there, and I'm standing freely here, but even so, let me make this a little easier for ye to grasp. I'm neither God nor the Devil; I'm just trying to be yer conscience; ye ken, the whisper that tells a man what's right and what's wrong? But since it doesna' seem as if ye've ever been ruled by a moral compass—evidenced by yer complete lack of direction in these matters—perhaps a wee bit of fear of the consequences will teach ye to go and sin no more. Ye may not be able to choose good over evil, but since yer main concern has always been self-preservation, after tonight ye'll end up doing right once ye've tasted the blood and pain that comes from doing wrong."

I let those words sink in for a moment and then continued, "So, Owen, what does the Good Book tell us about avoiding sin?"

Expanding his chest as if he were preaching from the pulpit, he began, "Matthew, chapter 5, verse 29: *And if thy right eye offend thee, pluck it out and cast it from thee; for it is profitable for thee that one of thy members should perish and not that thy whole body be cast into hell.*"

"Well now, I suppose leering at a little girl would count for offending the laws of God, but dinna fash, I'll not blind thee," I said soothingly as I stepped closer to him. "I'll just impair thee," and with that, I accelerated my arm and thrust my fist into his eye socket, following it up with a second and third blow. I'm quite certain his cheekbone cracked under the force of my punches, and his eye swelled and began to close almost immediately after impact.

Triumphantly, I announced, "We're on the road to redemption, are we not, Reverend Gilchrist? What say ye next?"

"Well, the biblical text tells us that *if thy right hand offends thee…*" At this, Owen raised his eyebrows in collusion.

"But, Reverend," I said to Owen, "in this case I believe it was both hands that did the offending. What shall we do now? Hmmm." After snapping off a branch from the nearest tree, I touched it to the fire and slowly walked the glowing torch behind Campbell. Wrapping my arm around his neck, I told him, "I willna' go so far as to dismember ye, Campbell, but ye do need something that'll remind ye of the consequences of puttin' yer hands where they shouldna' be."

Campbell shrieked in pain when I scorched his restrained hands with the lit branch. Inhaling the smell of charred flesh turned my stomach (an appropriate parallel to the disgust I felt for his actions), and I held the fiery implement in place long enough to ensure his agony but not the total removal of those hands at a later date.

Owen's eyes were enormous at the contrast between Campbell's screams of anguish and my relaxed demeanor as I went about exacting punishment. "Does the Bible say anything about what to do regarding other body parts if they 'offend'?" I inquired of Owen.

Placing a finger on his chin, Owen responded, "I'll need to ponder that one. Can ye give me a space of time?"

"Most assuredly," I replied to Owen. "Campbell, we'll be going for a little walk so that Reverend Gilchrist here can mull this over." Leading Cerwyn over to where George was standing, I took the lengthy rope from my pack and secured it round his waist. With Owen leading us to the broch where Brodie and Ross were waiting, I dragged our penitent along, forcing him to run or else be dragged along.

Campbell had to tilt his head to the right in order to see out of his left eye since the other one was useless, and he had great difficulty keeping his footing when I quickened the pace. It was not long before we came upon the other members of our crew, and I noted how they had managed to have everything ready that we needed. The canvas bags were filled with stones, a pile of boulders formed a kind of step ladder toward the wooden seat, and spikes protruded from that wooden perch.

After seeing Ross and Brodie, Campbell started to cry out, "What's this, Donn? What do ye need all yer fellows with ye to take down one man, ye filthy mongrel? Ye always were a sneak and a gutless coward. I've done nothing to deserve any of this, and I swear I'll be coming for all of ye, and ye, Donn, especially. I'll not rest till I see yer entrails pulled out before yer eyes, yer body chopped into pieces, and yer head mounted on a spike."

Jumping down from my horse, I moved toward him, "Ye ken, George, I've got to be honest with ye. I'm getting a wee bit tired of listening to yer prevaricating and yer protesting, especially after all we've done to help ye to mend yer ways. It so disappoints me that, despite all my efforts to save yer soul, ye've still learned nothing about yer own baseness.

"So I'm sorry, but I canna hear yer irritable voice anymore," and after saying that, I inserted a piece of soiled cloth into his mouth and tied it behind his head, silencing him for the remainder of the night. "And George, ye'll be sure to notice that my fellows here never laid a hand on ye at any point during our little visit. Unlike ye, I do not ask others to do my reckoning or fighting for me, nor do I ever run from the fray. I always settle my own scores."

Pushing him toward the boulder ladder, I called out to Owen, "Reverend, it wasn't the eye or the hands that did the most offensive thing in Campbell's case. It really starts with his perverted, twisted desires. It seems he finds the greatest arousal in accosting young virgins and forcing himself upon them. So, I'm thinking that he needs to make restitution for trying to ride the young fillies by being forced to ride something else instead. Something that'll make him think twice the next time he wants to mount anything. Up ye go, George."

There was no coherent protest, only squealing and whimpering that came from his gagged mouth. After I forced him to climb the boulders, he could see the narrow gaps in between the spikes and, moving most gingerly, tried to seat himself carefully into that narrow space. Once aloft on this high beam, his feet dangled in the air, and I affixed ropes on each leg that were weighed down with the loaded canvas bags, one on his right leg and one on his left. The weight would prevent him from being able to fall from his perch, unless he was willing to rake his *bawsack* on the protruding spikes in the process.

Sitting atop the wooden horse with his right eye pummeled and his hands burnt raw, Campbell moaned incessantly as he tried to endure the pull coming from the boulders fastened to his legs. Unable to resist a parting comment, I stood before the front of his "horse" and addressed him one last time. "I'll leave ye now to yer private meditations, George. Reflect on the errors of yer ways, man. And let this be a warning to ye: if ye ever try to force yerself upon any unwilling maiden again, next time I'll thrust my sword so deep inside ye that yer shrieking will reverberate in the halls of hell for all eternity."

The four of us mounted and rode away, the bleating of one wayward sinner echoing in our ears.

Double Meanings

Mary sat on her quilted bed, reading and rereading the poetry Donal had written for her. The only sounds in the room were the crinkling of unfolded paper and the soft rumbling of her furry friend who was curled into a tight ball beside her pillow, nose resting on his back paws. Like a priestess conjuring a spirit from beyond, Mary willed her lover's presence into her chamber by repeating his words aloud. The passion contained in the verses bridged the distance between them, and he became as alive to her as if he were standing there before her in the flesh, head tilted to the side and hand outstretched, seeking her own.

Caught up in this reverie, Mary did not hear the gentle knock. It was only when the door began to creak open and a voice said, "Are ye in there, Mary?" that the vision evaporated, and reality, in the form of the intrusion, reasserted itself.

Annag's face peered around the door. "Am I bothering ye, Mary?" she asked, noticing the opened papers lying on the bed. "Och, I can see yer blanketing yerself in the warmth of yer man's love. I'll not disturb ye," and she pulled her head back as if to go away.

"No, no, please. Come in, Annag," Mary said as she began to collect the strips of paper and return them to the storage box where she kept her most precious trinkets along with her own recorded musings.

While Mary was gathering this together, Annag entered the room, knelt down on the floor near the head of the bed, and started stroking Thor who had briefly lifted his head to acknowledge the new visitor, only to place it back down again to resume his nap.

Dreamily, Annag said, "'Tis a comfort, no doubt, to have his words when ye canna have his person, aye?" She gently caressed the pup's long, floppy ear while she spoke. "Tell me what he says to ye. Can ye share one with me?"

Somewhat embarrassed but eager to evoke the feelings from before, Mary agreed. "Well, I've told ye about the ones he left for me like bits of buried treasure in the forest, but this one in my hand didna' come from there. He gave this one to me directly just a few days ago when we walked together by the shore." Clearing her throat, she read softly:

Never wander from my side,
Be my love, be my bride.
Wedded now, we are as one.
My breath with yours will always run.
Thoughts of ye I canna escape
Dreams and visions, asleep or awake.
So lay down yer heart with me right now
And hearken to this, my solemn vow:
To hold and guide ye everyday
And lift all pains and cares away.
Be with me now, today and ever.
To live and love as one forever.

"Mary, those words, they're just so tender… 'lay yer heart down with me'? Och, ye get poetry, and I get grunts," Annag complained. "I'm not asking for ballads and rhymes, just some simple conversation once in a while, but with Hamlin 'tis only my own constant monologue that fills the gaps." She shook her head from side to side in disappointment. "What's worse is, I've not seen nor heard from him for three days now, and I was starting to think that maybe he was put off by my chatter. Perhaps he'd be wanting a more quiet, reserved maiden—like empty-headed Elspeth Greer who says nothing because nothing is happening inside that pea-brain of hers."

At this, Annag rounded her eyes into big saucers, made her mouth gape open, and let her tongue go lax as if mimicking the idiot she purported Elspeth to be. With a note of relief in her voice, she finished, "But then he sent a message for me through Devin explaining the reason for his absence."

Mary scrolled up the poem and placed it with the others in the box and then spun around to face Annag. Twisting her limbs to sit cross-legged on the bed, she asked, "Well, where has the man been these three days? If he's not been keeping away in order to rest his ears, then was he traveling for work, to deliver something maybe?"

"No, not traveling but yes, work. Actually he's been busy with a task yer father set out for him—a special project, ye might say." She stopped petting the dog and, still kneeling on the ground, leaned in toward Mary as if to confide a deep secret. "He's asked Hamlin to make him two gibbets for the prisoners. After Drew and Blake are hanged, they're going to be placed in them and left there to rot. A powerful message to any other blackguards roaming the glen who are thinking of causing trouble."

She shook her upper body as if an evil spirit had cast its shadow upon her. "So that's why he's had no time for me. I can stop blaming my running mouth for his disappearance, and I do not have to keep practicing silence anymore," she added with cheer.

Mary giggled at the thought of Annag ever holding her tongue. "Take heed, Annag, if yer man is skilled enough to make a gibbet, ye can wager he's probably already fashioned a Scold's Bridle for ye as a wedding gift!"

"Verra funny, Mary, verra funny. Seriously though. It kind of sends chills through me to think of Hamlin constructing such a thing—the gibbet, I mean. Ye ken he had to gain entrance into the dungeon in order to measure the sizes of the two scoundrels? Told me they were not big men at all and found it quite remarkable that so much wickedness could be contained in bodies so small and scrawny." Annag stood and made her way over to the fireplace where she stared into the rippling flames.

"Size has naught to do with it though," Mary countered. "Take George Campbell, if ye will. He's no grand specimen with his feeble shoulders and sunken chest, yet there is more darkness in his soul than in the *Nuckelavee's,* the devilish man-horse with its black blood and lethal breath. And speaking of breath, if ye've been in close proximity to the man, ye too would agree that the foulness that spews from his mouth leaves a coating of odor so thick on ye that ye canna get rid of the fumes till ye dive headlong into the loch."

"That may be," Annag conceded, "but those other two villains, after the hanging, with their bodies decaying and crumbling, will be giving off a stench just as offensive." The two girls grimaced at the mental image of corpses leaking fluids, clothes tattered and soiled with excrement, and skulls skinless and hairless.

"The execution is tomorrow, ye ken," Mary tilted her head to the heavens as if looking for guidance. "I saw the single candle lit outside the prison cell tonight. Strange thing about candles. They're a comfort in the darkness, but for the prisoner in the dungeon, they're a portent of death. Funny how the same object can take on different meanings depending on the circumstances, aye?"

Mary's voice grew fainter as she continued to explore these morbid paradoxes. "Take a rope, for example. It's what yer praying for when yer floundering at sea, and the current is pulling ye down to its dark depths. It becomes the slender thread that tethers ye to life itself. But tomorrow, it'll be the instrument that chokes it off and hastens those men to hell…"

"Och, Mary, how dreary. Spending so much time with a poet like Donal has made yer own imagination run wild, though I much prefer his rhymes of love to yer meditations on death," Annag declared. Marching back over to Thor, she smiled when he rolled onto his back exposing his speckled belly and asked, "And what say ye, little fellow? Do ye not prefer passion to pain?"

"Are they not but one and the same?" Mary's question tantalized them both, as each girl privately lamented the absence of her beloved while silently acknowledging the suffering that comes when the heart lay open to love.

***

The next morning Undlay Castle was shrouded in fog so thick that objects and people were only discernible by touch or sound, not sight. With no wind to lift or carry it along, it hung as heavy as the dampened wool that clung to a traveler's body after a full day of walking in a steady rain. Mary wondered if it were nature's way of protecting the spectators from having an unmitigated view of the wickedness inside the two criminals who would be on the scaffold later that day.

There was still some time yet between the early hour and the appointed time for the hanging, so Mary made her way to the stables, leaning on stone walls when they were present and stepping slowly and carefully over the terrain when they weren't. Thanks to her slackened pace, she avoided a more forceful collision with the wagon in front of her and only thudded against it with her body when it obstructed her path.

"Careful there, lass, ye'll not win any ground against a foe such as that," Devin called out to her from what seemed to be the front of the cart. Examining the structure from a closer position, Mary saw two large spoked wheels on either side and the waist-high planks of wood that formed its walls. This was to be the conveyance that would deliver the Camerons to justice. "Will ye be wanting me to tack a horse for ye, then? I've pulled Arwen for yer mother and Bedwyn for yer father. Robby says he's well enough to handle Hubert, so would ye be content with Mirain, perhaps?" He came around to the side where Mary was standing, bringing with him the tools he had been using to secure an additional wood plank behind the driver for the man's safety.

"No, thank ye. I'll be walking with Deirdre and Aidan. Mother wants me to take care of them as she'll be at father's side and not able to get them through their first acquaintance with death." Mary paused to consider this assigned responsibility. "I dunno why she thinks I'd be a proper guardian for a task such as this. I have no real recollection of being especially brave at the burning of Agnes Menzies during the witch hunts of '61 and '62. In fact, I only remember the fear she stirred up in me with her final curse upon us all before she was lit aflame. Her words haunted me, playing over and over in my head, and I remember thinking her ghost was pursuing me any time I ventured into the woods and I'd hear the breaking of twigs or the rustling of leaves."

Lost in the memory, Mary grew more pensive while Devin continued to affix the plank in place. "I swore she was trying to take possession of my body since her own had turned to ashes and her bones scattered. When the terror would take hold of me, I'd dash to my secret hiding place and cover the opening with branches and wait there—praying to St. Michael to save me from the spirits of darkness—till the woods grew silent and my faith was restored. So, a farewell malediction today from the Camerons might send me scurrying back to my safe haven, only this time with two more people in tow."

Without being conscious of it, she slipped her hand beneath the left side of her blouse so that her fingertips could brush against the rowan cross Donal had given her for protection.

"If that's yer main worry, ye'll do just fine then," Devin consoled her, "for yer Da' has refused them a final word. So it willna' be the little one's ears that ye'll have to protect from hearing. 'Tis their eyes ye'll be needing to shield instead." He began to bring the horses out, one by one, to the area beside the wagon.

Mary walked next to him while he maneuvered each animal from its stall to the outdoors, but the task wasn't enough to distract her from worry.

Hesitantly, she spoke, "I'm scairt to ask ye, but since I've never seen a hanging before, perhaps 'tis better to have knowledge of what to expect than not to. Maybe then I can be calmer when 'tis actually taking place. What exactly would we be seeing that'd create nightmares for us all later?"

Looking directly into her eyes to assess if she would benefit from such information, Devin explained, "Well, they'll be using a short rope today, so the dying will take some time, ye ken? Yer father wants the crowd to enjoy a lengthy contrition of sorts from those men—if not from their words than from their suffering. 'Tis the only way to set things right. The pain they endure must equal or surpass the pain they've caused. Ye understand?"

Devin then went back into the stables to get the final horse who would be pulling the wagon, an even-tempered mare who'd be able to block out the jeers and insults directed at her cargo as she brought them to the gallows. Harnessing the animal to the front, Devin concluded, "Ye'll be fine letting the children watch the Camerons climb the ladder, but after 'tis pulled away, that's when ye may want to gather them closer to ye. The process of dying 'twill be painful and drawn-out for the likes of those two. They'll be gagging and gasping for air while their legs will be jiggling and twisting in a grotesque dance of death. Could last a few seconds or much longer, there's no telling the length of time."

Everything was in its place: the wagon was prepared, the horses were primed, the ladders stacked on either side of the cart. Swiping the dust and moisture from his hands, Devin offered one final recommendation. "So if I were in yer place, that's what I'd cloak from their vision. I've known people to snicker and find humor in the convulsive movements of those dangling from the rope, but that laughter in the day turns to panic at night when it's just ye and yer thoughts alone together before a sleep that refuses to come…"

Devin turned his head to the side, straining to hear footsteps in the distance. With no gaps in the mist for them to peer through, Mary joined him in listening intently, surmising that the cavalcade to Craigmonie Hill was assembling. The march to the scaffold would soon be underway.

***

Deirdre and Aidan clasped hands and swung them together in unison as they trotted along and sang the words to an old rhyme, their lilting voices and intermittent giggling in stark contrast to the seriousness of their journey.

He led her down the path alone
To take and have her for his own.
She fell for him and all his lies
Believing one day she'd be his wife
But soon it came, he'd had enough
And thrust her from the edged-bluff.
Rising from her watery grave
Her ghost returned to haunt the knave.
"'Tis vengeance I seek, yer life is mine
I willna' rest till ye dangle from twine."
Her body they found and upon it they swore
To search for this man like no one before.
Pulling him out of the forest one night
They ken what to do to make this right.
Around his neck, they tightened the noose,
Pushed aside the ladder, and there he swung loose.
His legs were a-dancin' and twitchin' non-stop
And his body spun round and round like a top.
Her spirit left earth and could then rise above
Once the man paid the price for playing with love.

Their feet were dampened by the moisture that clung to the grass, and the water droplets in the air dotted their faces with sprinkles of wetness. Thanks to the fog that still lingered and surrounded the meadow, they seemed to exist in a world of their own making, impervious to the adult one they were advancing toward—a world marked by the insidious presence of crime and its requisite punishment.

In front of them were Annag and Mary who knew full well what awaited them all once they reached their destination, and it would certainly not be some sing-song, nursery rhyme ballad. "Don't ye think it's amusing," Mary commented to Annag, "how innocent fairy tales and nursery rhymes often have the most dreadful themes running beneath them? Like 'Mary, Mary, Quite Contrary'? What child ever thought it was about Bloody Mary Tudor and that her 'garden' was the graveyard she filled with Protestants? Or that those 'silverbells' were thumbscrews? Or that the 'cockleshells' were instruments of torture which were attached to—"

Halting Mary in her tracks, Annag interrupted abruptly, "Stop right there! I'll have ye ken there are children about us here. Ye need not be telling me what the 'cockleshells' were meant to squeeze! I can surely figure that one out for myself, thank ye verra much."

"I'm just saying," Mary turned to face Annag and countered, "when we were young, we'd just say the words without any thinking going into them. Like these two behind us. To them, hanging from a bit of twine is just a clever rhyme that keeps the song moving along. Nothing more than that. But it saddens me to say that it willna' be long before they have to see it in a whole other context, and once that happens, I do not think ye can ever go back to the world of enchantment anymore."

Annag mulled this over before trying to formulate a response. "Maybe not to the childhood world of charm and innocence, but there are other enchantments available to us as we grow older—thrills and rushes that we had no thoughts of in our younger days. We no longer have to listen to a story about a prince who will capture a maiden's heart. We can live it, and is that not more satisfying to have it in real time than to dream it in your imagination? Ye can hold Donal's hand, ye can caress his face, ye can touch his lips. Ye can't do that with a man on a page who lives in a world of make-believe. So do not be wistful. Each age has its charms, and we're just learning about the ones available to girls in the prime of their days!"

She wrapped her arm inside the crook of Mary's as the two walked together, fortified by the blessings of life as they prepared to witness the wretchedness of it.

***

Aside from the harvest gathering, the only other grand calendar event for the inhabitants of the glen was an execution. A festival of sorts, it drew together people of all stations and was the topic of discussion before and long after the ceremony took place. All work was suspended. The old showed signs of renewal by reminiscing about former hangings and beheadings, challenging each other with embellishments tacked on to the original details. The young moved with an eagerness and lightness in their step, congratulating themselves that they were being included in this very important grown-up affair. And the faithful asserted their righteousness, feeling validated that the mighty hand of

God was at work in the tangible blows of the executioner's ax or the manipulation of his rope.

A large crowd had already assembled, making it a challenge for Mary and her group to push their way through the shoulder-to-shoulder bodies so that they could take their place at the front with the other esteemed members of the McElroy clan. The knot between Dierdre and Aidan had been broken; now Aidan's hand was fastened to Mary's and Deirdre's to Annag's as they bumped and steered their way closer to the scaffold. When they reached the open space, they halted, and Mary's eyes were drawn to the two suspended metal cages that were intermittently visible in the shifting mist. They hung there emptily, patiently waiting to house their lifeless guests.

An occasional light breeze shifted the apparatus, causing the bars that outlined the vacant space to creak with a yearning to be filled. To the left of the metal enclosures was a crossbeam, supported by two iron bars of wood on either side. Over that crossbeam, two ropes were wound, each ending in a gaping noose that lifted every now and then with the touch of the wind.

And standing centered between the two structures was the hooded executioner—his legs firmly planted, shoulder-width apart, his head held high and unmoving. He lent a dignified, orderly presence to this theatrical show, and it was his carriage and composure that would ensure the smooth resolution of this upcoming drama of sin and redemption. Clearly, he was an experienced player on the stage.

The mob was surprisingly subdued, maybe in deference to the gravity of what they were about to witness, but a distant rumbling from the nether end of the group soon spread to the middle and then ultimately to the front where Mary held post with her charges. Like a pestilence that spreads from cottage to cottage until it results in the total upheaval of a village, the arrival of the criminals sparked an assault of curses and insults that ran rampant through the crowd.

First to come through, however, were Mary's father and mother, followed by Robby, who was trying to give the appearance of looking solemn when, in truth, his face was blanched and his body haggard from illness. The catalysts for the raucous noise were not the members of the McElroy family, but the passengers in the cart which was inching its way through the spectators. Shouts bounded through the air: "Die covered in yer own shite—how fitting for ye both!" "When ye're in Hell, then ye'll ken what it feels like to burn!" "May ye dangle and spin for hours before Death comes to release ye!" "Couldna' keep yer *bigealas* in yer breeches so now the birds will make a meal of it!"

With their backs to the driver of the wagon, Blake and Drew stared down the individual speakers, but when the horde began to sling the deprecations more rapidly and with greater frequency, the prisoners' heads kept swiveling, making their threatening looks seem more comical than intimidating. When the wagon pulled up alongside the scaffold, the driver placed the horse whip in his belt, jumped down, and removed the two ladders, placing each one against the wooden crossbeam in alignment with the ropes.

While the driver was busy with the ladders, a slight disturbance came amidst the front row of observers as Robby and George Campbell left the ranks of the onlookers to make their way over to the wagon. Campbell, donning gloves and wearing a patch over one eye, expanded his concave chest as much as physically possible while he strutted toward the villains with an arrogance that masked his feeble frame.

Only those privy to the truth of the arrest would know which man was the leader and which was minion because, to view them now, one would have reversed their roles. For Robby's uneven gait (caused by his inability to bend his wounded leg), coupled with his pale countenance, outwardly reflected both weakness and fear.

Knife drawn, George stepped onto the bed of the wagon and shoved each prisoner to move. With their legs bound together and their hands tied behind their backs, the men glowered at George with loathing and walked forward awkwardly because of their abbreviated strides. Awaiting them at the back of the cart was Robby who held his claymore in full extension in their direction. Robby would lead the procession to the stairs of the scaffold and present them to the laird of the glen, his father. Teague had already ascended the steps and stood at the foreground of the platform while the executioner and the guard positioned themselves at the rear.

The shouting and yelling had ceased, and a hushed sense of decorum blanketed the villagers. Mary felt the clasp on her hand grow tighter, a sure sign that Aidan felt the suspense intensify. A killing of this kind required a certain degree of pageantry, and those in attendance knew that, with the scene set and the actors present, the climax of the performance was about to unfold. Robby presented the two criminals to his father, bowed in deference to his overlord, and then stepped aside to join George at the far left of the platform.

In a booming voice, Laird McElroy declared, "For these, thy crimes of thievery, pillaging, rape, and murder, I, under the jurisdiction of our sovereign, King Charles II, ruler of this land, hereby sentence ye, Andrew Cameron, and ye, Blake Cameron, to be hanged unto death. To which, afterward yer bodies will be placed in yon gibbets to fester and rot till there be no flesh upon yer bones, at which time, those bones shall be scattered to the four winds upon unconsecrated ground. And may the Lord have mercy upon yer wicked souls."

As promised, there was no accommodation for the convicts to speak their final words. Instead, the guard and the executioner stepped behind each one and gagged their mouths so that their tongues were restricted from making any intelligible sounds. There was a peculiar calmness that lighted upon the two who were about to die, perhaps a kind of acceptance that they were without recourse and had to ultimately accept the inevitability of death.

Teague made eye contact with Kendrew Barclay, who stood on the ground inches away from the platform, seething with hatred and rage. Beside him were the members of his family, including a young maiden whose eyes were cast downward and whose body was trembling profusely. Refusing to lift her gaze throughout the entire ceremony, she folded her arms upon her chest and wrapped her hands in a vise-like grip toward the back of her ribcage in order to stop the shaking.

Back on the stage, George and Robby bent down behind the men and severed the rope that had restricted their feet, allowing them to march freely toward their doom. As they began their trek to the gallows, this time George went first, nudging Drew from behind until they reached the first ladder. The executioner lifted the noose over Drew's head, settled it on his neck, and secured it snugly while George stood by with his weapon drawn. Robby followed the same pattern with Blake, and after the hooded figure tightened Blake's noose, the two brothers began to climb the ladders, rung by rung, timing each step together.

As they stood poised on the uppermost rung, the executioner seized Drew's ladder first, and with one swift action, pulled it away. The audience inhaled on cue as the man dropped. His body began to spin uncontrollably, and his legs flailed in the air while he gasped and gagged for breath. Although the sight was fascinating in a gruesome kind of way, the crowd's attention strangely shifted from the dangling man to the commotion that started to erupt from behind the gallows. Shrieks and whoops accompanied an influx of armed warriors who began slicing and clouting their way to the prisoners. Over twenty men stormed the rear of the platform and chaos ensued.

Fearing his duty foiled, the executioner struggled to find a way to bring at least a portion of his job to its proper conclusion, so he darted around to the front of Drew's suspended body, and with his massive arms, encircled Drew's legs and pulled down hard, sending the sinner to the underworld with the snapping of his neck. No sooner had this been done than one of the invaders attacked the hooded figure from behind, plunging his sword into the man's back not once, not twice, but three times as if trying to spear an elusive trout in a stream, only in this case, the blade found flesh every time. When the executioner's body fell to the ground, his masked head came to rest in an ever-growing puddle of crimson fluid.

Panic was immediate. The alarmed spectators added to the confusion by attempting to run from the melee, but they had been packed together so tightly that there was little room to move with any sense of purpose. It was as if each person were captive to the swell and sway of the stampede and at the mercy of whichever direction the rush followed. Mary and Annag huddled the children into themselves, forming a shield of protection while they were jostled and turned about.

Trying to yell above the tumult, Mary leaned closer to Annag and commanded, "Take the children now. Head back to Undlay. Stay to the front of the platform and avoid the thick of the crowd. These savages have no interest in ye three. It's the Camerons and Robby they want. Go!" And with an impassioned push from behind, Mary sent them on their way.

In the few seconds it took for the mob to churn and for Mary to send her companions home, another clansman had crept up behind the guard. Grabbing a handful of the man's hair to pull back his head and expose his throat, the vandal carved through the sinews and muscle until the blood bubbled and gushed from the slit. In seconds, the guard's hands were saturated as he struggled in vain to hold his two flaps of skin together.

Although Drew's soul was already condemned to perdition, Blake's was still very much alive and filled with a yearning to pay back all who had done him wrong. One of his comrades had cut the bindings from his hands, and he used those liberated hands to loosen and lift the noose from his neck and remove the cloth from his mouth, laughing at the audacity of these people who thought they would have the final say in matters pertaining to himself. With one thing on his mind, Blake turned to see the guard lying on the ground after bleeding out and reached into the man's belt to snatch the whip.

Leaving behind red footprints wherever he walked, he headed straight for Robby McElroy. Robby was entangled already with one of Cameron's kin and was getting the better of him until Blake shoved his own man aside and brandished the whip before Robby. "Yer a lucky sot, aren't ye? More boy than man ye are, and too foolish to ken when yer in way over yer head." Licking his lips with a lust for blood and violence, Blake cracked the whip in Robby's direction. The lash thwapped against Robby's wounded leg, its fibers wrapping around the newly-opened sore as tentacles around prey.

The boy's screeching howl of pain elicited no help from any allies he may have had on the platform—the executioner and the guard were dead, George was nowhere to be seen, and Teague was being held under his armpits by two men while a third landed blow after blow until the laird had collapsed to the ground. Robby, like a wounded creature who curls up into itself in agony, went down on one knee to cradle the leg that had just been struck.

A fresh flow of blood poured from the gash and through his breeches, and Robby could do nothing to impede the surge. Blake coiled the whip again and struck the defenseless boy with a vigor that comes from a man who, as a child, reveled in doing the same to helpless animals. Again, the crack and snap of the lash upon Robby's flesh and again a cry of torment.

Unbeknownst to any of the McElroys, at the back of the crowd were Donal and his crew, and when the execution had gone awry, they sped toward the fray. Their delay up to this point was no fault of their own; it was simply the challenge of riding forward into danger when everyone else was running from it. Now that the path was clearing, Owen and Ross stabbed and punched their way toward Teague, disposing of two of Teague's assailants by ambushing them, tackling them to the ground, and kicking them repeatedly until they had lost all awareness.Clunking their heads against the wooden platform to ensure they'd be out for quite some time, Owen and Ross then turned toward the remaining fellow who had been pummeling the laird of Undlay just moments before. Ross, his red hair curled and aflame with ferocity, dived headlong into the man's gut, flipping him onto the dirt. Once the scoundrel was pinned beneath him, Ross set free his pent-up anger, battering the man's face until his features resembled a slab of meat carved by the dull blade of an unskilled butcher. Confident that Ross was doing just fine on his own, Owen had returned to Teague, hoisted the laird upon his shoulder, and carried his inert body down the scaffold steps and over toward his horse.

Donal and Brodie had to fight their way through the other Cameron clansmen before they could get closer to Blake. Preoccupied with the men who had killed the executioner and the guard, they heard Robby's wail in the distance and doubled their efforts to do away with their attackers. But Donal and Brodie weren't the only ones mobilized into action at the sound of the boy's anguish. With no care for her own safety, Mary ran toward the platform, lifted her skirts, raised a leg, and clambered over the edge until she had scaled the elevated stage. Her clothing still in disarray, she caught a glimpse of the shiny blade of the dirk that she always kept tucked inside her skirt for protection.

Gripping its handle fiercely with a determination that erased all fear, she crouched in a low position, trying to remain undetected as she made her way closer to Blake. Meanwhile, with a deliberate flick of his wrist, Blake had cast aside the whip and replaced it with a dagger that he had conveniently found discarded on the floor. Raising the weapon above his head, he took two large strides toward Robby, but before he could bring the blade into the boy's flesh, Mary, like a coiled wildcat who springs from the ground to pounce on the unsuspecting field vole, lunged at Blake from the side, seized upon his lower legs, and thrust her knife into the slender ribbon of muscle at the back of his ankle.

Now it was Blake's turn to shriek as he tumbled to the ground, his predator still holding fast. Peering down to see his assailant, he was incensed when he observed the long hair, the skirts, and the feminine shape beneath him. In one quick maneuver, he twisted his torso and accelerated his arm toward the prone figure that had sacked him, his dagger ready to puncture the wench's neck.

But before the pointed edge could penetrate her skin, Donal emerged from the fog and kicked Blake's arm with such force that the man's shoulder dislocated from its joint, sending both dagger and Blake himself to the floor. While the scoundrel squirmed and writhed in agony as he struggled to force the injured arm back into place, Mary lifted her face from her knotted position to look up into the eyes of her love. And only after seeing the concern and worry on Donal's face did she realize the kind of danger she had been in.

Droplets of Blake's blood dappled her face like grotesque freckles, the ones upon her eyelashes, she tried to blink away. Donal, bending low, scooped her up into his arms and sprinted with her toward his horse. Brodie did the same for Robby, tethering the injured boy to his body in the saddle, before commanding Dewey to a full gallop.

The remaining Camerons assisted Blake in hobbling off the scaffold and onto one of their awaiting horses. As they rode away, mangled corpses lay upon the platform in their wake; another dangled lifelessly from the rope. And while one of the two gibbets would soon be laden with the weight of a single decaying occupant, the other would remain empty, twirling and creaking with the shifting of the wind.

Mary – Changes in the Air

I couldna' lean in any closer to him. My arms were already fastened tightly about his body, and my cheek affixed beneath his shoulder as I tried to meld my being into his. The jolting of our movements in the saddle pounded a rhythm in my head, the only stability amidst my swirling thoughts. The intensity of what had just occurred was still with me, and I felt myself prickling with urgency. I was afeard that any softening of my grasp round Donal would allow me to tumble backward into the hands of Death, where he would whisk me away into the underworld as Hades did Persephone when she stopped to admire a flower.

Once again, Donal had saved me—only this time it was not from the dangers of the forest but from the murderous hand of the devil's servant. I owed my life to this man who sat in front of me. He rescued my soul when it was moments away from darkness, and I was now impatient to repay him in return. And so, as we rode together over the hills and meadows, I kept pulling myself deeper into him, hoping to immerse myself completely inside of him.

Only when the horse's speed began to slow did I detach my cheek from his shoulder and lift my head to see the familiar surroundings of Undlay. But in truth, I was not yet ready to go home. "Donal, wait. Can we not ride into the forest first? Let us take some time to sort out what's happened." I spoke these words to him as he twisted his head slightly back toward me in order to listen.

"I canna do that, lass," he spoke with regret. "Ye need to be with yer family who, no doubt, have been worried sick about ye. Believe me when I tell ye it's not that I wouldna' wish to stay with ye longer; in fact, every part of me is rebelling against saying farewell, even for a few hours, but I'm sure ye'll be wanting to look in on yer father and yer brother, and they'll be needing to see ye as well, back here safe and sound." Although he was trying to sound convincing, I was pleased to detect the underlying struggle he was battling between his emotions and his message.

Before the path that led to the castle entrance, Donal ushered Cerwyn to a halt, dismounted, and then, patient while I untangled my foot from his crossbow, raised his arms to help me do the same. Beneath the canopy of the trees, he reached his hands under my hair on either side of my head and brought me into his chest, "*Mo ghradh*, ye have no thought of what ye mean to me. My heart is not my own; it lies within yers and goes wherever ye go, moves wherever ye move, and remains wherever ye are."

Using his hands that anchored my head, he moved me away from his chest and pointed my face up to his. Bending to me, he placed his lips upon mine— first, with ravenous hunger as he strove to prove his need for me, and then with tenderness to prove his concern. "No harm can come to ye; I'll not go on without ye, Mary. When I saw ye in such peril, I ken there was no living for me without ye, and I prayed I would die first before ever having to walk this earth without ye by my side. I was either going to die alone, die with ye, or save us both, because there's no life for me without ye."

At this, he returned his lips to mine and then began making his way from my mouth, to my cheek, to below my ear, and then down my neck. I wanted no barrier between us, so I undid the laces of my bodice in invitation. His lips continued tracing a path downward to the swelling of my bosom, till his head nestled against my heart. Delicately cupping one breast in his hand, he moved his tongue upon my skin in a way that tantalized and excited me. I was aroused with such desire that my only thought was how much I wanted him--needed him--to take all of me.

Feverish with yearning, I placed my hands upon his head, drawing him in even closer. But a rush of breath from his mouth and a slight pulling back left me puzzled. Disappointment enveloped me, and I silently looked into his eyes to question why. He explained, "I want ye so bad, lass, I can barely control my need to have ye all to myself." He placed his kisses intermittently between his words and stopped only when his fingers found the rowan token pinned inside my clothes.

Upon touching it, he lifted his head and smiled with a blend of relief and joy. He vowed, "Whatever this life brings us, be assured that we will go on. No force can rend us apart. For I pledge aloud to the Almighty above, I say yes to this love. If it comes with agony, then agony will be my circumstance. If it brings punishment, then torture will be my fate. And if it ends in eternal damnation for me, then the fires of hell will be my dwelling. For I have found in ye the very spark of life for me. I canna and will not ever be without ye, Mary McElroy. I've shown ye that already in spirit, and verra soon I'll prove it to ye in body."

Moistening his finger, he wiped away each dot of dried blood that speckled my face as if he were erasing any fear or doubt I'd ever had concerning his devotion to me. Renewed by this sense of love's unconquerable power, I felt equipped to face whatever sorrow or tragedy awaited.

As he rode away, I wished he would turn back once more so that we could lock eyes and silently communicate our feelings one last time. But unlike Orpheus who couldna' stop himself from looking back at his lover, Donal, true to his word, kept moving forward while the only stones I was left to contemplate were the walls of the castle before me.

***

Crossing the threshold of the metal gateway, I nodded to the keeper, and before I could turn the knob of the great wooden door, someone opened it from the other side, and I came face to face with Hamlin Balfour.

"Och, ye're here!" he said in surprise, and with one hand, he pushed aside the hair that had tumbled over his face when he had abruptly stopped to avoid running me over. At the same time, I was greeted by another creature pleased at my arrival; my faithful friend came bounding through the door and began spinning in circles of jubilation.

"Well, hallo, little fellow," I said as I bent down to hug Thor, and to Hamlin I added, "yes, I am here." When he continued to just stand in silence, I lavished the pup with attention waiting for Hamlin to elaborate. But aside from the frolicking dog, the quiet lengthened between Hamlin and me.

"I was being sent to find ye," he offered and nothing more.

"Okay, well, thank ye. I've been found now. So I suppose there's no need for yer errand then, right?" At this point, I would've simply continued on my way, but Hamlin still occupied the space I needed to cross.

"Annag told me to go to Craigmonie to look for ye," he explained.

This was getting tiresome. "Yes, well, I thank ye for yer concern, and I'll tell Annag the same, but I'm here now, so I guess I'll just be getting along. I need to check on father and Robby and go see mother and the children. Come, Thor," I said, hoping my words sounded like something of a dismissal.

"Aye." He still stood.

"Thank ye again, Hamlin." I started to move forward with Thor wagging his tail and waiting to prance alongside me.

"Yes, well, I'd better head there anyway," he continued.

"Where? To Craigmonie? Why?" I didna' really want to stand here extracting words from Hamlin, but I figured I'd have to allow him to finish this conversation in order to get him to move. And it *was* puzzling to me why he still needed to go to the scaffold when the object of his quest was standing right in front of him.

"To bring back Devin," he uttered, leaving the cryptic words hanging in the air.

"And what might Devin still be doing back there?" I was growing impatient at this point.

"Oh, yer mother sent him out to look for ye, and when there was no word, Annag told me to do the same," he looked worried, and Thor looked confused as to why we were not moving forward.

I assembled the pieces for myself. "I see, so yer going to tell Devin that he can stop searching for me as I'm already back at the castle. I understand. Well, thank ye, Hamlin, truly, for both finding me and for telling Devin."

And with no other word, he headed out to fulfill his mission. I shook my head and thought how he and Annag were the perfect match then. While Hamlin had a natural propensity toward silence and introspection, Annag was one to always speak first, then think later—a true pairing where one supplies what the other is missing. Turning to my furry confidante, I concluded, "I suppose they've said yes to love as well!"

I moved with alacrity through the courtyard because, based on what Hamlin just told me, I needed to see my mother right away in order to allay her fears over my absence. After I climbed the steps and moved past the Great Hall on my way toward my parents' chamber, I heard a deep intake of breath come from the connecting hallway and a anxious yell of "Mary!"

Could this sound be coming from my normally placid and dignified mother? Tears glistened in her eyes as she placed her hands on my face and said, "I've been so worried for ye, child. There was so much confusion, and I wasna' sure what became of ye!" She then embraced me and held me tight. "When Devin took hold of me and seated me on Arwen, he galloped us back to safety, but I had no knowledge of what had happened to the rest of the family."

She stroked my hair as she went on. "Both yer father and Robby were returned home, and Annag brought back the children, but we'd had no sense of where ye'd gone." She kissed the top of my head in a display of affection I was not used to seeing from her. "I'd sent Devin back out again to find ye, but here ye are," and she pushed me from her in order to scan my person, "and ye've not been harmed in any way, aye?" She looked at me with concern.

"'Tis true, mother. I'm fine." I didna' wish to disclose what had transpired between me and Blake Cameron. "And Hamlin Balfour is on his way to tell Devin the same." I too found myself blinking back tears when I thought how close the day had come to leaving my mother to be clothed in black and grieving over three freshly dug graves.

"It makes me glad, child, to see ye safe and back at Undlay. Yer father took a terrible beating from those villains, but ye ken there's no keeping him down unless ye chain him to his bed. He's vowing an all-out hunt for Blake Cameron, but more pressing than that is the condition of yer brother. Yer father is in with him now, and I've just come from asking Fiona to make Robby some broth and gather some clean fabric to rewrap his leg."

She gently tucked a stray hair behind my ear and continued, "Yer Da' will be so pleased to see ye, child. Go to him now so that ye can give him at least some cause for joy." With that, she kissed my head once more and headed back toward the kitchen.

Oblivious to anything other than delight at having his mistress back, Thor padded excitedly up the staircase with me, his nails clicking on the stone steps. 'Twould be simple to define the world in terms of being with or without the one ye love, I thought. Nothing else really matters beyond that. Maybe, in some way, we humans were more like animals than we realized. For when ye strip away the politics and possessions and titles, the only thing that truly does matter to both is the welfare of the ones ye love.

At the top of the landing making her way to Robby's room was Annag, a crock of broth in her hands and some rags draped over her shoulder. "Annag, wait. I'm coming with ye," I called from behind.

With relief, she exhaled and said, "Mary! O, praise be, yer home! I sent Hamlin to go back and find ye. After I'd brought home Aidan and Deirdre, I waited for ye in front of the castle gate, but ye didna' come. What happened today was dreadful!" As her emotions intensified, Annag struggled to keep her hands steady to prevent the broth from spilling. "Hamlin told me everything he'd witnessed, took a beating himself too till a group of men wound up chasing away that despicable Cameron clan—blood all over the scaffold, bodies strewn about, yer father besieged, and Robby attacked by that demon who cheated death."

Annag started to swallow back her sobs. "And now look at the poor boy in there, barely clinging to this world, teetering between here and what's to come. I hope they hunt down that Blake Cameron, hack up his flesh, and let him bleed his way to a long, agonizing death. What a scoundrel for refusing to accept his own punishment and penance and trying to cheat death by exchanging your brother's life for his own." She nodded her head up and down for emphasis.

"I tried, Annag, I tried to save Robby myself, but I couldna' do verra much against a brute like Blake. Thank God for Donal and his men. It was they who came to the aid of the McElroys—all three of us are still alive and breathing, thanks to them." We continued down the hallway toward Robby's door.

Annag responded with a lilt of surprise in her voice, "Is that right now? Hamlin couldna' tell who it was, but he did say that they were all fine warriors, strong enough to send that vile gang scurrying away like a pack of long-tailed field mice."

Annag stopped me before I could push open Robby's door and whispered. "I do have some good news for ye in the midst of all this tragedy. Hamlin was called into yer father's chamber and asked to tell yer Da' all that he'd seen. The subject of George Campbell came up, and well, Hamlin had to report that he'd not seen George at all. Didna' come to anyone's rescue, never lifted his sword to fight. The man simply vanished. Hamlin told me that yer father's face turned purplish-red, and that wasna' from the blows he'd endured neither."

A tiny sliver of hope then! I tried to restrain the optimism that bubbled inside of me at this revelation that reinforced Campbell's wretchedness. I even laughed silently to myself when I wondered how many hours had to pass in my father's chamber before my Da' was able to pull all those words from Hamlin's mouth! But no matter. Whether it came out in a rush of conversation or in dribs and drabs, Hamlin's story was significant; there was no denying or disguising George's cowardice now. With this disclosure tucked away for safekeeping, I braced myself as I opened the door to my brother's suffering.

A single candle by his bedside and a subtle fire in the hearth were the only sources of illumination in Robby's room, despite the fact that it was still only mid-day. The one window in the room was covered over with a tapestry, the idea being the need to keep out the chill and moisture from the outside air. Strangely enough, although the fog blanketed the glen, there was a thicker cloud indoors, one of sickness that cast a pall over everything and pressed down heavily against my chest. My instinctive reaction was to rip down the tapestry and lift and shove that cloud right through the open window.

The oppressiveness of the air was accompanied by a toxic odor like that of rancid cheese. Blinking my eyes rapidly and breathing only through my mouth, I came up behind my father, knelt down on one knee, and placed my hand gently upon his shoulder. He had been sitting on a stool, hunched over and leaning toward the bed where Robby lay inert. My father's hands were clasped together in prayer, and his forehead tilted downward toward the connection his fingers had formed. When my hand brushed against his shoulder, he started and spun round to me quickly.

"What? O, my *nighean bheag*, where have ye been?" He stood up slowly and engulfed me in a big embrace, but when I squeezed back, he let out a small gasp which he immediately tried to disguise as a cough. With a little softer clasp that allowed for more distance between us, he continued, "Yer mother's been worried sick about ye. Everyone was home except yerself. What delayed ye, lass? Ye do not look as if ye ran into any trouble with anyone along the way, aye?"

And as he scrutinized me for injury, I too did the same with him. His left cheek was red and raised and the eye above it nearly closed shut. His lower lip protruded from the top one and was marked with cuts and gashes. He must have taken the brunt of the blows, however, not on his face but on his trunk, as he couldna' stand fully erect and kept one arm bent across his stomach as if in a perpetual protective stance.

"Father, I am well and was delivered to Undlay by the bravest of men, someone named Donal Donn, I believe. He saved me from the blade and put me on his horse and returned me home safely. I need be of no concern to ye at all as I'm fine and unharmed, but I come to see how Robby's faring since he took the worst of it," and after gently tapping my father on the arm in reassurance, I moved closer to the bed where Annag had given up trying to ladle a taste of the soup into Robby's mouth.

His lips, firmly closed, stretched in a thin line across his waxen face making me feel as if I were looking at a body lying in a coffin not a bed. The wounds on his face stood out against the pallor of his skin. Still raw, they had not yet scabbed over, perhaps because there was so little energy inside of him that could be devoted to healing when it was doing all it could just to merely survive.

Although Robby's body was covered in a thick quilt, I could see a pulsing beneath the blanket, and when I moved toward the end of the bed and lifted the cover, I could see his right leg involuntarily quivering. His boots had been removed, but no one had detached the fabric of his kilt from being stuck to the bandage on his leg. Verra gently, I pulled the cloth away from its adhesion and then slowly peeled away the bloodied bandage.

With my dirk in hand, I began slicing through the fabric near the top. Immediately, I was hit by the stench of infection. Green and yellow pus oozed from the gash and mingled with the blood that flowed from the lashes of the whip. Streaks of red traveled from the wound both up toward his waist and down toward his ankle. Clearly, Robby was in serious danger, not just of losing the leg but of losing his life.

There was a basin of cold water by Robby's bedside, but I told Annag to boil up some more and fetch it to me as quickly as possible while I began trying to clean out the putrid residue. When my cloth made first contact with his leg, Robby swung his head side to side as he lay there moaning in pain. I started at either end first, allowing him to get used to the sensation before I went after the more inflamed, sensitive parts—kind of the way I had cleansed his face a few days ago. Comforted to see something concrete being done other than the airy prayers he had offered skyward, my father felt at ease enough to respond to my last comment.

"Now, ye'll be staying far away from that Donn character, ye mind me, Mary?" He pointed at me in emphasis. "While he did ye a good turn by bringing ye back to us, he's a worthless vagabond. Ye'll be wise to never deal with the likes of him again, eh? He's not worthy of yer time or yer attention." Throughout this speech, my father's voice rose from a whispered recommendation--in deference to his ailing son--to an outright command at the finish.

While I continued to dab at the pus and grime, the door creaked open once again, and my mother stepped cautiously into the room. Gliding past me with a soft touch of appreciation on the back of my head, she crossed over to my father and said quietly, "One of our guards has returned, and he brings good news. While he and the others were gathering up our dead for burial, word came that Blake Cameron was killed. A single arrow plunged straight into his heart. May not have been the way ye'd quite envisioned it, but justice has been served nonetheless, and the world is rid of two of the blackest souls who ever walked among us."

She bent her head to kiss her husband's hand after reporting the welcome message and then added, "Och, and George Campbell has come to consult with ye as well. He is in the Great Hall awaiting ye."

The triumphant look on my father's face immediately clouded over with thunderous anger upon the mention of George's name. "I will meet with the guard to discuss any further details he has about the killing of Cameron, but as far as Campbell is concerned, tell him I'll not speak with him today. I canna be in the same room with a milksop who deserts his own men because he's too soaked up in his own selfish needs. The poltroon still lives while my boy here strains for every breath. No, tell Campbell to come back tomorrow. Maybe then I can make him understand that he's dead to me without literally making him so as I'm wont to do right now. I'll not taint my bloodline with his blighted one. We'll find a more suitable match for Mary in the months to come. Titles or no titles, the man who marries our daughter must, at the very least, be a man."

I wanted to jump up and rejoice at hearing these words, but I restrained myself and focused on what I was doing. After my parents left the room— father to see the guard, mother to address Campbell—I placed both of my hands upon the streaks of red that coursed down the bottom of Robby's leg and tried to absorb the heat emanating from them. Closing my eyes, I listened to my breath, and with each inhale, I tried to lift the warmth of the infection from his body and into my own. And with each exhale, I released that impurity into the air.

While awaiting the fresh water Annag would bring, I continued this measured breathing and kept my eyes closed, which seemed to signal to Thor that it was nap time for him as well. Leaping into Robby's bed, he lay down under the bridge created by my arms with his face between his paws and drifted off to sleep. While the pup dreamed of rambling over the meadow and Robby dreamed of being without pain, I just concentrated on healing my brother since my own dreams seemed to already be coming true.

***

For four days, we—Annag, my mother, and I—kept vigil at my brother's bedside as he lay suspended between ascending or returning. A trio of female knights, we went beyond the traditional evening watch to commit ourselves to continuous devotional observance, splitting up the day into thirds. When the moon dominated the sky, my mother dabbed away the beads of sweat that gathered on the brow of her bairn, cooling his forehead with a moistened cloth and whispering petitions to Saint Margaret. Placing her faith in the patron saint of parents who've lost their children, she beseeched the holy one to refrain from adding her son to that mournful assembly and to grant her more time with the boy whose beardless face lay motionless on the pillow.

When the rim of the sun peeked above the horizon, Annag would tap gently upon the door and change places with her, and the ceremony would continue. Equipped with medicinal nourishment, Annag shunned invocation, placing her faith in the herbal concoctions she administered: coriander mixed with milk and honey for the fever, and a balm made of oil, honey, and dried wormwood for his aching joints. Later, when the room heated up with the warmth of the mid-day sun, it was my turn to extend our observances at this altar by calling upon both divine intervention and curative measures.

Pleading with St. Raphael, "God's healer" himself, I recited words of prayer while applying the mint leaf juice to Robby's leg, hoping to soothe the irritation and close the wound. For the time I was with him, I aired-out the gash, being sure to blanket all other parts of his body that still trembled with chills. Every hour of my watch, I administered a mixture of water and vinegar to the area and held it in place while I begged the Archangel to intercede and heal the infirmity that lay within this body, a body that housed the spirit of a brae warrior despite having the look of a vulnerable child.

After two days of these rituals, we were rewarded with our boon when the red streaks on Robby's legs began to fade from thick ribbons to fine tendrils, till by the third day, they vanished altogether. His mind, which floated beyond us during those long, silent hours, started to reengage with its surroundings, and although he did not speak, it was a victory of sorts when his eyelashes began to flit and flutter with awareness.

By the fourth, he was taking in bits of food and drink—broths and tea mostly—and soon his words started becoming more fluid and regular. Only then did my father return to visit Robby's chamber, probably because 'twould have been too distressing to have come earlier just to watch helplessly as his eldest boy slipped out of his grasp like water running through his fingers. I've no doubt my mother had been keeping father fully apprised of the slow, incremental improvements Robby had been making, so it took this long to reassure my Da' that he'd not be needing to say a permanent farewell when he next walked into son's room.

Robby was sitting up in his bed when the door swung upon, and Teague McElroy, in full regalia, filled the space with his formidable presence. If I'd ever doubted the depth of my father's love for his children, I'd never question it again after witnessing the scene that played out before my eyes. This most intimidating ruler of the glen ran with unbridled joy toward the bed and nearly crushed my newly-recovered brother in an embrace that lasted as long as 'twould have taken me to race up and down the castle steps four times.

Letting out little snippets of laughter, my father relinquished his hold and pulled himself back to look into the face of his prized boy. Biting down on his lower lip and blinking his eyes rapidly to prevent any tears from forming he rejoiced, "Ye've come back to us, lad, despite having one foot planted in the other domain. No doubt ye must've felt the force of all of us pleading with yer soul to return to us. God has preserved ye to carry on the mission ye've already begun as a soldier of truth and justice. The good Lord has answered the prayer of an aging sinner who finds himself renewed and restored by the daring and bravery of his eldest son."

Careful not to squeeze the slender reed that was now my brother, my father drew him in toward his heart and, resting his head upon Robby's, he whispered, "Born of my blood, pride of my den, this young lion will continue to roar."

A single ray of light from the unobstructed window settled upon the joined bodies of father and son, and I felt myself an intruder in this most special homecoming. Careful not to disturb the halo that enveloped the two spirits, I drifted away silently through the doorway, leaving them to revel in this blessed reunion.

Mary – Revelry and Risks

Once 'twas clear that Robby was out of danger, father reinstated the harvest festival to coincide with Michaelmas Day the following week. As soon as he made the announcement official, preparations began in earnest. Cooks, overseen by Fiona, butchered and seasoned what would later become delectable dishes of mutton and pork. Servants chopped leeks, cabbages, onions, and peas with the speed and precision of master craftsmen. Fishermen who trawled the waters of the loch deposited their bounty of eels, trout, and pike to be salted and smoked for the banquet.

Throughout this frenzy of activity, I found myself splitting time between overseeing Robby's resurgence and assisting Annag in the kitchen. When I could break free, I would fly like a chaffinch from the confines of the castle to light upon the place in the forest where I could find my nourishment. There beside the hollowed-out tree, I satiated my hunger by pecking around the opening and drawing out a morsel or two that had been left behind for me by my love. Although I did not have the good fortune of being held in his arms, I savored the verbal embrace he offered through his poetry. Alone at night in my chamber, I'd cherish his ivory pages like a bird proudly displaying its white-striped wings and place them, along with my own recordings, in the strongbox-nest beneath my bed for safekeeping.

On the eve of the celebration, I was, as eldest daughter, put in charge of the baking of *Struan Micheil*, the large scone-like cake some refer to as Michael's Bannock. Fashioning the dough from the oats, barley, and rye from our land, I moistened it with sheep's milk, enfolded cranberries and bilberries inside, marked it with a cross, and heated it on a fire of sacred oak, rowan, and bramble wood.

The task took me longer than expected because the first one broke while being baked, so I quickly reassembled the ingredients and tried again, hoping to avert the projected bad luck by speedily creating a second. The remains of the first I discarded with immediacy, tossing a piece of it into the fire as a tithe to the devil.

The raised pitch of anticipation and excitement kept many in the castle from sleep, and so in the early morning darkness, the kitchen fires began to burn brightly long before the sun kissed the meadow. In the Great Hall, attendants were assembling and arranging tables, later to adorn them with trays and platters of apples, quinces, and plums. Barrels of ale were made ready and strategically positioned in the four corners for easy access to quench the thirst of the guest whose throats were parched from telling stories and sharing gossip about the events of the season.

By noon-tide, the visitors began arriving, staking claim to parcels of land where they'd set up camp for their families. Father boasted that an entourage of British emissaries on behalf of our most sovereign King Charles II had sent word that they would be joining in our festivities and residing with us for the duration, and he was most anxious to make certain they felt welcome and at ease. Apparently, this was the King's way of showing his appreciation and gratitude to the laird who was stamping out lawlessness in the Highlands by arresting and doing away with bandits like the Camerons.

And speaking of the Camerons, I had seen nary a glimpse of their supposed captor, George Campbell, throughout this time, and my heart was indeed greatly lightened by his absence. During the most recent hours I spent with Robby, my brother informed me of my father's confrontation with George and his subsequent castigation of him. Holding nothing back, my Da', like a ravenous bear, sunk his teeth into George and flung the man's ineptitude in his face as if he were shaking a carcass back-and-forth with devious pleasure.

Lying about his deeds, taking credit for another's feats, abandoning his post, refusing to assist a comrade—the allegations came fast and grew in intensity till—according to Robby who heard it from my father himself—my Da' stood nose-to-nose with the coward, exposing the man's true nature, and just barely restricting himself from denting George's pathetic face with imprints of his fists. Campbell would still remain on watch, but Bryston would be elevated to first-in-command until Robby could assume that mantle upon his return to full health. Reports of any engagement or activity would be verified and corroborated by Bryston since Campbell's word could no longer be trusted.

To pass the hours till the feast, I took an empty basket, and with Thor by my side for companionship, roamed throughout the glen searching for white, pink, and purple Michaelmas daisies. While the pup was easily distracted by the sights and sounds of the landscape, my eyes were drawn to these splashes of color amidst the brown furze and grasses that reflected the emptiness and gloom of autumn and impending winter.

Blossoming so late in the growing season, the flowers stood like soldiers bearing the colors of the warrior Archangel himself, bestowing upon the viewer a shield of hope and protection against darkness and evil. When my container overflowed with stalks and petals, my little friend and I trotted back to the castle where I organized small bouquets that could be placed in the center of each table—a nod to the vibrancy of the past harvest and a promise of the ones to come.

Aware that Donal was to be in attendance that evening, I took great care to get myself ready. Starting with my hair—an untamed and unruly mess that my Ma often said mirrored my spirit—I dipped my brush in rose water, and with long, deliberate strokes, combed it until it captured and reflected the surrounding sparkles of light. Rather than tie it back into a single braid, I let it fall free past my shoulders, affixing a headband while I submerged my hands into a basin of cold, refreshing water. Placing my tingling palms and fingers upon my face, I scrubbed away any dirt or residue, and using a cloth, did the same to the remainder of my body until I stood as cleansed and invigorated as if I had bathed in the early spring waters of a bubbling creek.

The dress I had chosen for this day was a rich, emerald green, the color of Loch Ness when it welcomed the last rays of departing sunlight before the night sky changed it to a deeper purple and black. The velvety texture of the fabric was soft upon my skin, and its cut transformed my wiry, youthful body into that of an alluring woman by magically conjuring voluptuous curves in places where before there were none.

Removing the plain headband from my hair, I replaced it with a crown of daisy petals whose alternating colors formed an appropriate garland sitting atop the green of my dress. With an approving tail-wag from Thor, I took a deep breath and departed from my chamber to join the banquet in the Great Hall.

The din grew louder with each step I took down the stairs, and I could feel a lightness of nerves in my belly as I drew closer to the sound. Outside the main doors of the hall, my father and mother, Robby, Aidan, and Deirdre waited for me as we would all make our entrance together. I could sense my mother's endorsement from the brief nod she gave me, and my father's eyes lit up with pride when he recognized that his wild and winsome daughter could indeed carry off some semblance of being a lady after a wee bit of proper cleaning and dress. Offering his arm to my mother, he clasped the one she inserted into his own, and with his other, pulled the latch that opened the enormous, two-panelled door to the Great Hall.

Conversation ceased when the air resounded with the notes of a trumpet played by a musician who, along with his other mates, occupied the balcony above the main dais where we McElroys would sit. After the pairing of my parents, the rest of us filed in singly behind them: Robby, then me, Aidan, then Deirdre; for despite birth order, Robby would be my father's primary heir over me as would Aidan over my sister. I may not have liked the unfairness of it most times, but in these circumstances, after almost bidding Robby farewell forever, I had no care for who was where in terms of procession or inheritance.

I kept my eyes fixed straight ahead attempting to maintain a regal and dignified air, but I could feel the eyes of the glen upon us, upon me, and I longed to turn to the sides in order to find that face in the crowd that I yearned to see.

When we arrived at the front and stood before our chairs, my father reached down to the table, seized his goblet, and raised it aloft. To the gathered assembly, he announced: "Welcome, friends and family to Undlay and to this harvest celebration. We come together to rejoice in and pray for the continued prosperity of the people of this land. Blessed indeed by the bounty of the season, we have remained unified as one against those who look to pillage or undermine that bounty. Thus, on this feast of St. Michael, when the nights will soon grow darker and the days colder, let us bid farewell to the productive year we've enjoyed and ask his protection during the wintry months that lie ahead. Principal angelic warrior and protector against the powers of evil, we offer thanksgiving for these gifts of yer abundance and rest easy, trusting that yer abiding love will continue to safeguard us in the year to come. *Slainte mhath!*"

The individual voices of over one-hundred people blended together in a single response of "*Slainte mhath!*" with each person raising his cup and taking a deep, hearty swallow. Throughout my father's speech, I scanned the audience, letting my eyes register the familiar faces in the crowd. Mrs.

MacAra, Mrs. Nairn, and Mrs. Ruadh sat together with their children at the table farthest in the back, and I smiled internally with relief when I saw little Meggie giggling, playing, and mixing in with the other young ones despite her recent encounter with adult corruption.

A little closer to the front were William and Kirstine Donough, William standing tall despite his fall from the ladder a few weeks ago and Kirstine looking ready for the midwife to visit her table in between dinner and dessert perhaps. Seated among their clans, Ollie Mac Cain and Bryston MacLeay had their eyes fixed upon my brother, their unspoken joy conveyed by their sunlit countenances. The Barclays had journeyed from Avochmore to partake of the excitement, and it seemed to me that even Edina herself seemed to be immersed in the merriment of the occasion, comforted by the fact that the Cameron brothers had been disposed of and, in time, the memory of what they'd done to her would hopefully be erased as well.

Moving forward from there, the Gordon and Waterson families were placed together, Shannon gazing lovingly at Malcolm who still seemed an innocent yet willing victim of the love potion he had imbibed. Fiona and Annag sat at the center of yet another table and were surrounded on all sides by the Balfour tribe. Hamlin had inclined his head down toward Annag as she began twittering about something as soon as my father's toast had concluded. Although I couldna' see Hamlin's eyes, his body deferred to Annag's in such a way that I already ken he was thoroughly lost to her charms.

Nearest to the front and to my right was the table reserved for the visiting English diplomats, four men engaged in animated conversation whose topic, while unknown to me, was clearly one of great import. Despite all being past middle age, they argued and gestured with the kind of passion and intensity associated with youth, and I found myself wishing to be close enough to overhear what exactly they were debating.

On my left, two adjoining tables were comprised of McKintys and Campbells. Perhaps this proximity to us was a good thing as 'twould allow my father to keep a watchful eye on what they could be plotting now that one clan had been offended by my broken betrothal. This thought had barely formed in my mind when a distinct sense of discomfort swelled deep within me. As I looked at their seating arrangement, my eyes settled upon George, and I understood the reason for my unease.

His eyes pierced me with an odd combination of disgust and covetousness, almost as if he hated me as much as he wanted to possess me. It wasna' love, no, nothing like that at all. It was more of a sick determination that if he couldna' have me outright, then no one could, and he'd simply have to find another way to seize me for his own. I found myself struggling to bring air into my body at the thought of this, and as I panicked, my hand went to my throat to fight off the restriction his animosity caused me. I had to wrest my vision away from his area just to regain my composure.

Turning to seek refuge and strength by locating my savior, I once again took the entire assembly into view while I visually hunted for him. And there, at a table in the back, nearest the widows and their families, sat Donal along with Devin and three men I did not recognize. I wonder if he had been waiting all this time for me to finally connect with him over the laughter and shouting that rose from the benches, for in that moment when we exchanged eyes, every noise faded into the background, and the only sound I heard was the silent call of love. I responded in like terms and felt my face flush with longing for him. My heart beat with the same rapid drumming ye hear inside a rabbit ye've just liberated from a snare. Despite my quickening pulse, there seemed to be a steady, unshakeable bond that extended right across the room, erasing the distance between us so that we were the only two people occupying the hall. With the slightest movement, he took two of his fingers and tapped them twice upon his heart, all the while keeping his black, dancing eyes anchored to my own. I could make no overt gesture in response, but I hoped that he would understand the language I was speaking when a warm, knowing smile broke out on my face, a smile that was meant for him alone.

I was frantic to rush toward him to close the gap between us, but I realized there was a grand feast to endure first before I could slip away. Servants dashed back and forth from the kitchen to the tables delivering the literal fruits of their labor. First, the soup was paraded out and ladled generously into bowls that steamed with mouth-watering aromas. Then after a short delay, they returned with an array of seafood dishes seasoned with the herbs and spices from the castle gardens.

Like a musical piece building to its crescendo, the meal reached its pinnacle when they settled before us roast goose and pork and the featured main course of lamb in commemoration of Michaelmas. Succulent morsels were carved and placed onto dishes by attendants careful to preserve the drippings upon the plate of each guest. While those around me indulged in these entrees with gusto, I found that I myself had very little appetite and took only scant portions, leaving a good bit of it untouched on my trencher.

The plucking of lute strings brought me to attention, and my heart leapt with the knowledge that soon it would be time for the musicians to play. And once they did, people would start standing and moving about, giving me the chance to slink away from my seat. Because of the vast number of guests im the hall, I should have no trouble making my way to the table in the back.

Cups overflowed with spiced ale and wine, and the tenor of the evening became less stiff and more relaxed; people left their chairs and started socializing with friends and neighbors from other tables, comparing notes on their harvests and catching up on the latest news. So as the musicians continued tuning their instruments and the people migrated to different areas, I stepped down from the raised platform and walked briskly across the open floor on my way toward the rear of the hall.

My vision was cluttered by bodies shuffling about and greeting one another, so I couldna' see Donal at all, but I hoped he would notice my empty seat and trust that I was headed his way. Mid-stride, I felt my arm yanked from behind which forced me to spin about from the direction I wished to go. At the other end of that hand was the lurid face of George Campbell. "And where are ye going, Mary, with such haste? Hmmm?" He raised his scanty eyebrows at me and tightened his clasp as he spoke, "I believe the dancing is to begin, and I'm afeard ye'll be left without a partner if I do not step in and offer ye my services."

His subsequent wink during his feeble attempt to appear flirtatious made my stomach twist inside me as I tried to discreetly shake my arm free. My hair shook with this movement of defiance, causing the garland on my head to loosen and nearly fall as I tried to pull away from him. At this point, other Campbells at the table started to take note of what was unfolding, so I realized I'd have to bury my disdain and grant him this one dance in hopes that I could liberate myself thereafter.

With contempt, I snapped back, "I'm only joining ye because I do not want to disrupt the good fellowship that surrounds us." My words were meant to demean him and expose him for the hollow straw of a man that he was, but instead they had the opposite effect. Criticism only emboldened him, his desire to take possession of me swelled. Using the strength of his grip, he commanded me to the floor where two lines had begun forming once lute players strummed the opening notes of "The Canaries." Thankfully, this was a dance where partners were exchanged, so I was comforted by the fact that I'd only be forced to endure him for a small portion of the melody.

Partners stood across from one another, men in one line facing the women on the other. I averted my gaze from him and let my eyes wander, taking note of all the other pairings—Annag and Hamlin; Shannon and Malcolm; Devin and Mrs. Nairn; William and Kristine. Although I was smiling at the warmth they shared, I couldna' ignore the chill that rushed up my spine when I sensed Campbell's unrelenting stare upon me. His eyes empty and neutral, his lip pulled up and back on one side, reflected an air of superiority as he stood there smug and proud over his ability to subdue my will.

Each person in line stepped toward their partner as the music played. On the change in melody, we placed our open palms into our partner's, and through that connection, we turned about in a circle in one direction and then switched hands to move in the other. Although he was trying to will me to look at him during these moments of connection, I refused and instead kept scanning about the room. I had to swallow repeatedly and turn my head to the side to stop myself from being stifled by his breath that reeked of onions, garlic, and leftover remnants of food lodged in the nooks between his teeth.

After two turns, we resumed our positions in the parallel lines, but the ladies shifted one space to the right while the men remained in place, and I now felt cheery when I looked at the face of a more pleasant partner, Will McDonough, who must've mended quite well from his injury in order to be stepping like this. Free to enjoy myself now at least for a short while until I had to return to George, I felt a jolt inside of me when I saw Donal two partners away.

Counting back to assess the couples, I noted that he must've asked Mrs. Balfour to oblige him with this dance as everyone ken that her husband, Scott, had suffered a terrible accident some years ago when he was welding a large set of metal gates and one of them fell and crushed his leg. The music continued to swell and just a few moments later, Donal and I stood across from one another, gazing into each other's eyes.

When I came to touch palms with him, a thrill vibrated from my fingertips straight through my body, fanning a flame of desire deep within. His sable hair was combed straight back away from his face, and its ripples and waves shined with light as we moved together. He wore a plaid of navy blue and gray which was gathered and draped across his left shoulder, and the undone laces on his shirt gave a hint of the muscles that were simmering beneath its surface. The entire time our hands were connected our eyes remained fixed upon one other as we searched to discover the depth and nature of this passion we shared.

Without breaking the bond, he bent toward me and whispered, "Ye look stunning, lass," and when we reversed direction, he added, "I canna take my eyes from ye." Much as I wanted to remain, the melody continued, and I had to forcibly break the link we had forged and move on. I tried to replace the emptiness I felt at our separation with the lighthearted joy of the dance itself, but superficial happiness was a poor substitute for the intense desire I felt when in his presence.

Comforted by the thought that the night was really just getting underway, I heard the final notes of the tune and stood across from my abductor. When the music stopped and George was immersed in his deferential bow, I scampered away so that he couldna' physically restrain me to demand a second dance.

The musicians allowed for only the slightest space of quiet before they struck their instruments for the next tune. But instead of staying with the other dancers, I hurried to the outstretched hand of Donal and walked with him back toward his table where he wanted to present me to his other companions. Before we arrived there, however, I pulled him to me and whispered gently, "I've missed ye so. I've read everything ye left for me, and yer words give me so much comfort during the hours and days that I canna be with ye."

"Mary, my love," he said as he bent his head toward the side of my own, "it pleases me to hear that my verses bring ye joy, but even I ken that words can only go so far. Trust me. Someday I will prove my feelings to ye with something that goes far beyond mere rhyme." The warmth of his breath upon my hair made me crave his touch even more, but thankfully I was able to keep that hunger in check when he merrily announced, "Come along now. and meet my fellows." His enthusiasm reminded me of young Aidan's when he'd share something precious—like his toy stallion with a stick for a body and sea grass for a mane—with me.

But before we arrived at their table, I pulled Donal's hand back toward me. "Wait," I said. "I need to ask ye something." I searched his face while I asked, "Blake Cameron?"

His eyes sparkled, and the slightest hint of a grin formed upon his lips. "Aye," he responded. "The arrow was mine." Making light of it as if 'twere as simple a deed as delivering a letter rather than a death stroke, he added, "I told ye I had some business left undone, did I not?" He winked at me and squeezed my hand as if sealing a tacit contract between us. "Come."

Words were flying back and forth as I listened to three men engaged in a heated argument over the final resting place of William Wallace. "No, no, no," boomed the largest of the trio. "His head was spiked on London Bridge, and the four quarters of his body put up on display in Scottish towns for all to see. The pieces just rotted there, and that's the end of that." He folded his bulky arms across his chest as he concluded.

Agitated and spirited as his fiery hair, the second fellow spoke up, "Then what about the WW that's engraved on the stone of Cambuskenneth Abbey? Hmm? Wallace's uncle was a priest, ye ken, and had ties to the monks in that abbey. I say they took those chopped up pieces and buried them on consecrated ground. Makes sense, no?" He jostled the shoulder of the friend sitting next to him for further validation.

"Aye, so it does," piped up the third. "Ye've got it all wrong, Brodie. He had to have been buried there, ye fool. How else do ye account for how the stone points straight in the direction of Abbey Craigs, the site of Wallace's finest battle?"

But the first man wouldna' be convinced. "Nah, couldna' happened," he shook his head in disbelief. "They'd not allow some cowled clerics to come creeping at night to Stirling Bridge to take the man's chunks of flesh, place them in the earth, and say some magical holy words that would grant him eternal peace. Nah, the English seek their vengeance beyond the grave, they do."

At this, the third man punched the speaker in the arm and ordered, "Ssssh, ye daft eedgit," as he nodded over to the group of British envoys who were standing within earshot.

Preoccupied with the proximity of the foreign guests, they were completely unaware of our approach till Donal cleared his throat, and at that sound, they scrambled from their chairs to stand up. It was a bit comical how they jumped so quickly to assume this respectful posture as if trying to make amends that I may have overheard the content of their conversation. Little did they ken that I wasna' one to stand on ceremony and had certainly heard my share of gruesome and grisly tales from the servants and stable hands at Undlay, people I often sought out for their lack of pretense. I much preferred their company to that of the pampered girls of the glen with their phony, affected behavior and insipid conversations.

Donal proudly announced, "Ross, Owen, Brodie, I'd like ye to meet Miss Mary McElroy, daughter of the fine host of this grand feast." He ushered me forward as I extended my hand to each one.

"Thank ye kindly, milady, for this fine celebration," said the one with the hair as rich as the ripest pumpkin in the field. "We Gregors look forward to this gathering every year." As he said this, he waved his hand further down the table toward two young girls who were deep in conversation and two men who were deep in their drink.

Next came the slender, studious gentleman who kissed her hand as he declared, "Ah, virtuous lady, *your price is far above rubies.*"

Somewhat bewildered by such a greeting, I turned to Donal who explained, "Probably a biblical verse, no doubt. Owen is a preacher's son whose been delivering sermons since he was a bairn, pulling himself to a standing position in front of the water trough that doubled as his pulpit." Good-natured laughter was exchanged among the group although Owen feigned being offended by this revelation of his precocity.

As the third fellow stepped forward to greet me, I thought I detected something familiar about him. I seemed to remember crossing paths with this burly, heavily bearded man before, but I couldna' place when or where. With a tenderness that belied his immense size, he bowed to me and said, "'Tis a pleasure to see ye again, Miss Mary, all grown up as ye are now. I met ye once some years ago when I sought yer father's advice about managing my homestead. His counsel helped me and my family verra much, and I pledge myself, Brodie Munro, to be yer loyal servant should ye ever have need of my assistance." He nodded his head to reinforce his vow and clasped his hands together in front of himself in deference.

"'Tis my pleasure, indeed, and I hope that the upcoming winter months will be kind to us all. If ye or yer families are ever in need, please do not hesitate to seek me out, and I will do everything in my power to provide sustenance." I looked into the eyes of each man, hoping to convey that this oath was not just an empty promise but a true commitment to action.

I still had the nagging inclination that I had encountered this Brodie Munro somewhere more recent than the scene he had just described, but when the strains of "The Baffled Knight" began to play, I gave it no further thought. Instead, I seized Donal's hand and dashed with him back to the dance floor.

He snickered as we spun around. "For sure, ye'd have us dancing to this ditty of love!" I joined him in laughter as we both acknowledged the story behind the song: a knight sees a lady and wishes to lie with her, but she convinces him not to touch her till they reach her father's gate. There, she locks him out and scolds him for his base thoughts. Our hands were criss-crossed, and we leaned out and turned in circles with abandon.

He continued, "Ah, yes, the lady's skillful manipulation of her lover! Ye've done the same to me, haven't ye, lass? I suppose I'm no different than little Thor, lapping up whatever scraps of attention ye'll send my way."

I felt so exhilarated in his presence, not just from the bouncing about but from the sheer joy of feeling truly alive. All the sights and sounds and smells were more vibrant and defined as if the veil of monotony that had enveloped every prior day of my life had been removed, and I was experiencing the world for the verra first time. I was so immersed in the moment that I took no notice of things happening on the periphery, like George Campbell sidling over to Ross's two drunk brothers or my father fixing his glare upon me. Only later would these developments mar my bliss. I did manage to notice one of the Englishmen petitioning the players in the loft to perform "Bessie Bell and Mary Gray" and wondered if their animated discussion earlier may have been about the pestilence that was supposedly sweeping through London. Despite the song's morbid theme of two girls who retreat to a bower to avoid the Plague but are later infected by the boy who loves them both, the melody didna' stop people from swaying and stepping along.

I do think, though, most of the revelers were pleased when it came to an end and a fast-paced reel ensued. I remained with Donal throughout the entire evening, and when the musicians later performed "Geordie"—the ballad of a man whose wife begs the judge to stop her husband's execution—he turned to me and asked, "Would ye plead for me on my behalf, Mary, if it should ever come to that?"

Before I could answer him, my father appeared directly in front of us and inserted himself into our private world. "Donal Donn. I believe I'd be owing ye and yer men a most sincere thank ye for what ye did for my daughter and my son and myself." At this, he extended his hand to Donal in an expression of his gratitude. "Should ye ever be needing anything in the future, all ye need do is ask. If I can oblige ye, ye shall have it." Without waiting for a reply, he demanded, "Mary, yer place is with yer family. Come, the evening is drawing to a close."

My father marched away abruptly, but his command echoed in my ears. I reached out my hand so that my fingers could brush Donal's one final time, and as the notes of the concluding song filtered through the air, he whispered its words to me:

Her rosy cheeks and ruby lips
I own she has my heart in thrall
Then fill to me the parting glass
Good night and joy be with ye all.

Donal – Promises and Plans

When Mary was taken from the Hall, I felt cold and lifeless, as if I were camping outdoors and the fire had gone out. The room had lost its glow, and I fumbled about trying to fill the chasm in my heart with other distractions—one of which happened to be the sight of Campbell at my table.

"To what do we owe the pleasure of this visit?" I asked him sarcastically, striking an imposing stance. I stood to the left of his shoulder while he was seated below, situated between Derek—whose head lolled back into a drunken sleep—and Angus—who stared unfocused at the empty cup in front of him.

Campbell wielded a nearly empty bottle of whiskey in his bandaged hand as he gestured to Angus. "This man works for me, Donn, so mind yer own affairs." He stood up from his place and continued, "And as 'tis, my business here is finished." He directed that last comment to Angus, and to me, he said, "But I'm not through with ye, Donn, or yer other mongrels either. Watch yer back, eh? One move out of line, and I'll devour ye faster than a falcon does its prey, leaving only yer bones behind."

"Och, George," I said with the tone of an exasperated parent, "when will ye learn that in order for ye to frighten me ye'd have to be a man first, ye ken someone who keeps his word. And the only thing I see in front of me right now is a coddled, spoiled child who spends so much time satisfying his own needs that he's never cultivated a sense of anyone else's. Face it, George, no one'll come to yer aid since ye've never done the same in return. So that means it'll just be ye against me, and I do not think that's much of a battle at all, now is it? Keep yer empty threats and move on." I inched closer to him to reinforce my statement.

But George would have the last word, and he sneered at me before departing. "A man has no need of friends when the law is on his side. Remember that, Donn."

I watched him stomp away and then turned to my friends who were also unaffected by George's threats. As we gathered up our belongings to head to our camp outside the castle, I noticed Angus still staring at his place setting. *Drunken trance,* I thought to myself as I observed Ross trying to rouse both brothers so that they could leave the hall together. I did not realize at the time that I had supped with Judas.

***

Under the watchful eye of her father, Mary was unable to come to me during the remainder of the festival, so I had to be content with stolen glimpses of her walking about the grounds or attending the sports and games. It was a kind of torture to be so close that I could hear her voice ripple with laughter yet be so distant that I couldna' share in her pleasure. But like a desperate soul wandering in the desert, I considered these visions of her to be like prized trickles of water that I drank in for sustenance and sheer survival.

The next morning, able-bodied men organized themselves into teams, and in two separate waves, we set out on a hunt for wild boar. In the first session, my men and I took the prize, chasing the beast to near exhaustion, cornering it, then spearing it through for the kill. In the second wave, success was had by Hamlin and his boys, but it came at a cost, as one of his men had his arm mauled by the creature's tusks when the fellow's spear didna' penetrate deeply enough and served only to rile the beast even further.

During the afternoon hours, there were archery contests, shinty games between competing clans, and unofficial wrestling matches that broke out between disgruntled losers and boastful victors from the earlier competitions. When the shadows lengthened and night set in, we supped individually at our own camps on the open field and later gathered round the central bonfire where whiskey, wine, and ale flowed freely thanks to the largess of Teague McElroy.

In and out of the dancing flames, I could see a pair of green eyes flashing in rhythm with the fire, and I shifted my position to get a closer look. Mary, standing between Devin on her right and a young lady and her companion on her left, was singing along to the tune everyone was crooning, the one about fair Helen o' Kirkconnell. Far as I could tell, I didna' see Teague anywhere near his daughter, so I moved decisively toward her with the same secrecy I brought to reiving—only this time my desired prize was much more alluring than my customary plunder.

It was impossible for me not to jostle a few bodies in order to get closer to Mary, but I tried to move as slowly as possible so as not to appear to have a destination in mind. I would take a few steps and then linger to sing a verse or two, take a few steps and then linger, until I stood right behind her. She wore her auburn hair pinned up, and the paleness of her long, delicate neck stood out against the flames of the fire and the black edges of the evening. Boldness overtook me for I couldna' resist brushing my lips against the side of her neck, and when she sprung up in alarm, I placed my hands on either side of her waist to settle her.

I saw the glow of pleasure in her eye when she recognized that it was I who interrupted her so intimately, and I basked in the warmth of her affection. She took a quick glance round and then gently pushed my chest backward to signal that we should leave the gathering. Once through the people, she grabbed hold of my hand, and I let her lead me wherever she would. We soon left the crowd and the melody behind.

The air surrounding us grew chill as we departed from the heat of the bodies and the fire, but the outward coldness could do nothing to diminish my fever for my wanting her. Passing through the first set of trees as we entered the forest, I felt as if the curtains of Nature parted for us, welcoming us to lie upon her bed of earth and fallen leaves.

Neither of us uttered a word; our understanding of this moment was beyond spoken language. Her body and mine declared all that we needed to say. Beneath me she reclined, glistening under the light of the twinkling stars and the orange moon. Placing my hand under her neck, I raised her lips to mine while the other hand unlaced her bodice and brushed the soft skin there known only to me. Pulling my face away from hers, I burrowed under her clothing to gently explore the beauty that lay beneath. Her back arched in desire, and I returned my lips to the softness of her neck, covering it with layers of tender kisses.

Although mad with longing, I did not want to do wrong by her, so after returning to her lips for a long sensuous kiss, I looked deeply into her eyes and whispered, "I'm thinking ye can feel what my body is wanting, but I willna' go any further unless ye believe it to be good and true for ye as well."

With a slight nod of her head, she placed both of her hands on my shirt and drew me back down onto her. My head now buried in her neck, and my lips fluttering upon it, I slowly lifted her skirts, and as I raised them higher, I felt my own manhood nearly bursting within. When I was certain that she was still accepting this next step, I turned my hand to my kilt and was much less gentle pulling aside its folds.

When I placed my body atop hers, I anchored my arms upon the earth to keep my weight from pressing down too hard upon her. She let out a slight moan when I entered her, so I ceased all movement to make sure I wasna' hurting her. It took all the strength I could summon to hold myself in abeyance like this, but my concern for her superseded my longing. When she grew accustomed to accepting me there, she drew me toward her once again, and I began to move inside her a little more deeply. With gentle thrusting motions, I let the sensation build, and only after I felt her body rise and saw her head fall back in ecstasy did I surrender and give all of myself to her.

For some time after, I continued to touch her, playing with the strands of her hair that had escaped its confinement and tumbled freely about her shoulders. She spoke hesitantly, "Ye ken that I do not want to leave, but it'd be best to return before the singing and revelry end." Her eyes, wide and round like a fawn's, looked at me for a sign of confirmation.

"Aye," I said in agreement, but before we departed from this earthly Eden, I bent toward her once more and said, "I felt it the first time I held ye, and it's growing stronger with every touch. For me, there will be no other." I sealed my vow to her with one more passionate kiss.

On our return, the crunching sound of our own footsteps upon the leaves and twigs was the only noise in the air until I heard Mary's breath tighten into irregular spasms. Grabbing her wrist, I made her stop and compelled her to look at me. "Mary?" I said as I saw her face twisted in pain. "What troubles ye, lass? I havena' made ye do something ye're already regretting, have I?" I placed my hands upon her face and wiped away the falling tears with my thumb.

"No," she shook her head from side to side, "I have no sorrow over what we've done. I'd been wanting this and I was ready for this and it was everything I'd imagined it to be and more." She dropped her head and ceased looking at me as she went on to explain. "It's just that...it's just that...I was so relieved and excited when my father called off my bond to Campbell that I

178

started to envision a life together for us, and before my dream could even take form, it's now gone dark—like a candle whose wick is so short that its light snaps shut right after igniting."

She took a deep breath and revealed the rest to me. "This morning, one of the British lords spoke of me to my father. Seems his wife passed away last winter, and his household is in disarray. He's needing someone to manage his domestic affairs and wants a woman young enough to provide him with plenty of children as his first union was barren. Father says 'twould be a fine match for me as he is a duke or an earl or some other titled landowner from Northumberland. He and his consorts will remain with us for the rest of the week, and I'm to become 'acquainted' with him during that time.

"But, dear God," and she broke down completely here, crumbling to the ground and covering her face with her hands, "I do not want to become 'acquainted' with him. I want nothing to do with him. I ken that before what we did here tonight, and now after what we've done, I'm so certain of it that, if my Da' forces me to do this, I will have no choice but to run away from Undlay. I canna pretend to be another man's wife when my heart belongs only to ye."

She looked so intensely into my eyes that I felt she had penetrated the deepest recesses of my soul and ken that what she found there reassured her. Feeling more at ease once I learned that her sadness had naught to do with the threshold we had just crossed, I agreed that she and I had to take action.

Taking her hands into my own, I declared, "Run away with *me* then, Mary." The suggestion had a ring of impulsiveness to it, but in truth, it was a plan I had been fleshing out for some time now. "I have kinsmen in Ross-shire in the village of Knockfarrel. They'll help us. And, I've put aside a good amount of revenue as well. We can go and set up a place together there."

My grip on her hands grew tighter, and my breath pulsed with excitement. "'Tis a fine land, 'tis, along the River Peffrey whose waters are as shining and radiant as yerself. It may seem like a bold step right now, no doubt, leaving behind yer family and friends, but ye wouldna' have to be parted from them forever. With time, they'll come round and realize that ye had to be true to yer heart."

I pulled her to my chest and smiled while my chin rested atop her head. "And someday, they'll all come and visit. There'll be room enough for Deirdre and Aidan to explore like they were settlers in the New World itself, and there'll be plenty of fine steeds for Robby to groom and ride. And yer mother will come and help ye when yer bringing our children into the world, and yer father will be impressed with how I've cared for ye and made ye happy. He'll come to learn that his daughter's contentment canna be bought with meaningless titles or frigid castles."

At this point, I broke our embrace in order to read her feelings. When I lifted her face to mine, I saw splotches of joy breaking through the path of her tears, and I sensed she was envisioning the dream I had laid out before her. In her mind's eye, perhaps, she was seeing the rolling fields of purple heather that would surround us, the sparkling starlight that would shine above us, and the soft bed that would welcome us. There, each night, we would fall into each other's arms and let the cares of the world simply melt away. Although we wouldna' be living in a castle, we'd be monarchs in our own rite, living according to our shared edict of love.

As she let her sadness slip into the darkness, I caressed her face once again and said, "Just bide the time twixt now and Samhain so that I can make the necessary preparations. On All Hallow's eve when everyone else will be carving lanterns and hiding from ghosts and goblins, you and I will be cutting a path in the darkness, unafraid to be moving in the shadows." With this, I kissed her deeply in an attempt to seal her fate with my own.

Donal – A Final Ride

The surface of the water
'Tis a glass that shows to me
The image of the clouds
Rolling fast and moving free.

As they swirl before my eyes
Pushing beyond what I can see
I feel the pull of wind and change
Coming now to ye and me.

'Tis not a time to stay and wait
For here together we canna be.
And so we run just like the clouds
Testing a fate we canna foresee.

But place yer hand and heart in mine
And hear me now make this decree:
Our home resides in our embrace
And has naught to do with land or sea.

So though we journey near and far
Over hill and dale and lea
Trust that wherever we shall wander
Home consists of ye and me.

The hours turned to days and the days to weeks as the world round me
marched on toward wintertide. The golden hues of autumn which had clothed
the countryside in a cloak of perpetual sunset had given way to the more

somber colors of the approaching season. The deer grass on the moors, once russet red, faded now into a rich brown, then to an even softer shade in a gradual dwindling of its vibrancy.

Of course, there still remained a solitary day or two when the warmth of the sun tried in vain to reassert its dominance, but its triumphant mid-day appearance was short lived, and darkness overran the fields faster and earlier, forcing the glimmer and glow to retreat and give way to the spikes of bristling frost.

The breath from my nose and lips materialized in a vapor before me, and I rubbed my hands together for warmth as I waited for my companions to arrive. A few feet from me, Cerwyn foraged the ground for what little grass he could graze, and the vision of the horse scouring this way made me think of my own methods of finding sustenance. Tonight would be my last raid; hereafter, I'd be leaving with Mary for Knockfarrel to earn my living solely by farming and building.

'Twasn't going to mean much difference in lifestyle for me though, since I only used reiving as a method of payback—a way of hurting unprincipled nobles who oppressed the poorer folk beneath them. And it was great fun, in a way, playing the role of an anonymous judge and enforcer who sentenced these bastards to a special kind of punishment by the loss of their property and vanity. It gave me deep pleasure to bestow a few cattle, a spare goat, a fine mare, or a couple of chickens upon a God-fearing man, widow, or couple who had been left destitute by the unjust machinations of a depraved, greedy lord.

I'd not told a soul of my plan to head north with Mary for fear the news would leak and our plan be scuttled. We needed to move fast, however— probably have to set out in a few days' time—once tonight's mission was complete and this final profit added to my purse. The McElroys were planning a trip of their own come Martinmas, a journey south to Northumberland where they would proceed with Mary's nuptials to the earl residing there. I suppose Teague felt this match would do well for him politically, linking his lineage to that of British blood and ensuring King Charles' favor, but there were many who looked upon a union with an Englishman with the same distaste and repulsion one would feel when watching a limb dismembered from the body.

Aye, this would be my final outing, and I savored this opportunity to close the door on my enemy and former rival, George Campbell, principal clan leader of the Campbell estate. George's father had not properly recovered from the injury he had suffered during our raid on the McKintys, and local gossip reported that he'd grown feeble in his mind from having spent endless days and weeks sequestered away in his private chamber with no company other than the occasional servant.

It was said Campbell called out to his attendants using names of those already dead and buried, and he himself seemed about ready to join them in the churchyard. Word went round that George was hastening the man's departure by refusing to supply his own father with restorative food and drink. Subsisting on crusts of bread and limited ale, the old man passed the hours straddling a line between here and the hereafter while George slithered his way into power, seizing the finances and the control of the property. It was fitting that this final venture of mine would involve settling the score with a wretch who had sucked the lifeblood out of everyone who crossed his path in life, including the very person who had given it to him in the first place.

A thump of hoofbeats upon the ground interrupted my thoughts, and I looked through the darkness to discern the identity of the rider. Thick and bulky, Brodie sat astride Dewey, streams of mist rushing from the beast's nostrils. "Hint of snow in the air, do ye not think, Donal?" Brodie asked as he swiftly dismounted and strode forward. "Seems a bit early in the year for that, no?"

"Aye," I agreed. "Might make the trail a wee bit slippery, I suppose, but these creatures are more nimble than ourselves when it comes to staying upright and secure." I patted Dewey's broad neck and shoulder as I spoke.

"No doubt. I've been known to have my own trips and tumbles as a boy, and even as a grown man, I've taken many a misstep and ended up flailing about! 'Tis a good thing I have no problem laughing at my own foibles, otherwise I'd be sorely embarrassed by the many times I've upended myself," and, as if in recollection of one of those memories, Brodie placed his palm upon his forehead and shook his head at the image of his own clumsiness.

I had set no fire, so we stood enveloped in the darkness, discussing some of the details of the plan when distant sounds grew louder in volume as two more riders drew near. Owen and Ross burst upon the scene, and in his haste to dismount, Ross bellowed, "Bloody hell! It was some ride coming here!" Complaint and impatience marked his tone.

"What do ye mean? On account of the icy rocks and frost-covered ground?" Brodie asked, but before he could answer, Ross was already darting off toward the bushes, his red hair flapping as he ran.

"Nae," Owen stepped in to respond. "I mean, aye, 'twas a bit treacherous at times, but 'twasn't the frozen landscape that troubled him most. 'Twas his sister's cooking that's caused his discomfort. He thinks she fed him tainted venison because he's been struggling the whole time to stay atop his horse without soiling himself. 'Tis the third time he's had to empty his bowels— ugh—*O man of God, there is death in the pot.* 2 Kings, chapter four." Owen shook his head from side to side in support of his scriptural declaration.

"Hmmmm. Do ye think he's gone enough times for it to be empty now then?" Although the question sounded amusing, I was asking him seriously. "We've got quite a bit of a ride to Campbell's and do not forget, back again as well…"

Already I was trying to sketch out a plan in my head that would require only three hands instead of four in case Ross wouldna' be able to join with us. Postponing the raid was not an option.

Before Owen could wager a guess, Ross crawled out of the brush and responded to my question himself. "Dinna fash. I'm fine now. I've gone so many times that there's nothing left inside of me except my own innards, and I'm certainly not ready to be parting with them any time soon, thank ye verra much." He smoothed out his kilt, placed his hands on his hips, and spat upon the ground before continuing. "Besides, I wouldna' miss roiling Campbell for anything. Do not forget, he still holds two acres of my property—courtesy of Angus. To speak the truth, I wouldna' mind taking a wee bit of Campbell's own property to keep for myself, ye ken."

"I'm sure we can arrange something like that for ye, my friend." I grinned as I envisioned it playing out. "It'd be quite satisfying to see Campbell twist with rage when eyeballing his finest mares being boarded in the Gregor stable, no?" My eyes shone with mischief at the thought.

Ross countered, "Well, since his prized girl has already been stolen from him by the likes of ye, I figure I could be content with taking possession of some of his four-legged ones, for sure." We shared a hearty laugh at the thought of my having lured away Campbell's finest filly, but only I was aware of just how far away I'd be taking her in the days to follow.

The journey to Campbell's property would involve more miles than we'd ridden in the Cunningham raid or the McKinty raid or even on the night that we "helped" George with his penance, so we didna' linger verra long once Ross had emptied his bowels. Based on the recent information Ross had secured from his brother, the watch was still being conducted in the same location as before—by the broch near the McKinty boundary. I was confident that we'd have no trouble passing by the area undetected, and I was certain we could round up the Campbells' livestock and valuables with little resistance, but returning with the goods was what concerned me.

It's not easy to keep cattle, sheep, and goats moving together as one and in silence, so we'd have to disable the guards first before moving past their camp. To complicate things further, Angus mentioned that George had added more men to his crew, mercenaries of the verra worst kind who were motivated solely by the hint of coin or the promise of liquor. These rogues did not interact with the established guardsmen, like Ollie or Bryston or Robby, but rather kept to themselves, huddled together in the brush as they once did when they were on the other side of the law working as marauders.

Their loyalty to George was as meager and flimsy as the silk of a spider's web, and I'd no doubt it'd snap and they'd drop him straight away so long as they felt there was something lucrative in it for them. But still, I didna' want to have to deal with unnecessary confrontations or encounters, so we would proceed with more caution than usual.

The hint of snow Brodie had smelled earlier arrived now in tangible form, not as soft, downy flakes but instead as a freezing sleet that pelted the clothing on our backs and clacked against the rocks upon the ground. With the wind blowing from behind, our vision was clear and uncompromised, but the conditions did not bode well for our return if the weather remained the same.

On the horizon, I could discern the unsteady leaps and flashes of a single fire. Its presence indicated to me that it must have been positioned under some kind of tarp that the guards had raised. After making that assessment, I squeezed with my legs against Cerwyn's sides to signal a turn to the right where we could detour under the forest canopy. Behind me rode Owen, then Ross, then Brodie, all of us keenly aware of staying alert should we come upon any vagabond-turned-sentry.

Like a carpenter creating a spiral staircase, I sculpted an intricate winding path through the woods that would keep us safe from the guards and yet not be too circuitous as to waste time. Concentrating on guiding Cerwyn over the glazed and slippery undergrowth, I didna' hear Ross call out till Owen pulled up alongside to inform me so.

"Donal, Ross is needing to make a deposit. He says he'll do so and catch up with us in no time." Droplets of ice fell from the brim of Owen's bonnet while he delivered the news.

I nodded my assent but kept my eyes fixed upon the unlevel ground. We had not gone much further at all when Brodie broke the silence of our cover and cried out, "Something's gone wrong with Ross; I'm turning back." Without delay, Owen and I did the same, retracing the same boulders and brambles we had just traversed. Where once there was stillness, the glade now erupted in a tumult of striking blows and grappling bodies. Ross, whose hands were covered in blood, held fast to the coat of his assailant and was jamming his bent leg deep into the man's gut.

To his side, Brodie wrapped one hand round the neck of another fellow, lifted him up in the air, and threw him down, just in time to field an assault from a second attacker. Laying out that second man with a single punch to his face, Brodie then turned back to face the first who had risen from the ground, and bending his arm at the elbow, Brodie clubbed the man so hard that he went airborne for a few moments before crashing and landing with a thud upon a rotted tree stump.

Jumping down from my horse, I darted over to Ross where he sat with one hand pressed to his neck. "Let me take a look," I said as I knelt down beside him and tilted my head to examine the wound more closely. "What happened?" I saw the slice in the side of Ross's neck and directed Owen to go into my saddle pouch and rummage up whatever might be useful so that I could bind the gash. Thankfully, the villain had not severed anything major, and although there was a good deal of blood both in the area and on Ross's clothes and hands, the boy was in no immediate danger so far as I could tell.

Owen brought over to me a few shreds of fabric that he had found, and as I tied the pieces together, Ross explained. "I was squatting down over yon when I heard the sound of twigs snapping from behind my back. I ken it couldna' have been ye fellows since it come from the opposite direction, and as I stood and turned about, I was jumped by three knaves who tried to rob me.

One of them held a knife to my neck, while the other two started rummaging through the saddlebags on Bran.

"I was sure I could take care of the dwarfish troll on me, but I needed more hands to dispose of the other two. So I called out to ye and spun round at the same time, but before I could flatten my attacker, he nicked my throat with his blade. And then, of course, ye just saw what Brodie did to the other two, aye?" Once Ross finished speaking, I wrapped the cloth around the slice, tying a knot on the side to hold the bandage in place.

"I did. Can ye still ride with us?" I asked Ross while Brodie, looking invigorated and even larger in stature than normal after crushing both of his attackers, strode over to where we three had gathered.

Looking at me as if I'd made the most preposterous suggestion, Ross answered emphatically, "Of course! I might be spewing out liquid from both ends of my body, but I'll not turn back." Slapping the ground with both hands, Ross marched directly toward his horse, and after the four of us had mounted, I took the lead once again, directing us toward the Campbell estate, leaving in our wake the three swindlers whose only spoils were the crystals of ice forming on their sprawled out bodies.

***

Not only did Owen have a way with words, he also had a way with animals. He continually healed whatever was ailing our mounts—like Dewey's vision weeks ago—and right now, he was the primary voice responsible for soothing and directing a panicked herd. Just as I had thought, rounding up the cattle, sheep, and goats was a simple task with George not at home and his father an indoor prisoner. I'd wager we had lifted about a hundred beasts, mostly cattle, but we'd helped ourselves to two lovely mares and two ponies as well. Unlike the trouble we ran across in the forest, this part of the plan went smoothly, despite the driving chips of rain that felt like pin pricks upon our faces. Ignoring them as best we could, we waited for the numbness of the cold to dull the sting.

I rode at the front, and from time to time, I could hear Owen's soft whistle serving as an eastern boundary signal to bring back to the fold any animal who strayed. He had the more challenging terrain, the area was edged by a trackless bog, dotted with pools and overgrown tussocks of grass. A momentary lapse of attention and a wayward beast would be heard from no more. Judging from the frequency of Owen's trills, he had his hands full with creatures longing to wander. Ross patrolled the herd on the western side, a more even and less swampy ground.

Already compromised a bit from his injury, he needed all of his stamina to see this night through, especially since I had altered the plan by changing our route. Rather than having to deal with the guards on watch, I'd decided to expend the energy we would have used fighting for riding instead. It seemed wiser to me to tack on more miles on horseback than to risk Ross's well-being and our own by clashing with five men just to take a shortcut. Of course, 'twould add two more hours of traveling—and whistling—but I figured that freezing hands and discomfort in the saddle were a small price to pay for safety.

As always, Brodie rode at the back of the procession and was our first line of defense should there be a hot trod in retaliation. Like a miser whose appetite only grows at the sight of gold, Brodie's hunger for combat was stirred after his tussle with the two thieves. If Campbell's family and friends *should* sound the alarm and try to attack our hind-most man, they would be stomped out and swept away like sinners in the great flood. Comforted by that thought, I allowed myself to ponder the days ahead.

Once we were safely back home, I'd bring two sheep and two goats to Mrs. Nairn, and we'd let the rest of the animals graze for the remainder of the day. There was a sizeable pastureland near Undlay that was unused this time of year, so we'd keep them there till the following morn. 'Twould also give Ross a wee bit of time to recover before we'd need his help again when bringing the beasts to market. After they'd been delivered, we'd split the profits, and with that money added to my savings, 'twould be time for Mary and me to depart.

By tomorrow evening then, we'd be on our way to Ross-shire. I'd be needing to send word to her about that, but how? Perhaps I'll send Owen with one of the mares to the smithy at Undlay—what was the fellow's name? Hamlin, I believe? Aye, that's what I'll do. I'll have Owen tell Hamlin there's some problem with the mare's shoe, and then have him slip Hamlin a note to deliver to Mary. By the shoreline near those twisted trees, she'll come to me, and we'll forge ahead into the future by releasing the bindings that chained us to the past.

Just then, a shrill sound pierced the air, and Cerwyn's ears flicked back in response. Immediately, I pulled back on her reins, and once we halted, I cocked my head to the side to listen. No longer the gentle warning to corral a stray, the noise this time meant something greater was amiss, so I galloped with haste to the east. Careful to tread upon solid ground, I darted in and out of the animals who were at the border of the herd until I came upon Owen.

"Look," he gestured to the straggling cattle and sheep, "the flock's thinning out. Brodie mustn't be driving them no more. Something's not right."

"Take the lead. Keep moving north. Tell Ross to swing over to this side for the remainder of the way." I sped off to discover what could have become of Brodie. The herd was in disarray. In separate, distanced bunches, I saw a few goats in one area, some cattle foraging in another, and a number of sheep drinking from a western burn. We'd lost the tightness needed for travel, and this would delay our arrival significantly. More important than that though was the welfare of my good friend.

Farther and farther I retreated, but still, there was no sign of the man or his horse—impossible when ye think of Brodie's size and presence. It seemed as if he had simply vanished from the scene, and there was no chance he'd ever do that intentionally. He'd never be so distracted or selfish to shirk his duty. A shiver rippled through me that I assigned to the weather, mainly because I did not want to confront the reality that Brodie had been harmed. After finally coming to the end of the herd, I continued my search even farther beyond, looking for any indication as to what may have happened to the man.

With a kind of desperation, I continued to ride over hills and meadows, trying in vain to bury my increasing panic. But as the distance lengthened, my hopes diminished. A spike twisted in my heart when I realized that I had to abandon my search. I had no choice but to try to salvage what we could of the raid by getting the plunder back to Undlay. Once secure, I'd ride back again and scour the area more carefully. I'd either find him outright or, at the verra least, discover some clue or hint as to where he may have gone.

Changing direction, I returned to the rear of the flock and channeled my worry and frustration into the job of driving the herd back together. The wind had picked up considerably; its power pressed against me with such force that it thwarted my efforts to gain ground, and the eerie sound it made as it drove through the branches made me think it was a chorus of demons laughing at me and the folly of my grand plans for the future. With the howls and screeches I heard whipping round me, I slipped into darker thoughts, wondering if Brodie had fallen victim of the *Sluagh*, the spirits of the restless dead who kidnap unsuspecting travelers and carry their souls away. I shuddered with dread when I fought the gale long enough to raise my head and see a whirlwind of flapping wings fill the sky above me.

A Debt Repaid

Aside from the scuffle a few hours ago, it had been an easy run, Brodie thought to himself as he trotted along, keeping the animals in transit. Sure, the weather was a bit nasty and he was longing for a taste of stew to warm his belly—maybe one of chicken and pork, seasoned with a bit of pepper and saffron—but overall the venture was a successful one indeed.

Rounding up the beasts came natural to him and required very little concentration on his part, so he busied himself instead with thoughts of home. It was only a matter of days now before the priest would be summoned for his mother's burial. Until he had visited Hilda all those weeks ago, he still held out hope for her recovery, but the seer had told him otherwise.

In the softest of tones, she explained to him how his mother's spirit was ready to move on, yearning to hold the hand of the man who had chosen her to be his wife above all the other pretty girls in the glen. She longed to be with him again, silly and frivolous and exhilarated by life instead of battling to bring breath into that sunken and withered chest of hers that lay covered beneath the bedsheets. But Brodie's mother felt obligated to remain. Hilda was aware of this and counseled Brodie to let her go; he had to relinquish his hold on her. When he could do that, his mother would shed the heaviness of her sickly body and recapture the airy spirit of a young girl in love.

But it was very hard for him to surrender, especially when he defined his entire life by force—whether it be physical strength or will. He found himself feeling like a traveler in a foreign land: he could not find his way, he didn't know the customs, and he couldn't speak the language. For Brodie, submission was unfamiliar territory.

There had been a period of brief improvement after he administered the medicine Hilda had given him. The tincture had helped, lifting his mother to a kind of peaceful, intermediary country, removed from the pain of this one but not completely settled into the next. Only now could he appreciate that suspending her between two worlds was selfish of him. He had been holding onto her so tightly because he was too afraid to let her go, too afraid to confront his own grief, too afraid to admit that he was beaten. But if he had been less focused on himself and more attentive to her, he would have realized that her spirit was gone long before he sought out the witch's remedy. The frigid night brought him clarity, and he was ready now to grant her release. And so he prayed.

"Blessed Mary, Mother of us all, bring yer child—and my mother—home. Let her dwell in serenity and joy with ye and all the other saints. May she find comfort in my Da's embrace and in the laughter that spills from my twin sisters whose bodies were buried in the earth just weeks after they had been placed into her arms. Hear my prayer, Queen of Heaven, and grant her the deliverance that she seeks."

Lifting his chin upward and closing his eyes, he commended these words to the heavens above, and in so doing, immediately felt an enormous weight ascending from his own chest as well. The driving wind and pelting rain seemed of no consequence to him. Perhaps it was this complete immersion into a state of grace that made him oblivious to what was happening around him and vulnerable to what next ensued.

A filthy, nearly toothless scamp had been tracking Brody for some time, crawling then sprinting, scurrying then hiding alongside the distracted rider. Darting ahead to a better vantage point, the villain tucked himself behind a tree and loaded into his sling a rock about the size of his palm. Pointing the weapon at the head of the man on horseback, he pulled back the band and, waiting for the right moment, released the tension.

With the same force of a bullet fired from a pistol, the rock clouted Brody in the center of his forehead, and the man tumbled straight to the ground with a loud thud. Unimpeded by any front teeth, the thief's tongue slithered forth as he licked his lips in anticipation of the riches he would find on the body that lay inert on the ground.

***

Despite the fact that no alarm had been sounded, Robby had an uncanny feeling that something was awry. It was his custom to ride about and canvas the area during his hours on watch, mainly because he found it terribly dull to just sit back and wait for trouble to come to him. *Far better 'tis to seek it out,* he thought, *rather than allow it to overrun ye, like the dolts who think setting up camp is a valid form of protection during a Highland blizzard. At least the snow is light tonight.* He consoled himself with this, God's small favor, although he did believe it was the kind of evening you'd rather pass indoors, in front of a roaring fire with a warm blanket, a pretty lass, and a bottle of whiskey for sharing.

Even though some weeks had passed, his right leg still vexed him, stiff whenever it was cold and throbbing whenever he rode. *Twas still worth it,* he proclaimed to himself, especially since his actions provided a kind of retribution for what Blake and Drew had done to Edina. When he was younger, he had met Edina on a few occasions when her family joined his for celebrations, and whenever he thought of those days, the first image that came to his mind were those soulful eyes of hers. They were the defining characteristic on her face—large, soft gray pools that were as warm and welcoming as the glen before dawn. They held the promise of untold mysteries that would reveal themselves to you the longer you spent in their presence.

But after the assault, those eyes had turned within themselves, and their secrets were locked away forever, leaving in their stead the skittish and flitting movement of an animal on high alert. Maybe, with the right man beside her, Edina would return again to those lighter days when the world was exciting and full of possibility. *Maybe,* he thought, *I could teach her to trust again.*

Trust is a fine gift, but it must be carefully bestowed. Place it in the wrong person or in the wrong situation, and you're doomed. Robby understood, however, that trust must first be cultivated from within; it was a lesson he had mastered already for he continually listened to and was guided by his instincts, and right then, his gut was telling him that there was danger in the air. Increasing his speed yet moving as quietly as possible, he soon came upon a mounted rider who, despite his wide girth, moved with ease and fluidity.

A distant animal sound here and there convinced Robby that he had stumbled upon a raid in progress. Although the man on horseback appeared to be twice his size, Robby spurred his mount with a determination that justice needed to be served, no matter the consequences to himself. A momentary wince crossed his face when he thought of his leg, but he forged ahead to perform his duty, that is, until it was his duty no longer.

Robby witnessed what then transpired. With a sudden jolt, the big man toppled sideways off his horse and straight to the ground, making Robby pull up short and bide a moment, contemplating his next move. Guiding his horse over to the brush, he watched and waited. Sure enough, a hunched-back creature pounced on the fallen man and began rummaging through his pockets and sporran. *Two thieves in one night?* he celebrated silently to himself.

At the prospect of such good fortune, Robby commanded his horse to gallop, and as he dashed toward the scene, the greasy-haired footpad looked up from his pillaging and trundled away into the undergrowth like a rat scuttling away to find darkness when a torch-bearer draws near.

Rather than pursuing the lone bandit, Robby chose to arrest the grander thief who lay at his feet—if, in fact, the man were alive enough to even be arrested. If they had been closer to the border and the castles therein, Robby would've wagered it was a *redcap* who did this man in, for beside the fellow's body was a large stone, most likely the implement of his undoing. Bending down upon his knees, Robby pulled the body from its side and onto its back, and when he did so, he inhaled deeply at the sight of the man's identity. It was the fellow who had preserved his life, the man who had rescued him from the blade of Blake Cameron. His Good Samaritan was a common reiver?

Robby's world turned upside-down as he recognized the beginnings of a moral dilemma, but the struggle didn't last as long as it probably should have because, in Robby's mind, some things were more important than the law.

***

By the time Donal's men reached their destination, the rain had stopped, and the sun broke through the line of clouds in the battle for domination. A single ray of sunlight, like a spear, pierced through the gloom, gaining strength as more beams burst forth until radiance won over the day. Worn out by the miles they had traveled and the weather they had endured, both the animals and the men longed for rest, and while the creatures themselves could mull about and take repose, two of the men still had more business to tend to.

Faithful to his word, Donal rounded up the livestock he was gifting to Mrs. Nairn and, once he had delivered them to her, he would immediately ride forth again in search of their missing comrade. Ross, too, remained in the saddle, turning toward home to tend to his wound, leaving just Owen behind to enjoy a restorative nap. The plan was that once Ross returned to relieve Owen, the young preacher would then bring one of the mares over to Undlay under the pretense of needing her shoe examined, allowing Owen the opportunity to slip into Hamlin's hand the message intended for Mary.

The celebration the men should have shared at the conclusion of such a profitable night was replaced with an emptiness, the somber acknowledgement of Brodie's absence. Though none of the three spoke of the matter aloud, their movements communicated sorrow and resignation.

After carefully folding the paper and handing it to Owen, Donal gave these instructions. "Once Ross returns, be on yer way to Undlay. Give this to Hamlin only. Be sure no one sees ye doing so, and say nothing to anyone else. I'll be back with Brodie before sundown, no doubt, to spell Ross. Do yer errand today and be back here at dawn so we can drive these beasts and exchange them for revenue at Drummondshire." Clapping Owen on top of his shoulder, Donal moved quickly, tethered two goats together, along with two cows, and pulled them toward his awaiting horse. Once mounted, he trotted away with the beasts in tow.

Owen stared down at the folded letter in his hand, pleased with the gravity of this assignment and the trust Donal had placed in him. Awash in pride for himself and admiration for his leader, he thought, *The messenger shall go forth, prepare the way, and make straight the path. But even the good Lord rested on the seventh day, and so this humble messenger shall do the same.* Finding a particularly thick and spongy patch of grass beneath the shade of an alder tree, Owen dropped his cap over his eyes and settled into a peaceful slumber.

***

"Can ye not hear me, ye dunderheid? Do not make me yell as it'll split my head in twain," the man tapped his foot into the lump reclining before him in an attempt to stir the pile into consciousness. The heap on the ground shifted and squirmed, but it took a second real kick before the sleeper's hand slowly dragged his bonnet down from his face. That being done, the man blinked his eyes in rapid succession, attempting to ascertain his whereabouts.

Seeing only a blurred face above him with a single bump protruding from its forehead, the newly roused man gasped in horror, "I've awakened on the isle of the Cyclops, I have." He shook his head side-to-side as if to make the vision disappear. But there it remained. The overwhelming size of his assailant, coupled with that singular protrusion, led Owen to believe he had become a character in one of the many stories he had taught his students. Only when his vision cleared did Owen realize that before him stood a being—yes, of gigantic proportions—but a friend nonetheless. Brodie. He had come back! Terror transformed to jubilation as Owen leapt to his feet to embrace the man he had supposed gone forever.

"Ho, ho! Ye're back! And what happened to ye? Where'd ye go? Who did that to yer head? When did ye get here? How did ye get here?" The questions spun out from Owen's mouth one after another without pause.

"Hold off, now. Do not spin me around. My head is not steady and my belly is not constant." Brodie placed his hands out evenly at his sides in an attempt to ground himself.

With a gentler touch, Owen brought Brodie over toward the shade and offered him a swig of his drink. "Here, come sit. Tell me now, what's gone on?"

Brodie accepted the bottle and lowered himself to sit upon a rock across from Owen. "Well, I do not have much to say on that account. One minute I'm riding along, thinking about nothing in particular, and the next I'm falling from my horse. From there, I've no recollection of anything except waking up on the outskirts of Undlay Castle with Dewey grazing nearby. What happened in between is but darkness to me." He placed his hands on either side of his head as if to keep the pain contained and under control.

Narrowing his eyes to scrutinize Brodie's head, Owen said, "Judging from the likes of that, ye've taken quite a shot. Ye're lucky to be standing and not lying dead in a ditch somewhere."

"Take a lot more than that to keep this man down," Brodie proclaimed, letting his two fingers gently stroke the mound that stuck out from his forehead.

Moved by a sudden idea, Owen stood up quickly and said, "I must go tell Donal the good news! So long as yer okay then, I'd best be intercepting Donal who's out searching for ye. I'm thinking ye'll have no trouble watching over the cattle and sheep—I mean, after all, shepherding is in yer blood, is it not, big fellow?" With a wink and a smirk, Owen set off on the first of his two errands.

***

George Campbell was livid. The whole world seemed pitted against him. His feeble-minded father threatened to disinherit him; Teague McElroy revoked the marriage contract to Mary; and now someone had the audacity to steal his property. It was time he took control of each situation and showed them all who was in charge. The circumstances regarding his father had already shifted in his favor—the old dottard was hidden away and slipping deeper into oblivion with each passing hour. And, as far as the other matters were concerned, once he captured and did away with the scoundrel who plundered his possessions, Mary would then be his. All would be set right once again.

Seething with rage, he drove his horse unmercifully toward the castle. This would be the last time he would ever be victimized by a lowlife scum like Donal Donn. Now he had concrete proof that Donn was behind this raid, for a single albino cow—the only one of its kind in the glen—turned up at the Nairn homestead, and it was his.

He thought to himself, *Unless Widow Nairn or her ripe young daughter turned into Maid Marian, the beast was surely a prize given to them by some other reiver—Donn, to be sure. The man's more slippery than an eel the way he slinks in and out of trouble, but this time, they'll be no room left for him to glide away from me. I've got the evidence, and now I'll secure the sentence.*

Congratulating himself on the formulation of his plan, George was almost too smug to notice the scene that was unfolding in the blacksmith's shop. A chestnut mare that looked just like one from his own stable was staring straight ahead in George's direction while the smithy examined the hoof on her rear right leg. *Is that not Storin?* he wondered, feeling his heart pound in his chest.

Anger increasing, George fixed his eyes upon the man who had brought the horse to the farrier. *And is that not the bible-quoting preacher from that horrid night some weeks ago? I'd like to get my hands on him now when he has no one else beside him to protect his scrawny arse!* Looking down at his scarred hands, he vowed, *They're both going to pay for what they did to me that night.* George kept his fury in check so that he could observe what was transpiring between the two men. He watched. And waited.

***

With one hand around the man's cravat and the other pointing in his face, George demanded, "Give it to me. Hand over what he gave ye. Now!" Spittle sprayed from George's mouth onto Hamlin's neck and shirt.

Locking eyes with his aggressor, Hamlin refused to back down. "I dunno what yer talking about. And git yer hands off me." With a burst of movement, Hamlin thrust both of his arms upward to break George's hold. Not to be deterred, George swung his arm down, pulled out his dagger, and drove its point swiftly to touch the hollow spot in the center of Hamlin's throat.

"Och, yes, ye do, but maybe ye need just a wee bit of convincing, aye? If ye want to play the mute, perhaps I shall help yer lassie do the same as well, and the two of ye can grunt yer way through life. I see where she goes to do the laundering, all alone by herself by the burn in the meadow. No one'll hear her screams if I cut out her tongue first, aye? And ye can have her all to yerself...but only after I've had my way with her first. The only sounds coming from yer wedding bed'll be the rutting of two pigs if yer so hellbent on having no words to give me now." George's eyes flashed with malice as he relished the details of the scene he had just narrated.

Hamlin continued to stare into those black, lifeless eyes, trying to detect even the slightest hint of bluster and bravado, but there was none. Campbell spoke the truth—a harsh, unequivocal truth. The man would perform such deeds without hesitation, since his soul was devoid of any feeling. Only seconds passed, but to Hamlin, the draining of his will was as painfully slow as having to manually blow air onto a fire in the furnace without the use of bellows.

Never shifting his glare, Hamlin reached into his apron pocket and brought forth the folded paper. Reluctantly extending it toward George, he strove to embed into his memory every word George had uttered. Just the suggestion of what Campbell intended to do to Annag was enough to calcify Hamlin's heart, and as the man snatched the letter from his hand, the blacksmith promised himself that one day he would render this miscreant voiceless forever.

Rather than turn his back toward Hamlin and leave himself vulnerable to attack, George slowly backed away from the man until he was close enough to reach out and touch his horse's hide. Although the letter was beckoning him, he stuffed it into his pocket and rode toward the stables by the entrance of Undlay. Impatient to speak with Teague about the theft of his property and the undeniable appearance of the albino cow and stolen mare on McElroy land, he flung his reins toward Devin without greeting or acknowledgment. Devin responded in like terms, raising only a single eyebrow in disdain at Campbell's arrival.

Unable to wait any longer, George opened the letter as he marched toward entrance gate, and what he read stopped him in his tracks:

Twisted and entwined the two are now one.
Together they reach toward an unknown shore.
Where the roots were once anchored, there will I be,
Under the protection of our beloved rowan tree.

Meet me at dark on the morrow's eve,
We will cease being limited to visions and dreams.
As those branches reach northward side by side
That same course we will follow when we ride.

He stood still, pondering the content of the message. *There's only one fool who'd write such doggerel as this—stuff that would grate upon the ear of any self-respecting lady. But I must remember how simple-minded Mary McElroy is—not refined enough to be offended by such pedestrian verses, empty words penned by a groveling lackey. So, they're planning to run away, are they? And the meeting place involves water, a rowan tree, and a pair of conjoined tree limbs.*

George tilted his head, considering these details. *He must be referring to the site near the loch where the two alder trees fell and criss-crossed in last year's storm. What a surprise it'll be for him when instead of wrapping his arms round Mary and riding off to freedom, those arms'll be bound by chains and his journey'll be ending at the gallows.* Returning the folded paper to his pocket, George smiled, confident that he had all the evidence he needed.

With single-minded purpose, he cut across the courtyard, paying no mind to the people coming and going within. Anything happening around him was a blur because his sights were fixed on vengeance alone. He took the steps two at a time, eager to lay before Teague all of the information incriminating Donal. When he arrived at McElroy's chamber, the laird was sitting at his enormous table, looking over the documents spread out before him.

Responding to the sudden rush of sound that accompanied George's entrance, Teague lifted his head imperceptibly and continued on with his work. Begrudgingly, he spoke to the figure standing before him, "What is it, Campbell? I've much business to attend to here."

Given permission to speak, George plunged right in. "Laird, the man's fate is sealed. He and his ruffians have struck again, and this time there'll be no condoning his actions. He's plundered my possessions, over one-hundred and fifty head of cattle, sheep, goats, and horses. But like a dog leaving its scent upon the territory it trod, he's sprinkled the stolen goods on McElroy land, yer land. The only albino cow in the region—which belonged to me—now resides on the Nairn homestead, and my prized mare, Storin, was just shod by your very own blacksmith."

George's voice gained strength when he noticed Teague look up from his papers and consider his words more deeply. He pressed on. "Ye canna sit by and allow this villain to lift livestock and then besmirch yer own good name by planting the loot on grounds owned by yerself." George went a bit too far, however, when he added, "What would the villagers think if they saw ye harboring property stolen by a reiver? T'wouldna' look—"

George never had the chance to finish that sentence because Teague erupted, slamming the table with his open hand. "Mind yer tongue, Campbell. I certainly do not need ye telling me what I should or should not do about my reputation or my standing with my people. If ye had looked better to yer own affairs, ye wouldna' find yerself about as welcome as a soiled dish rag on a banquet table." McElroy took a breath to steady himself. Placing his thumb and forefinger to rest upon his chin, he asked, "I'm to assume that the man in question here is Donn, then?"

"Aye," George responded with enthusiasm and, inhaling deeply in order to deliver the final seal upon the reiver's fate, he added, "And, I've intercepted this note from the blackguard intended for yer daughter. Seems the devil has bewitched yer own child into thinking he's worthy of her." Coordinating his pronouncement of the word "devil" to coincide with his placement of the note onto the table, George folded his arms triumphantly across his chest and finished, "Next evening he plans to steal her too."

McElroy's face remained blank and emotionless as he reviewed the contents of the letter, but his voice was thick with feeling when he spoke. "How dare he! *Bheir an Diabhal mise a mo bhrogan mar teid Donal Donn a chrochadh!* [The devil may take me out of my shoes if Donal Donn is not hanged!] Florrie!" he yelled to the servant outside the hall. "Fetch Mary to me. Now!" To George, he commanded, "Set an ambush for this scoundrel tomorrow night at the place he specified in this letter. Take as many guards as ye see fit. This time he's gone too far."

"Verra good, my laird," George nodded, "it shall be done." Once his back was turned, George could no longer conceal the venomous sneer that spread across his face. Phase two of his plan was underway, and with Donn out of the picture and himself back in the laird's good graces, Mary would be the recompense he'd demand. The world, which moments before wanted to shrink him into obscurity, had now just expanded, offering him all of its glory once again.

Mary – To Live or Die

I lifted Thor from my lap once my tears had dried and the lump in my throat had dissolved. Stroking his fur had served to ease my pain, but I ken that I must not waste any more time grieving like this, so I placed him gently back down on the stone floor where he glanced once over his shoulder to affirm his work was done. Assured, he curled up into a tight ball and rested his head upon his crossed front paws, melting into a self-satisfied sleep.

The pup could easily slip into such a relaxed state, but I, despite being a virtual prisoner in my own chamber, couldna' wallow in inactivity. On this paper then, I would recount what put me in this predicament, and then create and devise a plan for how to escape from it.

My father has learned everything. There are no secrets any more. My love for Donal, our hope to be together, our need to escape from here—yes, everything has come to light. And under the brightness of his scrutiny, my world has diminished to the confines of these four walls. I'm not to leave the castle without a guard to accompany me. I'm not to be trusted. Indeed, my father knows me too well, for if I had my freedom, the first person I'd run to would be the forbidden one. But, oh, how close Donal and I once were to leaving all of this resistance behind!

Perhaps that paper my father was brandishing in front of me was about our departure. Maybe it contained details about when and how we would leave. Or perhaps it was yet another love poem addressed to me, one that featured the unlikely pairing of a simple farmer to a laird's daughter. Well, whatever was written on that paper does not matter now, for its contents are forever hidden from me. I must refrain from spending too much time in conjecture.

I may be restricted to this room, but I can wander in my mind wherever I choose, and I choose to see myself and my love far from here on the hills of Knockfarrel in a small cottage of our own, surrounded by those fields of swaying heather. Our days are filled with tasks done side-by-side, where we learn more about one another with each passing hour—family, friends, hopes, beliefs, dreams—these conversations enliven the most tedious of chores. Shoeing horses or milking cows or plowing fields provide the background music to the lyrics written upon our souls.

And in the evenings, as we lie together, we continue to explore the mysteries of our bodies and revel in unlocking those secrets, one by one. As I sit here, quill in hand, I try to capture with words the thrill beneath my skin when he brushes against me or places his hands tenderly upon me. How does one write that? What expressions can describe the rush that I feel when he presses his body against mine? Is it ever possible to explain how I long for him to fill me with his essence? And are there any ways to convey the hollowness I feel inside when we are apart?

Emotions canna be compressed into sentences and paragraphs; passion resists such neat and ordered packaging. It flourishes only in the expansiveness of the soul, yet here I am trying to limit and restrict it to fit onto a piece of paper. Foolish lass am I…

Shaking myself from these visions of ecstasy, I am grounded once again when I recall my father's parting words: "Our journey to Northumberland at Martinmas has been cancelled." He certainly was not delaying the trip as a means of punishing me, for he already knew my heart felt nothing for that match. If anything, he should have hastened our travel southward if he really wanted to see me suffer.

No, this pronouncement dropped me into even greater despair because it could only mean that he was renewing my contract to a former suitor, and that man was George Campbell. If my father wished to inflict upon me the most severe punishment, he has chosen the best form. For I might have been able to eke out survival had I been transplanted to a new country and set up amongst foreigners—the distance perhaps helping to dull the pangs of my heart—but to reestablish my betrothal to Campbell was to silence that heart forever. And if that was his master plan for me, then I write this pledge upon this paper: Death shall be my only bridegroom.

Just as I finished writing that final word, Thor's ears pricked up, and I heard a light but insistent tapping upon my door. Scrambling to put away my papers, I called out, "One moment, aye?" and stowed the chest beneath my bed. I barely lifted the latch on the door when Annag burst in, wide-eyed and disheveled, strands of hair falling from her bun and her hands shaking.

"Mary, O, Mary. I've just spoken to Hamlin. It was Campbell who wrested yer note from him, and while Hamlin did not ken what it said, I overheard the conversation between yer Da' and that awful man." Annag reached out to grab both of my hands and led me over to the bed where we sat down next to one another. I waited for her to continue.

Placing her palm against her chest as if to steady her breath, Annag explained, "The note was from Donal; it was delivered to Hamlin by one of Donal's friends, I suppose. Judging from what I overheard, it was telling ye to meet him tomorrow evening. Where, I dunno. But yer father commissioned George to bring a full complement of guards to go to that place and to capture him. Do ye see? Donal will be waiting and looking for ye and instead they'll seize and arrest him." Annag took in gulps of air, having told her story without pause or break.

Puzzled by my father's decision to deploy such an inequitable display of force, I wondered aloud, "Just for loving me? There's no crime against that now, is there? My father's own political designs may compel him to reject Donal as a future husband for me, but surely that does not mean he can imprison him just for loving the wrong girl?"

"Och, no, Mary. Ye didna' ken, nor did I, but Donal and his gang are reivers! They're the ones everyone's been searching for since the McKinty raid. Yer father and George said it. It's not just his love for ye that's calling forth all these guards, it's that he's a plunderer. Just yesterday, he lifted one-hundred and fifty head from George himself!" Annag's eyes flashed with delight when she revealed Campbell had been duped.

I digested this new information with immediacy because my mind already leapt to what was most urgent. "We must warn him." I stared at my door remembering my imprisonment. "I must find him."

Before I could fully stand up from the bed, Annag grabbed my hand again to set me back down. "Ye canna, Mary. Ye're being guarded, and even if ye do sneak out, someone'll be sure to follow ye, and ye'd wind up leading them directly to yer man. No. Hamlin will go for ye. Where can he find Donal?"

A sense of futility washed over me as I realized that I had never met Donal on the grounds of his own home. We met in the forest, by the shoreline, at the gathering, but never where he actually lived. "Och, Annag! I dunno where to find him because I've never seen his dwelling." I placed my fingertips on my forehead, massaging the thoughts inside as if trying to conjure up an alternate solution.

"Dinna fash, Mary. We'll figure out something." Annag gently patted my leg, attempting to console me with these empty words of promise. Both she and I sat in silence for a few moments till she bubbled with an idea. "Wait. What about the messenger? Do ye ken Donal's friends? Hamlin said the fellow was small, thin, blondish hair, and kept dropping bible verses into his conversation."

"Owen!" I shouted. Joy over this viable option burst within me. "It was Owen. I met him at the Harvest Festival. He's the son of the Lewiston preacher. When he introduced himself to me, he told me I was worth more than rubies, and Donal said that came from something in the bible!"

Clasping both hands together in triumph, Annag announced, "Hamlin will find him and tell him. And this Owen fellow will warn yer Donal not to go tomorrow night."

The plan was far from foolproof, and I dreaded to think of all the ways in which the message wouldna' get to Donal in time. With a level of intensity I had not realized I had possessed, I gripped Annag's shoulders firmly with my hands. "Hamlin must not fail, Annag. Donal canna be caught. If they find him, they'll hang him…" I stopped myself from finishing the rest of the sentence out loud. Remembering the vow I had written on the paper just moments before, I almost said, "…and if they do, it'll be a death sentence for us both."

Donal – In Abeyance

Patience may be a virtue, but it's certainly not one of mine. Even when I was a boy, I found it verra hard to wait for anything. How often did I scorch my mouth on a steaming bannock because I didna' have the patience to wait for it to cool. As I grew older and situations became more complex, I still didna' master the necessary discipline to remain composed till desire came to fruition. Impulsive, headstrong, spontaneous—these words best describe the kind of person I am. I suppose I'm just not good at sitting around, and yet this is what I am forced to do for the time being.

It was a fine stroke of luck that the blacksmith found Owen and told him how George intercepted my message for Mary. Well, that part—the fact that George discovered it in the first place—was not so lucky of course, but thanks to good fortune, Owen was able to get that information to me. By the time he came upon me in the field, it was well past midnight, and I was in a sleep so deep I had to crawl out from its velvety layers in order to fully grasp the meaning of his warning.

Owen's sincere disappointment in himself affected me deeply; he blamed himself for putting me in harm's way. It took a great deal of talking on my part to convince the man that I harbored no ill will toward him for this strange twist of fate. In fact, I owed my life to both him and that Hamlin fellow. Imagine falling into the hands of George Campbell under those conditions? How inglorious. I'd have died of shame right then and there, long before any executioner's rope tightened round my throat.

Needing time to secure a few belongings from home and to travel to this safe hideaway, I was relieved from my duty of watching over the flock. Owen took my shift, and this morning he and the other boys drove the animals to market without me. After splitting the profits equally, Ross will ride here tomorrow to bring me my portion. Only my men are privy to the location of my new dwelling, the place where I will be putting my patience—or lack thereof—to the test.

If one were to come upon the area, ye'd give it no further thought, for 'tis yer typical open moor, lightly dusted with snow and assorted piles of rocks that edge the stream which runs from the top of the hill and bubbles downward. The boulders grow bigger as ye climb higher and higher, and as ye near the top of the ridge, three enormous rocks come together like an ill-fitting puzzle of sorts. But again, the configuration itself would give ye no cause for further investigation. If ye did continue to explore, ye'd find a very narrow opening that leads into the cave I now call home.

Once inside, toward the right, ye'd hear the sound of the trickling stream running over the pebbles and granite as it makes its way downward to where it expands to the size of the burn that travels down the rest of the hill. To the left, ye'd see the few possessions I'd brought with me—a blanket roll with my bedding, flint and steel for making a fire, some dry oats along with a spoon and cup, my harp, and my writing. I spent the afternoon hours busy gathering tree branches and heather that I'd later flatten and smooth out to serve as a mattress to go beneath my blanket, and as I walked about, I could feel the weight of the sporran at my waist, heavy with coins. It made me smile to think 'twould be even more bulky tomorrow after Ross's visit.

'Tis true, my accommodations were stony and damp, but it provided me with a fine vantage point from which to view any unwanted guests. But tonight I sit in silence before my tri-turreted castle, gazing above at the luminous full moon. So often in the past I had felt comforted by the soft glow that kept the shadows of night at bay, but this evening it offered me no solace.

Its cold, impersonal light exposed the folly of my life. For tonight's moon was to illuminate the journey I was to take with Mary, a journey that was halted before it could even begin, a journey, perhaps, that would never be undertaken because a lady does not risk everything to run away with a commoner. And so, it mocks me, this moon does, by forcing me to take stock of who and what I truly am—a vagabond and outlaw who, for a brief moment, had the audacity to think he could capture the rays of the sun. Instead, this silvery, frosty shine rests upon the tiny crevice in the rocks that I must later crawl into and hide— the pathetic truth of what my life has come to.

I tell myself that I canna continue to dwell upon such ominous thoughts unless I wish to perpetuate them further and lose all sense of fight. Shaking this grim foreboding, I creep through the aperture, reach for my harp, and return to that same spot upon the hillside. Sitting upon the damp ground, I tuck my plaid more tightly around my legs and place the instrument against my left shoulder, letting my left hand strum the upper strings and my right the lower.

As I pull a string with one finger, I use another to stop the vibration so that the sound is crystal and pure. I play in defiance of the moon and any other elements that stand against me. I play to bring myself back to my center, my core of strength and determination. I play to remind myself of the bravery of all those who've gone before me, who didna' give in or surrender when the odds were set against them. I play on the verra instrument that only a few years ago had been banned and destroyed by the capricious whim of an unjust ruler. Yes, I am an outlaw, an outlaw playing the forbidden *clarsach*. Yet here we are, both of us, alive and well, despite the wishes of those who want to silence us to the grave.

A haunting melody lifts and wafts away from my fingertips like a burnt offering to the heavens where resides that indifferent orb which casts its detached luminescence upon us all. And I smile contentedly when I realize that beneath that same cold-hearted moon stands a frustrated George Campbell, who, with his legion of guards, continues to wait empty-handed by the twisted trees near Loch Ness for a visitor who will never come.

***

The days passed slowly. It was easy to satisfy my physical needs for there was lots of fresh water nearby, the weather wasna' too harsh, and plenty of game roamed the region. When those demands were readily met, I spent my solitary hours writing and playing music. I tried to settle into a kind of rhythm with this new existence of mine, and before long, a schedule started to form that involved even the visitation of friends. A few days ago, Ross came by to fill me in on the details of the exchange at the market, and it was a lucrative endeavor, no doubt. He placed into my hands a handsome profit that, with my current savings, would go far toward establishing my new home with Mary.

Brodie visited nearly every evening, arriving before dusk and remaining long after dark. He supplied me with both the latest news and the finest whiskey. It was from Brodie that I learned of George's vexation at the failure of his ambush and of his relentless commitment to discover who leaked the information of the arrest. According to reports, George's primary target of suspicion was Robby, but Campbell couldna' lay a hand on the laird's favorite son without jeopardizing his own flimsy grasp on McElroy's approval. Besides, he had no proof that Robby was ever in contact with me, his only piece of evidence the fact that the boy's sister was preparing to elope with a rogue such as myself.

On one of the more dreary nights when the rain slapped against the roof of boulder above us, Brodie told me of his mother's passing. There was no sadness in it though, and he recollected her final hours to me with a detachment that suggested serenity and acceptance, far different from our conversation months ago when he agonized over her departure from this world. Sitting there with him as we talked about life and mortality, I found myself intrigued by the concept of time, and after he rode away that night, I thought long and hard about how we measure a lifetime.

From birth to childhood to maturity to old age and death, it's the same cyclical journey. But what if there were something more enduring, something that shattered the idea that we passed these milestones only once? What if there were a way to transcend the progression so that we could live on and do it again and again? Religion, of course, suggests this to us as our souls ascend to heaven and thereafter reside in the company of the angels, thus breaking the cycle, but what if there were a chance that human spirits—not celestial ones—could conquer death because their love superseded the limitations of mortality?

I felt inadequate trying to put these questions into words and phrases, especially when many of them were based solely on feelings and emotions rather than logic and reason, but I puzzled them out nonetheless and continued to wonder.

In a peculiar way, contemplating ideas such as these brought me a certain kind of contentment. I wouldna' call what I found "patience" exactly, but more like a kind of permission that whatever the future held in store for Mary and me would be agreeable. I arrived at this acceptance once I truly came to believe that my love for her and hers for me would never die. Do what they will to either one of us—hang me on the gallows, marry her away to another, force us to live apart—it does not matter, for there is one thing that they'll never touch, and 'tis the only thing that endures. Love.

Bide and wait; that is our command.
So we follow a set course and stay true.
But if the time should come
When our chance has slipped away
Do not grieve and think we are through.

For ye'll feel me each day, in the wind on yer face.
And ye'll hear me in the rumble of a storm.
And when ye think ye're all alone
In the forests of the night
Let the memory of me bring you warmth.

Time will come with notice or without
To steal away the life we've been given
But a love that is as true
As the one we have shared
Will free us both from this mortal prison.

Aside from Ross and Brodie, Owen too made the trek up the ridge providing much-needed diversion in the late afternoons by regaling me with more stories about his students and their lively discussions. They had finished Vergil and were now on to Aurelius, and I found myself entertained by Owen's smooth transition from self-righteous preacher in the pulpit to engaging instructor in the schoolroom—both manifestations witty, knowledgeable, and enthusiastic.

One afternoon, he went into greater detail about the lesson they had covered on Aurelius' *Meditations*. "There's a section, ye ken, at the end of Book 10 where Aurelius tells himself, 'Remember that this which pulls the strings is the thing which is hidden within.' When we translated that line in class and coupled it with Aurelius' recommendation to never include 'the vessel,' or what surrounds it when contemplating the self, we found ourselves in a powerful conversation about what is real and what is not.

"And I thought of ye, Donal, because Aurelius mentions how that vessel is as empty as a weaver's shuttle, a driver's whip, or a writer's pen. So, if the pen *is* empty, as he says, then what is it exactly that fills it up when ye write? Where does it all come from? Those ideas and rhymes and such? It canna just come from other books ye've read, aye? There must be something pulsing deep within ye, no?"

This question, so simple on the surface, led us into an intense consideration of the power that resides within us all—whether we're creating pieces of art on a canvas or maneuvering over treacherous ground on a raid or facing an enemy on a battlefield. Sometimes it has naught to do with outside details and external happenings but rather with listening and trusting that little voice inside of ye that lights yer way. That's what great men do; they hearken to that voice inside of themselves, the spark ignites the fire of truth. And once they step in the direction of that light, they never find themselves in darkness again.

'Tis funny, but I'm sure that conversations like these, the kind I have with Brodie and Ross and Owen, would astonish the more 'educated' noblemen who preside over kingdoms. While they scoff at our backgrounds and are quick to label us as barbaric Highlanders, we ourselves believed differently. For though we may not have university degrees or status associated with the well-to-do, I'd match our wits and wisdom against any of those pretentious lords who frequent the palaces of London, the salons of Paris, or the courts of Rome.

Beyond such philosophical considerations were topics more personal and immediate, like those pertaining to developments at Undlay. Wisely, Owen had fostered a friendship with Hamlin, securing a way of getting information about Mary for me. Although Mary herself was being held under strict surveillance, Hamlin could get word to her and find out details about her by way of his betrothed, a girl named Annag.

Owen told me what he had recently learned. "Mary was frantic with worry over the thought that ye'd stumble into George's trap if Hamlin couldna' get the warning to ye in time, but once she heard of the bungling of George's ambush, she was relieved and overjoyed. The McElroys postponed their trip to Northumberland, so at least she's not being wedded off to some British fop below the border, at least for now."

He did continue to say that she longed for a kind word from me, and upon hearing that, I gave him my most recent verses to be delivered to her. Although I wanted nothing more than to head north with Mary immediately, I was aware that it'd be impossible to liberate her from Undlay at this time. In a few weeks, when the night hours stretched longer than the daylight, I'd be able to devise a way—with Hamlin's help—of using the darkness to our advantage. And so, one afternoon after Owen went back to Lewiston with a promise to return in two days' time and before Brodie arrived with his news and liquor, I started configuring another method of escape.

Sitting in front of my rocky enclosure, I was momentarily distracted by the red stag who was foraging amongst the dwarf-shrubs of heather and bilberry. Wearing his three-branched antlers like a majestic crown, he seemed accustomed to ruling over this territory and must've been surprised that someone had infiltrated his realm. *Dinna fash,* I wanted to tell him as he scrutinized me with his enormous brown eyes. *I'm not biding here long.* And in order to convey this idea, I stopped paying him any mind and returned to planning, allowing him to resume his grazing.

To that end, I reviewed how I had already taken steps forward by asking Owen to find out from Hamlin exactly where Mary's chamber was located and how many guards she would need to elude in order to exit the castle. Later tonight I'd ask Brodie about Cerwyn's condition—he'd been caring for all my livestock—and let him ken when to bring my mount to me. I hoped that by the end of the month I could put the plan into action, and then…

I looked up at that moment and, instead of seeing only the animal in the foreground, I beheld a solitary female figure slowly climbing up the hill. Her sense of urgency implied that she was not simply out and about for an amble in the countryside. And like the stag who then galloped away into the brush, I too couldna' take any chances, so I bolted through the opening of the cave and leaned my body against the side of the stone, craning my head round to observe her movements.

Much as I hated to think of harming a young lady, I had a pistol at the ready to warn her away. She walked with such purposeful manner that there was no question in my mind she was equipped with the knowledge that someone did, in fact, reside in this cave.

As she came nearer, she seemed more hesitant, more fearful. With a trembling voice, she called out, "Hallo? If ye're in there, sir, I've a message from milady for ye, a message from Miss Mary McElroy of Undlay." She kept looking back over her shoulder toward the way she had come, signalling to me how she hoped to be retracing those steps as soon as possible.

Pistol still in hand, I stretched my arm into the opening so that she could see the gun's silver shape and form. Sounding as menacing as possible, I shouted, "Leave it on the ground right where ye stand, and be on yer way."

Without taking her eyes off the weapon, she bent to the ground and placed the letter on the flat stone at her feet. Backing up several paces with her eyes still fixed straight ahead, she stumbled and lost her footing once or twice in retreat. After she'd moved far enough away, she spun round and sprinted downhill till all that remained of her was a small dot on the lower knoll.

Hooking the pistol into my belt, I walked toward the paper that seemed to come alive, pulsing with a hope that sprung directly from my heart. Unable to restrain my excitement, I ripped open the seal and read:

My Love,

Ross told me how to find ye so that I could get this message to ye. Our time has come.

Ross's sister Nora is here at Undlay creating a portrait of my mother. I've been granted permission to see Nora home tomorrow night as ye ken she canna ride a horse alone nae more.

Meet me at the Gregor's. I'll be waiting for ye there…

And just like that, after days of stagnancy, life began to stir once again. Questions of mortality, deliberations on time, discussions regarding the transcendent within—such examinations do enrich our existence, but sometimes, as Aurelius pointed out, it is a precious privilege to simply be alive, "to breathe, to think, to enjoy, and to love." And for Mary and me, in just one day's time that precious privilege would be ours once again.

Machinations

All night long, George had waited and waited for a felon who never came. Growing more irascible and indignant with each passing hour, he began to think he had been purposely misled in order to be played for a fool. He considered that the letter had been a contrivance, meant only to lead him on this bootless quest and to diminish his standing with Teague McElroy. Once again, his bold declarations had proven to be as insubstantial as words upon the wind.

But when George recalled Hamlin's resistance in surrendering the note and the secret way in which it had been passed, he ruled out his earlier idea that it was a setup and focused instead on figuring out who could have warned Donal about the impending arrest. When the skies began to lighten from sable to gray, George dismissed the men but commanded Angus Gregor to remain behind. Pacing back and forth, George tested the man's patience, speaking not a word and forcing him to sit there and wonder why he had not been permitted to return home like the others.

Beads of sweat dotted Angus' forehead, and his hands shook involuntarily. It had been a long night of waiting, and Angus yearned to grasp a bottle to bestill those quivering hands. When the craving overwhelmed him, he interrupted George's march, "Did ye need me for something more, sir? I was hoping to be on my way like the others, if it's all the same to ye." Angus waited a moment longer, then slapped his cap upon his leg to shake off the dew and placed it back upon his head as a sign of his wish to depart.

George stopped pacing. Turning back toward Angus, he then stomped directly toward the man, coming to a halt mere inches from his face. "Do I *need* something? Do I *need* something? Yes, I *need* something. I *need* ye to do a better job of watching the comings and goings of yer brother and his vile friends. That's what I *need*! Now go home and trail that brother of yers, and do not let him out of yer sight. Find out where Donn is hiding, and do not let me see yer pockmarked face and pickled body until ye do. Ye've got two days to get me what I *need,* and if ye canna fulfill my command, I'll call in every one of yer debts to me and seize all of the Gregor lands, and ye and yer brothers and sisters can live like gypsies in the woods for all I care! Now git on with it!"

George shoved Angus forcefully, and the feeble drunk fell backward onto the snowy ground. It took Angus some time get his feet properly situated, but after some twisting and contorting, he managed to stand upright and started walking slowly back to where his horse had been hidden with all the others. As he trudged away, he began to think: if he could ride home with any sort of speed, he might be able to catch Ross in time before his brother began his chores. And if he could do that, then he could follow Ross wherever his errands took him, but--he needed to secure some liquid company first. With that dose of courage in hand, Angus was sure he could trail his brother undetected. It was imperative, though, that he obtain his traveling companion sooner than later, so with that incentive dominating his thoughts, Angus rode home with wild abandon.

***

I shoulda' been a soldier at the courts of intrigue, Angus thought to himself, so proud of what he had accomplished in such a short period of time. He had arrived home just as his brother was saddling up to ride forth, and after they nodded to one another by the barn, Angus darted into the house to snatch two flasks of whiskey while Ross cantered away down the road. Following his brother at a calculated distance, Angus observed Ross and two other men bringing their lifted cattle to market and then watched his brother take an unusual path on return, one that did not lead to their home.

The course was uphill, but a good deal of the climb open to view, so Angus had to pull his horse off to the side and go on foot in order to witness what was happening above. At the crest, a second figure emerged, seemingly from the rocks themselves, and Angus spied the two men engaged in conversation.

If his eyes could be trusted, Angus was certain that man who'd sprung from the boulders was Donn himself. He saw Ross hand him a pouch, and then watched the two men shake hands and bid farewell. Angus had to move quickly to return to his horse and ride away before being noticed by Ross who had already begun his descent from the ridge.

Thoroughly pleased with himself, Angus broke into his second flask of whiskey, toasting his own ingenuity. He had conquered the first obstacle by locating the whereabouts of the wanted criminal. But Angus realized that Donn had the advantage of position and that, from above, the man could gun down or attack anyone who dared attempt to cross that open area to get to his cave. *No, we canna go after him here. We must lure him out. And I must use Mary McElroy to do it, for she would be the only prize worthy enough for Donn to risk his life and venture forth.* Another deep swig and the wheels of invention began to spin. Angus had a plan.

***

People are always being bought and sold. The price depends upon one's desperation. And of all of the servants at Undlay, Florrie was truly the most desperate. Her meager wages barely put food on the table for her, her five siblings, and her broken father who had been bedridden and unable to work for years. A mere child herself, Florrie walked the seven miles from her hovel to Undlay every morning and evening just to quell their pangs of hunger and was known to often scavenge for the scraps and bones left on plates at the McElroy table, snatching them before they were discarded into the trash or passed on to the dogs. When presented with the opportunity to earn a piece of silver just for delivering a letter to someone, she seized it without hesitation.

How easy it was to devise such a plan, Angus thought. This was the first time in many years that he was actually proud of something he had done. It was as if everything was destined to be this way, to fall into place in just the right manner so as to allow him to save his family from ruin and elevate his own name in the process.

Earlier that day when Angus had returned home, he was surprised to see Nora shuffling in and out of the house, loading up the cart with her art supplies and food provisions. As she limped in that uneven way of hers, concentrating on maintaining her balance while hoisting her belongings into place, Angus, without offering a helping hand, stood there watching. After a while, he asked, "What's all this?"

Putting the heavy bag down upon the ground, Nora caught her breath in order to respond. "When Ross comes back from his business later today, he's taking me and Sara to Inverness for a few days. I've been commissioned to paint the portrait of Gillian MacIntosh, wife of the chief of Clan Chattan. We'll be heading to Moy Castle by mid-day."

Placing her hands upon her hips and speaking like a disappointed mother to a wayward child, she added, "Do try not to gamble away any more of our land while we're gone, eh?" Bending to lift the final bundle of supplies, Nora grunted as she swung the bag over the side railing and into the cart. Once finished, she hobbled back into the house to await Ross's return.

Angus remained motionless, staring at the packed cart. He marveled in disbelief over his good fortune. For once, the stars in the heavens had aligned in his favor. The extended absence of his brother and sisters sealed it. He now knew exactly what he would write in the letter, and once that too was sealed, it was only a matter of time before Donn was captured, and he himself was free of his debt and duty to Campbell.

Though his tongue throbbed for another taste of liquor, he had to keep his wits about him in order to pen the message and send Florrie on her way. Then, he'd have cause for celebration.

Donal – Duty vs. Choice

Flakes of snow dusted my eyelashes, but I didna' brush them aside. They seemed a kind of benediction for the journey I was undertaking, so I blinked away the ones that hindered my sight and let the others remain as if they were the placement of holy hands upon my person. The whiteness of the landscape illuminated the night, casting everything in a kind of celestial glow. And with that light surrounding me, I rode toward the Gregor home where I could soon bask in the warmth of Mary's presence.

My few belongings were stored in saddle bags, and my purse was filled with the foundation for our dreams. Those final hours up in the cave were a true test of my fortitude as I fussed and fidgeted, each minute lengthening immeasurably as the day dragged on. At least I had Brodie's company last night to preoccupy my thoughts, and he told me of his courtship of Lorna now that his mind was liberated from grief. It amused me to think of him catering to the whims of a lover when he seemed so bold and domineering, not just in voice but in presence and opinion as well.

But I suppose that's what love does to a man—it allows him a glimpse into the softer side of himself that's mostly shielded and kept hidden from view. Love allows ye to open those closed doors where ye've tucked away yer dreams, yer fears, and yer weaknesses from everyone. And though it requires a great deal of bravery to permit yerself to be so vulnerable and exposed when ye're not sure yer listener even accepts ye, once ye take that leap and the feelings are reciprocated, ye wonder at yer own cowardice for having refused to venture into those hidden corridors ever before.

Yesterday, I confided in Brodie about this upcoming reunion with Mary and our plan to leave the glen. No doubt there was sadness on both sides this morning when it came to taking leave of one another, but I told him I couldna' remain here and be expected to carry on without her by my side. So, after delivering Cerwyn to me, he bid farewell with a robust embrace and a promise from me that I'd send word once Mary and I were settled. And after his departure, Time then decided to taunt me with its sluggish progression.

I'd been in the saddle for almost two hours and was now on the border of Ross's property. The snow had mixed with rain, glazing everything with a sheen of ice. Sure-footed Cerwyn paid it no mind, but I worried about how well Mary would be able to navigate the hills and valleys with these slippery conditions to consider. As long as we were able to ride as far as Beauly tonight, we could set up camp and then tackle the remaining portion of the journey with the morning light.

I felt desire building inside when I imagined an uninterrupted night with her in my arms; I envisioned what 'twould be like to wake and be filled with her fragrance. How intoxicating 'twould be to feel the strands of her silky hair delicately brushing against my shoulder and the softness of her body enveloped in my own. I could feel the wanting start to overwhelm me, so I suppressed these amorous thoughts and replaced them with concerns about the matters at hand.

The path that led to the house was strangely undisturbed; no hoof marks, no sign that anyone had ridden upon it. The layer of white upon the ground was still fresh and unmarked. Perhaps Nora and Mary had returned earlier in the day, before the snow had accumulated? Careful to remain in the shadows, I pulled Cerwyn off to the side and dismounted, keeping in view both the house in front of me and the barn on my right.

The setting was blanketed in silence with the exception of an occasional wind gust that made the iced tree branches twist and crackle. Nothing moved inside the house or around it, which meant that its occupants must all be asleep—except, of course, Mary who was waiting on me. I was assuming she was there, but was it possible that the weather had slowed them and that they had not yet come home? There was no sign of her horse about, but maybe that was part of her plan. Perhaps the horse was already sheltered in the barn so as to appear that she was intending to stay the night, as one would expect.

The wise thing to do would be to simply sneak over to the barn and have a look inside. After I thought of this and shifted my gaze from the house to the barn, my eyes alighted upon a red deer that stood in front of the enclosure as if he were a sentry positioned there to keep vigil. He looked straight back at me with unflinching stare as if he were trying to connect with me somehow.

His antlers were the same height and configuration of the stag I'd seen just yesterday, and I wondered if this could, in fact, be the same creature.

If 'twere, the animal would've traveled quite a distance—the same as I— to bring himself to this destination. Once he ken he had my attention, he turned to nuzzle the ground before the barn door, tapping his hoof against it a few times as if seeking entry. I watched this display but made no attempt to move from my place of hiding. After performing this action three times, the deer glanced back over his shoulder and looked fixedly at me.

Fer some unknown reason, I chose not to investigate the barn and instead considered sending a signal to alert Mary that I had arrived. Staying where I was, I cupped my hands round the edges of my lips and whistled a soft trill into the air, hoping it would carry toward her. My decision to do so and the sound I made caused the stag to jump and gallop away into the darkness, but not before looking back once more at me as if in disappointment. Other than hooves patting the snow, I heard no other sound in response, but I did see a flash of movement inside the house, and then a single candle was lit and placed into one of the windows. She knows I've come. Just a few moments more and we'll be in flight.

My eyes bore into the doorway, focusing my concentration on the moment it would open and Mary would rush through. I could hear a growing rumbling in my chest as my heart beat with intensifying speed at the thought of our embrace and subsequent escape. But from the barn came an even louder pounding that soon drowned out my internal one—the doors burst open and ten to twenty pairs of legs started crushing the ground beneath them, all of them sprinting toward me.

The door of the house then flew open as well, and more men spilled out to join in the hunt. I spun about quickly and fled, hoping to get to Cerwyn in time before they overran me, but in the distance, I saw that my horse had already been snatched by one brute who was currently whipping him into a trot, so forlorn was the animal to leave me behind.

With no chance of escaping on horseback, I had to rely on my own speed and knowledge of the terrain, so I turned rapidly into the brush to carve my way to freedom. Many of my pursuers slipped and fell on the uneven, icy ground, but a few dogged ones remained close. I turned back to survey my odds and saw that at least three were coming near, although there were sizeable gaps of space between the trio.

Darting behind a thick tree trunk, I awaited the first, and when he tried to pass, I jabbed the butt of my gun into the side of his head to lay him out cold. I ran some paces further ahead and awaited the next man. When he was nigh upon me, I thrust my fist into his belly, and then when he bent over, I propelled my knee under his chin with such force that his head seemed to snap almost right off his neck. After rushing ahead for a third time, I took out my dirk in anticipation of the arrival of the last fellow. Once he drew parallel to my hiding spot, I jumped out, grabbed hold of his legs, and flipped the man over.

With my knife raised and ready to strike his thigh to prevent his further pursuit of me, I began its downward motion but stopped when I heard my victim cry out, "No!" Whether it was the tenor of his voice or the youthful innocence underlying his plea, I cancelled my strike to look directly into the eyes of Mary's brother, Robby.

"Och, no. What do ye think ye're up to, ye darn fool? Did ye not have yer fill of chasing down outlaws after tangling with the Camerons? Ye should ken better than to arrest a fine gent like me when there are blackguards like George Campbell running amok. Now, go on, and turn yer weapon on the real leeches who suck the life out of these lands, and leave me to my vagabond ways that harm no one."

I lifted the boy from the ground by planting my two hands on either side of his coat and hoisting him upward. After I dusted him off a bit, I dashed headlong into the wild, leaving him standing there speechless. What I did not realize though was that Campbell had arranged for another group of men to seal off my escape because when I ran only a mile or so farther, I came upon a line of ten more men outfitted with pistols, every one of them pointed at me.

There, protected behind the blockade of his armed contingent, was George himself who called out, "Bind the bastard, hand and foot, and tether him to my horse. I told ye, Donn, a man need nothing more than the law to be on his side."

And as they coiled the rope around my body, I looked into the eyes of these men who performed their duty without any sense of allegiance to their leader, for many of them looked back at me with a sort of request for forgiveness, as if they were begging pardon for what they'd been forced to do. But there was one man standing stationary at the end of the line during all of this movement, a man who refused to raise his eyes at all. And I wondered to myself if Angus were busy staring downward to the hell his soul was bound, having just exchanged it for a symbolic thirty pieces of silver.

As one guard reluctantly secured my rope to the back of Campbell's horse, another had absented himself from my capture altogether. Instead, he went back to bind my horse to his own, and later, I was told, he brought the animal and my belongings to Brodie, a gesture of gratitude for preserving his life a second time. Let George say what he will about the law needing to be a man's only companion; his claim will prove all too true when he goes to his grave a lonely, despised wretch.

Enforcing written laws out of duty alone creates no sense of brotherhood amongst men. For I've learned that brotherhood goes beyond duty and obligation; it is an unwritten code based on love, respect, and sacrifice for one another. Often penned in bloodshed, brotherhood is the chapter in life's book that George Campbell never has, and never will, read.

Mary – Undercurrents

For days now, I've struggled to find peace. Like a sea vessel caught in a tempest, I'm battered on all sides: the past haunts me, the present confounds me, and the future crushes me.

I should've escaped with Donal when he first suggested the idea, for had I done so, we would've been far removed from the troubles that plague us now. Perhaps we'd have already chosen the little plot of land that was to become our home; maybe we'd have even begun preparations for the building of it. But instead, the distance between us is insurmountable and our shared dream but an illusion, as he runs frantically to elude capture, and I beat my wings against a locked cage.

When night falls, I lie awake, waiting for a sleep that willna' come. My eyes close, extending invitation, but I canna stay still long enough for it to visit. Regret, doubt, and fear I wrestle with every toss, flip, and turn, and when dawn breaks, I've been denied yet again the restorative power of repose. Each hour bleeds into the next, seeping trickles of pain and suffering till every day is soaked in sorrow.

It was during one of those evenings that I finally gave up and stopped pretending slumber was nigh. Extricating myself from my twisted blanket, I sat up in my bed and stared into the darkness. My sudden movement disturbed Thor who had been largely unaffected by my fitful behavior, but now, however, he too was awake—somewhat groggy but alert nonetheless.

I thought a bit of air might do me good. Realizing I couldna' actually leave the castle now or any time unattended, I wrapped the blanket tightly round my body and patted out softly from my room to the hallway where the windows therein faced Loch Ness. My friend trotted beside me as I walked along the corridor, my bare feet tingling from the touch of the cold stone. Once I reached the window, I leaned my elbows on the casement and drew in a series of long, deep breaths.

The pup curled up upon my toes, enveloping and warming them with his furry hide. Although it was still far from dawn, I could see the water bathed in the moonlight and gazed into its depths, wondering about the mysteries that lay beneath its veneer. The surface of the loch churned with a fury powered by the wind and freezing rain. Whitecaps battled one another for dominance, swirling in confusion over their lack of control. The scene was in turmoil much like myself.

But there's always so much more to something than just its external appearance. Not just with water but with people and circumstances as well. I thought to myself how my father had judged Donal solely because of his low rank, never really giving him the chance to prove his honor or the nobility that resided within him. My Da's eyes were trained to see only in terms of status and politics and wealth; they were blind to all else. So he would forever set his course with superficial checkpoints in mind, never realizing those outward manifestations were short-lived and ever-changing.

As I continued to study the watery expanse, I marveled at the strength and power of the current below that drove everything above. And what was it that drove Donal to be the thief everyone was calling him to be? The outlaw they now hunted? The label itself was an odious one. Surely there must be some underlying reason or force that compelled him to engage in such wrongdoing? There was too much goodness, too much tenderness in him for me to think otherwise.

As the wind shifted, icy raindrops slashed against my cheeks, but I did not pull away from the view. It was only when Thor lifted his head and began to whimper softly that my meditation was broken. The pup scrambled to his feet and then started wagging his tail vigorously in anticipation of someone or something. Shortly thereafter, I discovered why.

Trudging down the hallway came Robby, weary and deep in thought. As Thor ran down the narrow corridor to greet him, I offered, without prompting, my reason for being here. "I couldna' sleep."

Robby's appearance at this hour seemed odd. "What're ye doing home so early? Did ye not have the overnight watch?" I tucked the blanket around me more snugly while I watched Robby bend down to stroke Thor's coat in welcome.

"No, no need for that tonight. 'Tis done. The men've made an arrest, so our work is over for the time being. Probably will not see any more reiving in this glen for quite some time, I'd wager." And as he stood to walk away toward his chamber, I clutched his arm when he tried to pass.

"An arrest?" I asked in desperation. "Was it Donal?"

He looked searchingly into my eyes before answering, and then dropping his own toward the ground, he uttered the single word, "Aye."

My mouth immediately went dry; I had nothing to swallow back the anguish that ruptured inside me. My hands trembled uncontrollably, and my breath turned shallow and rapid. "No! Robby, tell me no. Tell me it's not him!" I heard my words come out in choppy gasps as I begged and pleaded with him to rewrite the truth.

"I'm verra sorry, Mary. Campbell set up a false meeting between the two of ye and had the men ambush Donal there. They seized him and brought him here to the dungeon. He's still alive for now, but I dunno for how much longer." Robby tried to deliver this information with gentleness and compassion, but the import of his words drove a dagger deep into my chest. An awkward silence lingered between us till I impulsively grabbed his coat with my hands.

"Ye must help me. I must speak with him," I was near frantic now and feared my voice would soon become unintelligible with keening. "Brother, please. Bring me down there. Let me talk to him. Just a few words. Please. I must see him. You must help me!"

"Mary, ye ken I canna do that. There'll be a guard already stationed there. And what am I to do with him? Besides, the man's not good enough fer ye, Mary. Father will be outraged at ye and me both if I do anything to put ye in that man's company yet again." He tried to break free of my grasp, but I clung to him as if I were dangling from a ledge, the intensity of my grip marking the difference between life and death.

"No, please, Robby. Ye do not understand. 'Twill not be yer fault. It'll be mine. Just take me to him. I do not need much. I just want to see him once more. Please." I choked out those last words when I felt the finality of their meaning. I started to believe I had succeeded in getiing Robby to at least consider my request once he began to shake his head from side to side as if yielding. I had to press further.

"Just tell the guard ye're to relieve him till morn, and I promise I'll not stay beyond a few moments. As long as ye do not mind serving as sentry during those remaining hours, then there's really nothing else ye must do. And I'll never ask anything more of ye, brother, and I promise I'll do anything for ye in the future, anything! I'll not forget what ye've done for me. Ever."

Robby pursed his lips and took a moment before answering. "Hmmmph. I suppose I can sleep there as well as I can sleep in my own chamber up here, but I mean it, Mary, ye're asking much of me to defy father's edict. That's not a betrayal I take lightly. Still, I suppose I wouldna' even be here—having this conversation with ye—if ye hadn't wrenched me away from Death's embrace and nursed me back to health."

After a slight pause, Robby added, "And I suppose I wouldna' had any need for healing had Donal not saved me from Cameron in the first place. And, if the truth be known, the man did much the same for me again earlier tonight." Stroking his chin with his index finger and thumb, he considered their chances. "A few minutes of conversation shouldna' be too hard to arrange. Come, I'll take ye to him."

***

Squatting in the alcove, I cuddled Thor close to my body as the two of us sat together in silence, listening to the verbal exchange taking place at the bottom of the staircase. We were tucked into a small niche off the landing, waiting for the guard to pass us once he was relieved of his duties by Robby. When I heard plodding footsteps drawing closer, I tightened my hold on the dog, hoping to seal off anything that might stimulate his curiosity. The man trudged by, but still, we did not venture out from our hiding place. I murmured faint words of reassurance to the pup, but I suppose they were meant mostly for me as I tried to steel myself against what lay ahead. When the quiet was broken by more footsteps and the jangling of keys, I realized the time had come for us to move.

Once I stepped out from the alcove to reveal myself, Robby walked briskly toward me and whispered, "He's there. Do not take too long. Just say what ye've come to say, and be done with it. I'll remain here to give ye some privacy, but when ye hear me heading back down, then ye must be gone." I nodded my head in assent, and after I turned to go, I stopped, returned to Robby, and engulfed him in a brief hug. Then the dog and I scampered down the narrow, grimy steps of stone.

Descending into this foul-smelling pit was made more bearable only because of the promise of what I'd find at the bottom. With the storm brewing outside, the ground was especially wet with sea water that had oozed up from below the floor. One inhalation through my nose reminded me to breathe only through my mouth in order to avoid ingesting the stench of waste and decay. Pushing all of these vexations aside, I bounded with haste toward my beloved.

The earthen floor was thick with slime as I came to a halt in front of the lattice iron door. Through the open spaces dangled Donal's arms, and I reached out for them, caressing them to my face. With a deep sigh, Donal whispered, "Mary, *mo chridhe*." His calloused hands stroked my hair as he continued, "I hate for ye to see me this way." He shook his head in disgust. "Ye must understand I'm not what they're calling me. I'm not an evil villain, a rogue perhaps, but not a baseless criminal. Please believe me." He cradled my head while he looked with intensity into my eyes.

I was startled and fell back a half-step when I beheld the full view of his countenance. His boyish features were battered and distorted by swelling. Dried blood had crusted upon his face like splattered mud on a traveler's boots, and my shoulders drooped with pity at the sight. "Och, Donal, who did this to ye?" I reached my hands higher through the bars toward his face, but he pulled away from my touch.

"The only pain I feel derives from the agony I've caused ye by being the kind of man who's brought shame to ye. But ye must ken, I'm not a common swindler. I've done what I've done only on behalf of those who couldna' defend themselves. Reiving was the only way to settle scores against the privileged but depraved men who cheat the good people of our land. That's been the sole reason for my raids, and I've always distributed the plunder among those who endured the greatest hardship under tyrants like Cunningham, MacKinty, and Campbell."

He reached toward my shoulders, lifting them up from defeat. "But these wounds? They mean nothing to me. I do not even feel them." His attempt at a smile here brought no comfort, only despair. That once handsome and inviting grin of his was now twisted and deformed as it struggled to spread across the mounds and gashes upon his face. "No, 'tis no harm done," he said trying to make me feel better. Grabbing both of my hands and clasping them to his own, he said tenderly, "What hurts me most is knowing I'm the one responsible for the heaviness in yer heart that comes from seeing me locked away in this filthy prison."

He released my hands and put his head down in dejection, but since his arms remained extended through the gaps, I stepped closer to the bars, and pressed my body against the raw iron. He did the same, and we joined in a fierce embrace despite the immoveable barrier between us.

Cupping my face in his hands, he licked his swollen, bruised lips and began to speak. "Mary," he drew out the sound of each letter just as he had done when we first met. "Ye must carry on without me now. My time has come, but there's so much of life yet for ye to live. 'Twould give me a measure of peace if I were certain that ye'd not waste yer remaining years grieving over the memory of a dead man, a man who canna give ye the pleasures of the world such as the kind we've savored in our brief days together."

I began to shudder with sobs. I didna' and couldna' conceive of a life without him—an endless stretch of days and months and years that held no promise of joy, no flutter of excitement, only infinite emptiness—perpetual and unchanging. The soft whimpering of two voices filled the air as the little puppy at my feet echoed my anguish.

Donal lifted my downcast face, and tracing my lips with a single finger, he whispered tenderly, "I'll never be far from ye, lass. When ye feel the slight brush of the wind against these lips, ye'll ken that I'm sending ye my kisses. When ye taste the juice of the rowan berry that ye've plucked from an autumn branch, ye'll ken that I'm filling ye with the sweetness of my love. And when ye see the white flakes of snow dancing upon the air, ye'll ken the joy that ye infused into my spirit whilst I was with ye. Ye can treasure these visitations and moments, but ye must continue to live on. I've enough shame to take with me to my grave; I couldna' bear the guilt of stealing away yer chance at happiness as well."

He then took his thumb and swept it across one cheek and then the other to erase my falling tears. "I'll be waiting for ye on the other side, my hand outstretched, till ye reach for me when yer earthly time is done. Then our clasp shall never be broken again." He bent his head toward mine, and we touched there in a way that made me feel as if he were sealing our eternal bond by relinquishing our one in the present.

But I didna' want to share his vision of what was to come, so I broke the connection and thrust my hands through the bars to grab hold of his broad shoulders. Trying to shake sense into him, I declared, "How can ye ever expect me to 'carry on' as ye say? Not after I've been with ye, walked with ye, laughed with ye, made love with ye! I canna fill the years ahead with living if ye're not here to fill them with me. Do you not understand?"

Distraught over the impossibility of his request, I shifted my grip from his shoulders to clasp either side of his jawline. "Do not console me with the visitations of a phantom when I want the living, breathing man beside me. Can ye not see? I've had but a taste, but now I must drink full. Skin upon skin, caresses, kisses, desire, rapture—the world canna be so cruel as to give me a glimpse of those things and then wrench them all away! And if life is so brutal as to steal ye away from me, then my sole wish is to cross to the other side with ye *now* if that is where ye're bound."

He seemed shocked by my suggestion, but I was not. Wasting no time in deliberating over whether it was right or wrong, I spoke only of what resided in my soul. Emboldened by what I felt was true, I announced, "No. 'Twill not end this way. No! I'll not let it. We have a home to build and a family to grow. We have years ahead of us that will be filled with song and laughter and love."

His expression slowly changed from resignation to interest, so I persisted. "We have sunsets to watch and walks to take and friends to see and children to raise. Donal, do not give up hope. Do not let what ye see here, right now, color yer vision of the future. While there's still breath to be drawn, believe with me that the sun will come peeking through the window of our cottage, surrounding us with its golden embrace. It can all still be ours; it must be. I have a plan…" My mind was racing with the thrill of possibility for I realized what I needed to do, and I understood that it must be done right away.

Bringing his head closer to my own, I placed my lips upon his and willed my faith would restore his. The sound of a footfall upon the stair compelled me to momentarily break our physical bond, but I returned once more to drink deep of him before breaking our clasp and saying, "Tomorrow night." Holding my hand up to his, I let my fingertips linger a few seconds more until they were forced to flutter apart and separate. In defiance of that separation, I boldly promised, "I'll come to ye."

***

By the clock, 'twas day, but ye'd never guess it to be so. The slate gray sky was mirrored in the surface color of the water, making me feel as if I were swaddled in a cloak made of heavy, dusky wool. The clouds pushed down with leaden oppression, while the churning and swirling loch reached up toward those clouds in rebellious fury. And I was caught between these two battling forces who were doing their best to render me meaningless.

Liberation had been granted me on account of Donal's arrest. With him securely confined to the dungeon, I was no longer considered at risk, so my family—most notably, my father—returned to their accustomed manner of essentially ignoring my comings and goings.

Under normal circumstances, 'twould have been verra foolish of me to venture away from the castle at the height of a storm such as this, but the current circumstances were far from normal. Donal and I had one last chance to mount an escape, and if we didna' seize that chance tonight, it wouldna' present itself ever again. His next trip would be to the gallows and mine to hell—if I dared fulfill the oath I had sworn.

The wind whipped round me, howling so loud that I cinched my headscarf tighter to my skull to shut out the sound. Trying to make my descent from the rocky crest, I stepped gingerly down the steep incline already flooded with water that had overrun the banks. With enough power to defy the laws of nature, the sea rushed upward, climbing the hills in a mixture of spray, froth, and mud.

At times, I had to sidestep and move laterally just to avoid the surges that reached toward me like the outstretched arms of a wicked sea monster trying to haul me down to its murky lair. While wind and rain competed for dominance over me, the barely discernible hut in the distance became the tiny point of refuge I clung to in my quest to keep moving onward. As I drew closer, I noticed how it too was at the mercy of the elements, and unlike the last time I had visited here, there were no woodland creatures huddling beside it in fellowship. Like me—small and frail on the outside but willful and determined within—the house fought on, asserting its presence and jeering at the powers that were conspiring to destroy it.

I reached the door, and with the noise of the storm so deafening, I didna' trust that my knock would be heard, so I pounded on the portal and shouted, "Hallo? It's Mary McElroy. Please let me in." The speed with which the door opened indicated to me that Hilda was somehow already apprised of my arrival.

"Och, my child," she said in seeming surprise, "come in from out there. What possesses ye to be roaming the countryside in a gale such as this?" She took me by the arm, drawing me over toward the stool by the fire. "Here, come, take off yer cloak and give it to me."

I did so, and she laid it out before the hearth to dry. Placing a kettle over the flames, she continued, "I'll brew up a fine cup of tea to take the chill from yer bones." She didna' ask me any further questions but instead just quietly went about the business of preparing the tea.

I wasna' sure if I should jump right in and make my request of her or wait, but the coziness of the cottage and the serenity contained within made my decision for me, and I chose to be comfortable with the silence between us. Despite the quiet in the room, the rain continued to pound against the shelter, and the wind shrieked in frustration as it circled round the house, but neither could penetrate the inner tranquility of the dwelling.

Handing me my cup, she brought hers over and placed it upon the small table that stood next to her chair and slowly lowered herself down to sit. Before she could reach for her drink, a gray rabbit hopped up to occupy the empty space upon her lap and began nuzzling and sniffing Hilda's fingers in hopes of dislodging a leftover morsel of food.

Of all the things I could've said, I started the conversation with a comment that had nothing to do with my visit this day. "Where's Gunnar?"

The question hung suspended in the air for a few moments before she responded, "Here. There. All around." She gestured with her filmy eyes in each direction as she spoke. Reaching for her cup, she took a sip and swallowed. Only after letting the taste linger for a bit did she elaborate. "There's many other worlds beyond this one, ye ken."

I pondered her meaning as I held my cup with both hands and stared deeply into the liquid within. I recalled how I'd heard tales of wise women reading the leaves at the bottom of such cups, presaging events of this world and maybe of the next. Was that what Hilda was working toward, I wondered?

She dislodged the animal, gently placing him upon the floor, and then walked slowly toward the cupboard where she took out a collection of plants and herbs and brought them to her table. Laying them upon the flat surface, she began grinding them with a pestle. "'Tis the way of this world to come and go. But…ye never really do go away, ye see? Ye just manifest in other ways. That's why I do not fear death, nor should ye. Can ye hand me that bottle behind ye, my dear?"

I looked over my shoulder in the direction she pointed and stood to retrieve the requested object. Handing it to her, I watched as she scooped together the remnants of the first plant and sprinkled them into the bottom of the bottle. She continued. "We're here to learn certain lessons, aye? And when our learning is done in this form, we can come back to learn other ones in another form…Or not. Ye see, we choose. We can stay as mist and spirit and float above the cares of this realm, or we can choose to feel it all again—the joys and the sorrows, the thrills and the boredom, the triumphs and the defeats."

She started mashing the next bunch of herbs, pressing them into smaller pieces. "And," she paused to look directly at me, "if the bonds ye forge in one lifetime are strong enough, ye can shatter the manacles of time to journey again with those same spirits. Yer forms'll be different, of course, but ye'll have a knowing, a knowing deep within ye when ye recognize the other."

She poured this set of contents into the container and repeated the process one more time. "Somehow it springs forth—like the birdsfoot trefoil that bursts from between the rock, sending splashes of three-petalled yellow blossoms amidst the cold granite. 'Twill have its way. Soul recognition is like that. The knowledge ye feel of each other blossoms and 'tis a wonder to behold. It canna be denied, no matter how much ye try to bury it."

She dropped the final ingredient into the bottle and proceeded to blend its contents by sealing the top of the container and shaking it. "Ye asked me about Gunnar. He's with us now, here by the hearth. And when I go outdoors, he joins me in the garden and the woods. And when I sleep, he tucks himself in beside me, wraps himself close, and waits for me to join him in the land beyond where I'll then choose what's next to come for myself."

She stopped her work and peered intently at me. "And ye, dear, what's caused ye to journey here on such a foul day as this? Ye have worry on yer mind." She extended both of her hands toward me, and I willingly surrendered to her grasp and her compassion. She spoke gently, "The time is near at hand, is it not? Do not be afeard, lass, ye'll not lose what ye've found, but 'tis not easy to let life run its course without trying to shift its direction. I'll not stop ye from trying, but I must warn ye that what is to come will come, and 'tis a serious danger to yer soul's journey if ye try to change the course of destiny by hastening yer own departure from this life."

Although it was peculiar to speak to someone who seemed to already be aware of my intentions, I masked normalcy and just explained my reason for coming. "I was hoping to ask another favor of ye, one of great urgency." I stopped here and inhaled deeply because I could feel my breath becoming shallow as I was on the verge of crying. "Some time ago, I came to see ye about a man, a man I'd met but couldna' find, and ye directed me to find a secret place where our love was sown. And we nurtured it with laughter and affection and rejoiced in wonder at the bounty of our contentment. But now he's been hewn from me, withering away in an underground cell, the date of his execution drawing nigh.

"If I could free him from there, we could leave all of this wretchedness behind and revive ourselves and our love in a new land. Can you not see it with me, Hilda? His hand holding mine, our footsteps and thoughts carrying us down the same path, the white blanket of heath bedstraw waving back and forth to us in communion. Help get us there, can ye? Will ye?"

My voice broke with emotion and sorrow flowed forth. "We should've been there by now, Hilda. We were to have slipped away last night. Those images of bliss I canna erase from my mind, those pictures of what is to be. I can bear with a delay, so long as we still get to color in that portrait of our future. But I canna conceive that our chance has slipped through our hands forever. I need to free him tonight from the prison, but there'll be a guard on watch. So this is what I've wanted to ask ye. This is why I've come. I need a sleeping draught to administer to the sentry, one that would render him so benumbed that I could lift the keys from his person, open the cell, and escape with Donal without being detected." There. Now it was all out. I waited breathlessly for her response.

She looked searchingly into my eyes and said nothing. I canna explain for sure what she may have been thinking or feeling during that prolonged silence, but after a while she spoke again. "Hold true to yer visions. A time will come when ye'll see it through." She rose from her chair and shuffled over to the cupboard once again, but this time she took out an oily kind of liquid that she carried back to the table.

Once seated, she added the fluid to the contents of the bottle. "Doesna' always happen in the ways we wish or in the time frame we imagine, but hold fast to it. If the ties of passion are potent enough, nothing will stand in the way of its expression." As she began to stir the concoction, a rhythmic clicking filled the air, carrying the beat of her words:

Time doesna' conform
To the figure that we shape—
The emptiness of grief
An arrival that is late.

'Tis cold and dark and dreary
Remaining here when love is gone
But do not step into those waters
To hasten the journey beyond.

Death will come of its own choosing
'Tis not for ye to open the door.
For if ye sever yer thread of life,
Ye'll be a single strand evermore.

The liquid in the bottle continued to swirl like a spinning whirlpool even though Hilda had stopped mixing the material. "Pour this into his ale. After imbibing the tincture, he'll pass out rather quickly, but the deepest paralysis comes after about five hours' time. Although I do not believe ye should wait that long."

Before extending the sealed bottle to me, she offered these parting words. "Let fate run its course. Do not bring harm upon yerself if it doesna' conform to yer vision. Control what's yers to control, but if yer attempt at shifting circumstance falls short, surrender to its power rather than take vengeance for its failure to live up to yer dreams."

With the potion almost within reach, I only half-listened to these words of caution. So driven was I to shape destiny to fit my personal design, I grasped only the potion and not her meaning.

Departures

She couldn't stop herself from either pacing about her room or gnawing away at her fingernails, so energized was she about the hours to come. It was past midnight, the guards had already changed duty, and Annag had adulterated the flagon of ale that was delivered to the newly installed watchman. If Mary followed Hilda's counsel carefully, then the lovers' best chance of escape would coincide with dawn, so she continued to march and nibble away the intervening hours.

What belongings she could fit into her satchel were stored away, including the pages she'd written that recorded recent events up to her visit with Hilda this morning. Even so, there was much she was forced to leave behind. Comfort and luxuries that she'd grown accustomed to would no longer be at her disposal, not that she looked upon the loss of these items with regret. For who, in their right mind, would choose a bejeweled gown worn during a lifetime of misery over a simple shift that could be readily cast aside to join her lover in bed? No, it wasn't the possessions that she would miss but the people she must bid farewell to that made her wistful.

Once upon a time, she and Annag had roamed the glen together, building castles of pebbles and shells and imagining themselves to be the queens and princesses who ruled them. They went from skinned knees to broken hearts, from tumbling down hills to learning dance steps, from looking at Undlay as the entire world to feeling confined by its provincialism. She would miss their talks together, their shared confidences, and the mixture of titillation and horror she felt at Annag's suggestive humor and her whispered secrets about the ways of love.

While she could not yet reveal to Annag the place where she and Donal planned to settle, Mary promised to send word after they'd established themselves without consequence. But that would take some time, and Mary could already feel the hollowness seep into her bones at the thought of her friend's absence.

There was no doubt that her father would be outraged over what she had done—most likely her mother too, although her Ma's anger would soon dissolve into melancholy and depression. Her father's fury, however, would fuel him for years to come, and Mary carried an ominous sense of guilt over having burdened young Deirdre with a heavy yoke of suspicion that would restrain her from tasting any type of freedom. Short of abandoning her plan to flee—which Mary would never consider—there was nothing she could do to alter her sister's fate except pray to the angels above that Deirdre would, at the very least, be preserved from falling into the soiled hands of George Campbell.

Of her family, Robby was perhaps the only one who might understand and forgive her for what she was about to do. Regardless of her father's contempt for Donal, Robby seemed to have an unspoken, subtle appreciation for the goodness that resided inside him. When Donal stood before Mary's father, her sire could only see a thief, a commoner, an upstart who had the temerity to wheedle his way into his daughter's heart. But Robby could see the honor by which Donal lived, the tacit code that bound Donal to his men--and they to him--in an arrangement that would include dying for one another if need be.

Robby was like that too. He saw through things into the heart of the matter. He recognized George Campbell for what he was. Despite Campbell's outward display of fancy possessions and fine clothing, Robby knew the fellow was destitute inside, empty of compassion, integrity, or bravery. Donal, for all his devilry, was a man to be admired, one who was born to lead, one who, when he gave you his word, meant it in terms of his own blood and bone.

Mary trusted that her brother believed she would be cared for and protected by this man, and she knew that Robby was aware of the magnitude of their love, its depth so immeasurable that she was willing to give away everything she had ever known. Robby, too, had been cared for and protected by Donal, so if there were anyone in the McElroy family who could comprehend why Mary chose to take this daring step, it was he.

She thought about Hamlin, her ties with him forged but recently. Although he did not interact much with her, certainly not enough for her to truly get to know him, she felt deep gratitude to him for preserving this chance she had at happiness. For it was he who had saved Donal's life by searching for Owen and delivering the all-important message about George's planned ambush.

Were it not for the stoic but brave blacksmith, Donal would've walked right into George's trap, and while this same kind of surprise ultimately did lead to Donal's arrest later at Ross's homestead, that was no fault of Hamlin's but rather the unforeseen result of the treachery of a desperate sinner.

Everything about this night was made possible then by Hamlin's intervention, and beyond that, Mary loved how he brought such joy to Annag, restoring the twinkle in her eye and the lightness in her heart that had been put aside after childhood. Hamlin was a good man, a reliable man, and a worthy partner for Annag in the years to come.

Then, of course, there was Devin, the man who had always treated her as a person first and not some dainty, pampered daughter of a laird. His patience, his kindness, his willingness to take her on as a student shaped her into the adventurous woman she knew herself to be. From being fearless on horseback to being bold about the future, she learned his lessons well, for it was Devin who sparked the spirit of daring that burned inside her, and it was he who fanned its flames until it became so incandescent that it would light her way this very night through the darkness.

In the process of making all of these mental farewells, Mary had calmed her nerves to such a degree that she was no longer skittish. Instead, she had come to rest in a seated position on her bed, stroking Thor's fur with rhythmic ease. She thought of the animals that roamed Undlay, particularly all of the horses that she'd groomed, watered, and ridden. When she was younger and Annag was unavailable to play, she thought of them as the friends she longed to have, carrying on conversations with them and creating imaginary voices for each that matched their appearance and behavior.

Bellowing Hubert, high-strung Mirain, and grouchy Bedwyn, they were as unique to her as the gifts she had been given on the Christmases of her childhood. She took comfort in the fact that she would be taking honey-tongued Arwen with her tonight, along with the companion she was petting beside her. This present from Meggie had turned out to be the lifeline that connected her from her past to this unknown future, and no matter how many days this dog would be permitted to trot next to her upon this earth, she would never forget the solace he provided her on this night of sorrowful exhilaration.

The time had come. Mary lifted her bag with the pieces and memories of home that she would carry with her into her new world. With a firm slap of determination upon the bed, she stood tall, walked over to the solitary candle, and blew it out, leaving only traces of its existence behind.

***

After taking careful and measured steps down the stairs which led to the dungeon, Mary was somewhat stunned when she did not see the guard in his usual position of watch. The stool was empty—something she had expected—but there was no sleeping body outstretched on the ground in front of it. Panic arose inside her; her body quaked with fear. Leaning against the stone wall to make herself less visible, she slinked along the edges of the corner to where the gaoler kept his bed.

Craning her head around the angle, she could see the outline of the man, lying flat on his pallet, senseless to the world that surrounded him. *Strange,* she thought, *that he would have the wherewithal to walk these few paces from his stool to here before passing out completely.* She waited a few moments to confirm his lack of awareness before stepping closer to his body. Searching first solely with her eyes, she scanned his person for the key to the cell, but when she couldn't locate it, she was forced to use her hands to manipulate his body and clothes.

Only after flipping him over from one side to the other did she spy the key resting comfortably on the ground beneath his head as if it had been neatly and purposefully placed there. *Another odd occurrence,* she pondered, *that a sentry should leave in full view of any passerby the tool that could liberate his convict.* But there was no time to waste over such peculiarities. Mary snatched the key and hastened toward the cell.

With hands trembling, she inserted the key into the lock while whispering, "I've come for ye. *Is tuso gaol mo chridhe. Leatsa, tha mi criochnaichte.* [O love of my heart. With you, I am complete.] Everything is ready. Arwen and Thor are waiting outside the castle. Brodie has Cerwyn loaded up and ready near the cave…"

But Mary's voice trailed away as she creaked open the lattice door and saw the vacant space within. Empty. She was too late.

Undlay Castle – 2018

Caitlyn fluttered her eyes to bring the room into focus. Surrounding her were stainless steel cabinets, stocked with shiny silver instruments and bandages. A palpable heaviness pressed down upon her chest, making it nearly impossible to move, and when she did attempt to shift her position even slightly, she heard the crinkling of paper beneath her. The narrow cot upon which she lay was positioned so tightly against a cold, unfeeling wall that, when her body faced that direction, she felt the overwhelming sensation of being entombed.

Waking to the alarming thought of having been buried alive, Caitlyn summoned the energy to lift and turn herself in order to gain an unobstructed view of the space she was in and, relieved to still be counted among the living, exhaled a sigh of relief.

Laden with a sense of despondency, Caitlyn waged battle against the pull to surrender to it. Mining the small vein of her instinct to survive, she fought instead to delve into the reason behind this despair. Disconnected images of faces arose in spotty patches, surfacing then fading, as the echoes of names reverberated in the chambers of her memory. Devin, Annag, Hamlin, Robby, Hilda, Meggie, Thor—visitations so brief she could only absorb them as flashes of physical forms accompanied by sentiments of warmth and fondness. But two images kept reasserting their presence, refusing to be mere flickers of recollection. Each persisted in haunting her, one bringing rancor and disgust, the other heartache and sorrow.

Becoming aware of the moist cloth upon her forehead, Caitlyn wished that its medicinal properties could smother the torment roiling inside her mind. A cool hand upon her forearm startled her, launching her back into the room as she crawled out from beneath those memories to peer over the mental divide that separated past from present.

"Are ye okay, lass? I see ye've been opening yer eyes and moving about somewhat. 'Tis me, Graham." The words were a welcome anchor for Caitlyn to seize, one that could steady her mind that was adrift. She fixed her eyes upon him in a lengthy gaze, but she could do nothing more than stare, so puzzled was she in sorting out the identity of this kind man who sat beside her bed. Her face must've worn the look of bewilderment, for the visitor repeated, "Caitlyn, 'tis me, Graham. Ye swooned after the boat ride, and security brought ye here to recover. How are ye doing now?" He kept his hand upon her arm, reacclimating her to the present moment.

Caitlyn's first attempt at speech failed as she could form no intelligible words, only a slight gurgle followed by the clearing of her throat. Handing her a small cup of water, Graham waited while she sipped a few meager drops and uttered the words, "Where's the cave?"

"Cave? 'Tis not a cave we're at, Caitlyn, but a castle. Undlay Castle. I suppose ye fainted, lass, and now ye're in the first aid station. Maybe ye felt a little seasick from the crossing or perhaps ye did not eat a good Scottish breakfast this morning before setting out on our journey? Whatever the reason, ye're fine now, and ye can rest here for a bit longer till we have to return to the boat and continue the schedule for today."

He looked at her earnestly, his head tilting in deep concern. "Or…if ye're not feeling right about going back out upon Loch Ness, I can contact someone from the tour company to arrange for transport from here back to yer hotel. Whichever ye think best, lass."

Caitlyn wanted to return to the group and not continue to be the center of all this fuss, but she still wasn't sure her limbs would follow her mind's command to move. Starting by wiggling her fingers and toes and then bringing her knees to her chest as a kind of test, she felt reassured that, with a bit more time, she could reunite with everyone and follow the prescribed itinerary. "I can do it," she said, trying to promote a sense of confidence she herself wasn't so sure she possessed. Needing to play this assigned role, she bit down hard on her lower lip to prevent the unscripted question from escaping: "Where did they take him?"

***

The kindness of her fellow travelers overwhelmed Caitlyn as they offered up their snacks, drinks, candy, even Dramamine to help restore her sense of well-being. Paula tried to give her the extra sweater she was always carrying in her tote bag as a spare, and Michael nudged her conspiratorially, exposing the whiskey flask he had hidden in the inside pocket of his slicker. Thanking them all profusely, she held back from accepting anything for the moment, but promised that, if she did change her mind, she'd know who to turn to for whatever she needed. And after a furtive wink to Michael, she drifted off by herself and held firmly to the railing as the boat chugged its way from shore.

Graham kept a watchful eye upon her while he resumed his role as historian and tour guide. "Okay, folks, so the plan is to ferry back over to Clansman Harbor where we'll disembark and load up into the car for our trip to Beauly Priory. Now though, once we spin the boat around, ye might wish to take some photos of Undlay from this vantage point. Seems almost indomitable when ye look at it from here and see it rising high above ye, looking down upon ye in all its power and glory. A bit intimidating even now, despite it being in ruins. Can ye imagine how small the trespassers and invaders would've felt when approaching it from this angle?"

Caitlyn paid little attention to the details of the castle; instead, she was drawn to the water churning beneath the boat. While the hull sliced through the surface, kicking up foam and spray, she ignored the bubbles of white that danced and jumped as the vessel propelled forward. It was the depth of the water that fascinated her, that lured her in, that beckoned her. The unknown fathoms it would take to reach the bottom disquieted her, and that unease sent a ripple of chills throughout her body as if the waves themselves were undulating inside her very being. Her grip tightened as she resisted the pull of being swept into the black abyss carved into the bottom of the loch.

An undeniable presence was washing over her again, and she felt herself slipping away once more into another dimension. What *was* that sound she was hearing? A low, moaning wail, heavy with loneliness and despair. The kind of cry that comes from the heart of an exile whose home is fading farther and farther from reach. The desperation in the voice grew in intensity, forcing Caitlyn to seal her ears with her hands to deny it further entry.

Clinging to a tiny sliver of awareness to lift her away from the watery chasm, she raised her feet up and down on the deck and swung her loosened hair into the wind to help realign her mind and spirit with the events taking place on the boat, leaving behind the anguish of what must have occurred somewhere down beneath it.

"Would you like a piece of gum, Cait?" Christina asked as she was gathering together her belongings and removing her jacket now that the nautical portion of their tour was coming to its end. "I've always had a bit of motion sickness myself, whether I'm on a plane, on a boat, or in a car, and I find that chewing gum helps a lot."

She extended the pack to her. "You should've seen me on my bus rides to school when I was a little kid. I would get off looking pretty green, and my first stop in the building was always the restroom, not my classroom. But once I figured out the gum trick, I chomped my way back to equilibrium!"

"And to some pretty hefty dental bills as well, may I add!" chimed in Doris, Christina's mother, as the two of them joined together in laughter.

"Thanks, I'll take your suggestion on this one," Caitlyn said, unwrapping a piece and indulging in both the flavor and the rhythm of chewing. Hoping she could find the equilibrium Christina had mentioned, she took her seat in the car unable to shake the companion who was still traveling with her.

***

The car ride to Beauly passed rather quickly due, in large part, to Graham's gift for telling stories, the current one focusing on this *beau lieu*, this beautiful place. Not just aesthetically pleasing, Beauly offered the community of monks who built the abbey here in 1230 fine agricultural land and excellent fishing, and for three hundred years, the order thrived—that is, until the Reformation brought an end to monastic life forever. Beauly's wooded, riverside location in the Highlands provided the remoteness the cloistered sect had sought, but eventually the coffers were robbed and the buildings quarried for Cromwell's construction of the citadel at Inverness. The church continued to remain in use as a burial ground, and Graham explained how their group would be able to view monuments and headstones dating from the 1400s to the twentieth century.

When they stepped out from the car, Graham directed them to the grounds, pointed out the location of the tavern where they'd later lunch, and then set them free to wander at their leisure. While everyone paired up, Caitlyn stepped out seemingly alone, but she herself knew that someone—not outwardly visible—was still connected to her. And this someone, once upon a time and long ago, had every intention of journeying this same path from Undlay to here.

In front of Caitlyn was an inviting, narrow path that led directly to the arched doorway of the front facade of the abbey. On either side of the path stood tombstones—some upright, some tilted sideways, some drooping backward—each bearing faded inscriptions of lives that had come and gone. Before walking through the open portal, Caitlyn decided to investigate the graveyard first, stepping carefully from one monument to the next, reading whatever could be deciphered from the engravings etched upon the stone.

Surrounded by concrete reminders of her own mortality, she began to wonder about the point of it all, the point of living. *If from dust we are made and unto dust we return—basically the listed birth and death dates—then what truly matters is the gap between those two points. What do we make of this chance we've been given to live?* She considered this as she stood before the monument erected to the family of John Macrae and imagined the pain underlying the written numbers and words.

How did his wife, Isabella, bear the loss of her son James who died in infancy? How did she carry on when her husband soon joined their child in a world so far removed from Isabella's own? What did it feel like to watch the body of her twenty-six-year-old daughter confined to a box beneath the ground while she was left behind to walk upon that same ground, mired in grief and sorrow for years to come? Where did she find the strength to endure? To rise from bed in the morning to bake the bread and tend to other daily chores when none of it really mattered at all? Life is, indeed, sacred, but why must it be interlaced with such sadness? When days stretch on endlessly and each one is enveloped in such misery, doesn't the unspoken alternative hold greater appeal? Caitlyn marveled at Isabella Macrae's fortitude to carry on, but she would not have condemned the woman either if she had chosen otherwise.

Moving into the church, Caitlyn examined more markers on the stone floor and then walked deeper into one of the interior rooms to see the tomb effigy of a knight laid out in full form. For some reason, it was less disturbing to gaze upon this figure who, rather than being left to decay in the dirt, seemed to be relaxing in peaceful repose. Beholding this likeness, she could envision death more as the act of tucking oneself into bed and nestling under a blanket of slumber--a sort of serene and gradual transition from one realm to the next.

In that sense, death could be something as familiar as one's nightly journey from consciousness to sleep. Feeling comforted by this last image, she walked back outdoors toward the edge of the property that overlooked the bend in the river. A beautiful place it was. Patches of blue sky were chasing away the heavy clouds, and the extra light shone upon the bushes and shrubs so that they differentiated themselves in shades of emerald to forest green.

Leaning against the iron fence, Caitlyn gazed in between the tree branches that dangled in front of her to admire the unblemished reflection of the sky upon the still water. Taking the moist air deep into her lungs, she sat upon the grass and absorbed the entire scene into herself, and, unlike the buried around her who had to cross over in order to reach such tranquility, she let her mind find rest in the present moment.

When thoughts did come, she let them float past her like untethered balloons drifting with the wind. As the sun conquered the retreating clouds, warmth wrapped its arms around her, and she closed her eyes to accept its embrace. Empty of concern or worry, Caitlyn relished the stillness and remained seated there for quite some time, but she would have been lying to herself if she claimed that she had found solitude. No, someone was there beside her—indeed, maybe even within her—and the voice of this being gently encouraged her to open her eyes and truly see.

Disappointed at having to break the enchantment yet unable to ignore the plea, Caitlyn followed the command and looked at the landscape surrounding her. Reviewing again the same calm water, the verdant growth, and the brightening sky, she lowered her eyes to inspect the ground at her feet. Every now and then a flash of light would bounce up from the terrain beyond the iron fence. Drawing closer to the glinting light, she discovered a most peculiar rock made of glassy flint and containing a perfect circular hole right through its center.

Never one to collect things, Caitlyn, even as a child, eschewed gathering such objects as coins or stamps or seashells, so it was somewhat difficult for her to understand why she reached her hand between the iron balusters to claim possession of this stone. But collect it she did, and after turning it over a few times in her hand to examine it, she unzipped the pouch in her backpack and tucked it safely inside.

***

Lunch at the Lovat Arms maintained the same historical tone set by the visit to the Priory. The main lobby boasted vaulted ceilings, a spiral staircase, and an alternating color scheme of red, green, and blue tartan, the colors of Clan Fraser of Lovat. The draperies and the upholstery in the dining room area followed suit, and the table where the group was seated resembled the long, formal kind that would have been occupied by the host and his family at a medieval banquet. Like any wise establishment, the Lovat Arms was careful not to become too enmeshed in the ways of the past, so its menu reflected a wonderful blend of traditional and modern dishes. When the food was served, Michael's haggis was placed next to Ann Marie's quesadilla, and Vivian's shepherd's pie sat across from Graham's chicken fingers and fries.

Graham regaled his listeners with the history of Clan Fraser of Lovat, noting the first recorded reference to the name in the twelfth century and finishing with information about its current chief, Simon Fraser, the 18th Lord Lovat.

With apologies for upsetting our digestion, he told them of the valor of Sir Simon Fraser, the patriot during the Scottish Wars of Independence who eventually met with a most gruesome death by being hanged, disemboweled, beheaded, and quartered. "His head joined Wallace's on a spike on London Bridge, and the trunk of Fraser's body was lifted in chains to swing close by. Sorry, folks, for the graphic descriptions, but the English have not been verra forgiving toward us Scots." Graham finished his story with a flourish, pointing his ketchup-laden fry at his listeners for emphasis.

Vivian continued the thread. "And they weren't very forgiving toward each other either, you know. Paula and I went to London last year and visited the Tower. One woman—I forget her name, do you remember, Paula? She was sentenced to death just for being related to someone who had offended King Henry VIII. Even though she was sixty-seven—which was much older back then than it is now—they chopped off her head, and it took eleven swings, they said, before she actually died!" Viv's eyes were round with horror at the notion of such prolonged agony.

"Aye, 'tis true. Mike, can ye hand me the pitcher of water, please? And we Scots have been known to turn upon one another as well." Graham accepted the container, poured more drink into his glass, and continued. "I should tell ye the tale of the fellow who was forced to dive head-first into a barrel of boiling tar! Happened not too far from here at a place called Chanonry Point."

Graham munched on his chips while the rest of the group grimaced at the thought of such a death sentence.

"Yikes," Caitlyn responded. "What did he do to deserve that?"

"Offended the Earl of Seaforth's wife. Who was it that said, 'Hell hath no fury like a woman scorned'?" Graham looked around the table for an answer. "Shakespeare, I guess?"

Caitlyn clicked into teaching mode, "Sounds like Shakespeare, but it's not. It's actually a different English playwright, William Congreve. But wait, are you saying she forced the Earl, her very own husband, to meet that kind of death?" Caitlyn leaned forward, eager to hear the answer to her question.

"No, actually," Graham wiped his lips with his napkin and explained, "it was her seer, a man named Coinneach Odar—Dark Kenneth—the Scottish Nostradamus, he was. Predicted everything from the Battle of Culloden to the Highland Clearances to the building of the Caledonian Canal to the coming of the railroads. The fellow even foretold the discovery of oil in the North Sea when he claimed, 'A black rain will bring riches to Aberdeen'!" Graham leaned back in his chair while he waited for the power of Dark Kenneth's prophecies to sink in.

The table was momentarily quiet while everyone considered the far-reaching vision of the Scottish soothsayer until Christina asked, "But then, why? If this guy was so good at seeing the future, what did he do to deserve death?" Her furrowed brow bespoke of her inability to equate two such unlike things.

Graham smiled knowingly. "He told the truth. Is that not what gets most people in trouble?" He looked into the faces of his listeners for affirmation. "The man gazed into his adder's stone, and he told the Earl's wife the truth. She asked him to peer through the hole in the rock and tell her how her husband was doing during his visit to France. And Kenneth, to avoid angering the ugliest, meanest, most miserable woman in all of Scotland, told her simply that the man was in good health and refused to elaborate. When she demanded that he tell her everything on pain of death, he did, and she had him killed anyway."

The waiter interrupted at this point, asking if they needed anything further, and when they told him they had finished, he left the check on the table, promising to return for it later.

Graham resumed the tale. "So, Dark Kenneth, he held nothing back, telling her the Earl was having special cuddles with one or more women in France,

246

describing the mistresses as being much fairer than the Lady Seaforth herself. And so, into the barrel of tar he went!

"Well, Kenneth was right about the Earl, and he was also right about his prediction that the Seaforth line would end with the last heir being deaf and dumb. Sure enough, in 1815, Francis Humberstone Mackenzie, deaf and dumb from scarlet fever, who had four children that all pre-deceased him, breathed his last, and the Seaforth name was no more."

"That's an incredible story," Michael commented. "Dark Kenneth was totally authentic, not one of those psychic frauds." He shook his head in awe and disbelief.

As everyone started gathering their bags and belongings in preparation to depart, Caitlyn extended her hand across the table toward Graham. "Wait. What did you say about that stone? How did this Dark Kenneth use a stone to see the future?" While she was asking the questions, she unzipped the front pouch of her backpack and began rummaging through its contents.

"It was an adder's stone—a rock that some believe is formed from the hardened saliva of serpents who mass together. It has a hole in—" Graham was immediately silenced when Caitlyn showed him such an object occupying the entire palm of her hand. "Yes! That's it! In Gaelic, we call it *Gloine nan Druidh*, Druid's Glass. 'Tis what Coinneach would peer through to tap into his Second Sight. But where did ye come upon this?"

"It was underneath the branches of the bushes and shrubs outside the gates of the Priory, near the area that overlooks the river. It flashed every now and then when the sunlight hit it at just the right angle. So I traced the path of the light and found it resting there. Do you think I should go put it back?" Caitlyn asked with a hint of worry in her voice.

"No!" Graham said emphatically, "'Tis not a museum piece, 'tis yers. And plus, it was outside the property line anyway. It'll be good luck for ye, lass. Provides protection against evil charms and nightmares and gives ye the ability to see the true nature of fairies and witches that are in disguise. No, 'tis yers to keep, and ye could certainly use some good fortune after the trouble ye had this morning at the castle, aye?"

Caitlyn stared at the rock in her hand, marveling over the powers attributed to such a simple thing. Breaking the spell, Michael joked, "Well, if you can look through that hole and see into the future, what's the traffic to Inverness looking like?"

Whether or not it could have been foretold, the traffic to Inverness was heavy, making for a very tedious car ride from Beauly back to the hotel. To make matters worse, when they were less than five miles away from their destination, an accident in the nearby roundabout kept them stuck in one place for twenty minutes. So it was with great relief that they spied the familiar structure of their lodgings at the crest of the hill not too far in front of them.

It had been a long day—an enjoyable one, of course—but a long one nonetheless, especially for Caitlyn who, beyond the customary arrivals and departures of the tour, also had to recover from her morning fainting spell and later contend with the feeling that she was a bit off-center for the remainder of the trip.

Graham was either the best actor of them all or he simply was the stereotypical energetic Scotsman he purported to be, for upon their arrival, he bounced out of the driver's seat, lifted the hatch on the trunk, and proceeded to carry all of their bags and belongings to the curb. "Well now, rest up, everyone. Pick-up tomorrow will be 8 am sharp. Another castle visit is on the schedule; this time it's Cawdor Castle, the site associated with Shakespeare's Macbeth—even though, in truth, the historical king never lived there—and then in the afternoon we're off to the battlefield of Culloden."

Michael had joined in to help Graham with the baggage, handing each one to its proper owner. "Sounds like the British are coming," he announced as he delivered the last backpack to Caitlyn.

"I suppose you're right," Graham concurred. "With Shakespeare's writing and the Duke of Cumberland's troops on the horizon, we'll be needing to focus our attention tomorrow on our neighbors to the south." With a glance at his watch and wave of his hand, he quoted Macbeth himself upon departing, "I go and it is done; the bell invites me."

After Caitlyn trudged up the two flights of stairs, she opened the door to her room, dropped her bag upon the floor, and collapsed into the chair that faced the large window overlooking the River Ness. Despite it being early evening, the sun still shone brightly, and the path along the water's edge was busy with cyclists, runners, and pedestrians. Two floors beneath her, a wedding was taking place, and from her window, she could see some of the guests, the women in brightly-colored dresses and the men in traditional tartan kilts, clinking glasses and toasting the newlyweds. And what of her?

She felt guilty admitting that she hadn't even thought of Brian, her boyfriend of seven years, during most of this vacation. She wondered, can you still call someone your 'boyfriend' after such a long time spent together? It seemed to be a word for the young, a word for someone who made you feel like a smitten schoolgirl every time you heard his voice or saw him in person. It was a word that conveyed excitement, infatuation, and desire—emotions she never did, and never would, experience with him. No, she should call him something else.

After all, she wasn't some twenty-something who found his conversation riveting, his approval paramount, and his touch electrifying. She was old and jaded. When she thought of him, her pulse didn't quicken with longing but with exasperation over the half-full coffee cup with its curdled milk perched atop her school book. It irritated her to think that, to get to her own work, she must do his first. Not that he was a terrible person.

He was dependable and predictable and steady. Their relationship was adequate—she wouldn't necessarily say fulfilling—just adequate. It served a purpose, kind of like the way vacuuming the area rug gives the appearance of cleanliness—as long as you don't go peeking under the furniture or into the corners, you never have to see the dust balls, dog hair, and pieces of left-over potato chips.

Tonight though she was thinking of him, and she was delving into those hidden recesses to examine the detritus of their partnership. No longer could she ignore the vacancy sign posted outside the portal to her heart. What happened today when she stood before the dungeon at that castle she did not completely understand, but she did know that she had never felt that deeply ever before—about *anything*. If something tragic should ever occur between her and Brian, she would carry on and, she was certain, so would he.

Of course, there would be tears shed and a period of mourning as well, but it wouldn't be utterly catastrophic like the way she'd felt today. *Donal.* The name kept reappearing in her mind's eye. Pronouncing it reintroduced the hollowness she felt when her hopes of reuniting with this man faded further and further from reach until the spark within her own soul sputtered and went dark, leaving only nothingness behind.

Now that was love. A love to live for. A love to die for. Clearly, she—despite being with Brian for a fifth of her own life—had never truly been in love.

***

Tossing, turning, flipping the pillow over to one side and later the other—nothing was working. Although it was past midnight, noise from the courtyard continued to rise, indicating that the wedding celebration had not ended. Sounds of the revelers, singing and clapping along to the music, climbed like the ivy growing beside her window, reaching its vines through the sill and into her room. A quick trip to the bathroom, a cup of cold water, a snapping of the bedsheets to freshen them up, and then a resumption of battle to gain admittance into the well-defended gates of sleep. At some point in the early hours of the morning, Caitlyn must have gained entry, but what she experienced once inside could not be labeled restful or therapeutic.

A hooded executioner stood upon a scaffold, and bending down upon one knee, he thrust his hands inside the sliced belly of his victim. Gurgling and gushing was followed by tearing and ripping as the man slowly extracted the worm-like strands from the cavity of the traitor's body. He beckoned, then commanded Caitlyn to come forward, and after ascending the four steps to the platform, she extended her hands forward to him to receive the tangled, bloody tribute.

Mired in wetness and slime, the entrails slipped through her fingers, first one string, then another, and she had to perform a quasi-juggling act just to hold them all together in one clump. The bloodstains on her white bridal gown appeared as smudges of bright red and later deep maroon, but she toiled on, carrying the innards like a demonic bouquet as she processed down the aisle toward the graveyard. The ground before the headstone gaped wide and open, having been hollowed out by the gravedigger who stood next to the pit, leaning heavily upon his shovel.

As she stepped to the edge of the grave, Caitlyn spread her arms to dislodge the remains from her grasp, but instead of dropping and falling into the pit, the strands intertwined with her fingers, latching on and refusing to let go. Invigorated with an awareness of its own evil, individual strings lengthened and extended from her hands to the dirt of the tomb. The pieces that touched the earth burrowed worm-like into the farthest reaches of the trench, pulling Caitlyn down toward the crater.

Turning to the gravedigger, she tried screaming to him for help, but no words came forth, only the raspy sound of the forced exhalations of her own breath. Teetering on the ledge of the abyss, she felt the front of her body tip toward the opening, her legs quaking in defiance of the gravity that pulled her downward. Just before her footing gave way, the man holding the shovel whispered, "Ye must go into the cave." These were the last words she heard before tumbling into the darkness.

Caitlyn awoke with a start, immediately coming to a seated position and examining her hands and fingers to make sure that they were empty and unchanged. Her back was bathed in sweat, her hair damp and sticky on her neck and shoulders. Glancing at the bedside clock, she saw the digits read 5:05. Morning. She had no desire to even attempt to return to sleep, not with those horrid images so vivid in her mind. Closing her eyes was not worth the risk of being unraveled again by such nightmares.

Hold on a minute, Caitlyn wondered, *why was I plagued with such frightful visions tonight? What about that dumb rock? Wasn't it supposed to protect its owner from nightmares like this? So much for Scottish superstition, I suppose.* Thinking this way, Caitlyn decided to dismiss the dream as merely the jumbled bits and pieces of what she had heard and witnessed earlier in the day.

Comfortable with that determination, she reached over to the table beside the bed, took a sip of water, but instead of putting the matter to rest, she held the cup suspended in the air for a few moments and reconsidered. Walking over to her backpack, she removed the stone from its compartment and carried it with her back over to the bed.

She inspected its shape and texture, turning it over and over again in her hands. What was it Graham had said about the stone and the seer? She tried to recall what exactly Dark Kenneth did to have the Second Sight, the ability to see both this world and another. 'Peer through the hole in the rock.' That's what Graham said the prophet did. Scooting toward the headboard so that her back rested up against it, Caitlyn stared intensely into the opening in the stone.

The room and all of its distractions soon faded away.

Peering Through Time

George Campbell enjoyed manhandling Donal, especially since the miscreant posed no threat to him with his hands tied in front of his body and his legs bound together. It gave George a scintillating thrill to push his prisoner up against the filthy walls of the cell and taunt him without fear of retaliation. "I promised ye that one day ye'd join yer lowlife brethren on the gallows, and that day has come." Thrusting his forearm across Donal's throat, he gloated, "And I've always been a man of my word."

Being this close to Donal's face offered George the additional benefit of being able to survey the damage he had inflicted upon the man a day ago. The delight he took in surveying the cuts and bruises and dried blood balanced the irritation he had felt over the watchman's incompetence. In flagrant neglect of his duty, the guard had drunk so much ale that he passed out and couldn't be roused. *Shameful,* George had thought, remembering how he had to drag the man to his pallet and secure the prison key himself, *to shirk his responsibilities in such a way.* But his aggravation had shrunk and melted away like ice during the spring thaw because he was now swept away with elation and gratification at the recognition of his own power.

It was a day of destiny, for both the convict and himself—Donal had an undeniable appointment with death and he a much-deserved upgrade in McElroy's good graces. Teague had entrusted him with delivering the prisoner to Craigmonie for a hanging that would be carried out at dawn in secret. Not wanting to risk the chance of Donal's lawless cohorts interfering with justice— as the Cameron clan had done—McElroy had decided to act covertly, taking care of this business without anyone else knowing.

Two men-at-arms would travel with George to the gallows, the newly commissioned executioner had already been notified and would be awaiting their arrival, and Teague would trail them a bit later as he could travel much faster than could George who had to drag behind him this lump of depravity.

Tonight was the stuff of legend, and George could imagine people years from now reading of his exploits and recounting them for generations to come.

Removing his arm from beneath Donal's chin, he grabbed hold of the man's shoulder, turned it toward the lattice door, and, placing both hands on his back, shoved the criminal from behind. Barely able to contain his exhilaration, George decided to himself, *This will, indeed, be a day to remember.*

***

His finger, damp and filthy, outlined the edges of the unyielding stone as he sat in silence in the darkness. Just a short time ago that same finger had traced the inviting contours of his lover's lips.

And now?

He thought about all the bargains people make during the course of a lifetime, and the one he had made that brought him here—to this dungeon where the chill fastened upon his bones. And he knew, without deliberating over it for a second, that he would do it all again without hesitation, without regret.

Writing of stolen embraces and impassioned kisses was one thing, but living it was quite another. The taste of her lips, the feel of her warm breath upon his chest, the sound of her panting with desire, and the simultaneous release of their paired ecstasy could not be captured on paper. *And yet, that is all I had,* he thought to himself, *mere words, brief melodies to describe the indescribable. Tonight, they offer no comfort.* He clung only to images of her as clouds of his icy breath formed and dissipated with the rise and fall of his chest.

But then Donal had seen the guard look groggy, had observed him tilting on his stool, and had heard him fall with a thud to the earthen floor. And when he had witnessed these things, he knew that a plan was underway. *That's my girl,* he thought to himself. *Turning the tables on fairy tale endings with the princess doing the rescuing!* A broad grin stretched across his face, his laughter echoing in the cavernous cell. He shook his head from side-to-side in wonder at Mary's fearlessness and determination.

However, the hours dragged on, and nothing had changed. Perhaps she was delayed? Perhaps the delay was intended? Perhaps there was no delay, and she had been caught? He immediately expunged that last thought from consideration, for to exist without hope was to be dead while still breathing. *No, she will come. I may not ken when, but I ken she will come.*

Footsteps racing down the stairs—too heavy to be hers. A surprise visit from Campbell instead. Donal observed how George kicked at the rumpled body that lay on the floor and heard him shout, "Git up! Git up, you lousy sot!" But the man did not budge. "Pathetic excuse for a sentry. Wake up, ye bastard!"

Donal savored George's displeasure along with the extra effort the man had to expend in order to drag the guard's body down the darkened corridor. But when George returned to put the key into the lock, Donal realized that something was not right. Something had gone terribly wrong. This could not be part of Mary's scheme. He wiped his dampened finger on his ragged clothing and walked forward to meet his appointment with Time.

He silently prayed that Mary had not been intercepted and harmed. If it were time for him to go to his death for the sins he had committed, he would march boldly toward the scaffold without regret. But if his crimes had been transferred to Mary's ledger, if his sins had dragged her down with him to ignominious torture and death, then he did not deserve to have an end to his suffering. He would ask the Lord above for relentless, enduring punishment, like the kind one reads about in ancient stories—having his eyes continually gouged out, pushing a boulder uphill without ceasing, suffering his liver to be endlessly ravaged—something that would be excruciating and interminable. A simple forfeiture of his life could, in no way, ever atone for the wrong he had done to her.

Not knowing Mary's condition nearly drove him insane, and he looked upon Campbell with the contempt of a deranged madman. Donal refused to utter a single word even when Campbell began mocking him verbally and assaulting him physically. He glared at him in silence, remaining coolly detached as Campbell jostled him all the way up the winding steps to the outside of the castle where he fastened the rope from his horse to Donal's hands and started hauling him along.

Donal knew the path well; it led to Craigmonie, and in those early hours before dawn, he could smell a new day hovering just beyond him. The storm from yesterday had passed, but the wind persisted, ushering in a crisp dryness that wrung out the moisture from the branches and leaves of the surrounding birchwood. How often had he roamed these lands--woodpeckers and crossbills busily welcoming the morning, red squirrels scurrying from tree to tree in a frantic search of treasured seeds and berries. Nature's gifts brought him but temporary solace, however, because he could not crawl out from under the weight of his guilt when he remembered how miserably he had failed the only woman he had ever loved.

Even though a tear fell freely down his cheek, his grief remained private as he trudged behind his three captors, their backs toward him. He had no means to wipe away the wet trace of sorrow, not with his hands bound and the rope so taut. After the first, another tear soon followed and then another. They flowed from self-loathing; he despised himself for being unable to keep his vow.

With scorn, he derided the oath he had written, *To hold and guide her every day and lift all pain and cares away*. And what had he done? Rather than lift her away from pain, he had immersed her in it, tarnishing her name and endangering her life, and now he was leaving her behind to fend off the lecherous advances of a scoundrel like Campbell.

While he tormented himself with such thoughts, the journey continued, and soon the trail narrowed enough to require the horses to move in single file. In addition to becoming more limited, the path also involved a steady uphill climb, one that strained the lungs of both man and beast. And yet, despite that extra struggle, moving physically upward seemed to lift Donal's internal ruminations from despair to hope. He started to recognize that he wasn't leaving Mary at a disadvantage at all, really; she had been unconquerable before she met him and she would remain that way long after he was gone.

She had a spirit of independence that was unbridled and would never be corralled by vile cowards like Campbell or blustery overlords like her father. And despite Teague's refusal to allow Mary to join hands with a rogue like himself, Donal knew that McElroy loved his daughter too much to ever reject her completely. She may be reprimanded, some of her freedoms may be curbed temporarily, but she would not be harmed. Teague would not do such a thing. And so, like the survivor she was, she would carry on, and he would wait for her, however long that 'carrying on' might take.

They were nearing the top of the rocky crag where the platform and scaffold were waiting. To bide and to wait, that was his command to himself, for he knew that she would come to him—if not in this life, then in the life to come. The crunch of his feet upon the rocks and pebbles and the hush of the

255

wind through the pines was interrupted by the high-pitched creaking of a swaying metal cage. Looking up, Donal saw its contents: the hollowed out eye sockets, the single patches and strings of hair, the exposed teeth frozen in an expression of grotesque surprise.

The corpse of Drew Cameron had passed beyond the bloating, beyond the skunkish smell, beyond the shrinking and the shriveling to become what was now—just skeletal remains. Perhaps that was in store for him as well. He rationalized that, when he reached that point, it'd make no difference to him anyway what he looked like or what people thought of him. In fact, even now he didn't care about either of those things. Whatever people saw in him or whatever they believed he was, he knew himself that he was a good man, a simple man, a principled man, who had never dipped his hands wantonly in human blood.

He knew that there was more poetry in his heart than he could ever get out onto a page, and he knew that he was blessed to have been given such a sweet—though too brief—taste of love's nectar, a taste that he would savor for the rich and robust experience it was.

They had arrived at the platform now, and the executioner was already present, standing erect, hands clasped behind his back. Campbell dismounted and strode toward Donal, untying the lead rope that would liberate him to walk freely to his death. *What a paradox—to be liberated only to die!* Donal thought amusedly to himself. He wouldn't grovel or beg, and it was past the time for rebelling. He would meet this final appointment with dignity and honor. Hoofbeats coming up the hill meant that the laird of the glen had come to witness the administration of his justice. Donal regretted how the man had let wealth and status blind him from seeing Donal for who he really was and for what he had meant to his daughter.

Donal's boots clacked upon each of the four steps as he climbed up toward the scaffold. Once he reached the top, stretched out before him was the most spectacular vista of the countryside—a pair of hills on either side opened to display the rippling waters of Loch Ness, while a third mountain in the background enclosed the scene with charm. *How could a site reserved for torture and death be so picturesque?* he wondered. Maybe it was a tiny offering of Christian forgiveness bestowed as a final gift upon the convict about to pay for his sins.

Donal couldn't resist a little playful banter with the hooded man beside him. "Hope yer not too new to the job, my friend. Tell me, I'm not yer first client, am I?" He chuckled a bit as he said this, but his humor was met with grave silence.

Both men stood immobile on the platform, waiting for direction, when Teague shouted to Donal, "Have ye anything to say for yerself?" The laird had never dismounted from his horse, so his position, along with his voice, was imposing and authoritative.

Donal took some time to consider the question. "Well now, let's see. I have no stories to spin, no verses to recite. My music's been taken from me as well. But, I will hold out the hope of having one favor of ye…"

Teague shifted uncomfortably in his seat but said nothing. "I ask that ye honor the name of Donal Donn of Bohuntin and grant me something other than a traitor's death." Donal paused here to wait for permission to continue. When none was forthcoming, he spoke sincerely and bravely, "Having never done no harm to any of yer clan, other than to rescue two of ye and love one other, would ye grant that my head be taken from my body rather than the rope be looped about my neck?"

Teague looked off into the distance, breathing in and out in careful consideration. After a lengthy silence, his lips parted and he responded. "Dead is dead, no matter the method. The sentence still holds, for endangering my daughter's welfare. But…in gratitude for what ye did for me and my son, I'll permit yer choice of form."

George's eyebrows immediately went down in indignation, but the executioner was already on the move, returning the hanging rope to his cart and reaching in and taking out the axe. He then resumed his spot on the scaffold, only this time his hands were not empty; instead they held the weapon diagonally across his body, one hand grasping the bottom of the handle, the other holding the top, right beneath the blade.

Donal quipped, "A man prepared for all contingencies, are ye not, my good fellow!" He fidgeted with his hands, trying to drop and extend them lower toward his sporran. "If ye can indulge me a moment or two more, I'd like to reward ye in anticipation of a job well done." Pulling a single silver coin from his purse, Donal gestured with his bound hands toward the headsman and released the payment into the fellow's palm.

Just before dropping to his knees, he spoke to the laird of the glen. "Thank ye. I'm much obliged, especially since, now that Donal Donn will not be hanged, the Devil may come and take ye out of yer shoes, aye? Was that not what ye had sworn earlier?" With a twinkle of mischief in his eye and a smirk on his face, Donal then assumed an upright kneeling position, both legs coming to the platform with a thud.

A rustling of the trees gave his heart a jolt. Had Brodie and the boys come at this last moment to save the day, to save his life? But instead of seeing his companions, he beheld a single red stag crane its neck around the trunk of the tree to look mournfully in his direction. Neither the animal nor Donal blinked for fear of losing that palpable connection, but when Donal bowed his head, the deer scampered away.

Raising his eyes one last time, Donal looked northward and spoke his final words, ones that he had written just a short time ago. "Trust that wherever we shall wander, home consists of ye and me. Mary, come home to me."

The executioner pivoted on one foot, drawing back his weapon. George smiled smugly, Teague watched stoically, Donal gazed knowingly, and the axe sliced ... efficiently.

***

There was no time to delay. Mary slammed shut the door to the prison cell and sprinted up the stairs, dashing through the castle to the outdoors where Arwen and Thor were waiting. In one swift movement, she jumped and swung her leg over the horse, commanding the animal to action. Keeping pace with the mare was her devoted pup who sensed his mistress' urgency and darted along beside them, his ears pinned back with the speed of his run.

Her only thought was to get to Craigmonie and interrupt the fatal ritual; what other reason could there have been for the vacant dungeon? How she would stop it she did not know, but she didn't have the time to figure that out right now. Her only impulse was to ride and get there in time to prevent the execution.

For so many weeks, she had refused to delve deeper into the cryptic words Hilda had given her, resisting the urge to decipher some of the prophecies, especially the one about their love being cloaked in sorrow. The current circumstances, however, forced her to acknowledge the meaning of those words, but the fighting spirit in her softened the interpretation to denote temporary not perpetual sadness. Isolated events that caused grief could be managed as they surfaced, but the alternative—to have *everything* end in sorrow—was too much for Mary to bear. So she chose to ride on, clinging to the slim chance that, once she reached her destination, a solution would materialize, and this encounter with melancholy would be brief and overcome.

Her breathing became more rapid and shallow despite the fact that Arwen and Thor were the ones expending the physical energy required to fly over the fields and hills. Call it nerves, call it worry, but in truth, that struggle for air arose from the panic growing inside her as she confronted her dreams slipping away. The warmth of his laughter, the way he looked at her, the touch of his hand upon her face—each image brought tears because these visions were becoming finite; they had a beginning and an end. There was the undeniable chance that they may never again be replicated.

Now began the ascent up the narrow trail. She felt no need to hide any more, ignoring the thicket of trees that could have screened her approach. Let this then be her announcement to the world of her intention to bind herself to this man—this robber and gentleman—who would be hers both in life and in death. Spraying rocks and pebbles as they climbed, Arwen's and Thor's determination matched that of their mistress as they drew closer to the small gathering of people in the distance. Able to count upon one hand the number of spectators present, Mary felt a surge of hope because, since a large crowd had not yet assembled, then it was more likely that the ceremony had not yet begun.

After only two more strides of the horse, however, the bitter truth became known. Mary pulled back hard on the reins and the dog halted in its tracks when she saw a masked figure shoving an unstrung, headless puppet into a metal enclosure. With a sharp intake of breath, she recognized it to be the lifeless body of her beloved. His gibbet on one side and Cameron's on the other formed two hideous bookends that bracketed a pair of dissimilar haunting stories whose shared subject was sin and retribution. With her clenched fist in her mouth, Mary bit down on her fingers to keep from howling out in pain. Once again, she had failed him.

Quaking with sobs that shuddered throughout her body, she turned her horse away from the scene, directing their way back downhill. The noise of her retreat caused George and Teague to turn their attention away from the gallows to look back over their shoulders in curiosity. Only Teague noticed the flash of long, red hair that curled from behind the birch tree and snapped in the wind.

In a frenzy, Mary dashed from the horror as if speed could erase the pain of her heart being shattered into fragments. He was gone, and he was hers so briefly—a momentary encounter that led to secret meetings and ultimately love. The rainy day in the forest, the picnic by the loch, the dancing at the festival. The tilt of his head when he jested, the melody in his voice when he sang, the mischief in his eye when he teased—fragments now chipped and discarded, never to return to wholeness again. The outer shell of his body and now hers was all that was left behind as decades of future joy were erased by the single swing of an executioner's axe.

With nothing to look forward to and nothing to live for, she rode deeper into gloom. He had rescued her, and she had returned the favor by condemning him. She blamed herself for this tragic outcome. For if Donal had not been entangled with her—the laird's daughter—his punishment would have been more lenient, a period of imprisonment and a hefty fine, perhaps. But Mary reasoned that Donal's life had become the only recompense that would satisfy her father's vanity and pride, and so the justice enacted upon Donal was all her fault.

At some point, however, instead of riding blindly, she decided she would go to the cave, the place where they were to have picked up Donal's horse and escaped north. Clambering up yet another hill, Mary could discern the outline of Cerwyn grazing at the top of the crest not too far from the triangular arrangement of rocks that had formed Donal's former hiding place. The horse pricked its ears hearing their approach and lifted its head in her direction to observe her arrival.

Brodie had prepared things so well. Mary's tears fell with greater frequency when she touched the possessions that were Donal's—his bedroll, his harp, the small storage box containing his poetry. She inhaled deeply to catch the scent of him, but it was too faint to bring comfort. Everything had been so neatly packed, pieces of their future tucked away and waiting to be assembled, but now they would remain separated and disjointed forever.

She had nothing to unify them, nothing to show that their souls were bound together as one. But, as she considered this, she realized that she had their words to attest that they had lived and loved. There would be no bodies to bury, but she could bury what was inside their bodies—the visions, the hopes, the desires, the plans, the feelings they had shared.

With a lighter step, she walked purposefully over to her saddle pouch and withdrew the pages she herself had written, pages that recorded their growing intimacy over the past weeks and months. She joined them to his, commingling the two together in the box she had removed from his belongings. Bearing it before her as one would a coffin in a procession to the grave, Mary climbed through the aperture of the cave and found a corner in its nethermost region, where their love would forever be entombed.

***

What was she doing crawling into that cave? Was Donal in there? Had he escaped his sentence? If he had, there was no earlier sign that he had returned to this hideaway, was there? Angus, as he felt most often these days, was disoriented.

He had spent his hours here at this place, the site where he first contemplated betrayal. Unable to function in the daytime or sleep during the night, he was haunted by the choices he had made. Donal had never offended him in any way, other than to make him resentful that the man was a better brother to Ross than he himself had ever been.

Donal had always been kind to Angus and generous to his family, bringing extra supplies during the cold, winter months when they were running low and, more recently, rebuilding the railing around the property when he, in a drunken stupor, had smashed it to pieces. To Nora and Sara, Donal was the perfect gentleman, assisting Nora when she needed transport and complimenting Sara on her delectable scones and elderberry pie.

And yet, despite all those benevolent gestures, Angus had deceived him, played him for a fool, and turned him over to a rotten blackguard who wasn't worthy enough to lick the muck off Donal's boots. So what kind of man, then, did that make Angus? During these past two days, Angus had come to learn that there were many things that liquor could numb, but his regret over harming an innocent man was not one of them.

When Ross and his sisters had returned home and learned of Donal's arrest, the women sobbed uncontrollably, and Ross's fury exploded. From room to room, he hunted Angus down, throwing him to the floor and punching him with fists fueled by the years of abuse he had suffered at the hands of his older brother. Releasing that pent up anger with each blow, Ross beat upon Angus until his knuckles were bloodied. When Angus could barely unfurl his body into a half-standing position, Ross literally kicked the man out the door, pushing and shoving him until he passed beyond the Gregors' property line. Told never to cross that boundary ever again, Angus had wallowed here, a short distance from the cave, where he could face the constant reminder of his own baseness and depravity.

He had but one bottle remaining, having drunk the other five that constituted his reward from Campbell. A bitter tonic for his guilty conscience, the liquor granted him only a brief respite from his wickedness, never would it fully erase the fact that he was a traitor through and through. And so, when he had seen Donal's horse delivered to this place last night and now witnessed Mary McElroy arriving here this morning, he drove himself to climb out from the vapors of his own sin and cowardice to try to make sense of what he was witnessing.

His supposition that perhaps Donal had returned to this cave some time during the night was proven wrong when he saw Mary and her dog enter the cave and then later emerge from it without him. Strange though, that after exiting the hiding place and heading toward her horse, she did not then proceed to jump into the saddle and ride away. Rather, Angus watched her caress the horse's neck, touch her head to its mane, and then simply walk away with the pup trailing behind. She had moved almost distractedly, as if she were in a trance, possessed by some magnetic force that was pulling her somewhere.

Angus had done many things wrong in his life, things he knew were beyond forgiveness, but maybe he could take one small step toward the light by following this girl and ensuring her safety. Refraining from unplugging the cork to infuse himself with courage, Angus tucked the container away and teetered to his feet, trying to walk a straight and narrow course with Mary in his sights.

***

It was done. The only proof of their love was now concealed in the earth, protected and sheltered from a world that had conspired to keep them apart. Her fingernails were split and broken with clumps of dirt lodged beneath. She did not care nor did she bother to clean them. It had been cathartic, in a way, for her to claw and dig her way into the soil. It felt purposeful, intentional, at a time when she had just been shown how powerless she was over the course of fate. And she would continue to exert her will by choosing her own destiny rather than wait passively for it to unfold.

She was beyond sadness now; perhaps she had actually triumphed over it. Sorrow had no grip on her any longer because she would show them all, especially those who tried to divide them, that she belonged to Donal now and for eternity. They may have taken him from her in this lifetime, but she would be his in the next. There were no tears in her eyes as she strode through the countryside, but it was a delicate and tenuous optimism that could not withstand even momentary distraction.

This was why she had to ignore little Thor who had sensed her mood shift and was moving irregularly beside her. Any attention she gave to the pup would only reinforce her attachment and love for him, binding her more intensely to this world, and she could not open herself to such a connection— not when it could weaken her resolve to leave it behind.

The morning sun kissed the earth like the soft touch of a mother's lips upon her child's head. Gentle and nurturing, the light encouraged the trees and bushes to shake off their overnight frost to participate in the warmth of the new day. Mary had walked over these fields so often that she nearly lapsed into becoming nostalgic and wistful about those past excursions, but she canceled out the memories before they could fully form. She had to remain single-minded and driven; there could be no deviation. She quickened her pace.

The wind had subsided, and the waters of Loch Ness were calm enough to reflect the sparkles of sunlight as if diamonds were glistening upon its surface. As she stepped along the shoreline, she saw the two intersecting alder trees that lay half immersed in the loch. She switched her gaze toward the hill where the rowan tree stood, tall and bare awaiting winter's arrival.

She could almost see the imprint their bodies had left behind upon the spongy grass that once conformed to the shape of their union. The clusters of red berries along with the green foliage were all gone now, swept away by the passage of time, leaving but empty branches in their wake. If she remained here, life would be perpetual winter, as barren as those limbs that trembled in the cold. She stood firm then in her decision to shatter time's cycle by hastening spring on her own terms.

She had stopped walking by this point and stood erect, gazing straight out into the water. Reaching into her bodice, she unfastened the cross that she had kept near her heart. Not needing further protection from the God of this world who had been absent during her hour of most desperate need, she entrusted herself to those deities who presided over the life to come. After gently placing the charm on the ground, she smoothed out her skirts and stared northward. *I'm coming to ye now, my love,* she promised aloud. She closed her ears to the whimpering sounds that came from behind her and paid no mind to the murkiness of the water that shrouded its depths in mystery.

Mary did not flinch when she took her first step into the icy current, and she ignored her billowing skirts as they lifted and floated around her while she made her way forward. The muscles in her chest began to tighten, and her heart beat faster and faster as the cold reached upward from her toes to seize upon all parts of her body.

Soon, uncontrollable shivering overcame her and then numbness, making walking an insurmountable task. Her legs buckled from this lack of coordination, and she sank lower and lower into the loch. Unable to do anything other than surrender, she felt her head go under the surface, and as she did so, she involuntarily gasped one last time until her breath ceased forever.

Her body drifted downward, deeper and deeper, eventually coming to rest upon the rocks and shells at the bottom, but her soul was not as fortunate.

***

His hands began to flap up and down at his sides when he saw her take the first step, and when she continued to move forward without faltering, he knew he should do something. But he was paralyzed with fear and the need for self-preservation. Bottling up his urge to shout created so much pressure inside of him that his temples were about to burst. He couldn't believe what he was witnessing, and quite honestly, who would? They would blame him for her death, concocting some story that he, a lewd vagabond, had assaulted this unblemished maiden to satisfy his own perverse desires. They would accuse him of violating her and then killing her in order to silence forever any charges she could have made against him. He would be labeled a rapist and a murderer in addition to being a traitor.

The worst part was that they were partly correct, for although he had not harmed her in a sexual way, he was absolutely responsible for her death and did not need a judge or jury to tell him so. That is why, in tortured secrecy, he watched her gradually vanish under the surface of the water until she was no more.

Most people, when afraid, rush to seek comfort in the arms of a parent or loved one; they journey home to a place where they can find this unconditional support. But Angus had no one who truly loved him, nor did he have a home to return to, so instead he ran frantically back to his most recent dwelling by the rocks near the cave. He hoped to find solace in the company of his final bottle of whiskey which he planned to hold fast and cling to.

When Angus came upon the site, comfort and consolation were put on hold for someone had invaded his sanctuary. Despite appearing husky and muscular, the man moved with a kind of nervous vulnerability as he checked on the horses and investigated the surrounding area. The visitor sensed Angus' presence and swooped down upon him with alarm. "Where are they? What have ye done?"

Angus recognized his interrogator, Brodie Munro, both his brother's friend and Donal's, but despite that familiarity, Angus could barely formulate an intelligible response. "I-I-I...dunno..." He choked out the syllables as his hands continued to flail uncontrollably.

Brodie had no patience for such an imbecilic display, so he seized Angus by his jacket and lifted the man up to his toes, suspending him in mid-air. "What do ye think, I'm *doaty*? Now ye tell me what ye've seen, and ye tell it to me now, ye sleekit bastard. Ye may seem daft from drink, but ye're not so emptyheaded as ye appear. Ye ken more than ye're saying." Brodie held fast to Angus' clothing, jostling the man back and forth as if to jar the man's memory into some kind of working order.

"I-I...They're not here...She's...she's...she's..." Angus tried lifting one arm to point in the direction of the loch, but Brodie's grip was too tight to allow for such movement.

"Spit it out, ye scabby bum. She's where?"

"Loch...Loch Ness...She w-w-walked in...gone...she's gone..." Angus breathed out in relief that he was able to string together something that made a little sense.

"She walked into the water? Mary walked into the loch? Is that what ye're saying? Did she not come out?" Brodie loosened his hold and lowered his voice as he tried to piece together Angus' jumbled message. "Did ye see it happen? Where? Where is she?"

Swallowing gulps of air, Angus continued to speak in halting fashion. "By...by...the twisted trees...she...she...she did not come out." That was enough information for Brodie to fling Angus to the ground and spring into action himself. Since Brodie believed that there was a chance of finding Mary alive, he left behind his own horse and jumped upon Arwen and rode away.

When he came upon the site Angus had described, he saw a small puppy sitting tall by the water's edge, staring into the still waters, his nose twitching back and forth as if trying to detect a scent that had been lost upon the air. Nestled between the animal's two front paws was a cross made of twigs bound together with a single red thread. When Brodie reached down to pick up the object in order to examine it further, the dog emitted a low purring sound that rose to a snarl. Hearing that sound and seeing the pup's head bow down as if declaring ownership of the piece, Brodie backed away in silence, leaving the creature his trinket.

Walking along the shoreline, Brodie surveyed the ground and the water's surface for any indication of Mary's presence. When he could find none, he guided Arwen on the trail back to Undlay.

***

After gaining permission to enter the castle, Brodie was led to the room where Teague and his son were discussing the need for the watch to resume during the upcoming winter months when cattle rustling would become even more prevalent. While standing in the doorway, Brodie heard Robby describe how the two shifts of guards would work in coordination with one another and how they would decide which person would be in charge of each division.

Teague looked at the names on the paper that Robby put before him. "I would expect the reiving to die down now that we've done away with the most notorious ringleader of the bunch. With Donn dead, do ye not think the other fellows will put aside their thieving ways and just fade away? If that be the case, do we really need two separate watches per day or can we not just have one?"

Brodie was stunned. Up until now, Brodie had assumed that Donal was still in prison, but here he had just learned that his good friend had already been slain. The cavalier tone Teague had assumed when announcing Donal's death enraged Brodie with the desire to strike back. His imposing figure swelled to twice its size as it became engorged with vengeance.

Not usually one to take pleasure in another man's misfortune, Brodie, for a brief moment, was glad that he too had bad news that would shatter this man's heart in the same way his own had just been broken. But that vindictiveness did not last, for Brody did not operate from a foundation of evil, and he knew that playing one grief against another did not even up the score. Both ended up being losses. It was tragic—either way one looked at it— whether you had lost a friend and confidante or a daughter and sister. There were no winners when it came to who suffered more over someone's death.

After recognizing how pain would soon envelop them all, Brodie looked upon father and son at table and spoke gently and compassionately, "Pardon me, my laird, Master Robby." He took off his cap and fingered its edges nervously as he spoke. "I'm verra sorry to be disturbing ye, but it seems there's been a terrible accident involving Mary."

He had their attention now and saw how Robby had leaned forward to hear more, but Teague pulled back seemingly on edge at just the mention of Mary's name. Brodie cleared his throat and continued, "There was an eyewitness who said there was an accident." He struggled for the right words, but there were some messages that could never be delivered with any sense of correctness. "He says he saw Mary drown. In the waters of Loch Ness. The man couldna' get to her to save her. She's gone." He waited to see if he should go on.

Robby stood motionless and speechless, his mouth open in disbelief. Teague pushed himself away from the table and slowly walked over to the window, turning his back on both Robby and Brodie to face his suffering alone. Brodie explained, "I went there myself and couldna' find anything of hers except that little dog that was always following her about. I brought ye back her horse, but the pup wouldna' budge from the spot." Brodie paused again. "I'm so verra sorry to have to deliver such news, but ye never can tell, 'tis possible the witness got it wrong, and Mary'll turn up somewhere soon. I pray for yer sake that she does."

Like a statue, Teague remained unchanged, silent and still by the window. Robby assumed the mantle of authority by marching over to Brodie and shaking the man's hand firmly in appreciation. The young man could not muster any words, only a silent nod of acknowledgement. As he was dismissed, Brodie could hear the faintest whisper of a question coming from the other side of the room. "What have I done? O, what have I done?" Glancing briefly over his shoulder, Brodie observed how the statue had ever so slightly come to life, covering its face of marble with the palms of both hands.

And, later that night, while Brodie, Ross, and Owen gathered together to share their sorrow and the McElroys wept over the loss of their daughter and sister, Angus Gregor tripped and fell upon his whiskey bottle, its jagged edge puncturing his neck. No one cared enough to come and claim the body.

Bridging the Gap – 2018

It was as if someone had flipped a light switch and all had gone dark, only there was no clicking sound, and the scene didn't involve an entire room. Everything that Caitlyn had just experienced had been projected through a slender spherical opening in a stone. The "show" wasn't entirely real, but it certainly had the semblance of truth. Unlike with movies when audiences are merely entertained by the actors on the screen, Caitlyn didn't feel like just a spectator. She felt part of the action itself, immersed in the content, not just a witness to it.

That explained why she felt so incredibly exhausted, wrung dry from horror, frustration, and grief. The emptiness inside her was real, as were the tracks of moisture that ran from her eyes down to her chin. Her nose was congested and her head felt full, the story of forbidden love, self-destruction, and guilt weighing heavily on her mind.

No longer was this a case of coincidence. Something intentional was undoubtedly at work here, for how could the same cast of characters resurrect their roles for a second time? Unlike yesterday when Caitlyn could recall only bits and pieces of the visions she had when she fainted outside the castle prison, today everything came into focus. The players took definitive form, details unfolded with clarity. A tale was demanding to be heard, and she had become the purveyor of its voice.

The clock read 7:30 am. She had no plausible explanation as to how all of this could have occurred in such a short span of time, but she was coming to understand that time was a very tricky concept—especially the measurement of it. The 1600s had bled into the present; complicated, lengthy occurrences from the past had been condensed into two rather brief dreams. Regardless of the interplay between that era and this one, Caitlyn knew that she had less than a half-hour to explain to someone why she wasn't going to follow the current day's itinerary.

The phone receiver wobbled in her unsteady hand as she pressed the numbers for the extension to the room next door. After three rings, she heard Paula saying, "H-h-hello?"

"Good morning, Paula. So sorry to bother you and Vivian, but I'm not feeling so great after yesterday, and I'm just going to take it easy today and stay local. Would you mind telling Graham not to wait on me and that I'll catch up with everyone later on this evening at dinner?"

"Why, of course, dear. Is your stomach still troubling you? I can leave my bottle of Pepto-Bismol tablets outside your door if you need. I keep a supply on hand, especially when I'm traveling." Paula lowered her voice confidentially, "The food, you know, doesn't always agree with me."

"Thank you so much, but I'll be fine, I'm sure. I'm going to try to sleep a little longer and then grab a light breakfast here in Inverness." Caitlyn felt she had to round out her excuse with a little more information. "I just can't bear the thought of getting in and out of the van all day. I think I need to use my legs a bit and take in some of that fresh Highland air." And that was true; Caitlyn did plan to go outdoors and do some hiking later on.

"Sounds good, Caitlyn. Vivian and I will pick up any travel guides and brochures that are available at Cawdor and Culloden in case you want to read about what you missed. We'll check in with you when we get back. Feel better!" With that cheery closing, Paula hung up the phone.

Caitlyn waited until after 8:00 before leaving her bed to shower, spending the intervening time sketching out her plan for the day. There was no question she had to return to Undlay. She must return to Undlay. She needed to speak to someone there—some guide or docent—about the people who had visited her the past two days.

Well, actually, she couldn't very well discuss their "visitations" without being thought of as crazy, but she could simply ask about certain names and their historical significance. In that way, perhaps one of the representatives could confirm whether or not Caitlyn's dreams did have some factual merit.

A forty-minute bus trip on the 919 line brought her to the visitor's center at Undlay. She sat for the short film about the castle's history, the one that traced the evolution of the fortress from the 6th century to its demolition in 1691. But on the subject of Mary, Donal, or Teague McElroy, the documentary was silent.

Leaving the viewing room and heading outdoors, Caitlyn was astonished at how different the castle appeared when approaching it from land rather than by water. From the tourist center, the fortress sprawled out wide before her, a long, downhill path connecting them both. An enormous trebuchet on the right harkened back to the days when English kings besieged Scottish castles with catapults like this, hurling great stones of destruction at its ramparts.

That same strange sensation of familiarity washed over Caitlyn again as she drew closer to the bridge that spanned the ditch encircling the fortress—the ditch was a dry moat and the passageway once a fully functioning drawbridge, lowered and raised based on the motives of the visitor desiring entry. To her left, the Northern enclosure included the gatehouse and the stronghold's tallest tower, and to her right were the scant remains of earlier buildings. Although she was intrigued by the entire structure, her main objective was to revisit the prison cell and speak to one of the guides stationed there.

Finding her way as if by memory, Caitlyn crossed under the arched entrance and saw the murder holes above, the little spaces and gaps where the guards would shoot arrows or pour boiling oil on top of unwelcome callers. Passing through the guard room and the chamber where the constable would sleep, she heard a tour guide regaling his listeners with one of the many legends involving Undlay.

"…Highlanders believe that there are two cells hollowed out in the rock below the castle—one has a treasure of gold, the other a plague. Both chambers remain undiscovered to this verra day for fear of unleashing so great a pestilence…" The group of people surrounding the man nodded their heads with interest, but Caitlyn could not stop for long. She continued on her way.

She found the staircase. Like the swirling lines on a nautilus shell, it spiraled and turned so tightly that a person could see only three or four steps at a time. The steps themselves were made of slate, and the stone walls on either side created such a narrow walkway that only one person could ascend or descend at a time. A railing made of rope was a modern convenience, newly added to accommodate less surefooted and less nimble guests of the twenty-first century.

As she moved lower and lower into the nethermost region of the castle, Caitlyn could feel a fluttering again inside her body, the same panicked feeling she had experienced just yesterday. She must stay coherent. She must stay alert. Stopping completely to take a few deep breaths that she hoped would ground her in the present, Caitlyn struggled with an overwhelming compulsion to close her eyes. Willing them to stay open, she waited until her heartbeat levelled out before resuming her descent.

The lattice door loomed before her, copper-colored and rusty from age and moisture. The small amount of light that had accompanied her on the staircase dwindled to nothing so that the cell itself was mired in darkness. One had to grasp the bars of the entrance gate and peer intently through the gaps in order to discern anything in its recesses. Caitlyn continued to breathe deeply to steady herself, but she paid a price for such anchoring when the musty scent of desperation and death began to subsume her.

Despite the shadows, she could see the small patch of dirt floor that had provided barely enough room for two people to sit or lie down head-to-toe (the narrow confines of the walls precluded any chance of fitting side-by-side). Perhaps the physical encroachment of those walls was meant to force the prisoner to have no choice but to turn inward and face the blackness in his soul.

Her musings were interrupted when she heard a group of people above her coming—single file—down the stairs. Their leader at the front cautioned them to be careful. "Do not rush, take yer time, and leave some space between ye and the person in front of ye. The steps can be slippery and a bit treacherous on account of the dampness, so hold onto the rope as ye go."

After delivering those directions to his followers, the spectacled guide noticed Caitlyn examining the dungeon and called out, "Hallo, there! I see ye've come to the most sinister part of the castle, lass. Am I right to assume that ye're intrigued by Undlay's grisly past, like the rest of us?"

The tall, slender fellow spoke in a lilting voice that hinted at the undisclosed riches he would reveal to his listeners if they entrusted their attention to him. His silver hair—combed back and glistening with shine as if still wet—along with his dark suit, crisp shirt, and plaid tie, marked him as, perhaps, an accomplished but retired businessman who had made his fortune and was now finally pursuing a vocation doing what he truly loved.

After seeing his name tag, Caitlyn said, "Thank you, Mr. Gilchrist. Yes, I do find this part of the castle quite intriguing. Do you mind if I tag along with your group and listen?"

"Please, call me Lachlan. No need for such formality." As the five other tourists huddled together near the corridor that led to the cell, he spoke to the gathering. "As ye know, nearly every castle had its dungeon, and Undlay was no exception. Ye'll only be able to approach one at a time, though, to get a glimpse of the inside. Ye'll notice it's a pretty dismal chamber: a dark, dank, windowless cave of sorts.

"Prisoners were kept here while awaiting trial—if they were lucky enough to get a trial. Sometimes a laird showed no mercy at all, and a sentence of death was enforced without delay. That's what happened to the most famous inmate to ever inhabit this jail, Donal Donn of Bohuntin, the legendary Gaelic bard who had the misfortune of being arrested for cattle stealing."

Caitlyn felt her breath catch in her throat. While the other people shifted and took turns looking into the chamber, she stood transfixed, absorbing every detail of the lecture. He continued, "Donal's more serious crime though, according to history, was falling in love with Laird McElroy's daughter, Mary, and most likely that was the reason he ended up being executed. I suppose McElroy could have delivered a lighter sentence to Donal for doing a bit of cattle lifting, but when it came to stealing away his daughter, that's where the nobleman drew the line. And so, he beheaded him at Craigmonie Hill and left his rotting body on display as a deterrent to all other thieves and unwanted suitors."

Caitlyn yearned to hear more. She longed to bring up names and places and events for verification. There were so many questions she wanted to ask, but she had to proceed slowly for fear of sounding too unbalanced or too suspicious. Why would a tourist like her know so much about Undlay and its inhabitants? Maybe he'd think her some kind of troublemaker, planted there to stump him with her inquiries.

No, she would tread carefully around the subject and limit herself to the most significant question of all. "But whatever happened to the daughter?" No other members of the group were present to hear her question or the man's response, so busy were they jockeying for position to get their view of 17th century crime and punishment.

"Well, to be honest, no one rightly knows. Some say she killed herself. Others say she ran away north where the two lovers were bound. She simply vanished. Never heard from again. Some folks in the glen—my Grandmother among them—say there've been occasions when they've been out upon the loch, and they've felt a presence, something ghostly, lurking under the water's surface, seeming all distracted and forlorn. And they've heard the mournful cry of a solitary animal that often accompanies the vision."

He seemed to consider his words thoughtfully for a minute before finishing, "But I've lived in the region my whole life, and Mary has never shown herself to me. So who knows? When I was little, though, my Grandma used to sing a Gaelic melody to me called "The Broken Heart," supposedly attributed to Mary." He broke into the tune:

'Gur e m' athair rinn an do-bheartMise chumail gun do phosadh.'
'Tha mo run air a'ghille.'

"The words reveal the tortured soul of the grief-stricken lass. In translation, she laments, *My father did an evil thing, keeping me from marrying you. I love the lad.*

"At the time, I did not know anything about the history of the star-crossed couple. I only knew that this refrain felt verra sad to me, so I'd nestle in close to my Grandma for comfort when the melody seized upon my own heart and squeezed it so tightly that tears of sorrow tumbled down my cheeks. In any case, I guess we'll never know what really did happen to the lost daughter of Teague McElroy…"

Caitlyn was about to refute Lachlan's assertion, but before she could, he spoke gently as if thinking about this for the very first time. "Ye know, my Grandma may have believed in ghosts and in a good love story, but I come from a family with a long line of preachers in it. Men who put their trust in the word of God before phantoms and such.

"But ye know what's funny? Even the Bible recognizes the mystery of existence. *Ye do not know what ye're life will be like tomorrow. Ye are just a vapor that appears for a little while and then vanishes away.* That's from the Book of James 4:14. Since we really do not know about the life to come, can we say with certainty that we will truly vanish away? What if a soul canna go quietly or refuses to do so? 'Tis a question that remains unanswered for us living souls who are not privy to the secrets of the hereafter."

Now was the time for Caitlyn to speak up. "I believe I may have an idea about what happened to Mary McElroy, Mr. Gilchrist. Will you help me assemble the pieces together? Maybe, between the two of us, we can put an end to her wandering and release her soul to find love again. With a little magic and a little faith, I'm ready to explore the dark recesses of the cave. Can you help me find it?"

Epilogue

I don't know why, after all those years, Mary chose me to be the vehicle for her story. Maybe she had tried others before but was unsuccessful. Maybe she hadn't finished her penance until now. Maybe she was waiting for the right person, one she could help as much as that person could help her. I don't know for sure, but I do know that it was only by partaking in her love for Donal that I began to realize what a superficial life I myself had been leading: one that was infected by complacency and content with ease and comfort, one that knew nothing of the ecstasy and agony of true, sincere, real, unconquerable love.

Lachlan Gilchrist turned out to be a trusted friend, confidante, and devout believer in my tale. His wealth of knowledge about the McElroy family and his familiarity with the geography and landscape of the glen proved to be invaluable. I was incredibly grateful that, right from the start, he took me seriously, once I started to offer details and descriptions from my two "visions."

Some of the information he had already been aware of and was able to provide written documentation in support of it. Some of it he had never heard before, as the facts and stories were not recorded in any reference text or history book. Patiently, he listened—I guess that is all anyone ever really wants, someone to listen to them, to believe in them—and after a time, he felt we were ready to begin our search for Donal's cave. By this point, I had already taken a temporary leave of absence from my teaching job in Boston and a permanent one from Brian, to allow myself more time to complete our research.

In order to stay in close proximity to Undlay and to the neighboring countryside, I found a small room to rent in a house owned by a lovely widow in the quaint town of Drummondshire. There I found the peace and solitude I needed to write down everything I could remember of the scenes that had come to life during my fainting spell and my view through the stone. After his work

276

day at Undlay was over, Lachlan would meet with me at the local pub to go over the information that I had inscribed onto my pages.

As a local historian and docent, he had private access to archived information in the Drummondshire library, including the original copy of *The History of Undlay and the Glen* written by a fellow named William McClue back in 1848. We cross-referenced my recollections with the historically recorded ones and were able to verify quite a bit of the background on Donal and his penchant for reiving. There were excerpts of his songs and poetry and even comparisons made between him and Robin Hood.

What we couldn't find was any mention of his three cohorts nor could we locate any account—disparaging or otherwise—of George Campbell. One thing was certain, however; the link between the playful rogue and the laird's daughter surfaced time and time again.

A few weeks later, when the summer's grip began to loosen and the countryside slowly retreated into autumn's embrace, Lachlan and I began our exploration for the cave. We printed out a map of the region given to us by one of the local hiking clubs and proceeded to mark off each section as we went along.

On a crisp September afternoon, before the sun fully dipped below the horizon, the sky was awash in a rose-colored glow when I felt a tremendous pull leading me toward a rocky hill. At its crest, I saw the formation of three rocks stacked upon one another in a triangular shape and shouted to Lachlan to come join me. When a russet-brown deer lifted its head from grazing to tilt his antlers at me as if in greeting, I knew in the deepest part of my soul that we had found the place we had been looking for. Marking the location carefully on our map, we realized we had to write down exactly where we were so that we could return the next day, having neither the proper tools nor the equipment to begin digging inside the cave right then.

I remember vividly how impossible it was to sleep all that night, knowing that the story of Donal and Mary, verified by their own words, was awaiting me. After three centuries of lying dormant in some dark corner of that cave, their chronicle was finally going to be brought to light. Lachlan was taking care of all the legal ramifications of such a find, but we both agreed that, until we had our hands on the actual property, there was no need to alert any of the authorities in advance.

The spirit of a Highland rebel still resided in the bones of my dear friend, for Lachlan agreed with me that we could keep our search a secret until we had something noteworthy to report. Without speaking the pact aloud, we both wanted to examine its contents before turning anything over. Was that wrong of us? I know for me it had become so personal a journey that I felt I owed it to myself and to Mary to be the first to read about this love that seemed to conquer time itself.

And so, that is what we did. We found the chest buried beneath the dirt near a hidden nook at the back of the cave. Sheltered from the outside elements and protected by layers of rock, it was intact, and each page contained therein was as fresh and pristine as it had been on the day it was written. By flashlight, Lachlan and I sat down and poured through the contents, savoring each word and its accompanying emotion.

After a few hours, we reluctantly returned the documents to the storage box and then contacted the representative from Historic Environment Scotland who worked as the director of Undlay Castle. We delivered our findings the next morning and awaited the time when the transcripts would be made available to researchers like ourselves.

In the interim, I still had the necessary information to begin piecing together the story of Donal and Mary, a story of love that had no boundaries. Before I knew it, I had the outline for this book, and when Lachlan was able to secure us prolonged access to those pages, I took Mary's words and Donal's and then bridged the gaps with the scenes I had been shown during my momentary ventures into the past. That is why you will see chapters devoted entirely to her voice, some to his, and others that were supplied by the visions Mary proffered to me.

I am grateful for having been given this chance to learn what passion really is, even if I should never experience it firsthand myself. I know, beyond a doubt, that they are together somewhere, Mary and Donal, roaming the Highlands with Thor by their side, walking hand-in-hand by the shores of Loch Ness. Visible yet invisible, palpable yet intangible, a love like that never, ever dies.

It was the power of that love which compelled me all those months ago to turn the pages of Fulton's anthology and find Donal's haunting lament:

O where hae ye gone, O Mary, my luve
I'm here but I canna find ye.
In a place far beyond the world we'd known
I'm lost till yer heart comes back to me.

And it was Mary's voice that called out to me in the silence, beckoning for release from her watery grave until I became her witness. Sharing her story with me became her chosen form of confession, her way of atoning for the fatal decision she had made to take her own life. Released now from the torment of being separated for over three hundred years, Mary and Donal no longer walk alone. They have found their way back to one another. They have finally come home.

Chapter Notes

Undlay Dungeon 1665

Undlay Castle – Undlay is the fictional representation of Urquhart Castle.

Loch Ness – 2018

History of Loch Ness Monster – "Loch Ness Monster" from *History* on www.history.com

Fictional book and title Nigel Fulton's *Anthology of Poetry from the British Isles* is a fabricated book.

"O where hae ye gone, O Mary, my luve…" – fictional ballad depicting Donal's separation from Mary and his burning desire for their reunion. The opening line of the refrain echoes the introductory question found in the Anglo-Scottish border ballad of "Lord Randal."

Is tusa gaol mo chridhe. Leatsa, tha mi chriochnaichte – O love of my heart. With you, I am complete.

Donal – The Reckoning

Poem – this piece is inspired by the ballad "Johnie Armstrang" as recounted in Alistair Moffat's *The Reivers – The Story of the Border Reivers*.

Return to Undlay

Ghillie Dubh – this figure is a combination of Campbell's *Superstitions of the Highlands and Islands of Scotland – 1900 –* as recounted in *British Fairies*: Scottish fairies would "sometimes take care of children whom they found forgotten" and Scottish Folklore – Ghosts Myths, and Legends (www.britishfairies.wordpress.com and www.visitscotland.com).

Donal – Anticipation

Poem using thistle image – Scotland's national flower saved the Scots during a Norwegian invasion in 1263 when the enemy removed their shoes in a surprise attack and, because they eventually yelped in pain, they awakened the natives and were defeated ("The Thistle – National Emblem of Scotland" by Ben Johnson on www.historic-uk.com).

The Raid – Litchfield

Background information on reivers – Alistair Moffat, in *The Reivers – The Story of the Border Reivers* provides extensive information on horses, clothing, weapons, trysts, the hot trod, various strategies, etc.

Donal – Man and Beast

Dh'aindeoin co theireadh – the Donn battle cry comes from the Macdonald of Clanranald: "Gainsay, who dares" and their motto is "My hope is constant in thee" taken from www.renaissancekingdomfandom.com

Mary – A Leap of Faith

"Rise when the day draws, bed when the nicht fa's" – this old Scottish proverb is quoted by Alexander Hislop in *The Project Gutenberg eBook of Proverbs of Scotland* (www.gutenberg.org/files).

Keeping the Wolf at Bay

Craigmonie – the description of the landscape along with the history of the location come from "Mary, lift my head" on *Graveyards of Scotland* created by Nellie Merthe Erkenbach, (www.graveyardsofscotland.com).

1598 slaughter of the Donns by Campbells – this fabricated story in the novel is based on the true Glencoe Massacre of 1692, the historical event that involved the decimation of MacDonald clan of Glencoe by the Campbells; the tale Devin shares with Mary uses the material from 1692, switches the MacDonalds to the Donns, and changes the time to 1598.

Donal – A Ceilidh

Ceilidh – is "a gathering" with music, singing, and storytelling.

Petrarch's Triumphs – this book traces the triumphant procession of six allegorical figures: Love, Chastity, Death, Fame, Time, Eternity. While

Eternity is victorious over them all—even Love—Petrarch is ultimately reunited with his muse, Laura, in heaven for eternity—an apt parallel for Donal and Mary.

Red Stag – the red stag "personifies the power of the other world…forests…and untamed nature" (from "The Scottish Stag" from *Scottish Folklore* www.usakilts.com). Paul Kendall in "Deer Mythology and Folklore" also discusses the deity Cernunnos as "the horned one" and "god of forest and wild animals" (www.treesforlife.org.uk). Cernunnos is seen as the Celtic symbol of the union with female energy. From "History of the Legendary Scottish Stag," the stag "represents power, agility, and sexuality" (www.kiltsnstuff.com). Ross' gift of the horseshoe points back to Cernunnos' horns and the promise of virility and fecundity.

Sowans Nicht – this is Christmas eve, so-called because of the tradition of having sowans on this night (a mixture of fermented oats and bran) that can be served as a porridge or used to make scones. Sometimes sowans were smeared on the windows and doors of neighbors who were viewed as unfriendly. It is an example of a "traditional food [that is] linked entirely to folk magic and folk traditions of Scotland" from "Exploring Lost Scottish Folk Traditions" *Cailleach's Herbarium* (www.cailleachs-herbarium.com).

Song – the tune the men sing at the end is based on a story that Moffat retells in a section entitled, "The Perils of Winter Raiding" (*The Reivers – The Story of the Border Reivers* p. 163).

Donal – Meditations

Sithiche – fairyland or elfland

Mary – The Threads of Fate

Hilda's Nordic background – this was adapted from the story of the Viking Princess that appeared in Erkenbach's "Echoes of the Past" from *Graveyards of Scotland.*

Sallow Trees – the word given to the native willow trees that live between 150 and 300 years in Scotland; the terms *witch*, *wicca*, and *wicked* all derive from the word *willow*. It "bends without breaking" and it is often looked upon as "a supportive talisman." These comments from Stewart Borland contrast with Shakespeare's decision to associate the willow with death and mourning—as Borland observes—with regard to Ophelia and Desdemona

("Tremendous Trees – Sallow [Goat Willow]" – *Highland Titles – The Everlasting Gift of Scottish Land* from www.highlandtitles.com). Linking Hilda to the sallow evokes the more pleasant connotation, and later in the novel, Hilda tries to teach Mary that, like the sallow tree, Mary can "grieve deeply and come safely through acceptance without shattering under the weight of grief" (Borland).

Mary – Kindred Spirits

Donal's comment about witch prickers – "Scotland's Witch Prickers" explains how the job of this court official amounted to finding the witches' mark and then pricking that spot with a sharp implement like a needle to see if the victim felt no pain. "The witch pricker played a vital role in weeding out witches from the community" (*The Real Mary King's Close* from www.realmarykingsclose.com). From *The Witch of Inverness and the Fairies of Tomnahurich*, the infallible test involved forcing "a darning needle an inch into the fleshy part of their bodies. If the operation drew blood and gave extreme pain, the victim was released. If not, she was set down as in compact with the Evil One" (June 1662-3).

Mo ghradh – "my darling"

Mary – Of Crime and Punishment

Legend of Urquhart – in the book *Urquhart and Glenmoriston: Olden Times in the Parish,* William Mackay explained that there were "two secret chambers in the castle: one with gold and one with plague" (from "The Treasure of Urquhart Castle" www.lochnessmystery.blogspot.com).

Mary – Imminent Danger

Knob – slang word for "penis"

Reekbeek – "horrible, disgusting"

Baws – "balls, testicles"

Cu Sith – a spectral dog from Scottish mythology. "The Cu Sith was feared as a harbinger of death…[and] take [one's] soul to the feary realm or underworld…it would hunt silently for its victim…" ("Scottish Legends: The Cu Sith" www.folkrealmstudies.weebly.com).

Donal – Charm of Protection

Mo lachain – my little hero

Legend of the Rowan Tree – in Norse legend, the rowan tree was "the tree from which the first woman ever was made." It "saved the life of the god Thor by bending over a fast-flowing river in the Underworld in which he was being swept away." The poem reflects how Mary performed this same rescue, of sorts, for Donal. "In the British Isles, [the rowan tree] protects against witchcraft and enchantment...From Scotland to Cornwall...rowan crosses bound with red thread were sewn into the lining of coats or carried in pockets" (Paul Kendall in "Rowan mythology and folklore" from www.treesforlife.com). Thus, Donal fashions this kind of cross for Mary to wear in the presence of such evil men as the Cameron brothers.

Donal – Judgement Day

Blathaich mal – "blackmail"

Wooden Horse – the punishment for George Campbell came from the practice of the "wooden horse" as described in "Medieval Torture – Medieval Warfare" (www.medievalwarfare.info).

Bawsack – "scrotum"

Double Meanings

Nuckelavee – "a hybrid of a man and horse-like creature with added horrific elements...its intention toward all humans who crossed his path completely malevolent" from "Nuckelavee – the malevolent creature that terrorized Scotland's Northern Isles" (www.transceltic.com).

Deirdre and Aidan's Song – this is an original creation based on the tradition of tragic Scottish ballads. In "Murder Ballads," Dr. Tom McKean writes, "the murderer usually pays the price at the end of the song, often with a gallows confession, a warning to others, and a prayer for mercy." The song included here concludes with the killer paying "the price for playing with love" (www.historicscotland.com "Murder Ballads").

Bigealas – "penis"

Hanging as a method of execution – various sources were consulted for recreating this scene, including Daniele Cybulskie's "Medieval Executions: The View from the Scaffold" (www.medievalists.net) and Vasudevan

Munkuth's "Gruesome, Clumsy, and Irreversible: The Science Behind 'Hanging by the Neck'" (*Science Wire* www.science.thewire.in).

Nursery Rhymes – the more sinister take on children's verse came from "The Dark Side of Nursery Rhymes" from *BBC Culture* (www.bbc.com).

Mary – Changes in the Air

Mo ghradh – "my darling"

Nighean bheag – small girl or little daughter

Healing methods – "The Air of History (Part II) Medicine in the Middle Ages" by Rachel Hajar, MD (www.ncbi.nlm.nih.gov).

Mary – Revelry and Risks

Struan Micheil – "a type of bannock or unleavened bread" for which "it is essential to get the ritual and method exactly right, for baking disasters portend all manner of evil falling upon your family in the coming year" ("Michaelmas Eve" *The Old Foodie* from www.theoldfoodie.com). Another source elaborates, "many cautions are given to her who is making the struan to take exceptional care of it. "Were the struan...to fail...the omen is full of evil augury to the family" ("La Fheill Micheil" *Tairis,A Gaelic Polytheist Website* www.tairis.com.uk). The fact that Mary's first attempt fails foreshadows tragic events that will later ensue.

Michaelmas Daisy – "provides color and warmth to gardens at a time when the majority of flowers are coming to an end...the daisy is probably associated with this celebration because...St. Michael is celebrated as a protector from darkness and evil, just as the daisy fights against the advancing gloom of Autumn and Winter" ("Michaelmas" by Ben Johnson from www.historic-uk.com).

Slainte mhath – a toast meaning "Good Health"

Canaries II – "a popular dance dating from the mid-16th century, reputedly based on dances found in the Canary Islands" (Oscar Batet "Music of Scotland: *Canaries II* – David Tayler, archlute" at www.carbatet.wordpress.com). The dance involves forming facing lines and matching palm to palm with one's partner and then going through the line and later reversing the direction to return to the original starting position (Batet).

The Baffled Knight – "a knight sees a lady and wishes to lie with her. She convinces him not to touch her until they reach her father's gate, and she jumps in, locks him out, and scolds him for his base thought. She is the skillful maneuverer of her lover" ("The Baffled Knight" from *Folklorist* www.trad.appspot.com).

Bessie Bell and Mary Gray – Bessie and Mary are two pretty girls who have escaped the 1645 plague, but a young man visits them both and brings infection. They die and are buried in the churchyard "among their noble kin and bask beneath the sun" (Lesley Nelson-Burns from "Bessie Bell and Mary Gray" www.contemplator.com).

Geordie – there are different versions of this song, but in the Scottish one, Geordie is to be executed and his wife pleads for his life, begging the king with whatever money and possessions she can offer ("Geordie" (ballad) from www.folkworld.de). The Scottish version ends happily with Geordie's release; thus, Donal asks Mary if she, like Geordie's wife, would stand up for him if need be.

The Parting Glass – a traditional Celtic song that is offered as a final gesture of hospitality to a departing guest ("The History of the Parting Glass" from www.irishmusicdaily.com).

William Wallace's Grave – the men argue over the location of Wallace's place of rest, and the mystery surrounding that location is captured in "Sir William Wallace's Burial Place" from *The Society of William Wallace* (www.thesocietyofwilliamwallace.com).

Donal – A Final Ride

Sluagh – they are "spirits of the unforgiven or restless dead" who "took the form of gusts of wind" and searched for human souls to steal. "in other accounts the Sluagh appear as a whirlwind of flapping wings and undulating shadows, like a flock of crows or ravens" ("The Sluagh: Spirits of the Unforgiven Dead" by Anna Mazzola of *Folktales* on www.folklorethursday.com).

A Debt Repaid

Brodie's assailant – the troll who wounds Brodie with a slingshot and stone is adapted from a practice undertaken by Roman soldiers and supported by evidence unearthed during an excavation in Scotland ("Ancient Slingshot Was as Deadly as a .44 Magnum" by Heather Pringle from www.nationalgeographic.com).

Red Cap or Powrie – a type of malevolent dwarf, goblin, elf, or fairy found in Scottish folklore. They "murder travelers who stray into their homes and dye their hats with their victims' blood" ("Redcap" www.mythicalcreatures.com). In "Border Reiver Family Heritage and Genealogy," redcaps "fling huge stones" at travelers who try to take refuge in their domain. A redcap is described as "a short, thickset old man with long prominent teeth, skinny fingers armed with talons like eagles, large eyes of fiery red colour, grisly hair streaming down his shoulders…and a red cap on his head" (www.BorderReiverHeritage.com).

The albino cow – in *Urquhart and Glenmoriston: Olden Times in the Parish,* Mackay records how Domhnull had lifted a herd of cattle, including one pure white one that was "readily identified" by its former owner.

Bheir an Diabhol mise a mo bhrogan mar tieid Domhnull Donn a chrochadh! – "The Devil may take me out of my shoes if Domhnull Donn is not hanged!" These words, spoken by Mary Grant's father, the laird of Urquhart Castle, are recounted in Mackay's *Urquhart and Glenmoriston: Olden Times in the Parish*.

Donal – In Abeyance

Clarsach – "harp" – starting from the 1600s during English rule in Ireland and Scotland, "harps were burnt and harpers executed" ("Harp History" by Allison Vardy at www.alisonvardy.com).

Aurelius' Meditations – Book 10 – "Remember that this which pulls the strings is the thing which is hidden within." This statement from Aurelius leads Owen into a discussion with Donal about the power of the soul, and how the soul is that hidden force which drives one's ability to create.

Red stag – its reappearance in this chapter carries with it all of the earlier connotations as well as the hint that it may be embodying the ancestral spirit of Donal's father who has come to warn him.

Donal – Duty vs. Choice

Donal's capture – adapted from the historical account that appeared in Mackay's *Urquhart and Glenmoriston:Olden Times in the Parish*. While hiding in his cave, Domhnull received a "message as if from Mary, proposing an interview at the house of a certain individual…Eager to meet her, he repaired to the house at the appointed hour…at a signal from his treacherous host, his enemies, to the number of sixty-three, as he himself states in one of his songs, rushed in and endeavored to seize him" (Mackay 188).

Mary – Undercurrents

Mo chridhe – "my heart"

Departures

Is tusa gaol mo chridhe. Leatsa, tha mi chriochnaichte – here, Mary actually speaks the words that Caitlyn stated in the opening chapter.

Undlay – 2018

Headstone for John Macrae – there is an authentic tombstone at the Beauly Priory that records the death of John Macrae in 1934, along with that of his son, James, who passed away in infancy, and a daughter who perished in 1920. His wife, Isabella, survived them all, dying in 1960. Caitlyn wonders at how Isabella was able to carry on despite so much pain and suffering.

Tomb effigy of the knight – Caitlyn is describing the effigy at the entrance to the north transept of Beauly Priory belonging to Sir Kenneth Mackenzie of Kintail.

Adder's stone – this small rock with a hole in its middle was the magic talisman of Kenneth the Sallow of the 17th century, a man who was gifted with the Second Sight. Graham later discusses how some of the many predictions made by Dark Kenneth came to fruition. This "Scottish Nostradamus," however, met with a most gruesome death after offending Lady Isabella Seaforth with one of his prophecies ("The Brahan Seer – the Scottish Nostradamus" by Ben Johnson from www.historic-uk.com).

Gloine nan druidh – "the glass of the Druids," a stone with a naturally formed hole (see above).

Peering Through Time

Donal's musings – some of the thoughts running through Donal's mind while he is in prison come from information taken from William Mackay's *Urquhart and Glenmoriston: Olden Times in the Parish.* Domhnull "was the Rob Roy of his generation, but he had more poetry in his soul than the famous Macgregor had, and although his deeds brought him in the end to the headman's block, he died with the reputation of never having injured a poor man, or imbued his hands wantonly in human blood" (Mackay 188).

Mo Chridhe – "my heart"

Donal's execution – it is true that Domhnull was beheaded and not hanged. According to William Mackay, Domhnull "begged one favor before sentence of death was passed upon him—he asked that he should be beheaded like a gentleman, and not hanged. His prayer was granted…" (*Urquhart and Glenmoriston: Olden Times in the Parish*). Mackay also recorded Domhnull's last words to Mary's father: "The Devil will take the Laird of Grant out of his shoes, and Donal Donn shall not be hanged."

Mary's death – there is no historical evidence to support Mary's death by drowning; this was simply the choice I made as author in order to reinforce the restlessness of her soul and her inability to reunite with Donal in the next world. The science behind the process of drowning was explained by Dr. Dipak Chandry and Dr. Gerald L. Weinhouse in the article "Drowning (submersion injuries)" (www.uptodate.com).

Bridging the Gap

The Broken Heart – these words are attributed to Mary, and they appear on the inscription on the placard "The Private Chamber" on the *Historical Marker Database*. "The laird's daughter, Mary Grant, is said to have composed a defiant love song after her father held the bard and cattle rustler Domhnall Donn captive at Urquhart in the late 1600s. Domhnall was later executed…*Gur e m'athair rinn an do-bheart, Mise chumail gun do phsadh. Tha mo run air a'ghille.* (My father did an evil thing, Keeping me from marrying you, I love the lad)" (www.HMdb.org).